PRINCE'S

SON

Cowboys of Mineral Springs
Book One

DELSORA LOWE

The Prince's Son

Cover Artist: Karen Ronan of Covers by Karen
coversbykaren.com/
Cover Photo Copyright Credit
@pixabay.com and @periodimages.com
Edited by: JS Corcoran of Pink Pencil Editing
Formatting: Nina Pierce of Seaside Publications
ninapierce.com/book-formatting
Author Photo & Website Design
@JanDeLima2014

ISBN: 9781091276864

Dear Reader,

Welcome to Mineral Springs where lives are intertwined in a mountainous ranching community near Aspen, Colorado. And to the series where strong and independent women capture the hearts of the *Cowboys of Mineral Springs*.

The Prince's Son is a first meet, royalty and the nanny romance between a self-exiled prince with a royal chip on his shoulders and the local rancher's daughter who rails against any man who tries to tell her what to do. When she tries to tell the prince how to raise his son, tempers flare and sparks fly.

I hope you love watching Ari and Carla wrestle with their emotions and their need to not become involved with each other. But who can resist a sweet kid? Jaime is the apple of his father's eye and a child that Carla wants to help, despite her family's misgivings.

Read on and you'll find out how this struggle between the uptight prince and the loving teacher turned nanny ends.

As you will note, Carter, Carla's big brother plays a major role in this story, trying to keep these two apart. But wait until he meets a woman who gives him a run for his money in book two, **The Rancher Needs a Wife,** coming out in 2020.

Yes, he's still the overprotective big brother and getting ready to take over the ranch, as his father, the matriarch decides to retire, for good this time. Carter draws the short straw at a family meeting to buy his stepmom her sixtieth birthday present, never imagining he'll get zapped with cupid's arrow by a feisty southern belle, single mom, and lingerie shop owner who is so wrong for him and has off-limits written all over her.

In book two, you'll see more of Sheriff Quil Sanchez. He'll get his own story and find a woman who outwits him and out-rescues him in **Rescuing the Sheriff**, book three. What fun!

I hope you love the by-the-book prince and the feisty cowgirl nanny's story as much as I loved writing this book.

~ Delsora

Acknowledgments

To the many people who had a hand in this story. Among them, my critique partners, Luanna Stewart, Judi Phillips, and Susan Vaughan, who added much to this novel, including helping me see the light of deleting all the excess wording and descriptions. To my editor, Janet Corcoran, who is a goddess of editing. Not only does she help me with my comma-challenged punctuation, and gently nudge me away from over-writing, but she adds insight to deepening the telling of the story. To my cover artist, Karen Ronan, who always manages to interpret my inane mutterings about cover vision into an actual WOW cover. To my formatter, Nina Pierce, who beautifies the inside of a book better than anyone. And to family and friends who continue to support me in my endeavors. Love you all!

Dedication

*To my daughter Tanya, whose tales of life
in Colorado were inspiration for the characters
and many facets of this story. And to my
grandsons, Waker, Mason, and Jack,
who each have a bit of them in every child's
character I write, including adorable
Jaime Orula, the prince's son.*

Chapter One

Patience wasn't one of her best traits.

Carla Peters shoved her tinted sunglasses on top of her head. The ones that gave her a rose-colored outlook on the day. Only today wasn't one of them.

With her hand shading her eyes, she searched the parking lot for her last student.

Five more minutes.

Ski boots clomped on the trampled snow as she paced back and forth. She tapped her watch—six a.m.? Now the battery was dead. Nothing had gone right this morning.

Carla glanced back at her partner and tapped the watch face once again. Tina flashed the five-minute sign. At least the small herd of kids were on their skis, ready to rock and roll. She focused her gaze back on the twisting ribbon of road just beyond the Silver Mountain parking lot.

A cold, crisp breeze played patty cake against her cheeks and tunneled deep into her lungs. On this picture-perfect late March morning, anxious to be on the slopes with her little charges, Carla couldn't imagine being anywhere else.

At least for today. And the two more weeks left until her ski instructor stint ended for the season. Then she'd get busy on her next project, her new school and the rest of her life.

She scanned the horizon one more time. Snow-covered, craggy mountains reached several thousand feet above where she stood. The cloudless blue sky, an incredible backdrop to knife-edged, ice-encased rocks gleaming like onyx in the sun, made the breathy plume of exhaust winding its way toward her stand out.

A high-end, black SUV swung around the last curve into the parking lot and skidded to a halt. She hadn't seen this Range Rover Sport before. Jaime Orula? When his nanny or the gentleman who worked for the prince dropped Jaime, they usually brought the bright red jeep with the Silver Mine logo on it.

The son of the horse breeder up-valley from her own family's beef cattle spread was the only kid missing. She should have checked the day's roster to be sure they didn't have a new student signed up.

Ari Orula glanced over his shoulder into the back seat. "You must hurry. We are late."

"*Desculpa*, Papa." His son struggled with the seat belt.

"English, please. We reside in America now."

Jaime nodded. "Sorry, Papa."

Ari smiled. "You are learning English well, my son. One moment. I will come around."

When he slid open the back door, Jaime's eyes were flooded with tears. "What is wrong?"

"I'm sorry to make us late. And I'm sorry I had to make you stop working."

"Ah, Jaime, I am the one who is sorry." He patted his son on the head. "I should not have been mad. It is not your fault. I did not know Sénhora was ill. And that no one else could bring you today."

"Maybe we should have stayed at home, Papa."

Ari reached to untangle the end of the seatbelt that had caught in the buckle. Worry snaked through him. His boy, always so sad these days. He was certain the ski lessons, grouped with other kids, would help bring Jaime out of his shell. "You do not like your lessons?"

Jaime stepped out of the car and looked up, his black eyes wide. "I do, Papa. Only I'm not so good. I fear the others will make fun."

Ari straightened. "They make fun?" Should he talk to the teacher? Was that why she'd called and texted him so many times, wishing to speak to him? He had been busy and thought the teacher would talk to the nanny as Jaime's other teachers had always done.

"No Papa, but they're better than I am."

"Do you ask for help from the teacher?"

Jaime shook his head. Ari's heart dropped. His boy, so shy and withdrawn since the incident with his mother. And now afraid to go to ski school where Ari was sure he'd make friends. What was he to do?

"Why do you not ask the teacher? That is her job to help you."

Jaime shrugged before he cast his eyes downward.

"Is she not nice to you?" He must talk to this teacher who was doing nothing for his son. Or maybe he should withdraw him from this school all together. He worked to temper his voice so Jaime would not think again that he was mad. "Sit. We will go home."

"No, Papa. Please. I want to go. I have fun. I like the teachers, especially Ms. Carla. She makes me laugh. Sometimes."

Ari's gut clenched. *Sometimes.* His son did not often allow himself to laugh, to let go.

"This teacher, does she help you?"

"*Sim*, Papa. She helps, but I'm not so good."

Ari's chest tightened once more. He must ask the nanny if Jaime behaved this way everyday—reluctant. "You will be good soon. If you wish to go today, then you need to pick up your backpack. Come now."

"*Sim*, Papa."

"And Jaime. Do not forget how much I love you, even when I am cross at work. *Sim?*"

His son's grin was all he needed. He must remember to take more time away from his duties to be with Jaime during the day. Between their breakfasts and suppers, he was so wrapped up in running the ranch, he'd let go duty to his own son.

3

Squinting, Carla nudged her sunglasses back in place. The tall man she'd watched emerge from the vehicle and help Jaime alight from the back seat was yummy. Who was he? Certainly not the nanny. His black Stetson had bobbed above the roofline of the vehicle. Now, with his back to her, his black shearling jacket did nothing to hide the breadth of his shoulders. The gray lamb's wool collar lay wide, accentuating both the jacket stretched tight across his back and ebony hair brushing his collar. Faded jeans hugged strong thighs.

Whoa. Now that's some view. That cowboy had the nicest hindquarters she'd laid eyes on in a long while. The heat flamed up her cheeks, despite the whistling wind. She hauled in a deep breath.

Get your head on straight, girl.

The cowboy turned. The profile of a regal nose added to the mystique of who he could be. He clutched Jaime's hand and walked toward her, his boots crunching on the gravel pathway. Carla homed in on an angular jaw covered in a few days' growth.

She couldn't help the grin as she grabbed her fill of cowboy scenery. But a tiny pang of sadness wove into her enjoyment as she watched the man gently hold Jaime's hand and memories of the child she'd lost rose from the past.

She shook off the twinge of melancholy and strode the thirty yards to meet the man and boy halfway. The black Stetson, shading half his face, gave him a dangerous look. Between that and the black vehicle with tinted windows… She shivered. Way too rich for her blood. Even if the Peters Valley Ranch had extra dough floating around, she couldn't see her dad and brothers turning in their faithful beater trucks, for useless luxury.

The man tipped his hat back just enough to lift the shadows. She didn't recognize him, but he had a determined set to his mouth. Why the grim expression?

Carla glanced down at Jaime with his beautiful ebony hair and bright red coat. "Hey, kid."

4

Jaime's mouth tweaked up in a half-grin.

"You will refer to the boy by his given name."

She straightened her back, ready to take on the imported cowboy. Judging by his accent, he must be from Jaime's native country. She removed her sunglasses. Slowly, she scanned the tall body. From his hand-tooled leather cowboy boots planted wide, up the faded jean-covered muscled thighs, pausing briefly at the strategically placed worn spot along the zipper, and on to the leather jacket, detailed in intricate stitching, that screamed pricey. No run-of-the-mill cowboy. Must be one of the prince's higher-ups.

She paused again to lock her gaze on lips pursed tight, then scanned up to eyes covered by mirrored sunglasses that reflected the sunlight back, causing her to blink. She tried not to laugh at his attempt at intimidation. She stared back and without breaking eye contact with the cowboy, reworded her greeting with an exaggerated drawl. "Hey, *Jaime.*"

The cowboy removed his Stetson, then flipped his sunglasses to rest on top of his head. His dark eyes caught her breath, mesmerizing her for a moment. The bright sun overhead hit his features. Her mouth went as dry as the desert surrounding Grand Junction. It was *him*. Prince Ari Orula in the flesh.

She'd seen a few grainy newspaper photos. Eighth son of the crown prince of Portega, a tiny island nestled off the borders of Spain and Portugal. The baby of the family. According to the stories she'd read, the aloof brother with the royal chip on his to-die-for shoulders. Even though he played hooky from his homeland on U.S. soil and had tried to blend in with the natives in the year he'd been in Colorado, his entitled attitude always managed to get him in trouble with the press.

Didn't sit well with the area ranchers either—her dad and brothers topping the list of *not impressed.*

Oh, yeah, she'd heard *all* about the prince.

She contemplated why he'd chosen their little mountain ski school, instead of Buttermilk or Snowmass a half hour away. Rumor had it, his fortune could buy up all of Aspen Ski

Company, including their four mountains and considerable holdings of condos, time shares, hotels, and restaurants in the Aspen area.

Carla reached over to pat the head of the quiet little boy with the onyx eyes, tanned-bronze complexion from his days on the slopes, and eyelashes a woman might be tempted to kill for. Trying desperately not to act star-struck about her proximity to a for-real prince, she knelt. "You all ready for some fun?"

The boy looked up at his father. Carla's gaze followed Jaime's. *Dang.* The boy was a miniature replica of his father. The prince nodded before Jaime acknowledged Carla with his own nod.

A man of few words. Jaime didn't talk much either.

And therein lay the problem. Carla thought there was a lot more behind Jaime's reluctance to not only talk, but interact with the kids his age. She'd asked his nanny about the kid being shy. Closemouthed as a moated and gated castle, the nanny obviously didn't intend to spill the family secrets while on the royal payroll.

But Carla had a plan. Go straight to the deep, dark, and stoic source of the river. Be forthright with the prince. Find out exactly how she could help Jaime open up.

Trouble was, she'd tried and tried to contact daddy dearest.

Jaime stepped toward Carla, a slight grin working at the corner of his mouth. Hey, she'd take any hint of a smile. She stripped off her glove and reached out. Without hesitation, he clasped her hand. She gave his a friendly squeeze before standing and placing her palm on Jaime's shoulder. She really did like this kid. Felt for him. Wanted to help him escape his tiny prison of shyness. "Go with Tina. And don't forget to put on your mittens."

When he didn't move, she added. "I'm right behind you. Tina will help you stow your backpack."

Jaime glanced once again at the prince. And once again his father nodded, as if the kid had to have permission to move.

Dang. That was so wrong.

Squinting against the bright sun, Carla studied the man in

front of her. Rigid. Demanding. Forbidden. He swept his hand out, like royalty issuing demands of his servants. But when she looked into his eyes, there lay a hidden uncertainty as his gaze dipped toward his boots and then back to his son. The barest smile tipped the corners of his mouth.

Jaime looked up at his father, then spread his arms around the prince's knees in a quick hug. This time, the smile reached the prince's eyes. "Go then. Enjoy your day."

"*Sim*, Papa." The boy remained where he stood.

"Jaime. Honey, grab your skis from Tina. Gorgeous day—we're going to have some fun."

The kid moved slowly toward the group. Now was her chance. Carla stuck out her hand.

The prince's eyes widened.

Geez, royalty. How *did* you address them? Looked like she'd committed a faux pas as big as the surrounding mountain range. Should she have fallen to her knees and dipped her forehead toward the earth? *Yeah, no.* He was on her turf now.

Getting an *audience* with him had been impossible. She'd tried for the past three weeks, but not one returned call or email. Apparently, rich, royal horse-breeders mixing with commoners, especially *ski bunnies* teaching six-year olds in the back-mountain town of Mineral Springs, Colorado, went against his royal rule.

Carla tamped down a shrug and an urge to put the man in his place. Wouldn't help the kid. When in Colorado, do as the Coloradoans do. Good 'ole fashioned courtesy with a healthy dose of how-ya-doin' and a firm handshake.

She extended her hand again. After leveling a drawn out steely-eyed gaze, he thrust his big hand into hers.

An electric charge from the dry air zinged up her arm. She jerked her hand out of his. *Whoa.* As she rubbed her arm, she vowed to stick to her story—electrical charge. Nothing more.

Carla faced down the prince's stare. His onyx eyes, as dark as the craggy mountains behind them, caused another zap to zing through her whole body.

Oh boy. Trouble with a capital T. Attraction to her student's dad, so not good. Especially a full-of-himself prince.

She stepped back, pressing her hand to her stomach to stop the flutter that had a mind of its own. *Body, listen to brain.*

No time to think about men. Any man. Especially arrogant, entitled men. She had plans. As soon as ski school ended, she'd return to the old grind. Waitressing at Comfort Food. One more job to fight for the almighty dollar to help her realize her dream.

Nope, no man would get in the way of accomplishing her dream.

Shifting her glance away from the prince's eyes to land on the straight line of his mouth, she found her voice. "I'm Carla Peters, your son's instructor." Before she could utter any of the how-ya-doin' niceties to soften up the prince's hard stare, pressed lips, and attitude, her mouth spit out the demand. "You and I—we need to talk. You never returned my..."

Shut your mouth, Carla. Okay, so she'd learned the art of subtly from her brothers.

His chin lifted. A regal lift if she ever saw one. A don't-mess-with-me lift. A do-you-know-who-I-am lift.

All too well. She nodded, an instinctive reaction to the unasked questions written across his face, before she straightened, pulling forth her control to match his. Right now, her mission to help the boy did not include cow-towing to the man. Prince or no prince. She had to stand up to him in order to find out how she could help shy, withdrawn Jaime.

His eyes narrowed and darkened, as if coal could turn blacker.

She had her work cut out for her. Teaching children was her calling, her passion. And this boy was hurting about something. *I owe it to this little boy to find out what's eating him.* She wasn't about to let a little royal attitude get in her way.

"I beg your pardon, Ms...." He stared at her face. Then his gaze slid to her name embroidered across the fleece vest, as if it was beneath him to remember the name she'd moments earlier told him. "Ms...Peters."

His voice, diamond hard, scored a cut deep into her gut.

Another man who didn't take her seriously.

She was sick and tired of male attitudes. Like she couldn't fend for herself. Know what was good for her. *Holy hello.* As a rancher's daughter, she'd dealt with hard-assed men all her life.

Not least, her dad and brothers who *expected* her to settle down and do what women were supposed to do—raise kids, tend vegetable gardens, and bake bread. *No dang way.*

If she didn't allow her dad and brothers to sabotage her dreams, she wasn't about to let one prince get to her. Eighth in line, no less.

Now…she had him cornered. Determined to finally get her audience with him, she stepped into his space. "I said we need to talk. Your son—"

"I have no need to discuss my son with you."

Carla tilted her head and steeled her resolve to match his veiled contempt. Focusing on his eyes—the ones rimmed with eyelashes just like his son's—she did what her training taught her. Read beyond his glare.

Attitude much?

Or was it pain? Did he try to scare people off so they'd stop tying to figure him out?

"Do you love him?"

"Of course, I love my son. How *dare* you question me?"

Nothing better than a challenge to get a man to talk. She stifled a grin. "I don't question. I wanted to see your reaction. I know you love him. That's why you and I must talk."

His stiff demeanor told her to back off. Wrong place. Wrong time.

She wasn't one to back away from a problem, even if this was not the right time to speak to him. He never called her back. And probably wouldn't if she walked away. She pulled out her *compliment* card.

"Your son is very sweet—"

"Sweet?" The prince spat the word out like a rattler ejecting his poison.

She stood her ground, shaking her head. "What's wrong with sweet?" *Royalty, schmoyalty.* He was a man, like any other. "Ask any woman."

His glare turned to a furious stare. *Double dang.* Well, she dared to cross the bridge over that dark river. Go for it.

She planted her fists on her hips and widened her stance to match his, the same way she always stood up to her brothers. It usually worked. "Sweet is one quality women look for in a man."

He stiffened, as if there was any more leeway in his body to straighten. The prince stepped back and crossed his arms.

She'd stepped over the line—way over. But no backing down now.

"When can we speak?" Although nerves were two-stepping in her belly, Carla straightened and seized control in her best schoolmarm voice. "With whom should I make the appointment?"

He turned away from her.

Of all the... Okay, so sarcasm probably wasn't the best choice of communication.

Then he was on the move, his long stride eating up the gravel pathway leading toward his vehicle.

No way was she letting him get away without hashing out Jaime's issues. Carla strode after him, her long legs matching his pace. Used to chasing after her brothers, she reached the prince by the time he'd yanked open the passenger door, grabbed his leather portfolio, and turned back toward her.

She stopped short and stepped back to give herself much needed space. He was one of those men who outsized his piece of the universe with his attitude alone. He unzipped the case, removed his tablet, and tipped the screen toward her. He swiped through the days of March until he reached-March eighteenth. He tapped the week icon. His long, broad finger traced a line across the third week.

"Wednesday? Thursday? Call my secretary." The clipped words, in a rich, low lilt, rolled off his tongue in a majestic, albeit, pompous way—as if everyone had a se-cri-tar-*ree*. He handed her a card, shut the case, and tossed it on the seat, then he slammed the door and swaggered toward the driver's side.

Despite the admirable view of receding backside, she'd not

be taken in by the strut of royalty. So, the man had money and power and a title. Don't friggin' tangle with Carla Peters. She sure as Hades didn't have power, but she'd match Mr. Your Highness in attitude. She hadn't battled four brothers all her life for nothing.

Carla crossed her arms over her chest as he slid into the upscale vehicle. No, Mr. Prince had picked the wrong person to pull out his royal attitude.

Chapter Two

Ari folded his arms over the top of the steering wheel, wanting to beat his head against the blasted thing. Giles was right. If he didn't stop acting like he had a royal scepter up his ass every time he interacted with his neighbors, he'd never fit in.

He had reacted badly, flaunting his power like the Crown Prince. The one person he tried his hardest not to emulate. He came to Colorado so he could be himself—not royalty, but a cowboy caring for his stock.

Hard to do when everyone knew your name and pedigree.

He glanced out the passenger window at the receding back of *that* woman. The one who had glared at him with those hazel eyes that sparked with flecks of emerald. Watched the sway of her hips in perfect symmetry with the rest of her firm, lush body encased in form-fitting ski apparel, the thin stripe running up her side from ankle to torso accentuating every curve. All he wished to do was rail against her audacity in questioning his fatherhood. Instead, his body reacted like that of a pubescent school boy.

He'd been a horse's ass, trying to take control of the conversation. Hardly surprising she'd called him on it. *Did he love his son? Of all the nerve.*

Then he'd agreed to a meeting. Why she insisted on getting in his business when there were only two more weeks of ski school, he wasn't sure. But he would hash it out with her. If nothing else, get to the bottom of why Jaime seemed on the verge of tears this morning. His fear about fitting in and not being as good on skis as the others. And humor the ski teacher's need to save Jaime. *What did she know? Did he love his son? Of all the nerve.*

At least he would be on his own turf. This time he'd show his princely charm, while demonstrating who was in charge. Who did he kid? He lacked people skills. He must enlist Giles for help. But giving his big brother an excuse for another try at a regular-guy-makeover would not go well.

With a roll of his eyes, Ari revved the engine and slammed the gear into drive, peeling out of the parking lot. The distance in miles was no match for his overactive mind. The one consumed with fury and pride...and lust. All he must tamp down if he was to do right by Jaime. Giles would comment on the tall order he imposed on himself.

Down the mountain toward the piece of valley that was his sanctuary, the miles did nothing to obliterate the image of the woman who both angered and fascinated him. He must forget the latter and make sure she knew her place and her job—teach the boy to enjoy life and make friends—for the remaining two weeks. The service for which he paid her.

He crossed his private bridge, over the river that separated him from the town full of people who refused to accept him. Most of their reluctance could be attributed to what Giles called his arrogance. He preferred to consider himself a consummate introvert who'd always had trouble relating to people, except those closest to him. His family. His childhood friends. Those he-became accustomed to over the years.

He was the eighth son and had never had to put on a public face like his much older brothers. And when he did, he chose to do so in the most self-effacing of ways. But arrogance? He understood his manner reflected that attribute. He knew no other way, learning from the master how to shove that royal attitude in people's faces. Make everyone show respect. Whether they wanted to or not. His arrogance had been his self-protection for so long.

The method that broached no argument. *Great lesson.*

Except with Ms. Peters. Perhaps she'd learned her own lessons. Dole out respect only when warranted. Ari had met her oldest brother, Carter, the one who ran the ranch. And he'd had a few run-ins with Mitch, the patriarch of the family. Predictably, she too treated him in such a way. Perhaps, as he had, she had learned from the best.

As Ari drove up the winding, dirt-packed road leading to his ranch, he straightened, drumming his thumbs in a hard beat against the wheel that right now was a surrogate to his nemesis, Ms. Peters.

No, he could not cave to her demands. If he did so, he would fail Jaime.

Jaime, who stood off to the side from the other kids. Not unhappy, but not interacting. Yes, his boy had probably learned the same lessons from him that he had learned from his own father. A wrong he must work hard to right.

And she questioned him about his raising of his son. What did she know of what they had been through the last few years?

He must give her some credit. When Ms. Peters beckoned, Jaime moved closer to the group, though his eyes downcast. Ari's heart had beat out of his chest for the shyness his son exhibited over the past two years. It was as if Ari peered into a mirror at himself at that age. But Jaime had a reason. He had been a vibrant boy before the accident.

When the striking teacher chucked his son under the chin and Jaime's head rose, a small smile had spread across the boy's face. He had even reached for her hand. He could not blame Jaime for the reaction. No, his son was not unhappy, nor immune to beauty, only cautious and shy. So sure time would heal, Ari wished more for Jaime. But there had been little evidence that Jaime's normally sunny personality would lift him out of his depths of pain anytime soon.

As Ari stopped in front of his home, he spread his fingers wide and released the steering wheel. He did not want this solitary life for his son. But what was he to do?

Trust this woman who dared confront him?

The ski lessons should have been the perfect activity to bring his son out of his shell. Meet other children. Find joy in his life. Already at rope's end with what to do with his withdrawn son, the teacher made it worse with her insinuations.

God the almighty knew Ari's fathering skills proved less than adequate. He had tried. But his role model had taught him to tough things out.

Ari gripped the door handle, fighting to clear his head of ghosts. He glanced at the second story window—his office. Visualizing orderly piles of files on his desk grounded him. The work that would prove him to be as good as his brothers. Better maybe, if his ranch improvements confirmed the success rate he expected from these new breeding techniques. And maybe his work would gain him the respect of the area ranchers. Certainly, at home in Portega, no one had taken his innovative ideas seriously. *Not yet.*

But he had done his research, gone to seminars, framed discussions with breeders all over the world. His organizational plan would give new meaning to automated and efficient horse breeding. No longer would his father or the Portega cabinet ministers laugh at Ari's ideas.

Maybe laughter was not quite the correct characterization. Yet, on occasion, they looked over the rim of their glasses when he claimed horse-breeding would put Portega on the map and fill the treasury with much-needed revenue.

He pushed open the truck door. Reflecting on innovation and organization and efficiency always relaxed him. Being in his own head, put him in his element. He had control. Proving himself put a smile on his face. Control of and delight in his mission, both rarely found in combination in his day-to-day.

Then, thoughts of the woman in the parking lot who'd stolen his control with only a few words returned. How was he to arm himself against this woman who dug herself under his skin in a matter of minutes?

Her appeal was evident, that he could admit. In a purely physical sense. Until she'd opened her mouth to question him. He could not allow such behavior. Making him question his ability as a parent.

Tearing his gaze from the window to his orderly office, he understood success on his ranch would mean nothing without succeeding as a father.

Hours later, bent over his desk and intent on shoving the unfortunate conversation with Ms. Peters out of his head, the national anthem of his beloved country rang out. Ari groaned. Why he had chosen this piece as his ring-tone for his father never failed to give him pause.

Hitting speaker, he moved the phone closer. "Your Highness."

"Why do you do this, Ari?" The gruff voice deepened. "I am your father."

"You call on business?"

"Of course. It is what we do."

"Then what can I do for you, *your Highness*?"

His father's sigh echoed over the speaker-phone. Ari had been taught from an early age to respect the position of his father. They rarely talked father to son. Only business. Yet he continued to antagonize his father, despite the crown prince's frustration. As if, for once, Ari could gain the upper hand and get his father to sound like a father, not that of the ruler.

"I am sending you a prized mare we purchased in the middle east. You must breed her with King."

"I must?"

"Do not argue. King is the match for her. I tell you. She will arrive in two weeks. Take care of the matter."

The click told him the usual—his father signing off without a word of praise or respect. A simple thanks. Maybe a phrase of love—not that his father would ever say the actual words he longed to hear since he was a boy. For the second time in as few hours, anger bubbled to the surface.

Ari tamped down his distress as a thought came to him. Sending a prized mare across the ocean had to count for something. Without the words, his father did acknowledge his expertise. Ari unclenched his fist, sucked in a deep breath, and allowed a smile to take hold.

He snapped open his laptop and pulled up his breeding chart.

Now to make plans for housing the mare for the next two years. Maybe by the time she reached her estrous cycle in the spring, he would have perfected his breeding methods to his satisfaction. He'd barely scratched out a few notes when the e-mail detailing the mare's ETA and her stats arrived from his father's manager.

He read, deep in thought about strategies.

A heavy knock sounded against his office door, pulling him from details of his newest challenge. He scrubbed his hand through his hair. He had no time for more interruptions.

"Enter."

Giles, his manager, confidant, best friend, and older brother, strode through the door. "You sound distracted."

"Father. He sends a breeding mare from the far east."

Giles raised a brow but said nothing as he plopped down in the winged leather chair in front of Ari's desk.

"What brings you here to interrupt my day?"

Giles full-faced grin brought out his dimple. "You know I only interrupt when things are dire."

"Dire? Jaime?" He half rose from his chair.

Giles gestured for him to sit. "The only way I can get your complete attention. Ari, you must learn to pay attention to non-verbal cues. See my smile? Notice I am causally sitting?"

Ari sat down. He should have known. The one brother who used warped humor in place of out and out royal decree. Of course, in Ari's father's eyes Giles was a commoner, even though his own father was a member of the House of Lords.

"Why do you insist on giving me a heart attack?"

"For one thing, you need to be brought back into the real world once in a while."

"And the other? You always have an angle."

Giles shrugged. "The fun of it."

"Giving your baby brother a heart attack is fun to you?"

"Without a doubt. Sometimes you need to be jolted from wherever you have gone in your own head. You take yourself too seriously."

"I do not—" He stopped himself as Giles' brow lifted. "You

are right. I do bury myself in work."

"Not only your work. But your relationships with outsiders."

"What do you insinuate?"

"You came to America to get away from royal snobbery, to learn how to be one of *the guys.*"

Ari leaned back in his chair. He should have known his brother would go down this path. "I have not succeeded well in that quest, I am afraid."

"If you'd let me help. We'll go to town tonight. Listen to some cowboy music. Drink a beer. Observe and learn how to relax."

"I have no time for that nonsense."

Giles leaned forward, resting his elbows on his knees. "If nothing else, you need to learn to relax before you end up struck down by a real heart attack."

"When I must deal with my father's commands, there is no time to relax."

Giles shrugged. "You know your father."

"No, I do not. He never lets one get close."

"That's the way you see it?"

"And how else would I see it but through my own eyes?"

"Therein lies the problem, my good man. Our own lens is usually warped. He has responsibilities. Like you, he hides who he really is in favor of the persona."

Before Ari could reply, Giles stood and crossed the room to Ari's wall of books. Tucked sideways across the top row sat the family photo album. He reached high.

"Oh, no. You do not bring out that old and dusty relic of how life is supposed to look. Posed, most of them."

"I plan to prove you wrong. I spent summers with you, remember? Have a look. Here." Giles flipped through the pages. "A little older than Jaime, I suspect. Your father teaching you to ride." He shoved the open book into Ari's arms and leaned over his shoulder to point out the ones of Ari and his father. "Not many fathers who are Crown Royals teach their boys to ride. They leave it up to the staff."

"Once."

"But your first time on a full-sized horse. No more ponies. I was there. I remember how proud he was of you."

"Proud. My father has never been proud of me."

"A photo, they say, tells the story of a thousand words. Look at his eyes. They rest on you. And there—a smile. Well about as much of a smile as your father shows. And your face." Giles pointed to the boy atop a well-muscled horse. "You too are proud. Your shoulders back as you look at your father. Both of you proud."

"That is but one example. A fluke."

"Or selective memory, my man."

"My older brothers—they all had much attention from him. He groomed them."

"Or you could look at this a different way. He had to micromanage them. You, he did not. You were always full of ideas, ready to make them into reality, ready to prove yourself. As you do now."

"What good has it done?"

Giles sat back down, crossing his legs at his ankles. "You have your own ranch and business. Your brothers were raised by mothers who were royalty—they expected everything handed to them. You did not. You made your future happen through hard work."

"Despite mother's lunacy and constant badgering that I must act the royal I am. I swear she lived through both of us to ensure the status our fathers brought to her American upbringing."

"It did exact a toll out of her," Giles said.

"And drove father away. Mostly likely your father, too. Do you think this is the reason father pushes me so?"

"He did love your mother once. And, never for a moment has he thought you common."

"But never does he bother to say a word of praise to me."

"He sent you a prized mare. Some things are not said in words, but gestures."

"Yes, that he did." Ari sighed and rubbed his thumb against the black chunk of basalt he kept hidden in his pocket. It was almost smooth on one side from years of worrying the stone whenever he needed to sort through the happenings in his life.

"Enough of this." Ari secreted the stone back in his pocket. "Now, what is so dire?"

"Sénhora Miranda's mother is extremely ill. She must return to Portega immediately."

"Her mother will live?"

Giles nodded, the laughter from his earlier teasing gone from his eyes.

"Excellent." Ari held in the emotional gratitude that his nanny's mother would be all right and kept to the business at hand. "And your plan for replacing Sénhora?"

"The sénhora suggested the nice woman who is teaching Jaime to ski."

"Ms. Peters? Hell no. Absolutely not."

"Do you know her?" Giles leaned forward.

"Most unfortunately."

"Jaime likes her. I do, as well."

Ari worked at not reacting to Giles' comment. He slowly exhaled. He dare not mention his predicament with Jaime's teacher. Giles would have a field day, dragging him to town to *normalize* him. And then challenging Ari to pursue the tempting Ms. Peters. *No.*

"I've researched her professional background."

"Of a ski bunny?"

Giles continued. "Her training, education, and experience give her the credentials to deal with children Jaime's age. In fact, rumor in town has it she and her friend will open an elementary school soon. She'd be perfect as a nanny. And her job ends in two weeks. Until then, Cook and I can keep an eye on Jaime when he's not learning to ski."

Ari shoved his chair back until it collided against the wall, and rose. "Find someone else."

"It is temporary—"

"Find. Someone. Else."

Giles tilted his head before rising. "This is the reason you do not fit in like one of the guys."

"Must you always have the last word?"

Dimple flashing, Giles ambled from the room.

Ari strode toward the door and slammed it shut. Why must nothing go as planned? Not that he begrudged the sénhora her need to care for her mother. In fact, he would order his pilot to fly her in the ranch's jet, so she wasted little time getting home.

A new wrinkle in his once well-ordered life. Giles would refuse to let go of his idea to hire the ski bunny to care for Jaime. He was the Silver Mine Ranch manager for a reason. Despite his cavalier manner, Giles studiously plotted out solutions. And damn him, but he was usually spot on with his assessments.

A litany of Portega oaths spewed from Ari's mouth. This woman would not be a part of their lives.

His rigid shoulders slumped.

He knew his brother. Giles would see to it he would have no choice but to deal with this woman.

The one Jaime liked.

The one Ari had not stopped obsessing about since their verbal confrontation that morning.

Chapter Three

Carla's cell chirped an appointment reminder. *Shoot.* After a crazy week at work and then up half the night helping her brothers with early spring birthing at the ranch, she'd managed to shove the meeting clear from her head. She better get a move on or end up late for the meeting of the minds with his royal high-and-mighty.

Minutes later, on her fifteen-mile trek to the ranch-fiefdom, her racing mind kept pace with the speed of her truck. Her brothers would crucify her if they knew she was on the way to speak to the prince about his son. The man had never gone out of his way to know any of the town's people. He lived like a modern-day, entitled hermit. And Carter and her dad continued to hold onto their grudge that the prince had bought the much-needed grazing land adjacent to their ranch.

Lowering the window halfway, she let the cold air wash over her, clearing her head. Staring down the prince the other day was one thing. Confronting him head-on in his own home could turn into a huge battle of wills. Why was he so against listening to her concerns about Jaime? She adored the kid. She only wanted to know the best way to approach him and get him into his comfort zone with the other kids. She saw the way he watched them from afar. He wanted to join in. It was as if he didn't trust himself or others around him. A puzzle, for sure.

She lifted her shoulders and rolled her head clock-wise, then counter-clockwise, to release the tension. Having her head on straight was the only way she'd win this battle with prince charming. It wasn't that she had animosity toward him—not like her brothers. But she was upset that he hadn't *bothered* to return her calls.

A light snowfall had dusted the roads overnight, enough to make it slick. Carla gripped the steering wheel. The chill hung in the air as the sun made its ascent, but it promised to be a beautiful day, perfect for hitting the slopes. If she made it through this meeting in one piece, she'd reward herself with a few runs on new powder before joining Tina and the class.

The bumpy, dirt road wound down toward the river's edge and a cluster of Cottonwoods, across an old-fashioned wooden bridge and back up through scrub. The stand of Junipers ahead formed a shield of protection for the ranch house sitting atop an outcropping overlooking the Roaring Fork. Carla down-shifted to grind her way up the steep, winding road.

Five minutes later, she stood in what had looked like a three-story rambling ranch house. Now inside, a more apt description would be mansion. As the short, gray-haired woman dressed in black with a white apron scurried out of view after greeting her at the door, Carla scanned the open lobby. A wide stairway bumped into the middle between the great hall and a huge open living space beyond.

Holy hello. What had she signed up for?

She kept telling herself that the kid needed her. Jaime would work with her one-on-one but when she suggested joining with the others, he retreated into himself. He stood on the sidelines, looking toward the group. She'd worked with shy kids, but Jaime wasn't shy. He was reluctant to intermingle for another reason. One Carla planned to uncover. He was worth the trouble of this visit.

The scent of hot peppers and onions and heady spices filled the air, causing her stomach to growl. She'd forgotten about breakfast. One of these days, she'd learn to cook. Her stepmom, Madge, and the ranch cook prided themselves on nurturing the family and ranch hands with heaps of nourishing food. Left to her own devices, Carla forgot to eat right. So busy with ski school or helping her brothers in the barn or riding across the valley herding cattle, nutrition bars were her staple. Coffee her drug. Throw in a few rashers of bacon or a thick steak and baker on occasion and she was a happy cowgirl.

Heavy footsteps across the wooden floor directly above yanked her away from obsessing about her rumbling belly. She couldn't see beyond the curve of the staircase. But judging from the pounding of tooled boots against each step, and excellent ass coming into view through the intricate, wrought-iron banister, it was a good bet that his royal-ness remained on the warpath.

"I have ten minutes. State your business," Ari said, before stepping onto the marble-tiled floor of the great hall.

Carla steadied her breathing, modulated her voice to calm, and looked him straight in the eye. "I'd prefer to sit while we talk." She couldn't let him have the upper hand. Not until she said what she'd come to say.

He tossed his head toward the other side of the staircase and the opulent seating facing a wall of windows that showcased the breadth of the house, two three-story wings flanking a courtyard, one story across the far end, and the grand view beyond. The grand view that overlooked the valley her family had saved for years to purchase. The grand view now owned by the prince had plenty of water and, according to Carter, was the reason the Peters Valley Ranch had none. Her stomach soured.

Why did she insist on trying to help this small boy? Because her gut told her the sweet, quiet boy needed her, that's why.

Quelling her own anger toward the arrogant prince, she focused on the greater challenge of helping Jaime by nodding assent to his unspoken command to sit. Until they both sat and were on even ground, she wasn't uttering another word.

Never mind the tick-down of his decreed ten-minute limit.

Towering over her intimidated her all to hell. Crazy. She tried to imagine he was one of her obnoxious and overbearing brothers. In all fairness, she loved her brothers. But, they *were* her brothers. You had to hate them sometimes. Fight with them. Stand up to them. She'd learned to overcome their intimidating tactics. Now, she couldn't help being intimidated—a tiny bit.

"Just like my brothers," she muttered. So much for vowing

to speak only when spoken to.

"I did not allow you to come here to waste time discussing your family."

Half way to the overstuffed leather armchair, she turned, choosing to ignore the word *allow*. Obviously, the prince had a burr up his butt about her family. Good ammunition. "You don't wish to talk about my family. But you choose to act just like my stubborn and arrogant brothers. I don't know why I bother with the lot of you."

He looked stunned at her retort. His mouth formed a straight line, his lips pressed together so tightly she feared he would swallow them. And just as fast, he transformed back into his haughty royalness, his eyes blazing.

"I have no time for insolence. You were the one who demanded this audience."

"Audience?" She bit her lip. *Stop antagonizing the guy. The mission is the kid, not one-upping the prince.*

In slow motion, he drew in a deep breath, as if practicing a calming exercise.

She held up her palms. "Look, I'm sorry. We got off on the wrong foot." She tried to regain some dignity and not further piss him off. *Remember the mission.*

"Wrong foot?"

"We shouldn't argue. I adore your son and want to help."

His hand swept toward the seating area in a rather rigid attempt at a conciliatory gesture.

She sat in the deep maroon leather chair. He chose to perch on the sofa arm adjacent to her, still towering over her and crowding her with his proximity.

Carla sucked in a huge breath. *Big mistake.* The heady scent of cloves and pepper and something very male accosted her senses. His onyx eyes directed a royal stare as if to say, *well, time is running out.*

"Jaime. I'm concerned about him. Don't get me wrong," she rushed on before he could cop his regal-in-the-ass attitude. "He's a good kid. His skiing is coming along fine. He follows instructions and learns quickly. But…" How to say this without insulting the father? Again. "His social skills—he doesn't readily interact with the other kids. Or with the instructors."

As if possible, the prince's eyes turned blacker. Man, she wouldn't want to run into him among the dimly lit stalls of a barn. *Behind the barn? Oh yeah.*

Carla sat up straighter and lifted her chin, trying hard to yank her head out of the gutter of lust and concentrate on fighting for Jaime. But dang, he was good looking in a regal, self-centered, buff, pseudo-cowboy kind of way. Now, if he'd only learn to relax. Maybe act as though he enjoyed life. "I want to help Jaime. I can tell he wants to join the fun." Okay, she'd blurt it out. "What's holding him back?"

The prince stood. "This is not your concern." He strode toward the staircase, then turned back to her, legs widened into his I'm-going-to-intimidate-you stance.

Carla stood, leveling the playing field. She hoped.

"I must ask you to leave. No more interference from you."

Carla widened her stance. "I came to find a solution for your adorable son, not to fight with you."

"No, you are not *permitted* to argue."

"Not *permitted?*" She blew the errant bang off her forehead and sucked in her rage. He was royalty. He was used to getting his way. And…to *holy hello* with keeping her cool. She might want to remind him this was America. Colorado. Mineral Springs. A township in which *her family*, one among many big ranchers, ruled.

"I might remind you, I am not one of your subjects. I am a teacher. I care about my students. I care about Jaime." She tried to keep her voice calm, but one look at his hard eyes and her forced calm lost out to frustration, before it morphed into fury. "If you want to use arrogance and stubbornness against me, go right ahead. But I'd assume your first priority would be your son. So get out of your own head and figure out what Jaime needs for a change. And when you figure it out, let me know. I want to help."

Carla turned on her heel, stormed across the wide hall and out the door, as if a wildfire licked at her heels.

When she reached her battered, twelve-year old truck, she stood, hands on hips and stared back at the huge ranch house. She'd blown it—big time.

Who was she to march in and tell a prince how to raise his son? But she couldn't help it. She cared about the little boy. He might live in opulence, but apparently Jaime had no one to rally for him, least of all his stiff and arrogant, and *okay*, handsome, father.

She started back to the house then stopped. Now was not the time.

They both needed to cool down.

Her gaze rose to the window above the huge, oak front door. A shadow moved. Was Prince Orula watching her? A shiver tingled down her spine. *Dang.* She did care about the kid. And sad to say, despite his pompous attitude, the boy's father fascinated her. She wanted to dig deep to find out what made him tick. Get beneath the surface of his icy façade, for there had to be caring and passion buried inside. She'd seen the softening in his eyes before he hardened his glare. And she'd seen no fear from Jaime when Ari had dropped him off at ski school. Why else would Jaime be such a sweet child?

Ari moved beyond the shadows playing on the floor by the window and paced the length of his office toward the massive cherry desk at the far end and back again to the bank of windows. Again, he stopped and peered out. Ms. Peters truck had roared off minutes ago.

He imagined she'd stomped all the way to her truck as he climbed his stairs, two at a time. When he reached his office, he caught her standing in the middle of his drive, hands on hips, staring at the house. More like glaring.

She had a fiery temper. With a fiery temper came passion, of that he was sure. For a moment, he wished she had marched back to confront him. Only he may not have been able to hold off. Her wild rose and thyme scent had swirled around him when she'd stood her ground in the great room. For a flash, he allowed himself to smile, before he remembered his anger.

She'd radiated a wild-eyed fury when she questioned him downstairs. He didn't blame her. He'd perfected the royal attitude and when he needed to control a situation, he hauled it out.

Suspicion was as ingrained as haughtiness. Taught from birth.

Strangely, he trusted the compassion in her hazel eyes, the tilt of her head as she tried to explain how she wanted to help Jaime. But one whiff of her spicy, floral scent and the aroma ignited his libido. He reacted as any man would, despite the lecture going on in his head to ignore any visceral or emotional tug.

The moment before he pulled forth the haughtiness card, he'd been on the verge of telling her everything. That scared the hell out of him. In the end, his rigid upbringing saved him—keeping everything tamped down inside.

Don't let your enemy see anything they can use against you. Vulnerability is a weakness.

He learned the lessons well. Until Arianna.

So why did he fight so hard against Ms. Peters? For fear she might have ulterior motives. Like Jaime's mother.

Ari looked over the land he recently acquired. The ranchers nearby, including her brothers and father, were angry for his intrusion on *their* land. Soon, he would prove them wrong. Prove he could be one of them, care for the land as well as they did, and be a good neighbor.

But right now, he wasn't worried about neighbors. Right now, he needed to shore up the wall he carefully erected the day he lost Arianna. A wall to shield him from wanting another woman.

Not that he *wanted* Ms. Peters. She simply reminded him of what he lost and could someday want again—that was all.

He cursed at the lie. Neither this woman with the innocent blond braid slung over her shoulder nor any other woman, possessed the power to tear down his wall. Kick a large hole in it? She had done that on first meeting. But tear it down? No. He would work to protect his heart. And Jaime's.

His intercom bleated. Pressing his finger to the on-button, he bellowed, "Can this not wait?"

"Ah, I see you concluded the dreaded meeting with the *incompetent* Ms. Peters." Giles' British-accent mocked him.

"And this amuses you?"

"Indeed, it does. Right now, I have other concerns. I need you in the stables. King's temperature is up."

Ari disconnected and ran down the hall, down the stairs, and back through the kitchen. He was breathing heavily by the time he reached King's stall.

Giles emerged from the shadows. "The vet is on the way."

"Thank you for looking after him."

"What else would I do for your prized stallion?"

Yes, his prized stallion, despite no longer riding. Not since Arianna... Whispering words of comfort, Ari smoothed his hand along King's neck and down along the withers to his back. "I cannot lose him."

"You won't. He is strong-willed." Yet Ari saw the concern Giles tried to hide.

After the vet arrived, diagnosed an infected hoof, and administered a shot of antibiotics, Ari and Giles turned over the care of the horse to the trainer. As they strode back to the house, Giles pointed toward the snow-capped mountains. "The chill in the air remains. I miss the warmth of Portega's summer."

"So, you miss being home?"

"You forget Portega was never home to me. I don't miss London, nor do I miss Portega—just its heat."

Ari laughed for the first time all day. "Point taken."

They entered the warmth of the kitchen where Sénhora Domas, *Cook* to all of them, prepared the sauce for one of the seafood specialties of his island home. Ari inhaled the magnificent scent. Grinning at Cook he kissed her on the cheek and declared, "On days such as this, I do miss home."

"Ah, but I bring your home to you, my dear son."

"That you do." He had spent many childhood hours in the

29

sunny Portega kitchen, working on his lessons or helping Cook as she taught him the basics of cooking. He had loved every minute of getting away from the rigidity of being a royal. She had been his port in the storm.

He poured two mugs of rich, black coffee and handed one to Giles. Together, they settled in the bright, cozy corner of the kitchen. Jaime, once he returned from ski school, would take his usual seat there for lunch, while Cook showered him with love. Ari valued the connection his son built with Cook, just as he had as a child. Perhaps he should ask Cook her valued opinion on how Jaime was doing.

The alcove jutted out from the kitchen. The table seating six looked out over the valley and mountain range. And despite the snow-topped peaks and lack of ocean views, Colorado reminded Ari of his home with the craggy black rock that climbed the sides to the majestic heights.

"Hits the spot." Giles leaned an elbow on the table, cradling the mug. "Tell me about your meeting."

"Nothing to say, except Ms. Peters is bent on interfering with the raising of my son. I believe it is time to discontinue his ski lessons."

"What are you talking about?"

"They do him no good."

Giles put down his mug with a thud. "Do no good? Open your eyes, man. Jaime's a changed boy every day he returns from lessons. He chatters about Ms. Carla and what he's accomplished that very day. You would deny him this because your *pride* is wounded?"

"My pride is not—"

Giles held up his hand. "Don't humiliate yourself by denying the truth."

Ari gripped his mug with both hands. "You cannot understand, Giles."

"No, I can't. I didn't live in your boots. But I know Arianna left a deep wound. And I know that until you move beyond the pain that haunts you, you'll find no peace or joy. Neither will Jaime."

30

"I—"

"No more excuses, Ari. It's been years. You must find a way. Otherwise, you hurt yourself and your son. The lessons have done him good. Give Ms. Peters a chance. I'll warrant whatever Ms. Peters had to say, she's close to being right. She's astute. You might want to heed her warnings."

"There were no warnings."

Giles squeezed his brows together. "The fact she confronted you shows not only her courage and compassion, but...*should* serve as a warning. She's smart and experienced with children."

"All right. But what am I to do? She says Jaime speaks little and remains by himself. And Jaime was so sad when I dropped him at the mountain. He has no friends...still."

Giles' features relaxed. "Heed my advice. There is only one week left of classes. Jaime must stick it out. Despite what you saw in the boy, his insecurities in the morning give way to delight by the time he returns for lunch. You must hire this woman to finish what she's begun. She doesn't know Jaime well enough to see the improvement, but there's been improvement. You bring Ms. Peters here as nanny and she sees him in his own environment, I promise you Jaime will emerge from his shell."

Chapter Four

"Rough day, eh?" asked Tina, her best friend since the cradle.

Carla fingered the end of her braid, studying the foam on her draft beer. "He made me so mad. He's not an easy man to deal with."

"Why should he be? He's one of those foreign asses who think they own the world."

Taking a long draw, Carla waited for the cold bubbles to soothe her. They didn't. Her muscles clenched at the assault on her empty stomach. She couldn't quite put her finger on what it was about the prince that had her all tied in knots. "No. It's more than that. Sure, he's entitled and acts on it, but…" Did she really want to confide in Tina just yet? Or defend the prince, when the whole town didn't like or trust him?

Yeah, the morning had been tough, trying to haul any morsel of empathy out of the fool guy. Clearly, he loved his son. It showed in the pain etched around his eyes and in the grim set of his mouth. But what was causing mistrust when she only wanted to help? And why did he hold so tight to his misery, as if to show his pain would make him a lesser man? One thing for sure—he *was* in pain.

Carla tugged on the elastic restraining her braid and finger-combed out the knots of the day's turmoil, letting her hair fall free and easy over her shoulders. Between the beer and releasing her tightly braided hair, she hoped her body would relax and her anger would dissipate.

Maybe she should just leave Jaime's issues alone. Really. Not her business. After all, she only had him for one more week of lessons and then he'd be none of her concern. His sweet face floated through her subconscious and resurfaced to remind her of her goal. She could accomplish a lot in the next week, despite the prince's stubbornness.

"Hey, good lookin'."

Dang. Carla's head emerged from the clouds. She slowly turned on her stool, not really in the mood to face Shawn tonight.

He held a shot glass close to her lips. The sweet, heady scent assaulted her nose. "You look like you need this."

Whiskey. Yeah, she did. One thing about Shawn, he did know her better than anyone. He'd been her best friend forever. Next door rancher. On and off again lover. She found comfort in that, but that special spark she desperately wanted had never flamed, even when she found out she was pregnant and thought she might marry Shawn. After she lost the baby, she never told Shawn, because she couldn't marry him. They could be friends now. But a full-blown, married and madly in love type of relationship never would have worked between them. Not like the kind between her parents that had ignited the room. Nor the kind that her dad had found again with her stepmom.

And, she hated to admit it, the kind that sparked between her and the prince the two times they'd met. Perhaps the spark of lust was only one-sided. Most assuredly the prince didn't feel it. And if he felt any sort of spark, he'd explain it as a flame-thrower of ignited anger.

"Well, darlin'. You gonna take this whiskey off my hands?"

Yanked out of her reverie, she plastered on a smile for the red-headed, freckle-faced man who'd never let her down. "Yeah, thanks. Rough day."

"Then, I'm feeding you two lovely ladies. The best steaks the Rustler's Grill has to offer."

Her stomach rumbled. Tina hopped off the bar stool and headed toward the corner table occupied by three of Carla's brothers, before Carla could say *yes* to Shawn. She had to laugh. Tina used any excuse to get near that handsome and rugged lot.

As she stood, Shawn snugged his arm around her waist and kissed her forehead. "I'll take good care of my girl."

She adored him, but one of these days she had to let Shawn go.

Gravel spit off his wheels, as Ari roared into the parking lot. He brought his truck to an abrupt stop, smack-dab in front of the flashing green and yellow sign. With a smattering of bulbs missing from the letters spelling out Rustler's Grill, the sign reminded him of a haunting, toothless grin. He almost missed the turn off to the hole-in-the-wall tavern. Why had he agreed to meet Ken Duggans there? "Should have dragged Giles along," he muttered.

Jumping from the Jeep, he strode toward the low building and shoved against the heavy oak door, wishing he were anywhere but here.

As his eyes adjusted to the semi-dark, he squinted through the haze of tobacco smoke hanging over the jumble of tables. Despite the stale smell permeating everything, Ari's sudden urge for a cigarette overtook his common sense. He'd long ago given up the habit, but every now and again he craved the drag and burn of the pungent and spicy-scented smoke of his homeland as it shot down the back of his throat and straight into his lungs.

Ari rolled his shoulders before plunging his hand into his pocket to run his thumb and forefinger over the pitted stone to ease the craving. Better not to ruminate about his reckless days. They only reminded him of mistakes made and regrets gnawing a hole in his gut.

Duggans was leaning against the bar, flirting with the bartender. In no mood for this meeting, Ari had no choice. He must act as though he needed the slime ball rancher's help. He wanted nothing more than to string Duggans up, but for now he would play out his hand and wait.

He strode to the middle of the room and scanned the

darkened corners for a secluded table. When Duggans motioned him to the bar, Ari ignored him. No way would he get in the middle of the scum's flirt fest. He'd given up flirting long ago.

Turning his head toward the right corner to search out a table, he saw her. Strands of golden-copper hair streaming down her back. Unlike the buttoned-up, braided cowgirl he'd now twice had a run-in with. Both times, hands on her hips, breathing fire, getting in his business and telling him what to do. She looked different, softer, relaxed, and he imagined what it would be like to know her gentler side.

He couldn't take his eyes off her, and found himself a voyeur to just what he wished to avoid—a tall, red-headed cowboy hitting on his son's sexy ski teacher. Why would she hang out with a slovenly cowboy? And let him paw her. Another negative he could use against her employment when arguing with Giles. As he stared, a young woman next to her tapped her on the shoulder.

Carla turned, her gaze settling squarely on him.

He wanted to turn away, as if he didn't care.

Her eyes widened, her jaw dropped, and her hand reached toward the end of a strand of hair shimmering in the muted, dancing lights from the numerous bar signs. Apparently, he had shocked the flirting Mzzz Peters—showing up in this dive. Then as quickly as she registered his presence, she tossed the errant strand over her shoulder and turned back to the crowded table. Back to her boyfriend, the other woman, and three of her brothers. He'd met them all. Had no use for any of them.

As if on cue, her oldest brother rose to stare at Ari. A silent threat.

Carter tossed a wad of bills in the center of the table and headed straight toward Ari. He stopped just out of Ari's reach, spat on the floor, and slapped his dusty Stetson on his head, before striding past and out the front door.

The Peters family was one of many that didn't want to play nice and neighborly to the new foreigner they considered a hobby rancher. But the eldest Peters' behavior was over the top.

Ari could conceive of nothing he'd done to make the hatred personal.

Looked like Carla bore an affinity to her big brother. Although she'd identified what her fight was about, his son. And, at least she hadn't spit when she'd left his ranch in a fury.

For a second, Ari remembered the flash of fire in her eyes and the sway of her hips as she'd stalked away from him that morning. She was right. But he would never admit that to her. His and Jaime's business was none of her concern.

The red-headed cowboy had watched the entire exchange. He spread his big hand across the back of Carla's neck and began kneading. A jolt zapped straight from Ari's heart to his belly. He stepped back. He did not wish to be in the cowboy's place. She was a fine-looking woman, but her bite appeared to be deadlier than a rattler. He had no desire to be in striking distance. Not again. Giles would argue, but Ari would prevail in this battle of wills over a new nanny.

Yet he continued to stare. Carla shifted to the left and the cowboy dropped his hand before turning his attention to his friends. Shimmering waves of copper and gold caressed her shoulders where the cowboy's hand had been moments earlier.

For the beat of an irrational moment, his hand ached to replace the other man's. His groin stirred with a long-suppressed need. This physical pain was only longing for what he denied himself since the fatal end to his marriage. He had no need of a woman. *Yes, keep telling yourself this fable and soon you will believe.*

Ari forced himself to focus on business and away from the likes of Carla Peters.

A table in the left corner just off the end of the bar was empty. Duggans looked up and Ari nodded toward it. Striding across the room, he claimed the table. He removed his Stetson and balanced it on a hook behind him. He did not sit. He would not give Duggans the advantage. He waited, his boot tapping against the scuffed, wooden plank floor.

Duggans reached across the bar and fingered a lock of the pretty bartender's hair, then whispered in her ear. She smiled and nodded. Duggans straightened, locking his shoulders straight back in the ritual dance of a man who just scored.

She is a fool. Ari shook his head as he placed his hand on the top rung of the chair that backed up to the corner wall. He wanted Duggans' back to the room. He wanted Duggans to feel vulnerable, even though the idiot probably would not be aware of his lack of power or of Ari's strategy to make him feel powerless.

The man swaggered toward Ari, his smirk abrasive. The bartender followed with two frosty mugs in one hand and a tray carrying four shots of whisky in the other. Apparently, Duggans had picked his own weapon of choice.

He pulled his chair around, straddling it to lean toward the table. A power play of his own. Ari slid his own chair from beneath the table to sit with his back to the corner. The bartender set a frosted mug in front of each man, then lined up the four shots down the center of the table. She barely glanced at Ari. She tossed a sultry smile toward Duggans, then sashayed back behind the bar.

Duggans turned to watch the swish and sway of her hips.

He is a dog. Ari loathed having to deal with this man.

Duggans turned back to Ari and lifted his mug in a sarcastic salute.

Ari lifted his own mug and flashed his best haughty, royal smile. *Let the games begin.*

With a hefty gulp, Duggans set down the mug and reached for a shot of whisky. After letting the shot slide down his throat, he growled, like a mountain lion ready to devour his kill.

Ari lowered his beer, untouched.

"I have what you need. And you can afford to pay for it." The man's tone left no room for niceties or compromise.

As close to an admission as Ari would get, he did not let the veiled confession faze him. "Maybe." Ari smoothed his finger up the outside of the glass, the icy buildup giving way to liquid.

The man had no morals, playing both sides of the coin. If Duggans sold the water rights to the creek that Ari was certain the immoral man had damned up, he would win. Conversely, if

Ari did not take the deal, both Ari's Silver Mine Ranch and the Peters Valley Ranch south of him would dry up. Then Duggans could scoop up both properties for a song. A win for Duggans, either way. Ari suspected he wanted access to the natural gas that probably ran deep under both the Silver Mine and Peters Valley ranches. By depriving his neighboring ranches of water and buying the whole lot, Duggans was bound to make a ton of money off the mineral rights.

"Aw, come on, Prince. I don't like to play games." With that said, Duggans tossed a feral smile over his shoulder, aimed directly at the bar.

Ari did not utter a word. The fact was, he was here on pretense—to play the game, as well.

While Duggans ogled the bartender, Ari moved the man's empty shot glass to his own side of the line-up and replaced it with a full glass. Duggans made two strategic mistakes. He was already half-way to being drunk. And he'd let himself be distracted.

The man turned back. "Well, *Prince.*"

"I never play games, Duggans." Ari lowered his chin and homed in on bloodshot eyes. And just so the man understood he meant business, he drawled in his best American slang, "And I don't *cotton* to blackmail."

"Why you…" Duggans' palms pushed against the edge of the table as he started to rise. Glasses swayed and rattled.

Ari anchored his mug with his palm. "Sit down." It wasn't a request. The man needed Ari as much as Ari needed what Duggans had to offer.

Duggans sat, grabbed the next shot glass, and downed it. "We either start talking serious business, Prince—" He ground the word out in a long and deadly drawl.

"I will *not* be threatened."

"Five hundred grand—bottom line."

Ari shoved his chair back and reached for his Stetson.

"Four and a half." Duggans bit out the words in a mock capitulation to bargaining and downed a third shot. He'd lost count of the drinks. Ari hid his smirk. He had a job to do and that was to deal with this scum-of-the-earth—string him along, reel him in, and go for the kill. But not tonight. There was still work to do.

"One hundred," Ari countered.

Duggans stood and listed to one side. "You need me, Prince. Ain't telling you again. You pay my price or there'll be hell to pay." He picked up the last shot, downed it, and teetered off toward the bar.

Ari glanced at the bartender. A frown creased her forehead. Maybe she was not fool enough to tangle with a mean and cheating drunk after all.

Ari had what he came for—proof Duggans was up to something. He'd sit tight until the other man left. He sipped the warm beer and almost spat out the watery brew.

Duggans yelled an obscenity toward the bar and staggered out.

In the opposite corner, the group continued to enjoy their Friday night party. The red-headed cowboy leaned in and whispered in Ms. Peters' ear. Ari wished to hell he had saved at least one shot of that rot-gut whiskey.

What was it about this woman that both tormented and fascinated him?

"What?" Carla had lost all connection to the conversation around her. Cole, her youngest brother, had asked a question and she had no clue.

Shawn leaned over, his whisper tickling her neck. "You're distracted. Is it that handsome prince who's got you all in a lather?"

Carla ignored Cole as she looked at Shawn. "What're y'all talkin' about?"

"You've been glancing over there ever since he walked through the door, darlin'" The cowboy twang signaled Shawn wasn't happy about being ignored. No way he believed the prince was competition. Maybe Shawn cared more for her than she realized. Until now, it had been understood they scratched the other's itch. No complications.

"Curious. What the hell is he doin' in a dive like this?"

"That all?" Shawn traced his index finger up her arm, giving her a shiver that had him grinning. "You ready to leave?"

She recognized that tone. He figured he liquored her up and fed her, now he'd get his reward. She immediately regretted her thought. Shawn wasn't like that. He'd been a best friend all her life, sometimes with benefits. Right now, hope shined from his eyes.

"Look, Shawn." She laid her hand across his forearm. "It's been a rough day. Yeah, I'm ready to go, but I'm going home. Alone."

He nodded, as if he expected that answer. Probably because, of late, it had been her answer time and again.

"I'll walk you out."

"No need." She slid out of her chair and grabbed her jacket.

"You're not walking out back alone."

"I've done it a million times."

Cole leaned in. "He's walking you out."

She glared at her youngest brother. Hands on her hips, she countered. "I can take care of myself. I don't need any male to protect me. When are you guys going to get it through your thick heads that you need to trust me?"

"It's not you we don't trust. You saw Duggans stagger out of here, and in a foul mood. If he's in the parking lot, you're fair game. Plus," he tossed a look over his shoulder toward the corner where the prince sat, "If I let you leave here without one of us, Carter will have my hide." Cole grinned his baby brother manipulative smile. "Come on, Cal. Do it for me."

Shawn stood, shoved his hat on his head. "Calling it a night."

Cole winked.

Carla shook her head, then blew him a kiss.

She turned to say goodnight to Tina, but her friend was too engrossed in what Ore was saying. Ore lifted an eyebrow toward Carla and went back to charming Tina. Carla couldn't help but smile. Maybe her brother would finally do what was right and snag a decent woman for a change. Most likely not. Flirting was Ore's way of having fun while keeping his distance. All her brothers, except Jack, were the same—afraid of commitment.

Like she was any different.

Shawn slipped his hand across the small of her back. The gesture once gave her comfort. Tonight, it meant Shawn wanted more. A hook-up, yes, but he also wanted commitment. He was a family-man with an eye on the future. He wanted someone to take care of. He'd been her protector, even as a kid. Problem was, she no longer needed looking after. Yes, she loved Shawn. But he wasn't her future.

She glanced toward the opposite corner. The prince stared. She stared back, as if they played a game of chicken. From the moment they'd first spoken, they'd been at odds. Despite being one of the most annoying people she'd ever met, she was attracted. In a flash, she pictured what he might be like if he loosened up a bit. Let himself have some fun.

When his brows shot up, catching her in the moment of fantasizing, heat rolled across her face. Trying to rein in her imagination, she diverted her attention back to Shawn.

As Shawn guided her toward the door, she glanced over her shoulder. The prince watched her every step.

After the heavy, humid air in the bar, the cool night air hit her like a slap in the face. She needed the blow to get her head on straight. She didn't want Ari Orula…and she didn't want Shawn.

She'd known that part for a long time. Shawn had been comfortable, safe, always watching her back. But she witnessed the hurt in his eyes when she turned him down…again.

It wasn't fair to string him along. Allow him to hope for more than the friendship they'd shared most of their life. Right at that moment, Carla wanted nothing more than to lean into Shawn. Lean on him, as she always had. But she could no longer afford that comfort. She had to cut the tether. She only hoped she wouldn't lose her valued friendship.

But she couldn't prolong her decision. Shawn wasn't going

anywhere unless she pushed him into it. He deserved more than she was able to give. Deserved a woman who would flourish under his protective and sweet nature.

When they reached her pick-up and she lifted the door handle, he rested his palm above her head, keeping her from opening the door. She turned, and he leaned.

No kiss tonight.

She edged back, her shoulder snug against the solid metal. At that moment, she understood why being with Shawn never felt totally right. He was too much like her brothers. He *was* like a brother to her. He would hate knowing that.

"Let me drive you home, darlin'. You know you can't handle your alcohol."

"I had one beer and that shot. Then you ordered me the biggest danged steak on the menu."

He grinned. "You ate it all. You always do."

"Yeah, I always do."

He brushed his thumb across her cheek and down the side of her face to her chin. "I know you. Better 'n anyone."

She nodded, pressing her back against the truck door, trying to escape his warm, safe, comfortable touch. "Aw, geez, Shawn. Yeah, you do. That's the problem."

He straightened. "Problem?"

"I love you, Shawn. You know that. But you and me…we'll never make it."

"What? You and me, we belong together. Your whole family knows that." He stepped back, placed his hands on his hips, and puffed out his chest in a face-off. "When you gonna figure that out?"

Carla left the security of the truck door. She cupped his cheek. "You're a good man, Shawn Brown. Any woman would be lucky to have you. I'm just not the right woman for you."

He opened his mouth, and she placed her finger across his lips. "You know that. I imagine deep down you've always known that. I'd do you wrong before you could holler rock slide. It'd hit you that fast. I don't want to destroy you. I love you too much for that."

He stuffed his hands in his pockets and looked at his feet. The truth hurt. "Yeah, I've known it. I just hoped too much, that's all."

"Someday, you'll have the woman you deserve and a passel of kids hanging on her skirts. You'll be smiling bigger than Aspen Mountain. And then I'll be able to say—" she poked him in the chest— "I told you so."

He smiled, the wide grin she loved, white teeth flashing against his tanned, freckled face. He kicked the gravel. "I suppose you're right. I hope that day comes quick, 'cause right now my heart's breakin'."

Carla wanted to kick the dang gravel herself. Maybe dig a hole to China, like she and Shawn had tried to do as kids, and escape the ache in her heart. The ache caused by hurting her best friend.

She stood on tiptoe and kissed his cheek, then turned to climb into the truck. He grabbed the door before she could close it. "I'm driving you home."

"No, Shawn. I appreciate the gesture, but I need to be on my own. You and my brothers assume I'm helpless. I'm not. I can take care of myself. And this is as good a time as any to start." She placed her hand on the edge of the open window and pulled the door shut. "Night."

He nodded, backed up, and turned on his heel without a look backwards.

Chapter Five

Carla clutched the truck's steering wheel and swallowed a sob burning deep in her throat. Now was as good a time as any to be on her own—totally on her own, without Shawn or her brothers or her father looking after her. Despite the fact she hadn't been under their roof for years, their pervading attitude was that she needed their help in everything she did. She loved her family, but she didn't need them the way she had as a child. She had dreams. And those dreams would only come from *her* blood, sweat, and salty tears.

Then the tears came—full force. They flowed for her loss and fear and new beginnings. She cried so hard she blocked out everything around her.

Gasping for a breath, she opened her eyes. And screamed.

A man's shadow wavered beyond her blurry vision, right outside her truck window. She lunged for the lock button just as the door swung open.

"What is wrong?"

The melodic rhythm of the prince's accent quieted her fears instantly. "Prince Orula." She managed to squeak out his name between hiccups.

"What did that cowboy do to you? I will kill him with my bare hands." Contrary to his words, he reached in and swept her damp hair back from her face and absorbed her tears with the press of his thumb against her cheek. "Tell me what he did."

"Nothing. He did nothing. It was all me." Carla started to cry again. Orula stepped back, as if he had no clue how to deal with a blubbering woman. Most men didn't. She hiccupped a teary laugh and swiped at her eyes with her sleeve. The look on his face was classic male, oh-my-gawd-what-do-I-do-now? He might be a prince and he might be a foreigner, but he was all male, unable to deal with female hysteria.

When he reached into the truck and pulled her into his arms, she melted into his solid chest. All male. No denying it. And *maybe* able to deal with a bawling woman.

"Move over. I will drive you home. You will tell me what happened. Then I will decide whether to kill the cowboy."

She shook her head, her heartache replaced by determination and pride. "I'm perfectly capable—" She hiccupped...again. "—of, of, of driving myself home."

"You are distraught." He put his foot on the running board and hoisted himself up. "Move."

She didn't budge.

He balanced on one foot, his hand against the top of the door, his other on her seatback. "Why do I bother? You are stubborn. No, ornery."

"You're used to getting your own way. But not with me."

"You get into my business, but I am not allowed in yours. Foolish woman."

She pressed a palm against his chest, and he dropped back to the ground.

"I don't give a dang if you *are* a prince, you cowboys are all alike." Carla leaned over to turn the key. But before she could twist her wrist, he reached across her and plucked the keys from the ignition.

"You are not driving home."

She straightened. And glared. *The look* always worked with her brothers. "I. Need. My. Truck."

"Your truck will be parked by your home when you awaken in the morning."

Confident he'd back off when she gave him the you-are-crazy-and-arrogant-stare, she pulled a second set of keys from the glove compartment. Unfortunately, she couldn't get them in the ignition fast enough before he was balanced on her running board again.

Calmly, as if talking to a child, he said, "I will drive you in your truck. Giles will meet me at your home."

"Giles?"

"He manages my business."

"And is at your beck and call, night and day? I see how it is, your highness." She lifted a brow.

He placed his butt, his *luscious* butt, halfway on the seat beside her and shoved with his hip. "Move over. And call me Ari. I am not royalty here in this country."

The argument welled up in her, as did her denial she would ever call him Ari. But between arguing with him and crying her heart out over Shawn, she'd reached her limit. Right now, she wanted to crawl in a gopher hole. No more talking.

"I will see you home safe." Ari's tone carried both gentle concern and royal command. "Make sure you are all right."

Carla needed kindness and strength right now. She slid across the seat and watched him move into the driver's side. His profile, with its strong, straight nose, and eyelashes to die for, silhouetted against the glaring lights of the Rustler's Grill sign. When he glanced at her, heat shot straight through her. She'd only met him twice, but she now fantasized about running the tip of her finger through the tiny cleft in his square chin. *Dang.*

She was too tired to ponder this attraction to the prince. Too tired to argue. She wilted against the passenger window and stared into the darkness edging the shadowed parking lot. She twined her fingers through a strand of hair as she tried to quell the shake of her hand.

She'd just broken Shawn's heart, and now she was lusting after someone she could never have.

And didn't want.

At least, that's what she told herself.

She turned toward him.

He glanced back, with a lift of his brow.

No, I'm not all right.

The prince's Stetson angled low and to the left in protective cowboy mode. Redirecting his gaze to the road ahead, his prominent, regal features stood out in profile.

Nice.

What the holy hello was she doing? All her bluster with both Shawn and the prince about taking care of herself had ended with a royal cowhand chauffeuring her home. How had she let this happen?

This man was a force. One she'd have to contend with by rallying all her strength and determination.

He caught her stare. A grin, almost a smirk, lifted the corners of his mouth, before his face froze in a half-smile. "Do you want to talk about it now?"

"No." She turned toward the window. None of his business. Nor anyone's business. Only the whole town and her family had made their, what?—affair? friendship?—their business as long as she could remember.

She heard the deep intake of breath and the slow sigh of exhalation, as if he tempered his next words. She'd been rude. Carla met his gaze. "No. Thanks."

He didn't argue. "You know, I wanted to squeeze my hands around the neck of *your* cowboy."

She liked the deep, lyrical composure of his voice. And she hated to admit the fact he had come to her rescue when she'd been a babbling, basket-case. But still she countered, "He's not my cowboy."

"Most certainly, you could have fooled me."

She blinked away a tear. She'd fooled Shawn and herself for too long. "Not anymore."

"Ah, so you let him go."

"How do you know he didn't let me go?"

"One of my skills is reading people." There was no arrogance in his voice, only a statement of fact.

"And?"

"Your man—there is no doubt he wants you."

She nodded and waited for the haughty retort of I-told-you-so.

"Breaking a person's heart, even though you know it is for the best, is heartbreak any way you look at it. You have a right to be sad."

Surprised by his sentiment, Carla blinked back another onslaught of tears. "I—I didn't break his heart."

His concentration lifted from the road and he glanced at her. The steely set to his eyes allowed no room for argument.

"Okay, so I guess I did. He's my best friend—since we were kids. Everyone expected we'd marry." She gulped air.

"Ah, he wanted more than friendship. You could not give him what he wanted."

How the holy hello had they gotten into this conversation? Out of desperation, she countered with snark. "*Something* like that."

"What is it *you* want?" He was persistent. She'd give him that.

Turning in her seat to face Ari, she planned to put an end to the conversation. "I shouldn't have told you this—"

"But you need to talk. Simple. I sit right here. I do not know you or your family. And no one else wants to hear what you have to say on the subject. They have made up their minds. Is that not correct?"

He read her like a GPS. She could talk it out with Ari and get on with things or spend the night crying. Reluctantly, she said, "They'll all hate me. Shawn is the most decent man I know. But—"

"You do not love him."

Was he going to keep finishing her sentences?

She pointed toward the alley leading to her apartment above the grain store. As he turned down the narrow lane, she gestured toward the parking spot.

As soon as he parked, Carla struggled with the seat belt, trying to get out of the truck before he did the chivalrous thing. The last thing she needed was prince know-it-all, with a sensitivity she did not expect, to walk her to her apartment.

He pulled open the door and extended his hand.

Crappola. Not fast enough.

She bit her lip. *Be nice.* With her heart tap-dancing against her chest, she accepted his gentlemanly gesture. "Thanks."

"I will walk you."

48

"I'm fine. Thank you for the ride."

"Giles will not be here to take me to my Jeep for another hour. I have time to walk you."

"And then what?" She regretted the sarcastic question the moment she spit it out, but she was fed up with men trying to rule her life. And right now, she needed alone time.

He shrugged. "I sit in your truck and wait for him."

"For an hour?" The prince planned to cool his heels in her alley?

He nodded.

She blurted out, "I can make coffee." His quick smile made it clear he'd easily maneuvered her into issuing the invitation.

Unfortunately, she didn't mind.

Ari was not used to darkened, back alleys and rickety stairs that climbed as high as the stars.

The faint glow of the street lamp at the end of the alleyway emitted barely enough light to see. But the view was glorious. Not the dumpster across the way or the rusted screen door that clung to its hinges at the back entrance to the pizza joint. No, the view was Carla's backside as she climbed the steps in front of him. Her jeans hugged her well-rounded curves. He liked women with a bit of meat on them. And this woman had *meat* in all the right places.

He had no excuse for his lusty thoughts. His brain was not clouded by alcohol. The setting was not remotely romantic.

No excuses.

He almost slammed into her back when she stopped on the narrow platform at the top to dig in her bag for her keys. Once she palmed the ring of keys, he moved to her side. "Allow me." He waited for her reaction. He had already figured out no one did for this woman without an argument. He enjoyed baiting her, watching her struggle between being polite and standing up for herself.

Much to his surprise, she managed the high road, handing him the keys and then stepping back against the flimsy railing of the deck. He reached for her forearm. "Careful." Before she could argue against his protectiveness, he let her go, unlocked the door, and gestured for her to enter.

She looked over her shoulder after stepping over the threshold. "It's a mess."

"I am here for coffee and company. I will shutter my eyes to all else." But he did no such thing as he scanned the small space. Her space, so like her, discordant. Not neat, not messy— but filled with her energy. Lived in, and comfortable. In seconds, he'd sized her up.

She was a contradiction. He had not expected her to yield so easily to his chivalrous act. But the *act* was him. Maybe she recognized he couldn't help his upbringing. To be a prince meant you did for your people, all the while allowing few close. You assume responsibility, taking care of everyone around without fanfare or notice.

She had already called him out with her opinion of how much attention he paid Jaime. And there she was wrong. For some strange reason, he cared what she thought. He wanted her to understand him. But no. To make her understand meant opening up. Allowing her to see below the surface. No way. He let few close.

If he admitted the truth, she already pulled at him. His heart pumped and his nerves jumped with the urge to hold her close and protect her from her pain imposed by the cowboy. Without thought for propriety, he had hugged her close in the jeep. Then he let her go. He tamped down the urge to do it again. That was all the comfort he would allow himself to offer. There would be no touching.

"How do you like your coffee?"

He looked across the space to where she stood, tucked in an alcove at the far end of the same room. "Black and strong."

"You *are* a cowboy." She laughed, the tentative tease filling the air.

He liked her low laugh. "Working into that role, but I have much to learn."

"I bet, between culture and way of life. What did you do in your homeland?"

"The same."

"Cowboy?"

He shrugged his shoulders. "Not quite. We raise and breed Lusitanos, the native horse of Portugal, the country closest to ours."

She tilted her head. "I've heard they're beautiful. What made you bring them to the United States?"

"I visited Aspen as a child. I have always been struck with awe by the wild and rugged beauty of this state. Reminds me of my home, without our ocean and temperate climate."

"Sounds like a lovely place to live."

He stared at the argumentative Ms. Peters. The argumentative woman who now smiled and carried on a conversation about his *lovely* homeland. How things had changed in very few days. Or truth be known, in the last half hour. He would not have guessed he'd be standing in this small room that spoke of home and family and comfort. Her room.

Again, he scanned the small room to take in the nuances of her space. The wrought iron bed disguised as a couch sat against the long wall, lined in heavy bolsters propping up an avalanche of throw pillows. He stood in her *bedroom*.

"Do you miss your home?"

He blinked away the path his thoughts had traveled, to her bed and her lush body.

"At times, yes." His hand reached into his pocket and fingered the talisman. He would go home when he'd proven himself. Until then...

Stepping toward the wall to the left of the couch, he ran one finger down the edge of a frame holding a photo of a stick-slender girl standing next to a handsome strawberry roan. The girl was dressed in cream breeches, a black wool coat with a stock tie and a helmet, the harness tight under her chin. Her braids even with her shoulders, her hair golden yellow, lighter than now. Her brown eyes too big for her girlish face. He recognized the adolescent toothy smile, now a woman's wide and sensual one, and the spattering of freckles across her golden skin, a shade lighter than her hair. The girl before she developed her curves. "How old were you?"

Carla crossed the room and handed him a heavy mug of thick, black coffee. The aroma was heavenly after the stale odor of beer and cigarettes at the Grill.

"Eleven."

"You showed?"

"Briefly. My rebellion against western-style."

"Ah. Your father allowed this?"

"No." She smiled. "My mother grew up in Boston. She overruled him. My father—he would have done anything for her."

He hesitated for a moment. She had used the past tense. Did she not have her mother any longer? He would ask, but not tonight.

Ari moved to the next photo. "And this?" She was dressed in a hot pink, western-style shirt with rhinestones and a pair of slim jeans. The curves more evident now. The high chestnut-colored leather boots, handsomely tooled, topped off right below her knees, accentuating her long legs.

"Sixteen."

"And no longer the rebel?"

She twisted a strand of hair around her finger. "I wouldn't exactly say that."

"Once a rebel, always a rebel. No?" She rolled her eyes, reminding him of Jaime. One reason, he imagined, why Jaime adored her. Despite Giles championing her to be hired as the temporary nanny, he was more convinced than ever that he could not. He could not allow her to get close. Or closer than he felt at this very moment. *No.*

He returned his gaze to the photo. Her hair, now cropped, spun red highlights among the gold. At sixteen, her curves ripening, she was well on her way to becoming a woman. "Do you continue to show?"

She shook her head. "I did until I went away to college. Now I ride for ranch work."

"Never for fun?"

"It's been a long time. You?"

"A long time."

"Really? You breed horses. Why don't you ride?"

He wasn't ready to answer her question, so he shifted her focus. "Is this you, as well?"

"Teaching at the Mineral Spring's Therapeutic Center." When he lifted his brow, she added, "For troubled and ill children."

"Explain."

"This little girl, Mandy, had cancer. Riding gave her a companion, the horse, to talk to and cry with."

"*Had* cancer? She is better now?"

Carla's playful smile faded. She turned away to settle in the stuffed chair, covered in an earth-toned, western-style pattern. "She died when she was ten."

"Were you close?"

She sipped the steaming coffee, before nodding.

"I am, ah, truly sorry for your loss." He stuffed his hand in his pocket, found the stone and rubbed. What else could he say? Nothing to make her feel better after all these years. He gestured toward Carla's wall of memories before turning away. "Many ribbons."

She nodded, again sipping. An excuse against having to speak, he guessed.

He scanned the small area for a seat but found no place else but her couch to sit. He eyed the spot for a moment, trying to put out of his mind that this was her bed. He sat, set his mug on the coffee table in front of him, and picked up a magazine from a scattered pile. He flipped through the pages of knitting patterns, surprised. "My mother knits."

"It's something to do."

He quirked a brow at the woman who shut down as he did. Setting the magazine on the table, he noticed the cedar half-barrel tucked under the table, spilling over with colored yarn. "My mother says it relaxes her. The busier her schedule, the more she knitted."

"Knitting is calming."

She revealed nothing, as she stared at her pile of magazines. He said nothing. Waited.

She glanced up. Was he making her uncomfortable? He could say the same. Perhaps he should have spent this time sitting in her truck. Shifting on the firm mattress, he reached for his mug of coffee and swallowed a bracing gulp.

"Does your mother have many royal duties?"

He looked toward her wall again, not sure how to answer. "She and the Crown Prince are no longer married."

He was surprised when she failed to press him on his parents' marriage.

"And your father?"

Ari reached for another magazine—this one on riding. "A story too long for this time of night." Where the hell was Giles? He hadn't expected to get into an intimate discussion with this woman. His leg twitched, urging him to stand and pace the small space. He forced himself to stay where he sat, then tossed the magazine back on the table.

Carla stood and strolled toward the kitchen nook. She must be as restless as he.

"More coffee?"

"Thank you, no. The morning comes quickly." He stood and pulled his cell from his pocket just as it buzzed. "You are here?"

Thank the good god. In the last hour, he'd come to like Carla. More than that, he was attracted to her to the point he thought about strolling across the small space and taking her in his arms. Big mistake. Including the thoughts that spiraled through him about wanting to touch her, hold her, caress her lips with his. *No.*

As he tucked the phone away, Carla stepped in front of him. He reached for her, wanting desperately to finger the wisp of hair curling around her ear. Perhaps trail his knuckles across the soft skin of her high cheekbones. He pulled his hand back before he succumbed to his wants. "The hour is late. We both must sleep."

Carla moved to the door, pulled it open, and stepped aside.

Ari moved past her. Then stopped.

When the prince turned to her, so close that the heat of his body warmed hers and the spice of his scent tickled her nose, Carla struggled to maintain her equilibrium. Not reach out to touch him, stroke his cheek, step into his arms.

She stepped back and glanced at the wall clock, the hour hand now closing in on one a.m. Who'd have thought she'd be saying goodnight to the very prince she'd bolted on this morning? For good reason, of course. He'd tried to intimidate her. And succeeded. Now...

Ari lifted her chin with his forefinger. "You are all right to stay alone?"

How could she answer such a question? With a flippant, *of course I am, I'm a modern woman and no man needs to protect me.* Or did she put on a demure, *I-have-a-prince-at-the-door, I'll-be-fine* swoon. Oh for heaven's sake, he was just a man, like any other man.

But when she looked into eyes the color of rare black pearls and teeming with a blend of heat and compassion, she merely nodded. She didn't dare open her mouth. Dare to breathe. Dare to allow him to close the tiny gap between them.

When he leaned toward her, she couldn't will herself to step back.

Was he going to kiss her? *Jeez.* The I-can-take-care-of-myself woman made quick work of bursting the wild and romantic imagination bubble invading every pore of her body.

Carla stepped back, away from the warm finger and away from the mesmerizing, ebony eyes. This wasn't only physical. For the last hour, he'd shown concern. He told her about his family. She never imagined that someone like Ari had led the kind of life where normal things happened—like divorce and death and children who feared things bumping in the night. She'd put him on a pedestal, as if his lineage allowed him to walk on the waves crashing against his island shore without being affected by everyday life.

Finding her voice, she whispered. "I'll be fine." When his hand reached to hover near her cheek, she backed up once more. To distance herself. To let him go. She babbled on. "Thank you...for the ride. It was nice. Kind. You didn't have to..."

Taking a third step, she waited for him to duck out the door.

Ari straightened his back and squared his shoulders, transforming into his official persona. "Yes, very well then. I wish you good dreams."

When he finally walked through the door and began his descent to the alley, she stepped forward. Leaning her forearm on the doorframe, she wedged her foot against the screen to keep it open. And watched Ari. She thanked her lucky stars his friend Giles stood at the bottom of the steps, otherwise, she'd have been mighty tempted to chase after him. Drag him back in.

Okay...a bit dramatic. She wasn't the man-dragging type. Caffeine coursed through her veins, having long dispersed the relaxing effects of beer and whiskey. Wired from conversation and the memories dredged up, the events of the evening, and the ache of letting Shawn go came crashing back. On any other night she may have succumbed to the push and pull of warring emotions that had her disliking Ari one minute and wishing he'd kiss her the next.

I think not.

Ari reached the bottom and glanced over his shoulder. For one second, with the street light arrowed on him like a stage spotlight, silver glinted in his ebony eyes. Then he turned away.

Giles stood by the driver's door, keys dangling from his finger. She heard Ari say in a commanding voice, "You drive." Funny, Giles didn't seem put out about the whole bossing around thing at one in the morning. He closed his fist around the keys. As before, he climbed into the driver's side. He looked up at Carla and winked.

Carla smiled. Giles! He was the man who occasionally dropped Jaime off at ski school. So, not everyone quaked in the presence of the prince.

Without looking back, Ari climbed into the passenger seat and waited to be chauffeured off. The whole scene surreal, a formal parting, as if she and Ari had shared nothing in the last hour.

For the best.

Carla sighed, backed into her apartment, and flipped the lock. Turning, she stared at her tiny space. And leaned. The solid door at her back gave her strength to face the empty night ahead. Good thing the night would be short. Right now, she wasn't sure she could get though the dark hours before dawn without shedding a ton more tears.

Chapter Six

Carla dragged herself out from under the heavy quilt. She glanced at the clock and groaned. She'd tossed and turned worrying about her lost friendship with Shawn. The hardest thing she'd ever done—letting him go. Shawn spelled security. And losing security spelled scary.

She straightened and turned her thoughts to the mundane. Otherwise, she'd worry herself into breakdown mode. Already late, the three-minute shower did little to wake her from the fog. Pulling open dresser drawers, she found a turtleneck and ski pants, and dressed on the run. She vetoed heating up the night-old pot of coffee sitting on her counter. But nothing could veto thoughts of the prince-turned-friendly and the almost kiss.

Less than one week left of ski school. And then what? A dull month of unemployment until the seasonal restaurants opened up and Comfort Food beefed up its staff for spring and summer tourists. It was too early to get out her mountain bike. And this year, the early snowmelt meant spring skiing would be virtually over in another week or two. Plus, it meant no more interactions with Jaime and the prince.

On the way to the door, Carla stopped and reached toward her desk in the corner by her tiny kitchen. Fingering a thick file, she smiled. Over the next month, she'd spend time finalizing plans for her new alternative pre- and elementary school. They had pledges of interest, so the school would fly. Now to start the aggressive task of fundraising.

Sighing, she grabbed her coat, boots, and pack. No time to ponder dreams this morning.

Carla jogged down the back stairs to the alley. After climbing into the old pick-up, she headed toward the drive-through. Her muddled head needed a jolt of caffeine and her mouth watered for a cinnamon-laced pastry.

Ten minutes later, swallowing the last bite and licking teeth-numbing, sweet frosting off her fingers, she swung into the ski area parking lot and jumped from the truck cab. She wasn't about to leave behind half a cup of Joe. With ski boots and pack flung over her shoulder, she balanced skis in one hand and coffee in the other and strode toward the group of children.

Tina met her halfway. "I'll hold your coffee while you get ready."

"Rough night." Carla mumbled and headed toward the bench before shrugging the boots and pack off her shoulder.

"Yeah, I heard."

"Already? Sometimes I really hate small towns."

"No secrets here. How'd Shawn take it?"

Carla's gut clenched. "Better than I thought. He didn't get angry, which made me feel even guiltier."

"He's a good guy. He'll find someone who's right for him."

She fastened her left boot, then raised her head, surprised by Tina's enlightened wisdom. Not that the rest of the town would see the break-up that way. "Exactly what I told him."

"Your brothers are another story. They won't take it so well."

"Ya' think?" Groaning, Carla bent over to fasten the right boot. "You expect any differently? If they're not running my life, they're not happy." She stood to walk toward the children. "Only six—who's missing?"

"Jaime."

"Probably overslept too."

"What?"

"Nothing. Thinking out loud. Let's get started." As Carla gathered the children in a half circle, she heard the deep roar of the Range Rover Sport. Once again it was Ari who stepped from the driver's seat, catching her off guard. Normally, she would meet Jaime and his nanny half way. Today, she waited for Jaime to come toward her.

Ari didn't approach. He loaded the pack on Jaime's back. Carla watched as with large hands placed gently on the child's shoulders, he turned Jaime toward the group. Jaime glanced back at his father before walking slowly toward the other kids.

Try as she might, she couldn't help locking gazes with the dark and handsome prince. His nod, barely perceptible, sent a path of awareness tingling down her spine.

As Jaime neared, Carla strode toward him. She caught and cradled his small hand in hers. Without a backward glance, Ari turned and climbed into the Range Rover.

Fine. If Ari could pretend they hadn't poured their hearts out to each other, albeit it in a reserved, hold-everything-back sort of way, and forget he'd leaned toward her at the end of the evening, she too could forget the aborted kiss. Kissing *had* been his intention. She'd seen the heat in his eyes. Until common sense filtered through the fog addling both their brains.

Carla concentrated on Jaime, her mission for the week. All the other kids were comfortable on their skis and needed much less one-on-one supervision. Tina could handle the bunch.

"You and I are going on a special run today." Carla squeezed Jaime's hand before letting go and helping him off-load his backpack. He looked up at her, his eyes wide. He hadn't uttered one word yet. "What would be fun for you?"

He shrugged.

Carla knelt down in the snow. "Jaime, please tell me. What is the most favorite thing you learned?"

His gaze shifted downward.

In a whisper, she reiterated the plea. "Please, tell me. So we can have a special day."

He pointed to the left, toward one of the runs.

"What? Tell me."

"Going down the hill."

Carla breathed in the sweet victory at hearing Jaime speak a whole sentence. "You like the Ribbon Run?" She too pointed toward the gently sloping and meandering run designed for youngsters to practice downhill skiing. It had enough of an incline at the top to make it challenging for kids of intermediate skill, but not so hard toward the bottom that the smaller children would muster up too much speed to hurt themselves.

He nodded again.

"Then after we have our opening exercises, you and I will go all the way to the top and ski down."

Jaime's smile eased across his mouth and lifted toward his eyes. *Good. I've hooked him.*

Ari glanced toward the wide windows at the front of his office. The window from where he watched Ms. Peters storm off. Was it only yesterday morning? So much had changed in one night.

Despite his trepidation about Giles' idea to hire her as nanny, last night he'd found her to be a strong, principled woman. Stubborn, yes. A bit reckless, he suspected. He'd seen her at her most vulnerable, yet she rallied to stand on her own and not be rescued.

He smiled.

"A huge grin. I don't believe I've seen many of those."

Ari's head snapped up to glare at his brother. "What do you wish?"

"What do you think?" Giles wandered in and plopped into the chair in front of his desk, liked he owned the room. "You seem grumpier than usual this morning. Late night?"

"You had the same late night."

"At your command, I recall. So you could rescue the *hated* Ms. Peters."

"It was necessary."

"Care to elaborate?"

No, he didn't, but Giles was like a pit bull. Better to come clean. Not totally clean. "She had some problems with a cowboy at that disgusting bar."

"And you had to step in?"

"Or allow her to drive home and endanger herself."

Giles sat straight then leaned his elbows on his knees. "This cowboy was trying to hurt her?"

Ari swiped his hand through the air, like a karate chop. "I will not betray a confidence. A hurt heart, that is all I will say."

"Ah. You managed to wrangle that information out of a woman who appeared to despise you?"

"Despise? That is a harsh word."

Giles nodded. "That's how it appeared to me."

"She bristles and is opinionated and…"

"And?"

"I have work to do. Is this the only reason you barge in and interrupt me?"

Giles stood, his grin wide. Not a good sign. "Pulling your royal attitude on me does not work. Last night, you smiled as you jogged down her stairs, after spending over an hour with her. Have you not changed your mind on hiring her to care for Jaime?" Giles flashed his palms, before he could interrupt to deny the smile or anything else. "It is only for a short time, Ari. She is qualified and as far as I can tell, she is a good person. Reconsider. For the sake of your son."

For the next few days, Carla worked one on one with Jaime. At the end of the session on Wednesday afternoon, she watched as the boy ran toward his father who had picked him up all week. Ari settled on his haunches, eye level with his son. Jaime gestured, apparently telling Ari all about his day. Ari nodded a few times. Her heart thumped in an erratic pattern, watching father and son, their heads together. She couldn't tear her gaze away from the scene. She'd been so wrong when she'd essentially accused the man of neglect.

After several minutes Ari stood, grabbed Jaime's backpack, and waited for the boy to climb into the back seat of the vehicle. As Carla started to turn back to her charges, his head lifted, his eyes fixed on her. Again, as on Monday morning, he simply nodded.

Carla's heart threatened to explode. After the evening they spent in her apartment, she grasped enough about this man to understand the gesture required all his strength. She speculated any acknowledgement of her success with Jaime might make him feel exposed. Now, more curious than ever about the strong and silent prince, his nod reinforced her resolve toward her mission to help both of them.

She strode back to the few students waiting for pick-up, her mind focused on this week's challenge—Jaime—and beyond to the school of her dreams. If she could help Jaime with one-on-one attention, imagine what her teachers could do for the kids in this community.

The potential excited her. And she would prove to everyone she could make her dream a reality.

Chapter Seven

After grabbing dinner on the go, Carla hunched over her yellow legal pad, scratching out notes. With a deep breath, excitement curling through her, she grabbed her cell to return Betsy Sams' call.

"So, Kyle found the perfect location? I'm ready to move on this. If we can get more funding, we can open the school this fall."

She held the phone away from her ear as her more than enthusiastic friend screeched something on the other end. "I have no clue what you just said. You're worse than a three-year old." Carla laughed. "I assume all that shrieking means you're ready to get started."

Betsy described the place.

"Oh, my gosh—perfect. Can you set up an appointment so we can get into the building early next week?" Carla jotted more notes. "I've downloaded forms to submit to the state and town. I'll fill out what I can, then you can add in your information. We need our early childhood education transcripts and copies of our licenses. Plus, the transcript of the town's approval for the school.

"And Kyle...?" She hated talk of financing, but it had to be said. When Betsy married the new town doctor, he'd been so supportive of their ideas he volunteered to help raise money, including chipping in himself.

"Yup. He's in and has his feelers out for more funding."

"You found a gem, Betsy. Who could imagine in our senior year of high school?"

"A dream finally coming true. It was meant to be."

"Yeah. Remember Ms. Evans pooh-pooing our senior project idea that Mineral Springs needed a school of its own." Carla sighed.

"What? You going to let her negativity get to you after all these years? We'll invite her to the grand opening."

Carla burst out laughing. "So bad. You do realize, you're the yang to my yin—always the sunny, optimistic one. We make a great team."

"Except you're a looney-tunes. Tell me you don't believe you're not sunny—most of the time."

"In a mood."

"How's Shawn taking all this?"

"Does everyone know?"

"Only the whole town. What did you expect?"

"Yeah, yeah. Moving back to original topic."

She and Betsy ironed out the next steps so they could hit the road running once Carla finished up ski school season the next afternoon. A positive project to look forward to, rather than impatiently waiting weeks until Meloney rehired her seasonal waitresses at Comfort Food.

She was so ready to take on the huge responsibility of opening a much-needed school. She'd spent years in high school and college, and the last few dreaming and planning. No more juggling waitressing and teaching ski school to cobble together a living. Not that she couldn't go back to live at the ranch...

She shook her head. Nope, she was going to succeed on her own—no help from family.

It wasn't that her family didn't support her efforts or believe she could make a living around her passion for teaching, but they had been raised that family and the ranch came first. They wanted her committed to this ideal. All of her brother's, except Cole who would finish college this spring, had come home to work. She loved the ranch, but she couldn't imagine the rest of her life working with her brothers and father hanging over her shoulder watching every move she made. Somehow, they hadn't quite figured out that a twenty-nine-year-old woman could plan her own destiny without help from a man.

It was no secret her family struggled to keep the ranch going. Two years of drought and high feed prices had taken a toll. She helped as much as possible so they wouldn't have to spend so much on salaries, but she couldn't keep giving away her labor for free and maintain her own living space and build toward her dream. Plus, it seemed the faster her dreams edged toward reality, the more they asked, as if to keep her close.

Being the only girl sucked big time, even if the men in the family wanted to protect her out of love. Especially after their mom died. Thankfully now that Madge was in the picture, they had eased off a bit.

The ache deep in her heart assaulted her every now and again. She missed her mom. With Mom, she had an ally to gang up on all the guys. With Madge, she wasn't so sure. She hadn't spent enough time at the ranch to really get to know her dad's new wife.

Carla's swirling thoughts and plans and dreams collided into the makings of one big headache. She sank back against the deep cushions of the armchair and smoothed her fingers across closed lids and up across her forehead in an attempt to sooth away her worries. The dark edges of unconsciousness flittered behind her lids, as she drifted towards much needed sleep.

A heavy and insistent knock on the front door startled her into an upright position.

"Ms. Peters, answer this door."

A shiver zapped straight down her spine. What in goddess' green pastures possessed the prince to knock on her door at nine o'clock on a Thursday night?

The knock sounded again, louder and more insistent. "Your truck is here. Open."

"Hold your horses," she muttered, now fully awake. He did have a way of commanding her presence, even at her own door. "I'm coming." Carla took her sweet time before swinging the door wide.

"I must speak with you."

She covered her mouth, as she hit on the one reason Ari would be there. "Jaime? Is he all right?"

"Of course, he is fine."

Yes, of course. "Right. You wouldn't be here if he wasn't."

He strode through the door, uninvited. "I have need of your services. Starting immediately."

"Excuse me?"

"Sénhora Miranda has gone to Portega. Her mother, she is ill. And now Cook has the flu. I have no one to care for Jaime."

"I may know of someone—"

"I want you."

She stared at him. His demand surprised her before she understood his meaning. "I *have* a job." Okay, so it only lasted one more day, but he didn't know that. Although becoming Jaime's nanny intrigued her, she'd rather be caught in a hailstorm, miles from the ranch on horseback, than let Ari, or any man, dictate how she spent her time.

Maybe if he'd asked. But he did sound desperate. Scratch that, he *had* to be desperate if he was asking her.

"Ah, but that job only takes six hours of the day. I am certain it pays little. I will pay one thousand a week, twenty-four hours a day as nanny." Her mouth opened. "With Sunday's off," he added.

She wasn't often speechless.

"I must ask you to pack your bags and be ready to move in as soon as the ski school ends tomorrow."

She squared her shoulders, stepped into his space, and looked him in the eye. "Prince Orula, I have not consented to—" She was arguing over an offer of one thousand dollars a week? Was she nuts? *Yes.*

"Please, I have need of you." He dropped his gaze to the floor, then back up until his eyes locked with hers. "Jaime has need of you. He asks after you. Fifteen hundred a week."

Carla lifted her palms. "Whoa. It's not the money." She could feel her nose growing longer. Yeah, working was about the money. But she wouldn't sell her soul to the devil to attain her goal at any cost.

"Please. I beg of you." He turned and paced toward the door and back. "Twenty-five hundred."

Her heart dipped. Not about the obscene amount of money, but because Ari needed her—even if he didn't want to admit Jaime wasn't the only one with needs.

She sucked in a deep breath. He wasn't close to being the devil. Yeah, she wanted to believe the worst, if only to add much needed space between the two. Because no question, she'd wanted that kiss.

And now, he looked at her with those eyes. The same as his son's—lost and exposed.

He *needed* her.

"One week"

"Two."

"I have other commitments."

"Fine. We *begin* with one week. Giles will move your belongings tomorrow afternoon."

She ignored the 'begin with one week.' "No, Ari, I stay here."

"You must move in. You will see. The hours begin early and end late."

She shook her head. "Jaime doesn't need me as he sleeps. I'm more comfortable—" She couldn't be under the thumb of this man. He was demanding at the best of times, even when he slipped and showed the edge of his vulnerability. But living under the same roof? *No.*

Plus, her brothers would ride over the edge of the cliff if they learned she bunked out at the prince's *castle.*

"Jaime...and I...we both— He has nightmares. You will live at the ranch."

Her brain said no. But one look at his face and her heart said yes. How could she deny him, when he tried desperately to cover up his need with a royal command?

She could work on her school plans after Jaime went to bed. She'd sock away the week's salary to put toward school expenses.

Ari touched her arm, His palm hot against her skin. A shiver zipped down her spine. She nodded her agreement, knowing she stepped into a deep gopher hole of trouble by consenting.

Carla managed to get through the restless night and the last hours of ski school the next morning, despite thoughts spinning through her head and a thumping heart that beat out of control. Panic attack? Close.

And now, as kids bumped their way down the snowy path overloaded with equipment, her heart rate accelerated. The last day of ski school.

When Ari dropped Jaime off that morning, he'd done his usual thing—nod and leave. What the holy hello had she agreed to? How would she manage under the same roof? The man had let down his guard the night he drove her home. But now, he held his armor tight to his chest.

The day had dragged...and flown by. Carla couldn't help tearing up as the last students said their goodbyes. She loved this job and hated the end of season for so many reasons. But today's ending was different. She had a new adventure to face. And a new fear.

Her stomach jumped from a jumble of nerves that refused to quiet. With Jaime's hand in hers, the last to be picked up, they waited by the edge of the parking lot.

The big, black Range Rover swung off the highway and roared toward them. Carla expected Giles to alight and order her to follow him back to her apartment for her things. But long legs in familiar boots showed beneath the open door, as Ari stepped from the car. Wasting little time, he strode toward them.

She waited for the controlling and arrogant attitude. Nothing. Ari paid no attention to her, as he knelt in front of his son. "You had a good day?"

"*Sim*, Papa." Jaime's head bobbed in excitement. "I came down the big hill all by myself and didn't fall once."

"The big hill? My, my, that is quite a feat. You are proud of yourself?"

"*Sim*, Papa."

Ari stood and tousled his son's hair. "Good. You should be proud. Now, let us go. I have much to do this afternoon." Only then did the prince turn to Carla. "Giles will meet you in an hour. Are you ready?"

"Three hours." The last thing she wanted was for Ari to believe she was geared up for the adventure and waiting impatiently.

"Giles will help you pack. One hour."

She lifted her chin. "You understand I'm putting my life on hold for one week. I have personal things to take care of before I come. And, I will drive myself. Three hours."

His brow creased.

She shrugged. He'd live taking orders from her. After all, he coerced her into accepting his offer. He'd just have to cool his heels at the *castle* while she called Betsy to have her move the building inspection to the following week. Betsy would understand, especially when she found out how much Carla would make for one week's work.

Besides, the last thing she wanted Ari to know was that her anticipation had risen with each minute that passed since he'd left the previous night.

Chapter Eight

Carter quelled his anger by taking Carla's stairs one step at a time. Knowing his sister, if he approached her like a bellowing and bucking bull, she would never see reason.

He tempered his knuckle rap. Waited for her footsteps with a patience he did not feel.

"I do *not* need help," she said, as she opened the door. Her eyes widened. "Carter. What are you doing here?"

He pushed past her. "We need to talk."

Immediately, her hands went to her hips. "If you plan to get in my face about my business, you can turn right around and leave."

"What were you thinking?"

"What did I do *this* time?" Hands remained plastered on her hips as she strode toward him, backing him against the counter separating her kitchen from her living room.

He crossed his arms, anticipating her usual swat across the chest when she didn't want interference. "Shawn. What were you *thinking*? You two have been together forever."

"As. Friends." She raised her palm and with nowhere to go with the counter at his back, he braced. "I'm not going to hit you. Yet. But you have to let me live my own life. Shawn and I have always been friends. Not my fault he wants more."

"Carla, it's time you settled down."

"Says the big brother who remains single. And…." Her pointer finger jabbed him. "Still trying to tell his grown-up sister what to do."

He lowered his arms and grabbed the finger she again aimed

at his chest. "You hurt him, you know."

"Of course, I know. You can't imagine how bad I feel. But I love him like a brother. That does not a marriage make."

"Cal—"

"Do not say it. You know I love Shawn. I always will. But I am *not* right for him."

"You've always been—seemed—"

"Being the operative word. All of you decided years ago that Shawn and I *seemed* to be right for each other. Maybe on paper." She stepped out of his reach and hugged her arms around her waist. "You can't make me love someone, Carter. Shawn's been like family, always. But you can't dictate that I love him that way."

Her whispered words hit him in the gut.

She backed up and tripped against a large suitcase. "If it were that easy, I would have had you married off to Meloney by now."

He ducked his head and shoved his palm over his forehead, dislodging the hat he should have removed. "I want what's best for you, Cal." He'd watched her ogle the prince the other night. He behaved badly the way he went after Ari Orula at the Rustler's Grill, but he had to mark the Peters' family territory. Show the guy his family, and all they owned, was off limits.

"Fine. You've said what you need to. We finished?"

His gaze locked on the suitcase behind her. "Going somewhere?"

"Goodwill."

"That suitcase is brand new."

"What's in it, you nitwit. Now go. Leave me alone. And Carter?"

"Yeah."

"I do love you, but you need to learn to trust your family. You might run the ranch, but you don't run our lives."

By the time he got down that set of rickety stairs, the guilt had eaten a hole in his belly. Sure, Carla was a grown woman, but she needed him. He had to remember what a strong woman she was. But his family role was to protect and help out any way he could. It was time they ~~all~~ repaid all the help Carla gave the family, by coming to her rescue once in a while. Tomorrow, he vowed to round up his brothers to come over and fix these damn falling-apart stairs.

Maybe that would make up for all his blustering.

Chapter Nine

Ari paced from his desk to the window and back, impatient to see Carla arrive. The sun was close to dipping behind the mountain range across the river.

"Will you sit for god's sake. You're like a wild horse forced into his first corral."

He tossed a look, the kind that would fell most in his employ. Not Giles. "I should have sent you to retrieve her."

"Now you sound like she's some sort of possession. She will be here. You've got to learn to relax. Not everyone is on a strict schedule like you set for yourself."

Ari strode back to the window, pulled aside the sheer curtain, and stared at the empty drive. "What if she has decided she will not help Jaime?"

"She is not the type of woman who says one thing and does another. She'll be here. You gave her little time to prepare for a week away from home. Perhaps…" Giles grinned and stretched his legs out in front of him, slouching slightly in the big chair. "She has plants to water or a bird to house."

"She has neither of those. You forget I was in her apartment."

"That you were. And you no doubt noticed every detail."

"Of course, I did. I always assess. You think I would have hired her on your word alone."

Giles shook his head and stood. "You make me crazy, little brother. I could use a brandy. So could you before you wear a hole through the floorboards."

A truck engine roared up the incline that led from the river. By the time Ari jogged to the window, again, Carla's truck had bounced across the open space toward the house. This time, she didn't park at the far end. He let out a breath he was sure he'd been holding on and off for the last fifteen minutes.

"I guess you're on your own for that drink. I have duties. Greet our guest and get her settled." Giles sauntered toward the office door before he turned. "Are you okay now?"

Ari gave a quick nod, as his stomach settled. He *had* doubted she would show.

After Giles met her at the front door and formally introduced himself, Carla was ushered upstairs and into a bedroom overlooking the valley and mountains in back.

Her brothers would not be happy about this latest twist in Carla's childhood education career quest. More like a crooked turn in the road. She should have told Carter, but she hadn't dared. Already fired up about Shawn, he would have exploded if he realized she planned to spend the week at the Silver Mine Ranch. Eventually he'd find out. Then she'd pay her dues. The guilt ate at her. But right now, she didn't have the energy to fight with her over-protective, big brother. Even when everything he did stemmed from his love for and protection of his family, he wasn't a man who easily saw reason.

"Ms. Peters, Sénhora Adélia will be here in a moment to help you unpack."

Snapped from her thoughts, she turned from the magnificent view and faced Giles. "Thanks, but I won't need help."

Giles smiled, warm and wide. "Ah, but the prince insists on treating you as a guest—"

"And you don't believe he should?"

"I did not say that, Ms. Peters." For a moment, his British accent turned crisp, before it settled back into a comfortable lilt. "You are indeed a most welcome guest. I merely meant the prince stands on decorum." With a wink, he added, "It's in his blood. He cannot help himself."

Carla laughed. The few times she'd met Giles when he

dropped off Jaime at ski school, she'd been drawn to his kindness and easygoing manner. "Nor can he help his royal commands."

"There you have it, Ms. Peters." Giles dipped his head in a mock bow as he backed out, but nothing could hide his grin.

"Must you insist on this Ms. Peters deal?"

"Decorum." He winked again and disappeared down the hall.

With Giles to run interference between her stubbornness and the prince's royal attitude, it stood to reason the week wouldn't be so difficult.

Carla turned to face the room. Her suitcase lay on the queen-sized, newel-posted bed. The double doors to the closet were flung wide. Unpacking was an exclamation point—an end from which she had a feeling there was no return. She would need a backbone of steel to leave at the end of the week. Ari had ceded to her negotiations for a one-week limit. But now that she was *captive* in the prince's tower, she had a gut feeling he wouldn't let her go easily. Not until Jaime's nanny returned. She refrained from counting dollar signs if she did continue past the week.

And Jaime…would she be able to leave him after a week in close quarters? She was truly fond of the kid, and the challenge to help him pulled at her heart. She placed her hands on her hips. *Well, I have one week to make a difference.*

She unpacked and stowed the suitcase under her bed. Now what? Wait for the summons? She was sure it would come soon.

After wandering around the suite, she pulled out a novel and sat in the cushioned seat of the large bay window that overlooked pastures blotted with a patchwork of snow and spring green. She could totally imagine Carter, galloping across a summer landscape of hay-colored grass, herding the ranch's Australian Lowline Angus. He worked like a dog the last five years to help their dad pull the ranch back from the brink. It had been his idea to turn their business into fully organic, grass-fed cattle ranch. Area restaurants in Aspen now vied for their beef.

Expansion had been part of the ten-year plan. Expansion to the valley beyond—now out of their reach. Prince Orula had swept in a year ago and purchased the land.

Now she stood on the forbidden land, colluding with the enemy.

A soft knock sounded at the door.

"Come in."

A petite woman, wearing a conservative, beige, shirtwaist dress entered. Taking two steps into the room, she bowed her head. "Good evening, Ms. Peters. I am Sénhora Adélia at your service. The prince requests the honor of your presence at dinner. Six o'clock sharp, if you will. He plans to outline your duties at that time."

The woman backed out the door before Carla could respond to the summons. *It has begun.* She'd be lucky to last out the week without letting her sharp tongue get the better of her. This time, she did conjure up dollar signs—marching dollar signs. Her silent mantra of survival for every time the prince irked her, because she could guarantee he would.

When she arrived at dinner, one minute before six, Ari rose and pulled out the chair to the left of him. Jaime sat across from her. "Thank you for joining us. I hope you find your quarters adequate."

Adequate? The suite of rooms and luxurious bath, the size of a normal kitchen, was quadruple the size of her apartment. The bedroom alone equaled the square footage of her efficiency. Then there was the sitting room, dressing room, and a fourth room that doubled as office and exercise room, complete with a computerized elliptical machine, a treadmill, and weights.

She wanted to burst out laughing at his formality. She held herself in check and simply responded, "Thank you. Most adequate."

"Ms. Carla, may I come visit you in your rooms?"

Ari's eyebrows squeezed together in reprimand. "You will address her as Ms. Peters. And, inviting oneself is not polite."

"*Sim,* Papa." The boy lowered his head, but his eyes were

raised to scrutinize her as he peeked out from under his bangs. The child had a bit of feistiness in him after all. Carla had detected that spirit over the last few days when Jaime forgot people watched him. Or when he bit down on his lip in concentrated determination as he skied down Ribbon Run. She planned to capitalize on that quality to get him to open up.

She almost laughed out loud. This balancing act between the prince's code of discipline and her own desire to be less strict with the boy could prove difficult. "I'm sure we will have opportunity for you to visit once I settle in. I will invite you when I am ready to receive visitors. Maybe tomorrow—we will see."

"*Sim*—ah—yes, Ms. Peters."

"Jaime is used to calling me Ms. Carla at ski school. I would much prefer that, ah, if it is all right with you."

Ari nodded.

An uneasy silence settled around the dining table that could effortlessly seat twenty.

"Do you eat in here every evening?"

"No, often we have supper in my suite. When I am not at dinner, Jaime will eat in the kitchen. Tonight, we welcome a guest."

"This is special," Jaime chimed in. "But I like the kitchen. Cook gives me—" He squeezed his eyes shut and pressed his lips in a straight line so as not to expose the slight grin that fought to take purchase at the corners of his mouth. Or, Carla suspected, utter any secrets.

With a straight face, Ari arched his brow. "You finish your dinner first. Am I correct?"

"*Sim*, Papa."

"It is important to eat your vegetables and clean your plate—for all growing boys. Then you may accept treats from Cook."

"I try, Papa."

Ari winked at Carla, the first sign since she'd entered the dining room that he was human rather than a royal robot. Her heart expanded. Watching Ari interact with Jaime trumped all the hassle of living under the same roof and jumping to the prince's orders. But it was more than that. The strong, silent, and commanding man had a sweet heart underneath it all.

Giles was right. Royalty coursed through his blood. He acted out a part he'd been raised to take. In many ways, Ari reminded her of Carter—both serious about their standing in the family and their own obligation to protect and serve. But every once in a great while, they each let down their guard.

"That is all I ask, that you try and eat all your dinner." Ari's wise counsel to his son brought her back to the moment.

As if on signal, the swinging door to the kitchen opened. Sénhora Adélia entered carrying a soup tureen. Bending her knees, she offered Carla easy access to the ladle. "Crab and roasted corn bisque."

"Smells incredible." Carla filled her bowl. She'd had a power bar for lunch and prayed her stomach wouldn't rumble before she dug her spoon into the creamy creation.

Ari scooped half a ladle full for Jaime. The boy's nose puckered into a non-verbal do-I-have-to? "Try it. You may be surprised. You like the corn Cook makes over the grill, yes? This is the same corn."

The boy nodded.

Carla was impressed with the respect Ari showed his son. What she assumed to be an arrogant and condescending attitude turned out to be anything but. This was his way, so different from the raucous meals at her family's ranch. With a table full of growing boys, she and her mom had little peace and quiet at mealtime. Dinner at Ari's showcased a quiet civility she'd never experienced in this working-man's southwest town.

When Ari glanced her way, she smiled. His eyes twinkled, bits of silver swimming through the onyx, and her heart melted some more.

Carla and Jaime made it a daily habit to have breakfast with Cook. The two had developed a good rapport on Ribbon Run, but the last few days, Jaime started to come out of his shell. He remained reticent about some things, but his glee at daily life on the ranch inspired her. They'd settled into an unstructured and easy rhythm. Just the two of them.

Most mornings, Ari was already up and out in the barn working with the trainer and his insemination specialist. Growing up on a ranch, Carla understood herd management, ensuring a fresh crop of cattle each spring. She knew little about breeding horses, but assumed the operation was similar, and just as time-consuming. The fact Ari worked side by side with his staff upped his wow factor, as it negated her brother's arguments about the high and mighty prince, wannabe rancher.

Carla smiled at Jaime, as he gobbled down a third big pancake. "We'll have to work off all this food. Shall we go to the stables after breakfast?"

With his mouth full, Jaime shook his head.

"Where then? We need to get outside on this beautiful day."

"The gardens."

Carla buried her disappointment. Checking out the Silver Mine Ranch stables was top on her snoop-list. If nothing else, she could quell Carter's anger about her accepting this job. Not by divulging Ari's secrets, but by showing her brother this ranch was not in competition with the cattle ranches in the area. Maybe she could convince Jaime to wander toward the stables later.

When he finished the last bite, they helped Cook, who had suspiciously made a miraculous and speedy recovery from the flu, by stashing their plates in the dishwasher and wiping down the corner table by the windows.

Jaime ran across the kitchen. "Thank you for the yummy pancakes."

Cook bent and accepted a kiss to her cheek. "You're welcome, my sweet boy. Now run along."

"Come on. Ms. Carla." He offered his hand and she grabbed hold with a smile in her heart. Progress. They strolled out the kitchen door.

"Tell me why you like the gardens."

Jaime looked at her, his eyes wide with excitement. "The flowers, they are so pretty. And the gardens smell good."

"Do you ever plant things?"

Jaime shook his head as he lifted the wrought iron latch and swung open the wooden gate. They entered a garden surrounded by a four-foot high, old-fashioned stonewall, probably to deter the mule deer and elk.

"Once, a deer jumped over the wall."

"Oh, my goodness. What happened."

"He ate some flowers and got stuck in here."

"That must have been some adventure."

Jaime jumped and clapped his hands. "Indeed, Ms. Carla."

He sounded just like his father. Her mission was to bring Jaime out of his shell, but the tug of adoration for both Jaime and his father was at best an unwelcome intrusion. She could not afford to open her heart. Like she could stop the crack that widened daily.

"Pete had to open the gate and bang on a big pot with a wooden spoon so the deer would run out."

"Wow. I can see why the deer would like it in here with all these flowers. But he must have been scared, right?"

His earnest face with the tight lips and the bobbing head, showed how sympathetic the kid must have been for the poor, imprisoned deer. "But he's safe now."

As they moved slowly through the gardens, Carla breathed in the damp and pungent smell of rich earth. She itched to lunge her hands into the soil and sift it through her fingers. Pear trees and Aspens, providing a bit of shade for the blue, white, and purple blooms of the early Siberian Bugloss and Pasque flowers peeking out among the Rock Cress in the rock gardens, filled the space. Other plants along the winding paths, whose leaves unfurled their spring green, rose toward the sun. The wall protected the garden and held in the warmth from the sun, cushioning the area from the cool, early spring winds.

"Who works in your garden?"

"Pete." Jaime said the name as if Carla should have known.

"Is he the gardener?"

Jaime shrugged.

"Maybe you and I can get some seeds and plant them?"

Jaime catapulted into the air, a huge grin on his adorable face. "I want to plant seeds."

Carla's heart melted at his exuberance. Something he'd held in the entire time he'd been skiing on the mountain.

He looked to the skies, then scanned the garden. He bit down on his lower lip before he looked up. "What kind of seeds?"

"I don't know." She reined in her mirth as he mirrored his father's serious manner. "I may have to buy seeds. You can help me pick."

Following the flagstone path curving through the gardens, they came to an old shed at the far end. Out of a jumble of clay pots piled outside the weathered building, Carla chose a smaller one. "Maybe we could use this." She placed the pot on the wooden potting bench that stood underneath an expansive overhang perfect for protection up against the exterior wall. She handed Jaime a trowel she found resting on the edge.

After tugging on the door that dragged against the layer of crushed stone, she peered in.

"Wait here." Carla stepped through the door. Once her eyes acclimated to the deep recesses of the shed, she noticed the order. Bags of potting soil were piled atop a wooden pallet. The top one had been opened, but the edge was now rolled down and clipped closed with a row of clothespins. Tools were hanging from hooks on a pegboard. In a small, wooden box on top of the bench, she found several packets of seeds, evidently left from last year.

She grabbed a packet of seed and the open bag of soil before stepping back out into the sunshine. "Look what I found. Seeds." She handed the packet to Jaime.

He turned it over. "Sun, ah, flow...ers." He read the words slowly, sounding out each syllable as he worked out the pronunciation in his second language.

She tousled his ebony hair. "You are right. You're a good reader. I love sunflowers."

"Me too. Can we grow these?"

"I'm sure Pete won't mind if we plant a few in this pot."

The two sat on the grassy edge by the shed and planted five sunflowers. "We'll leave the pot right here. They'll get plenty of sun. We have to water the seeds every day."

"When will they grow?"

"It will take a few weeks, I'm sure." She reminded herself to tell Cook, since she wouldn't be there when they started to sprout. That thought twisted in her stomach with an ache she hadn't imagined she'd experience. As they walked back through the garden, Carla noticed an empty patch of turned earth about ten feet by ten feet. "Will Pete plant vegetables here?"

"No. We only have flowers in our garden."

"Maybe we can ask your dad if we can plant some lettuce and other things."

When Jaime scrunched up his nose, Carla added, "I bet Cook would love it if we grew her vegetables for the salad. We'll ask her first."

"She likes corn, too," said Jaime. "Could we grow that?"

"I'm not sure there's enough room for corn. It gets taller than me and takes up a lot of space."

"Can we ask Pete?"

"Maybe we should ask your father first."

Once in the kitchen, Carla asked Cook for a piece of paper and penned Pete a note about their sunflower pot. They spent the rest of the morning gathering twigs and stones for an art project, then went in for lunch.

The quiet time provided a chance to learn what Jaime liked, what he remembered from his time living on Portega, and all about his grandparents. Every afternoon, after they watered the seeds, she helped Jaime with reading and simple arithmetic and geography. He was up to par, even though Ari had pointed out the need for Jaime to catch up on his schooling since English was a second language. She'd be sure to point out his son was in good shape to be enrolled in an American school the following fall.

Every evening, the three ate dinner together, usually in Ari's sitting room.

Each night she helped with the bedtime ritual of brushing teeth and washing Jaime's face. When Ari arrived, he helped Jaime with his pajamas and tucked his son into bed. Carla's official day was done. She would have loved to stay for story times, but Ari reserved the private moments for the two.

On Saturday night, Ari sent Jaime in to brush his teeth and asked Carla to stay for a few moments. He gestured toward the couch, then sat in the nearby chair. "I know you agreed to a week. And tomorrow marks the end of your week."

Here it comes. "Ari, we discussed this. I have other obligations starting on Monday. And you did promise Sundays off."

"I must fly to Denver in the morning and spend several days. Unexpected. Giles and Cook have other duties. But we can work around your day off tomorrow and outside obligations, if you can stay on one more week."

She opened her mouth to protest, but he raised his palms. "I implore you. His nanny remains in Portega with her ill mother. This trip was not planned. We will accommodate any of your needs."

She couldn't say no. Truth was, in less than a week, she'd connected with Jaime and everyone else at the ranch. She wasn't ready to leave. "I will make some calls tonight, but there are meetings that I switched from this week to next that I cannot miss."

"Of course. I will schedule you to meet with Giles first thing in the morning. He will make arrangements to cover Jaime's care for all your obligations." He rose and extended his hand. "Now, you will come with me and share in Jaime's goodnight, so you know what must be done." He beckoned with the curl of his palm. "Come." When she stood, he clasped her hand in his and walked toward Jaime's room.

A frizzle of heat shot up her arm and imbedded in her heart. The weight of attraction only cooled slightly once they'd reached Jaime's room and he dropped her hand.

She stood in the doorway between the playroom and the boy's bedroom.

"You will say your prayers."

"*Sim*, Papa."

Carla's heart melted into a maternal puddle when the youngster sank to his knees and steepled his hands against the edge of the bed.

"Please look after grandmamma and grandpapa, Giles, Sénhora Miranda, Sénhora Adélia, Cook, Pete, and..." He opened his eyes and glanced up at Ari. "Especially look after Papa." He crossed himself and started to rise, then dipped back to his knees. "Oh, and please look upon Ms. Carla. She is my new friend and she needs your help to do a good job, so Papa will let her stay here with us."

She barely restrained herself from sweeping in to take the boy in her arms. Jaime was opening up. And he'd made a space for Carla in his heart.

Ari glanced back at her, flashed a rare smile, and motioned her into the room.

Together they tucked Jaime under the covers. Ari picked a book from the pile on the bedside table and settled on the edge of the bed while Carla sat in the nearby rocking chair. In his accent, the lyrical rhymes of Dr. Seuss sounded magical. Jaime followed along, every now and then his jovial giggle interrupting the story at an especially silly rhyme. As Ari closed the book, the boy begged for one more.

Ari pulled him into a bear hug. "You have been good today?"

"*Sim*, Papa." In his excitement, Jaime almost catapulted himself off the bed.

"Ah, but how do I know this?" Ari's eyes glinted with tease.

"Oh, Papa. You know I have been good. Read another story. Please."

They read *Goodnight Moon*. Carla noted the drop in Ari's voice each time he turned a page. Surprised he knew such a trick, she watched as Jaime's head drooped halfway through the story. Finally, his eyes drifted shut and his breathing evened out.

Ari was a good father. Not surprising that he'd been livid

when she asked him if he loved his son. She'd only meant to goad him. Now she understood the insensitivity of her question. Carla gave herself a mental slap about *assuming*. And watched as Ari leaned down to arrange the blankets and kiss the top of Jaime's head.

She moved into the playroom ahead of Ari. He pulled Jaime's door to within inches of shut, the narrow slant of a muted beam from the nightlight tunneling across the floor their only light. Carla's breath clogged her throat with unwelcome emotion. The whole scene of father putting son to bed had been—well, there were no words to describe the ache of longing.

To have a child like Jaime, so full of warmth and love, made her heart expand. To watch him emerge from his shell, nothing short of amazing.

And with it came her own sad memories.

She gulped back the threat of tears and thoughts of her miscarriage. The child Shawn knew nothing about. They'd been too young. He would have dragged her to Vegas—*done right by her*—before her brothers and Dad came out wielding the ole' shotguns. Seven years later, handling the loss of her baby did not get easier.

Ari approached. She started to turn before he could read the need on her face, but he stepped closer and reached for her.

"Carla?" His forefinger and thumb cupped her chin. His touch gentle.

A shiver of heat slipped down her spine. She fought to keep from leaning into him. At this moment of weakness and sorrowful memories and need so deep, she wanted nothing more than to rely on this man. She, who tried *never* to rely on a man.

She had no choice but to look into eyes so dark they blended with the night. Would he ask her what was wrong? She'd only known him a few weeks, but he saw things she tried to hide deep down.

"You have done much in this short time to help my boy. Hearing his laugh is music to me."

Surprised by his backward way of thanking her, she shoved down her own memories and concentrated on what he said. "He must have laughed before?"

"Of course. But not often. Not since—" As if a knife sliced through his sentence, he stopped.

"Since what?"

He dropped his hand and backed up a step. "Now is not the time."

"When?" She closed the small space between them. "You asked the same of me when I wanted to tell no one about Shawn." She mimicked his formal words but if she could get a reaction, she'd do what she had to. "When will you tell me what is bothering Jaime? And you?"

For a second, his breathe suspended. She thought he would open to her.

"Not now," he said. "It is not your business." He turned on his heel.

"Ari? Please." Her words followed him into the hallway, leaving her to navigate the dark room on her own. She shouldn't have pushed. It wasn't as though they were in a relationship and she had a *right* to know.

She worked for the man—nothing else.

Except, understanding what made Ari tick would help her understand Jaime.

Before tiptoeing out of the playroom, Carla peeked through the narrow opening in the door to make sure they hadn't awakened Jaime. His face, so angelic in sleep, made her ache

Chapter Ten

Fifteen minutes later, Carla paced her suite from one room to the next. As if pacing would dispel the ache from buried memories, or that persistent physical want.

Being so close to Ari stirred up many emotions she normally kept at bay. The past week had been busy, her mind off her own problems. But now, watching Ari and his son and getting to know each better, everything she thought she'd buried resurfaced. And along with it, a longing for a partner in life and children of her own.

She shouldn't have agreed to stay another week. Holy hello, in a span of a week she'd become attached to Jaime and Ari, and the entire household. And Ari…

Ari? Who knew?

Worry over the fragility of her heart far outweighed her concern about her brothers finding out about her latest, albeit, short-lived occupation. A roller coaster of guilt, hope, fear, lust, longing, and sorrow had her on a ride of ups and downs and twisting turns over the last few weeks. Since she first introduced herself to the prince.

Her head spun.

Pacing did nothing to quiet her mind. So, she strode one last length to the small table nestled by the window, booted up the computer, and readied her files in order to bury her head in preparing to open a new school. She hoped it would take her out of swirling thoughts that refused to quiet.

She glanced at the old Raggedy Ann sitting on the bureau— the doll that had traveled with her everywhere since she was a kid. Resisting hugging her childhood friend to her chest for the comfort she craved, she ignored the doll and concentrated on filling out school forms.

An hour later, as Carla backed up her paperwork, a knock brought her back to reality.

Ten p.m.

Her heart pitched to the pit of her stomach. Did Jaime need her? She had the monitor on, in case he had one of his nightmares, but she'd heard not a sound from his room.

She yanked the door open, readying herself for bad news. Ari stood in the middle of the hallway, hands stuffed in his pockets, looking as pitiful as one of her brothers when he'd done something stupid.

"I must admit to being sorry." His voice had that same royal tone, but his words... This was a side of Ari she never expected to witness. She opened the door further and stepped back into the shadows of the room.

The hard onyx stare unsettled her. The mantle clock ticked behind her.

He straightened, liberated his hands, and strode past her in typical princely fashion to stop midpoint in her sitting room. "I should not be cross with you. This is not your fault."

"Cross?"

"I have things I wish to keep to myself. You understand?"

"Of course, I do. I never should've asked."

"You care about people—that is why you ask. I understand this. But I cannot talk about such things."

"It's all right. Really. I, ah, I only asked because of my concern for Jaime. And...you."

He stood outside the circle of dim light emanating from her desk lamp.

"Do you want to sit?"

He shook his head as his gaze settled on her mouth. "I want..."

Like a moth drawn to the light, she moved toward him. He didn't hesitate. In a flash, the reticent and remorseful cowboy turned into the take-control prince. His palms cradled her jaw.

The surprisingly rough pad of one thumb moved against her bottom lip. He tilted his head and guided her face toward his. His warm breath, the slight scent of brandy mingled with peach pie, caressed her lips. And then his mouth melded with hers.

Neither gentle nor tentative as a first kiss should be, it was deep and needy, igniting smoky embers into full-fledged flames. She leaned against his hard chest and gave in to the moment. To warm, firm lips. To his tongue gliding a path across her mouth. To her own willingness to open, as he slipped in to explore.

When she joined in the dance, her mind shut down completely, focusing only on the sensation of his lips against hers. Hot and hungry.

A kiss like no other she'd ever experienced.

And as abruptly as the kiss started, it ended. The warmth of his hands cradling her face disappeared.

Ari pulled back as though he'd been singed. He swiped the back of his hand across his lips.

Carla's eyes, smoky and almost shuttered, suddenly widened. Her mouth dropped open, but no words emerged.

What had he done? Ari turned and strode out of her suite, rushing to the far wing of his home and headlong into his suite.

All he could think about was her rosy, plump lips after their kiss. The spicy taste of her that matched her spunky attitude. Her wildflower scent that lingered long after his escape down the corridor. Her multi-speckled hazel eyes, that widened even more, as he turned his back on her. That image would remain with him forever. He'd let his passion get the better of him, and hurt Carla as a result. And hurt the one chance he'd allowed for Carla to get close to Jaime. In one week, she'd made a difference in his boy's life. In their lives.

How had he let this woman get so close? He would crucify Giles for suggesting he hire Ms. Peters. Yes, Ms. Peters. He had begun to think of her as Carla. A very bad idea, which led to his stupid mistake. A kiss. For more reasons than he cared to admit, this kiss had been wrong.

He betrayed her trust. He was her boss—she his employee,

taking care of his son. He must let nothing get in the way of ensuring Jaime was safe, especially his lust. For that was all it was, lust—for a woman who did nothing but contradict him, rile him.

And…bring happiness to his son. Yes. Carla, ah, Ms. Peters, cared for Jaime. But she distracted Ari.

That distraction would not do. He must keep one, and only one, target in his sights. Jaime.

Punching the button on his intercom, he summoned Giles and then called his private pilot, before seeing to the task of packing his bags. His plan to eat breakfast with Jaime and *Ms. Peters* before leaving for Denver would not do. He must leave immediately.

When Giles sauntered in wearing running pants and a rumpled T-shirt, Ari realized he had awakened him. Nonetheless, he issued instructions. "You will find a new nanny."

"It's nearing midnight. What the hell is going on?"

Ari refused to answer. "As soon as you have the new nanny in place, escort Ms. Peters back to her home."

"Ari, you don't mean—"

Ari ripped the five thousand-dollar check from his checkbook and thrust it toward Giles.

Giles stared. "You're paying her off? And overpaying at that."

Ari pulled back the chit and ripped it in half. "Never mind. She will refuse to cash this, the stubborn woman. Get cash from the safe."

"What did she do?" For a moment Giles glared at him before his expression softened. "Rather I should ask, what did you do?"

"It is nothing. You were wrong, Giles. She won't do as Jaime's nanny."

When Giles stepped forward, Ari raised a hand. "No more discussion." He stuffed the check pieces in his desk, no longer willing to wait for Giles to see reason. "When Ms. Peters is home, give her the money. All of it. Do not take no for an answer. You will call me in Denver to report progress."

Giles pressed his lips together, crossed his arms over his chest and stood there. Ari would not discuss the situation. He had kissed the woman. If Giles found out the truth, he'd simply laugh and say *it's about time, old man.* But Ari could not bear to live in close proximity to this woman.

He would kiss her again. And maybe more. Yet, he did not trust her even as he lusted. He could not take such a chance.

Not appropriate.

Ashamed he had taken his grief and anger out on Carla, he could never explain to Giles or Carla that he continued to mourn his wife. And that he also hated his dead wife to the very depths of his soul because of her deceit. And that, no matter how hard he tried, he could not resolve this dichotomy of deep sorrow and hatred. He opened a bureau drawer and, without sorting through, grabbed a pile of clothes and threw them in the suitcase on top of his bed.

"Ari."

Ignoring Giles, he moved to his closet and selected several suits. Those he threw on top, not caring if they wrinkled.

How could he ever explain when he had no understanding?

And despite all the emotional turmoil of the past plaguing him, he had succumbed to Carla's charm. Kissed her. Wanted her. Desperately.

What was wrong with him? He had made a mistake bringing her to this ranch. Allowing Giles to persuade him and allowing the temporary nanny to get close to Jaime…and to him.

Ari hoisted the carry-on to his shoulder and instructed Giles to follow him with his suitcase.

"Now I am one of your servants?"

"I have no servants." Ari glared. "And I have no wish to speak of this."

Giles shrugged and grabbed Ari's suitcase. "You never do, little brother. You never do."

Carla helped Jaime button his shirt before they walked down the hall to Ari's suite. Today of all days, she had no wish to eat with Ari. She would drop Jaime off and fetch him later.

She knocked on the door waiting for the deep and commanding voice to issue his usual *enter*. The door swung open and Giles stood on the threshold.

Jaime pushed his way past Giles' legs. "Papa, what shall we have for breakfast?"

Giles caught him around the waist, swung him in the air, and tickled him. Jaime squealed. "Your papa is in Denver." He set the boy on the floor and playfully swatted his butt. "Go. Find Cook. She will feed you."

"What will I have?" Jaime asked, making a silly face.

"I don't know. Perhaps some *mushy* gruel."

Carla could tell by the exchange this was a game the two often played.

"No. No. I desire French toast with powdered sugar." The huge grin on Jaime's face reached his eyes in such a twinkle, Carla's heart squeezed.

Giles laughed. "I bet if you smile big and ask politely, Cook will make you such a dish."

The small hand clutched hers and tightened. "You will come too, Ms. Carla."

"Ms. Carla and I must talk."

The boy looked up, his big, brown eyes signaling he needed assurance she'd be there when he got back. She nodded, and he let go of her hand. When Carla's gaze rose to look at Giles, his eyes were on Jaime. The smile, as he watched the boy skip off, didn't reach his dark eyes. When he finally looked at Carla, a deep, hidden sadness was evident. He loved the boy.

As soon as the door shut, she asked, "Is the prince all right? He isn't ill, is he?"

"What happened between you and Ari last night?" The voice, harsh and accusing, pierced like a knife. So different from moments earlier when Giles teased Jaime, and so different than he'd ever been with her before.

"No-nothing. Why?"

"He was to leave this morning. He left last night. Most unusual. Prince Orula *never* changes his course of action. *Everything*…is planned ahead."

Carla said nothing. What could she say? *Your prince kissed me, like I've never been kissed before. And then wiped the most beautiful kiss ever from his lips and stomped away.*

"He is angry with you. What is it about?"

"I—I don't know."

"Oh, but you do, *Ms. Peters.*"

Uh-oh. Giles always called her Carla unless he addressed her in front of Jaime—then it was Ms. Carla. He really was mad. She'd better come clean. "Maybe it was because I questioned him."

"What about?" He didn't wait for a response. "No one questions Ari." His tone softened. "I know we wish to at times, but it is not done."

"No, you're right. I never should have asked him to tell me…"

"What? Tell me. If I don't know why Ari is angered, I can't help you."

"Help me?"

"Jaime needs you. Please." He stepped toward her. Not in anger but with his palm outstretched, asking for her cooperation.

"I asked what he hid—what made him ache so deeply." She swallowed, hard, to hold back the tears. "I know now I was wrong. I never hold my tongue. When he talked of how little Jaime laughs since…well, that is what he wouldn't tell me. The why of it all. Ari buries a sadness. What happened?"

Giles shoulders squared. "I am not the one to discuss a topic best left alone."

"But how am I supposed to help Jaime if no one will tell me about his problems? This is foolish. I should never have come here."

"Ah, and therein lies the problem. Ari believes the same."

"What?"

"He asked me to find your replacement."

94

Carla swiped at the tear trickling down her cheek as regret, then anger, bubbled up within her. "How dare he? First, he bullies me into moving in here, wants me to stay an extra week, then kisses me. Now he wants me gone."

"Kiss?" A smile flitted at the corner of Giles' mouth.

Whoops. Might have said too much. Shoot. She couldn't lie, not when Giles had already seen through her this morning.

"An accident." Dang it, she didn't want to have to plead her case. "Not an accident. A mistake. It won't happen again." She flipped her hand in the air as if swatting a pesky fly. "Is that what he's afraid of? A kiss? That meant nothing. Ari knows better. He was the one who wiped it from his lips."

"Ari?"

She placed her hands on her hips. "This is America. In America we don't kowtow to royalty. His name is Ari and that's what I call him."

"Artilio Jaime Arnaldo Otavio Eugenio Orula."

"Excuse me?"

"*That* is his name. But if he is fine with Ari, I'm sure I'm not one to argue." Giles' grin widened to meet the crinkle around his eyes.

"Oh gawd, not a surprise he's so headstrong and formidable. With a name like that—why would anyone do that to a child?"

"Someday when you meet his father, the Crown Prince, you will understand."

"I will not apologize for calling him Ari."

"Nor should you have to if that's what he accepts." Giles' eyes lit. "You do realize you are as headstrong as Ari?" His brows lifted, his lips pursed.

Carla could almost see the wheels turning.

"A good pair—the two of you. Here is the plan. You and I must work together to ensure Ari understands his mistake. And, we must make him believe it is his idea." He shook his head. "Not easy to do. He can be stubborn—"

"No shi—oot."

This time Giles laughed out loud. "You have spunk. Easy to see why Ari finds you pleasing."

"Pleasing? Isn't that a bit old-fashioned?"

"Oh yeah, but it fits. Totally fits."

Carla wasn't sure how she felt about being *pleasing* to his stubborn royal-ness. Good thing Carter or her other brothers weren't in on this conversation. Carter would have challenged Ari to a showdown for finding her *pleasing*—six-gun at dawn. She pressed her lips together to squelch her own grin. She could picture it now.

Despite her silly fantasy of two men fighting over her honor, tears threatened again. Ari hurt her by kissing her and then wanting her gone. And he didn't have the guts to tell her in person.

She turned her thoughts back to plotting with Giles. After all, the goal was to help Jaime, not assuage her hurt feelings...or for that matter, Ari's guilt. "What will you do to find my replacement?"

"The usual. Call agencies in Denver. Post help wanted in the local weekly and on the internet. Call home to Portega to see if someone on the Crown Prince's staff can be spared."

"How long will that take?"

Giles shoved his toe into the deep carpet before looking at her, as serious as she imagined Ari would be, except for the spark in his eyes. "*Weeks*...I should think."

"Until then, you need me?"

"I see your point." Giles was silent for a moment. "Yes, we will need your services for at *least* a few weeks."

"I only promised a week. And with that Ari assured me he could work around my schedule. I have other things planned for this next week."

"Cook and I can fill in whenever you need us."

"And when is Ari due home from Denver?"

"Two or three days in Denver, then three in California before returning to Mineral Springs."

"And what will he do when he finds me here?"

"I will communicate to him that I have kept you on until we find someone. I can appeal to his sensitivity around disrupting his son's schedule one more time. Especially since..."

"What?"

"Depending on how Ari's business goes in Denver, I may have to fly off to represent him in California. We've managed to overbook our business meetings. Cook cannot handle Jaime by herself and continue with her duties."

Carla steepled her hands under her chin. She looked skyward, then flashed Giles an evil grin. "I don't want to be here when Ari returns if you are off somewhere else. I believe I will have a *family emergency*." She tilted her head. "What do you think? An excuse that necessitates me going back to Peters Valley Ranch to help Madge, my stepmother, who has *suddenly taken ill*. I must cook the meals for the ranch hands."

"Oh, dear," said Giles, now beaming. "What will we do with Jaime with no one here to care for him?"

"The only solution will be for Jaime to spend time with me at Peters Valley Ranch where my brother and his son can help me keep Jaime occupied while I attend to my own business." She grinned, rubbing her hands together, "Seriously, I think this will work. It will give Jaime a playmate near his age. And Madge...she dotes on Aaron, my nephew. She'll do the same for Jaime. Win-Win. Right?"

Giles grinned. "Splendid. In the meantime, I will work hard to find another nanny. Around my other obligations, of course."

Carla grasped his hand. "Sounds like a plan. Will you be in hot water?"

"I beg your pardon?"

"Trouble. Will Ari make trouble for you if I take Jaime to the ranch?"

"Ah. Trouble I can handle. The prince and I go way back." He squeezed her hand.

"Really. How far back?"

"The cradle."

"Your parents were in the Crown Prince's employ?"

"Not quite." He paused, his eyes darting over her shoulder. "Ari and I share a mother. I lived with her in Portega after her marriage to the Crown Prince."

Well, this put a new spin on things. Could she trust Giles?

Or was there a bit of sibling rivalry?

"Maybe this is a bad plan." She dropped his hand.

"My younger brother has been stubborn since the day he was born. I can say that, I am seven years his senior. If you doubt my loyalty..." He let the sentence hang between them, then added, "I have looked after Ari always. I would let nothing harm him, including his father...or you. Do you understand?"

She didn't. Not entirely. But she nodded. This mysterious relationship with his father might explain a lot about Ari, but there was one thing she didn't understand. "Can I ask you something?"

"By all means."

"Why do you put up with his arrogance? You're his older brother."

Giles smiled. "It appears I put up with his arrogance. But nothing is further from the truth. You will see."

Again, she didn't understand Ari's convoluted relationships with his family, but she nodded anyway.

"I believe you're good for Ari and his son. I'm taking my chances on you. Don't fail me." He had turned the tables on Carla, with a directness she couldn't fault.

Giles might not be a crown prince's son, but he had the regal bearing of an aristocrat. And she believed him. "You can trust me to do the right thing by Jaime. And Ari."

After breakfast, Giles told Jaime the plan. The boy's gaze dropped to the floor as he shuffled his feet.

"You'll have fun at Ms. Carla's house."

Jaime continued to study his feet.

"We will follow Carla in her pick-up," said Giles. "You see our fields out back? Those touch the land on which Carla lives."

Carla circled her arm around Jaime's shoulders. Despite being adjacent, no way would she tell him the ranch house was twenty miles away, on the other side of town. "Madge will make you pancakes filled with chocolate chips and smothered in her homemade elderberry syrup. It's *yummy*."

Jaime's head lifted, a smile directed toward Carla. "*Sim*, I'll go with Giles to your house."

Carla helped him pack and added his stuffed stallion, a box full of books, and his very own miniature pillow meant for hugging. She tried to assure him. "I'll be in the room next to yours."

"Will I be able to see in the dark?"

"I have a beautiful night lamp that looks like a butterfly. We'll set it by your bed."

"And what if I have need of you?"

"The door will be open between our rooms. If you call, I'll hear you. Will that help?"

Jaime nodded.

"And you'll get to meet my nephew, Aaron. He's near your age."

"Yes then, I'd like to meet Aaron."

Giles helped Jaime, while Carla placed a call to the Peters Valley Ranch. Thank goodness her father was out of town at an auction in California, and Carter and Ore were moving cattle to one of the intermediate pastures. Madge was delighted with the news and ready to help with what Carla was sure would appear to Ari as a *nefarious* plan.

At the ranch, after Giles settled Jaime in and they all sat down to lunch with Madge in the large ranch kitchen, the boy relaxed.

Luckily, Madge was an incessant chatter. When she brought up the rabbits who loved to eat out of her garden, Jaime jumped into the conversation. "What do they eat, Ms. Madge?"

"Unfortunately, they love to eat my lettuce. I need to find a solution."

Jaime rested his chin on the palm of his hand, lips drawn tight, until a smile bloomed. "I know. At my house we have a wall around our garden. You should do that, Ms. Madge."

"You are indeed a smart boy," Madge said, as she leaned in to pat his hand.

As Madge cleared the table, Giles stood to leave. He ruffled the boy's head. "You are lucky. Tonight, at dinner, you'll meet real American cowboys."

"I know about cowboys. We have them too."

"Ah, but not American cowboys. This will be an adventure not many boys have."

Carla's heart rate sped up. Her brothers—how would they react to royal company at dinner? Luckily, she wouldn't face any but Jack for a few more days. A week in and she hadn't yet told them of her new position. After all, it was only supposed to be a week. And certainly not extended to include a visit to the Peters Valley Ranch.

What in the word had possessed her to agree to this farce? "Giles, we need to talk before you head out."

"Much as I would love to chat, I've no time. A plane to catch in Aspen." He tapped his watch. "We will catch up later. You have my cell number."

Before she could follow him out the door, he had climbed into his SUV and peeled down the road.

Dang it all. Now she had to face her brothers alone. At least today, Jack would be the only one around.

And maybe she could embellish the truth a bit. Tell them this *babysitting* was an extension of her ski school duties. The father of her student, desperate for help, needed her. Well that was true. But she would have to downplay her dealings with the prince.

And, she'd have to swear Madge to secrecy.

Chapter Eleven

Once Giles' SUV disappeared around the bend in the road, Carla grabbed Jaime's hand. "Come on, let's take a walk to the stables." Maybe she could introduce Jaime to Jack, so he could get used to the idea before all her brothers were at dinner together. Dinner might go better if she had one ally.

Jaime's hand tightened around hers as they approached the corral edging the great barn. Jack's little boy, Aaron, sat atop a paint pony. Her brother held the lead, walking boy and horse in an ever-widening circle. Carla's arm jerked back as Jaime stopped dead in his tracks. She looked back at him when he dropped her hand. She knelt. "Do you ride?"

Watching the corral, he shook his head. Worrying his lip, tears swam as he blinked to hold them back.

"Jaime." His head snapped around to face her. "What's wrong, honey?"

His mouth opened, but no words emerged.

"Tell me. Are you frightened of horses?"

He shook his head. "Yes," he murmured, at the same time.

"We'll stand right here and watch." She wondered why the reluctance, especially for a boy growing up on a horse farm. But then Jaime had been reluctant on the ski slopes at first.

He slipped his hand into hers again. "Can we go near the barn and sit?"

"Sure." Carla led Jaime over to the barn and, once settled on a bale of hay, pulled him onto her lap. Jack waved at them.

"That's Jack, my middle brother."

"How many brothers do you have?"

"Four."

"I have no brothers. Papa has many brothers in Portega and Uncle Giles. Where are yours?"

"Cole is in college. Carter and Ore are out with the cattle, so they'll be gone for a few days. So will my *papa*. He's at a horse auction in California."

"That is where Papa must go soon."

Great. Hopefully Mitch wasn't bidding against Ari at the auction. That would only heighten the rivalry.

"And who is that boy?"

"That's Aaron, Jack's son, on the horse. Remember, I told you about my nephew. He's only a year older than you."

"He rides horses?"

"He does. He's helping his daddy train Chess, the pony he got for his birthday."

"His own horse? My daddy has lots of horses, but I don't want my own."

"Really? Why not?"

The child's shoulders shrugged against her chest.

"You could learn to ride and then maybe you might want your own horse."

"No. I want a dog."

"We have several dogs. Would you like to meet one?"

He nodded.

She nudged him. "Let's go see Heidi. She lives in the barn. Soon she'll have puppies."

They sauntered through the wide doors into the semi-dark and waited for their eyes to adjust. Jaime's hand tightened around hers to the point of pain.

"Heidi lives in this stall." Carla gestured toward the middle of the barn.

"I thought stalls were for horses."

"Usually. But we have extra, so Heidi has her dog bed in here. She likes to help us with the horses."

Jaime didn't move.

"It's okay, all the horses are outside today."

Jaime looked up. A smile slipped across his lips to lift the corners of his mouth. Jaime hugged Carla's body, walking with his shoulder to her hip as they moved down the long aisle. "It's all right. Remember, the horses are in the paddock." He eased a few inches from her. "Here it is."

They peered in.

"Where is she?"

"Probably wandering around. She keeps an eye on everything that goes on in this barn."

"Is she a watchdog?"

Carla laughed. "I guess you could call her that. Oh, look." She pointed. A small black and white sheepdog trotted in at the other end.

Jaime giggled. "I love dogs." He ran toward her.

"Easy honey. Go slow. She's friendly, but she doesn't know you yet." Carla caught up with Jaime. Soon they both sat petting Heidi. When she finally tore Jaime away from the dog, they explored the barn, met Jack and Aaron, albeit a good distance from Chess, and planted peas in Madge's garden.

Later that afternoon, with Jamie asleep on the couch in front of Nick Jr., his favorite T.V. show, Carla wandered into the kitchen. "Can I help with dinner?"

Madge glanced up from washing pots. "Oh goodness, no. You've had your hands full all day with that darlin' boy. Sit down. I'll make tea. I have oatmeal lace cookies."

"My favorite."

"I know."

"I'll sit if you do. Then I'm lending a hand whether you want me to or not. Remember, I'm here under the guise of taking care of you through your *illness*."

"Cal, you need to tell me what this is all about. Why are you playing these games with Prince Orula?"

"Long story."

"I've got time." Madge brought the plate of cookies and the teapot to the table. "Sit. While I start bread."

Carla gave Madge the short version, excluding the kiss, and fabricating a little white lie about her meddling as the reason Ari wanted to hire someone else. Then, she focused the

103

conversation on Jaime and his issues. She told Madge what little she understood, and all she didn't, about why Jaime was so quiet and skittish.

Madge turned on her industrial mixer to mix the bread ingredients, kneading it with the paddle attachment. Carla set out tea cups and napkins. The steady and comforting *thrump, thrump, thrump* of the machine soothed her, and gave way to thoughts of Ari and the mystery of the man.

"What kind of kid doesn't like sugar?"

The paddles slowed, the *thrump* became a slow hum and then stopped. Carla was shaken from her thoughts. "I'm sorry. What?"

"I said, there's all kinds of therapy, sweetie. Depends on what's bothering that young soul. You can use art, plants, horses, even baking. I bet plunging his hands in a bowl of dough and kneading would be just what it takes to bring that little guy out of his shell. When Jaime wakes up, I'll let him mold his own tiny round loaf and sprinkle it with cinnamon and sugar. But I see you were lost in thought about that prince of yours...and his boy."

"He's not—"

"Can't fool Madge. It's written right across your face. You've got a thing for that handsome man."

"Handsome yes, but he's got an ego the size of the Rockies. He's stubborn. And he has no clue how to treat a woman."

Madge's eyes widened. "Did he treat you wrong then?"

Carla shook her head. How could she say he treated her wrong? He'd rescued her the night she broke up with Shawn, even though she didn't ever want to admit she needed rescuing. He'd been kind. And amazingly, he read her like a well-loved novel. He'd figured out things about her that even she hadn't figured out about herself. Or hadn't admitted. Like why she'd become the family rebel, stemming back to her young horseback-riding days, when she didn't want to be what her father and brothers expected her to be. He questioned every photo on her wall and made her think about why she'd become who she was. And in a flash, he'd figured out why she kept so much to herself, even from Tina, her best friend. This town and her family, so small and intimate, she had no life of her own, unless she rebelled. Or kept secrets.

And because of that, she had opened up to him. A perfect, ornery stranger. And poured her heart out about Shawn.

Yes. Ari, the outsider he claimed to be, had figured that out right away. Something her family and friends never had.

No. He hadn't treated her wrong. Well, except wiping that kiss off his mouth and wanting to fire her. Instead, he'd gotten under her skin.

"He thinks he has to be a knight in shining armor."

"What's wrong with that?"

"I can rescue myself, thank you very much."

As she sat, glancing around the kitchen on the ranch that had always been her home, a pang of longing for her mom squeezed her heart. If she were here, Carla could confide in her about the prince. And about how hurt she was when he walked away the moment her heart had decided to open. Man, she missed her mom.

She looked up to see Madge standing by the counter, wiping her hands on her apron. Worry etched her brow.

"You want to talk about it, sweetie? I'm willing to listen. Goes no further than here." Madge locked her lips with an invisible key.

Carla's chest expanded. She might not have her mom anymore, but she had Madge. No wonder her father loved this woman. How Madge put up with Mitch and all the boys and a mostly surly Carla, she had no clue. But this woman had a heart of gold. Swallowing, she nodded. "Thanks."

Madge pulled out a chair at the scarred, wooden kitchen table. "Tell me all about it."

"You must have some leads. You have had time." Ari shouldn't take his anger out on Giles. He should face Carla on his own and not make Giles do his dirty work. He hesitated to admit this, even to himself, but he didn't have the backbone to confront Carla for something that was clearly his own fault. His issues now all mixed up in emotions, not rational thought.

But two days into his trip, where he met with Federal authorities in Denver to continue discussions about how to go about reeling in and finally trapping Duggans, he was worn down. Like a fly-fishing expedition, patience and perseverance was required. Throw out the line, wait until the fish bites, reel it in slowly, let it roam for a few minutes, then reel in some more. The plan was for Ari to slowly give in to Duggans. A tantalizing small payment at a time, funded by the government. No longer stymied by the agents request of him, he had only to gather his courage. His anger was there and so was his willingness to play a part. Plus, he was perfectly capable of outsmarting the stupid, smarmy man responsible for holding the Mineral Springs' water hostage.

Now he must turn his attention to the way he'd left things at home. And still, he must head to California tomorrow afternoon. Which meant more time away from dealing with the Ms. Peters situation.

He rested his forearms on his thighs, leaning forward in the stiff-backed chair by the desk in the hotel room. With his head bent and his hands clasped tightly, he silently berated himself for being seduced by a pair of hazel eyes, copper-hued blond hair, and a body with all the right curves.

Giles' deep voice boomed over the speaker phone, pulling him from his worries. "You hired Ms. Peters because you were desperate for help. You're lucky to know such a person who can handle this position. It's not easy finding someone of caliber to replace her. And someone temporary, at that. Do you want just anyone to care for Jaime?"

"Giles. Stop. You are right. I am wrong to be so angry. It is my fault."

"Really?"

"Must you be sarcastic? This is serious business."

"Roger that, as the Americans say. But you must admit, when given an opening such as you admitting anything is your fault, I can't help but comment." Giles chuckled.

Ari's heart thudded. Without this man, his older half-brother who had been more like a father to him, he would not have survived his childhood. Maybe a bit of an exaggeration, but with seven haughty brothers who looked down on him because his mother was an American, and a father caught up in decorum of the job he'd inherited, his station as youngest made life unbearable at times. Like the child on the playing field who didn't fit in and never was called upon to participate. "Please. You must find a replacement before I return."

"I find this sudden change of heart intriguing. What aren't you telling me, mate? Has Ms. Peters done something so wrong you must dismiss her?"

Ari swallowed. Hard. He wanted nothing more than to use arrogance and his position to avoid the answer. Especially when Giles brought out his cockney accent. Except pulling rank never worked with Giles. He tried to sidestep the question. "You have not observed her with Jaime. She is wrong for the boy. *That* is all."

"That is all? You aren't fooling me. You never do anything, even last minute, without a well-thought-out plan. You studied Ms. Peters for two weeks as she schooled Jaime in his skiing."

"It is none of your business."

"Then if this is personal between you and Ms. Peters, you should be handling this. I know she is strong willed. Did she question a decision of yours? Is this your pride reacting?"

"I would not let pride stand in the way of helping my son."

"You are wrong. You have let pride overtake common sense many times in the last few years. I know. I've been with you through thick and thin."

"Yes, the only one. You are right."

"Then tell me." Giles' voice softened. No longer the know-it-all big brother, but his friend, his confidant, his lifeline.

"I have allowed this woman to know more than she should. I cannot permit it to go on."

"You're afraid? She understands you more than you want? Is that right, Ari?" Before Ari could respond, Giles continued, "You've hardened your heart for too long. Don't you understand how your actions affect Jaime? Ms. Peters is the one who can help you both."

Ari straightened. "*I* do not *need* her help."

"Excuse me?"

"I do not *want* her help. Is that clearer?" He stood and paced across the living room of the suite, much too big for one person. At the same time, the walls closed in on him, pressing at his head and heart.

"But you do *need* her." Giles' big brother tone switched from goading to conciliatory.

Ari recognized what he was up to—trying to convince him to give Carla a second chance.

"She's the one who can make a difference. She's the one who may set you free. And set poor Jaime free from a burden he doesn't yet understand."

Without so much as a *talk to you later,* Ari pressed the disconnect on the phone. Then he strode across the room to dispel his anger. As he scrubbed his hand across his face, he thought about what Giles had said.

Giles' insights hit too close to the truth. He didn't want to hear Giles observations, he didn't want to believe his half-brother was right. He wasn't angry at Giles. He was angry at himself.

It would be prudent to leave Denver and go straight back to Mineral Springs. Make sure Giles found a new nanny. Deal with the situation called Carla Peters.

His shoulders slumped. He dared not see her yet.

He would stick to his schedule and go on to California. The mare he prized was up for auction and he meant to have her. *Inês de Castro* would be ready to produce the foals Ari needed to prove his theory long before the Crown Prince's mare was ready to be inseminated. With Ines in his stables, he would make his country proud. His father and brothers would finally be forced to give him the respect he sought.

Ari swallowed his impatience with Giles and his unease about the hold Carla already had over him. He concentrated on his business strategy to get what he needed in the coming days.

He hoped more time away would give him clarity on what was the right thing to do. When he returned home, he would face both Giles and Carla. Put to rest this absurd dance of nerves assaulting his gut.

"Ms. Carla, will we eat in the kitchen again with Ms. Madge?"

Carla squeezed Jaime's shoulder, before slipping her hand around his. "Tonight we'll eat dinner in the big dining room."

"Oh. Why?"

His voice so soft, she knelt to face him. "Jaime, tonight we have more people at dinner. The last couple of nights it was only the three of us. Tonight, you'll sit right next to me. Aaron and his dad will be there, and my other brothers too."

Queasiness assaulted her stomach. She could totally understand his trepidation at facing her big family. Thank goodness her dad was in California and would be for a few more days. Maybe by then she could take Jaime back to Giles. Granted, Mitch would hear about her temporary job, but she'd be finished, money in her pocket.

Her hand tightened around Jaime's as they walked out of the bedroom and down the stairs. Her brothers would have to behave in front of a small boy. Wouldn't they? At least Carter and Ore hadn't shown up yet. Cole had breezed through earlier, heading to the stables, so she'd missed introducing him to Jaime. Hopefully, Jack would fill Cole in.

Gawd, I'm being ridiculous. Her brothers weren't cruel. But they had a tendency not to reason through an answer before they opened their gigantic mouths and inserted their dust-covered boots. The last thing she needed was for one of them to be insensitive toward Jaime.

Looking back when she had set out to introduce Jaime to her brothers one-on-one, not realizing they were all away from the ranch, Jack was the only one she'd been able to tell that she was employed by Prince Orula. He'd been cool about the whole thing. As a dad, he understood better than her other brothers that you couldn't blame a boy for his father's actions. He also understood why Carla agreed to help—the money had been the deciding factor, but helping Jaime was now a front and center priority.

Cole had spent the last few nights on campus, as he often did, and Carter and Ore were on the trail. Tonight would be a different story and she'd have no time for one-on-ones with any of them. Yeah, she was chicken. Years of listening to all her brothers' bluster had her playing the coward.

She sucked in a deep breath to calm her nerves. Time to tame the buckin' broncos.

"Come on, Jaime." She tugged on his hand and guided him downstairs.

The little boy stopped at the edge of the huge dining room, his grip crushing her fingers.

"It's all right. Remember, you get to sit next to Aaron at dinner." Before she could change her mind and grab dinner for both to eat in her bedroom, she tugged on Jaime's hand. Together they stepped over the threshold, under the carved molding of the arched entryway, to confront a dining room full of stares.

Carter, who had entered the dining room from the opposite door stopped while pulling out his chair and stared, too. More like glared. His brow rose. He surely suspected whose son's hand she held. No one who had met Ari could miss the resemblance between the prince and Jaime.

To avoid confrontation, Carla nodded. Tilting her head, she looked directly at her brother, a silent signal pleading with him not to utter anything derogatory in front of the boy.

Carter squared his shoulders. Standing at the opposite end of the expansive table, he looked every bit the proxy head of family while Mitch was out of town. But his blatant and silent message could not be missed. The conversation would continue once Jaime was out of earshot.

Madge must have picked up on the terse silence going on between their nods and raised brows. In a loud voice she announced, "We have a visitor. I suggest we all sit and show this young man what a happy family looks like." She pulled out her seat at the other end but before she sat, she scanned the table. Her glance rested on each brother, one after another, stressing her message with a look that spoke volumes.

Madge sat and the deafening scrape of chairs against the wood floor ensued as everyone followed suit.

Carla glanced at Madge and smiled. With Madge in her corner championing for Jaime, the guys would have to behave themselves.

Bowls and platters were passed family style and heads were lowered for a quick silent prayer of thanks, before silverware clanked against stoneware. Nothing like a hot and hearty meal after a long day's work to stop a cowboy's chattering. Once they'd consumed a few bites, deep voices competed against each other as each relayed the day's news about business. Family time—the few hours in the day left for talking shop.

After a week of quiet dinners at Ari's, and then with Madge, Carla needed a few minutes to acclimate to her family's boisterous ways. She glanced at Jaime. He'd barely touched his meal, as his head bobbed back and forth taking it all in. She reached over, cut and speared a piece of roast beef, and shoved the fork toward Jaime's hand. "Eat," she whispered.

Once the guys finished talking business, the teasing began. The brothers always found something to pick at and were ruthless with each other.

"Oh, don't give me that," Ore hollered, as Cole threw a jab about his most recent tumble while rounding up cattle from the winter pastures.

Jaime jolted at the loud voice right across from him. "Are they fighting?"

"No. See, they're laughing at each other. It's called teasing." She gave Jaime her biggest smile.

It was a minute before he finally giggled. "They are loud, aren't they?"

"My dad and uncles are the loudest ever," said Aaron, throwing out a brag once he realized Jaime was absorbed in the action around him.

Carla assessed the crew sitting around the table. She'd grown up with the rowdy bunch, and she wouldn't change a thing. The fact they were as merciless with her as with each other, meant they loved her. She should know that by now. But she couldn't help being prickly about their teasing and their need to control. Could that be the reason they continued to treat her like a kid, despite being able to ride, herd, and brand with the best of them?

Carla cut more roast beef for Jaime, encouraging him to eat despite being distracted by the entertainment. Leaning back in her chair, the talk surrounding her, Carla's stomach settled enough to shovel in her first bite.

A few hours later, after tucking Jaime into the trundle bed in the small room just off hers, Carla propped herself up in her bed. With her laptop open next to her and legal pad in hand, she scribbled notes. Despite years of dreaming, the nitty-gritty of planning a new school now overwhelmed her.

She glanced at the laptop, and the contractor's renovation schematic for the building they hoped to lease with option to buy down the road. She knew the building on the outside. Tomorrow, Madge would watch Jaime while she met with Betsy and Kyle to tour the building. She sketched out a timeline for renovations to make sure the contractor could stay on target for a fall opening. And…ensure they had the funding to afford the project. She reviewed their faculty and staff applications that they'd distribute to education job posting sites as soon as they signed a building contract. All in time to capture applications from the usual end of a school year contract period for those looking for a new fall job. Then tweaked curriculum ideas from years of planning as she sketched in a few new ideas. Once they hired staff, they would finalize curriculum details with staff input.

Supplies were the next step—educational toys and teaching aids needed to turn empty spaces into vibrant rooms of early childhood learning.

And funding, an ongoing process of writing grants and soliciting wealthy local donors. Tuition was determined, with enough wiggle room in the budget to allow much-needed scholarship dollars. Carla sucked in a deep breath to calm her nerves. Nerves of excitement that her dream was finally becoming a reality.

The stomp of heavy boots echoed down the hall. Not surprisingly. She'd been steeling herself for this confrontation. *Carter.*

She could tell by his walk, brisk and commanding. She wasn't ready to face her brother. He always managed to bark first before figuring out if the danger warranted the bark.

And she wasn't wrong.

"What the hell?" Carter stood in her doorway with his legs splayed, elbows out and hands inches from his hips.

She laughed. He looked like a gunslinger, ready for a showdown.

His glare, along with the stance, made him formidable. Obviously, he wasn't amused by her outburst. His hands curled into fists and settled on his hips. "Explain yourself." His voice boomeranged around the room.

She placed her forefinger across her lips like a strict school teacher keeping her student under control. "Keep your voice down." She hissed the order. "If you wake Jaime, so help me—" She stood and placed her hands on her hips, mimicking his stance. "He doesn't deserve to be caught in the middle of this."

Gesturing down the hall with a nod of his head, he lowered his deep voice to a low growl. "Then you might want to follow me."

He turned and strode out of sight.

Carla sighed. Her brothers were a ton of work—Carter at the top of the list. Pulling the door to her bedroom closed, she followed him to the end of the hall and the windowed alcove overlooking the outbuildings and mountains beyond.

"What the hell—"

"You're repeating yourself."

"This isn't funny, Cal."

"No, you're right." Keeping her tone level and low, she refused to rise to his bait. "But you will hear me out before you go off like a dang bronco with a burr under his saddle."

"You're the one jeopardizing this family's livelihood."

She wanted to slap her hand over his mouth. To make him stop his tirade and listen for a change. She knew her brother, so she leaned against the wall with arms crossed and waited for him to get the rant out as he continued, on and on, about dedication to family. She'd heard it all before. *Many* times.

Her brother was fiercely loyal.

His role as oldest brother was one he seriously assumed. After all, he'd been raised to take over for their dad, and it was a huge responsibility. Each of her brothers had been assigned a certain role in the family business, as had she. She'd rebelled. Her family, as with most ranching families, had a stilted and gender-biased perception of ranch life for their women. Despite the fact most were used to mucking stalls and riding round-up, they were also expected to manage the homestead. One of the reasons she pursued her own work passion.

She straightened her arms to rest against her legs when he stopped for a breath. "My business is my business alone."

He stared at her. "You're part of this family, Cal. Don't you forget. If you believe—"

"I live on my own and earn my money in the way I see fit. My degree is in early childhood education. Taking care of Jaime *is* my career."

"How the hell do you see that? You're starting a school. That's your career. Not friggin' babysitting for a prince who's stolen our water by damming up the creek on the prime grazing land he bought right out from under our noses."

The muscles in her back seized up. Arguing with her brother was one thing. But him not respecting, or understanding, her career choices sent the anger straight through her. "This has nothing to do with the ranch. And I am *not* babysitting." She emphasized each word. "I'm working with a child to help him get over some deep-seated fears so he can be a real kid—*that's* what I do."

"And you brought him here, why?"

"His father is out of town. The sensible thing was to bring

114

him here, where I can both help Jaime and be closer to town so I can work on the school. And—" She flashed her palm. "—help my family while I'm here."

"That's not the point. You're working for the enemy."

"I'm working for a child who *needs* me. I'll not punish Jaime because of some Hatfield and McCoy mentality. You'll have to get over this, Carter. I'm not hurting our ranch by working for Ari."

His eyes narrowed and his lips pinched thin across his face. She recognized her mistake immediately.

"Ari? You're *now* on a first name basis with a prince? What is this guy to you? Did you leave Shawn because this damn prince is paying a little bit of attention to you? He's using you. Don't you see it? You threw away your life with Shawn for a romantic notion that will get you nowhere."

He turned and left, his bootsteps echoing down the darkened hall.

"Stop being an ass, Carter. I'm not in love with Ari. Most times, I don't even like..." He was gone. What was the use? No one would listen to her when she told them she had every right to choose who she wished. Ari or no. Carla stared out the window as dusk overtook the rolling hills of their legacy.

Did all of them feel this way? Had she jeopardized her family's livelihood simply by caring about a little boy? And what the holy hello did he mean about Ari stealing their water? He hadn't given her a chance to ask. Not with his belligerent and bullying bellows and interference with her livelihood. And then stalking off.

No.

A full-blown shudder of anger surged through her. For gawd's sake, she was a grown woman. Just because she was the baby girl of the family...when would her brothers realize she could stand on her own, make her own decisions, understand what family allegiance meant, and sure as holy hello hang out with whomever she pleased?

Chapter Twelve

Carter shoved the screen door open so hard the wooden frame slammed against the side of the house. Containing his fury wasn't in the cards when all he wanted to do was shout it to the surrounding mountains. He jumped off the porch steps and strode across the grassy expanse to the barn. And through the wide-open doors oblivious to the chaos he brought with his noisy intrusion into the dimly lit stalls and to the quieted horses as they settled in for the night.

Stopping dead on a doornail ten feet into the muted light, his respect for his nightly sanctuary trumped his attitude. The peace and relative silence of the stables cloaked him in a protective and warm wrap. It quieted his beating heart. He inhaled the comforting scents of sweet hay and manure and leather.

Pulling off his Stetson, he tossed it on the peg by the door. His fingers scrubbed an anxious path through his hair to land at the base of his neck, before he cupped his hand and rotated his head to ease the ache that had worked its way into each muscle and tendon.

He never should have taken his frustration out on Carla. She didn't know the extent he worried about the future of the Peters Valley Ranch. The weight settled and pushed against shoulders and a back that was supposed to be broad enough to carry the family problems. It seemed he often carried an overload of stress and worry.

When you added Ari Orula to the mix, the man with enough wealth and influence to take down the Peters Valley Ranch if he wished... How could he tell Carla she colluded with the enemy even if she thought her only stake in the matter was helping the kid?

Carter rolled his shoulders to relieve the built-up tension. He understood deep-down Carla's motive. She'd always been spirited and motivated, even as a child. Add in her empathy for anything or anyone in need, he got her desire to help.

Yet, he continued to strive to protect her from the world and from herself. *Shit. Old habits.* A grown woman with aspirations of her own, he had no right to stand in her way. Especially her dream to work with children. But why Orula's kid?

And this—this thing with the prince. The foreboding uneasiness streaked down his spine, again stiffening every muscle he managed to relax in the last few minutes as he inhaled the familiar scent of his sanctuary—his barn.

Whatever the prince was up to would hurt Carla in the end. Carter knew this. And he saw it in her eyes. She was emotionally attached already. Not only to the kid, but to the man.

When Ari Orula brought Carla down, the possibility he'd also take down the family ranch was real.

Carter paced the length of the aisle between the rows of stalls, striding in and out of shadows cast from dim bulbs spaced along the way. In the largest stall at the end stood Redrock, his palomino. The one he'd raised since birth. Trained. The friend who always listened and offered wise counsel in the tilt of his head, in the nuzzle of his muzzle, in the flick of his tail, and the soft flicker of his ears.

"Hey, boy."

Redrock answered in his signature soft nicker, his *glad to see you.*

"You know me too well. Any chance you can help me out— give me advice?" Redrock's ears flicked. Carter leaned in and ran his palm down the palomino's forehead, more to offer comfort to himself than the horse. The comfort did ease through him, as his mind spun options on handling his dilemma with Carla.

"Advice?" The voice echoed from the entrance to the barn.

Carter turned, surprised to see his best friend since childhood standing there. "Awfully late for a visit. Something wrong?"

"Not with me. It's you I'm worried about." Quil wandered down the aisle between the stalls, in his lawman's bow-legged gait.

"And that's what brought you way out here?"

"My turn for the night shift. Making rounds. Figured you'd be out here, so I swung by. Must have been my sixth sense."

"You always did have that radar thing." Carter stepped back, one palm anchored against Redrock's stall door.

"You going to tell me?"

"Carla."

"What's she up to this time?"

Despite his mood, Carter couldn't stop a low chuckle. Quil had grown up on the ranch. They'd been playmates since the cradle, officially becoming a part of the Peters' family at age six when his dad passed away, leaving him an orphan. His mom had died in childbirth. He knew Carla as well as the rest of his brothers.

Carter turned back to Redrock. Grabbing an apple from his pocket, he pulled out his penknife and began to peel off slices and slip them to his horse.

"That bad, huh?"

"She's falling for *that* prince."

"*That* prince, huh."

"Don't bullshit me, bro. Or I'll consider you complicit by turning a cheek to his scheme to take over the valley."

"Whoa, that's quite an accusation. What's your evidence?"

"*A*. He snapped up the land we'd been saving for."

"And did he have that information when he *snapped* up the land?"

"How the hell would I know? But everyone in town did, including the real estate office."

"So, in your head, me and everyone you know is involved in a crime." Quil settled his hands on his hips above the gun belt that held his badge, handcuffs, baton, and everything else the town sheriff needed. "If anyone is complicit... I'm sure it's not Carla or me. Realtors are out for the biggest pot of money."

"You know damn well I didn't mean you...or Carla...literally." Carter reached for his hat and realized he discarded it at the other end of the barn. He didn't want to have this conversation with Quil, but he couldn't stop himself from spouting his frustrations. "*B*. He has water. We don't. If it's not trickling down to us, where is it going and why?" Okay, taking this out on Quil...and on Carla wasn't exactly fair. But he was mad and confused, and he had to take it out on someone. He couldn't discuss it with his father. And he had no special woman in his life. His best friend would understand.

"Look, man. We're checking it out. Don't go jumping to conclusions until you have all the facts."

"Then tell me what you know."

Quil skimmed his palm across the back of his neck. "You know I can't tell you anything about an ongoing investigation."

"Investigation? What the hell is this damn prince up to, anyway?"

"Whoa, back up cowboy. Try trusting your friends and family for a change. Now tell me about Carla and the prince."

Chapter Thirteen

After breakfast the next morning, Carla held Jaime, his belly wedged against the edge of the large sandstone sink as he reached for the faucet. She poured liquid soap in his outstretched hands, his long fingers working the lather into his palms and up his arms. Strong fingers, like his father's.

Where had that come from? Concentrating on the task at hand, she shoved away the memory of Ari's warm fingers resting against her lips, kneading her neck, grasping her hand.

"Good, get every inch all the way to the elbow," she instructed. "When cooking, you've got to make sure you don't spread germs."

"How long does it take to make bread?"

As Carla set Jaime on the floor, Madge answered. "Almost all day, dear heart. It's a lot of work."

The little boy's brow furrowed. "All day? I won't have time to visit Heidi. I want to see her new puppies." He turned to Carla. "How come they had to be born when I was asleep?"

Madge's spirited laugh filled the kitchen. "Dear heart, babies come whenever they want to. No mama can control that. Now, we'll start the bread, then it needs to take a nap. You'll have plenty of time to see the pups. When you come back from visiting Heidi, we'll knead the bread."

"A nap?"

Carla knelt beside him. "First we mix all the ingredients. Remember what we did when we made pancakes?"

"Measured the flour and put it in the bowl with the other things."

"Right. Then what?"

"We stirred it all up."

"After stirring, remember how Madge said we should let all the ingredients rest for a few minutes?"

Jaime nodded, his eyes widening. "Then we put it in the pan and cooked it."

"Right. But when we make bread, we must let it rest for a lot longer, like when we take a nap. Long enough to go out and see Heidi and play with the pups. When we come back, Madge will teach us how to shape the dough into a big ball."

"Okay," Jaime said as he climbed the stepstool in front of the opposite counter so he could help measure out the flour into the industrial mixing bowl.

Clearly, he was ready to move on—enough explanation. They mixed the yeast and water in the large bowl, then dumped in the rest of the ingredients, the flour last. With Madge's help, Jaime flipped the switch on the big machine. Once it was mixed, Madge dumped the ball of dough into a large mixing bowl.

"Now, we let it rest," Madge said, as she covered the bowl with a damp towel. "The towel is just like a blanket over the bread."

After washing counters and hands and little cheeks that managed to get covered in flour, Carla handed Jaime a towel. "Let's go see Heidi." She patted her pocket where she'd tucked her phone. She couldn't wait to show Giles, and soon Ari, the photos of Jaime's flour-covered cheeks and those she would take of him with the puppies.

Jaime skipped out the door ahead of her and headed toward the barn. Such a change in only a few days. Carla hadn't pushed him to get near the horses. Instead, she'd let him be to do what was comfortable. Today, she would encourage him to stand at Aaron's side as her nephew palmed sugar cubes and apple chunks. Each time Jaime watched the horse and the gentle way he had of picking up the goodies without biting Aaron, his fears eroded bit by bit. Maybe today he would dare to feed the horse.

They were half way to the barn when Carla heard Madge call her.

"Wait, Jaime. We have to go back."

"But Heidi."

"We'll see her in a minute."

Jack and Aaron strolled out of the barn, each leading a saddled paint. "Cal, we can take Jaime with us."

Carla shook her head. Her brother was a patient and excellent teacher, but Jaime wasn't ready to get that close to a horse. It was one thing to have the stall door forming a blockade when Jaime dared to reach out his palm to Chess. But this up close and personal—no.

"He can sit on the fence and watch us. Nothing else. I promise."

"I want to watch Aaron. Please, Ms. Carla."

"I, ah—"

"Carla," Madge called again. "It's important."

"Okay. But sit on the fence and do not go anywhere else. I'll be right back."

Jack held his free hand out toward Jaime and the boy ran toward him.

Carla couldn't help but smile. Jaime was loosening up a bit, first with Madge, now with Aaron and Jack.

As she neared the kitchen door, Madge thrust Carla's cell into her hand.

Giles' breathless voice radioed apologetic as he updated Carla. "Ari was called to our mother's side. I know you planned a day off tomorrow to go to your meeting, but I can't take care of Jaime. I'm at the airport. I'm sorry, Carla. An unscheduled trip. Will you be able to keep Jaime with you?"

Carla's heart thumped. If this was an emergency, wouldn't Ari want Jaime with him in Portega? She would dearly miss having Jaime around. And Ari. And why wasn't Giles leaving for Portega? "Your mother, is she all right?"

Giles laughed. "Most definitely, I assure you. Grace is almost certainly crying wolf. Only Ari knows how to handle her in one of her *crises*."

She released the breath she'd been holding. "Of course, I can keep Jaime here until either of you return."

"How is our boy doing?"

"At first withdrawn, but now he's having fun and making friends."

"So soon?"

It was Carla's turn to laugh. "You underestimate the power of Madge. She has Jaime cooking. Today we're making bread. He's made friends with Heidi, who just gave birth to puppies. And Aaron, my brother's son, is showing him the ropes."

"Ah, so this trip to your ranch has accomplished much already."

"He continues to be reticent about so much. There's plenty of work to be done. But he sleeps and eats well. That's progress."

"Well, you now have a few more days to work with Jaime and to show Ari, upon his return, this miraculous change."

Carla's heartbeat quickened. "You realize I only promised a week. Miracles take much longer than that."

"Ari never planned to let you off the hook after a week."

"How things change in a few short days."

"You are doing wonders for Jaime. Don't you want to stay?" Giles voice dropped in tone, now serious. "Jaime needs you and whether or not Ari admits it, so does he."

Carla's palm cradled her belly as she clutched the cell phone in the other. Was she doing the right thing? Did she really want to go back to living at the royal ranch? She adored Jaime and was proud of what they had accomplished together over the last month since she'd met him at ski school. But living up close and personal with the prince was a different story all together. Despite her claims to Carter of her disinterest in Ari, she'd told a big, fat lie.

She *was* interested in the guy.

She *still* thought about his kiss.

But it was more than that. From the moment he'd escorted her home that one night, she'd begun to peel away his layers to discover a vulnerability and passion that he kept hidden.

Dang it all, she wanted to know more. Dig deeper.

"When will Ari be back from Portega?"

123

"Portega? Grace resides in Manhattan. I assure you, he will make quick work of settling our mother's latest trauma. I expect not even a week. I shall return sooner. You will be all right then?"

"We'll be fine."

"You have my cell and you can call on Sénhora Adélia should you need a few hours of relief."

"I'll be fine. I have plenty of backup here. Travel safe." Carla placed the phone on the kitchen table.

"Is everything all right?" Madge looked over her shoulder, her hands plunged deep in a sink filled with sudsy water.

"Ari is now in New York City and Giles is flying to California. Looks like Jaime might be here longer. Is that all right? I can go back to the Silver Mine. We don't want to be in the way."

"Nonsense." Madge wiped her hands on her apron. "I enjoy having young ones underfoot. Even though Aaron, Jack, and Emma live close by, it's not the same as Jaime living right here at the house. Been a long time since my two were that age."

"Do you miss them? They're so far away."

A look of longing crossed Madge's face before she turned back to the sink. "My girls live their own lives, and I get up to see both often enough. I do miss them, but Cheyenne isn't too far a drive."

Living at the ranch for the last few days, Carla had witnessed the passion and caring Madge showed to her adoptive sons and now to Carla. She portrayed unmitigated strength. Carla tried to lighten the moment. "At least this family keeps you busy enough."

"You got that right." Madge scrubbed a pot. "Tell Jaime we need to punch down the bread dough in about half an hour."

"I'm sure he'll love that—being given permission to punch."

Madge glanced at Carla and lifted a brow. "Part of the therapeutic qualities in making bread. Now git. I have work and so do you."

Carla strolled across the dirt expanse between the front lawn and the barn and corrals. She spied Jaime sitting on the top rung of the high fence opposite her, a big smile spread across his face.

As Carla neared the fence Aaron jumped down from the paint, handled the lead, and walked toward Jaime. Jaime's eyes widened and his lips thinned tight across his face. With his hands anchored on the top rung to either side, he leaned back as Aaron drew near.

Carla broke out in a run. "Aaron, don't—" She didn't have time to finish the warning. Jaime fell backwards and landed on his back with a loud *thwack*. Jack ran across the enclosed corral and leapt over the fence as Carla raced around the outside, both arriving at the same time.

Kneeling, she reached out to scoop Jaime into her arms. Jack caught hold of her wrist. "Don't move him."

The boy's face was ashen and his eyes were closed. He lay motionless.

All common sense disappeared. All her first aid training recessed to the back of her brain. "Do something."

"His pulse is steady." Jack launched in with his EMT training. Leaning toward Jaime, he repeated the boy's name, while checking every part of him, feeling for broken bones and bumps. "Jaime. Jaime, can you hear me?"

The boy's lids fluttered open. He sucked in a deep, shuddering breath.

"Look at me, Jaime." Jaime's eyes focused on Jack's mouth. "Can you see how many fingers I'm holding up?"

Jaime nodded. "Three."

"Good. Good. You just had the air knocked out of you. You rest right there for a few minutes, then we'll get you up and walking around. Aaron, sit here with Jaime."

Carla kissed Jaime on the forehead. "Lie still, okay?"

She stood and turned to her brother. "I *told* you to be careful. I told you to watch him. He's afraid of horses." She strode past Jack, turned on a dime and paced back. "I should have taken him back to the house. This is all my fault."

"For blazin' sakes, Cal, calm down. It's no one's fault. He

lost his balance." Jack stepped in front of her, forcing her to stop. "And he's all right."

The hiccup of a sob bubbled up. "What if something *had* happened to him? Oh my gawd. He's in my care. I have to keep him away from all of you...and the horses."

"Do you hear yourself? That's the last thing he needs. Remember when you were his age and you fell off Fidelity? How scared you were? How Pop made you get back on her?"

"This isn't the same."

"How do you know? You haven't talked to the boy about his fears, have you?"

Carla swiped at her eyes and looked at Jack. Despite the raised tone, no anger laced his voice, only common sense and compassion. She shook her head.

"What are you afraid of, Cal? Getting too close to the boy? Or getting too close to his father?"

"What? Where did that come from?"

Jack cocked his head and grinned. "Bingo."

"You ass." If Jack could see the truth written across her face, then probably all her brothers could see it too. Pulling forth defenses against her brother's teasing, she shrugged.

He gripped her shoulder. "Do you trust the man?"

She nodded.

"Then don't let Pop or Carter interfere. See how this plays out."

"I can't. It's not right. I only promised a week, you know. And now, they all need me." She glanced down at Aaron holding Jaime's hand, their heads bent toward each other, talking. She really cared about Jaime. And by getting to know the son, she learned more about his father. That knowledge made Ari more down to earth. Not some untouchable royal.

And therein lay the problem.

She'd learned enough to understand he was a caring man, not the standoffish snob he insisted on portraying. And then there was the part of her that reacted physically. Something she couldn't explain, because he was so unlike anyone she'd ever known and anyone she'd ever been attracted to.

Something she wanted to explore.

Something she feared exploring.

Dang. Why did life and love have to be so complicated?

Double dang. Why did she keep imagining Ari in terms of love?

Jack patted her on the shoulder like she was a little kid. "You'll figure it all out. In the meantime, let's find out how to help Jaime over his fear of horses."

She nodded and wiped the tear tracks off her cheeks.

"We're in this together—we're family. As long as Jaime is with us, he's family too."

Carla followed her brother. Jack was right. And more understanding then she'd given him credit for. She hoped she could count on him to be the mellowing agent to counteract Carter and the others.

He squatted on his haunches beside Jaime, then cradled the boy's back and head to lift him to a sitting position. "You okay, buddy?"

"*Sim.*" Jaime's voice croaked. Was it fear or embarrassment?

"Happens to all of us. Did you know Cal, Carla, fell off a big horse when she was your age? Knocked the air right out of her, just like you. And look at her now. She loves to ride."

Jaime's spine locked into place. He looked directly at Jack. "I hate horses."

"Really, even little ones like Chess?"

Jaime glanced toward Aaron and past to the gentle paint. He bit his lip, as if considering the wisdom of his unbridled hatred of horses.

Carla sat down on the hard ground, her legs crisscrossed in front of her. Leaning her elbows on her thighs, she whispered, "You don't have to ride him. But maybe you could help Aaron take care of him. Chess loves to have his coat brushed. Would you like Aaron to show you how?"

When he hesitated, she added, "Jack and I will be right there with you."

Jack stood and extended his hand to Jaime. The little boy

glanced at Carla before stretching out his own hand to be pulled to his feet.

Aaron sidled up to Jaime. "I'm sorry I made you fall over."

"You didn't," said Jaime. "I-I'm not so good with horses."

Aaron's grin engulfed his freckled face. "I can teach you. Chess, he's a good boy. He loves carrots and sugar cubes."

Jaime scrunched up his nose. "I hate carrots. But I *love* sugar cubes."

"Me, too. Come on." Aaron skipped ahead of Jaime, gesturing toward the edge of the corral.

Jaime followed slowly, glancing over his shoulder.

"Right behind you, honey." Carla smiled. With Jack and Aaron, maybe they could help Jaime over his intense fear of horses. And maybe he would open up about what caused the fear to begin with.

At the most, she had less than a week to make this work.

Madge sliced two wide chunks of hot baked bread, slathered each with butter that instantly melted into pools, and placed one on each small plate. Both Aaron and Jaime's eyes widened as she reached for the shaker and sprinkled the bread with cinnamon and sugar.

"Let me see those hands," Madge said.

Both boys offered up clean palms, a stark contrast to the ring of dirt that circled their arms just below the elbows.

"Okay then, eat up."

"Where's mine?" Carla reached for Jaime's plate, teasing the boy. His grin, as he grabbed the other edge of the plate, told her everything she needed to know. The child had overcome a lot today.

"So," Madge said, hands on her hips. "Where were you when I needed help with this bread?"

Jaime glanced at Carla, who winked. He giggled, a musical sound indicating he understood Madge's stern look was all in jest. His sweet smile melted her heart into a pool, like the butter melting on his just-from-the-oven bread. Jaime let go of the plate and ran toward Madge. Flinging his arms around her, he looked up. "Can we make bread another day?"

"Of course. dear heart. I make a lot of bread. I know you were too busy with Aaron and Chess." She removed her apron and led Jaime back to the table, then sat down between the two boys. "Tell me all about your day."

Carla leaned against the kitchen counter, chewing on a warm slab of bread she'd sliced from one of the fresh loaves. She watched the interaction as the boys regaled Madge with stories of their afternoon.

"All you do is hold out your hand like this." Jaime demonstrated, holding his palm stiff in front of Madge's mouth.

Madge ducked her head toward the outstretched palm and pretended to lap up a sugar cube, before planting a kiss on the small hand.

Jaime giggled. "You do that just like Chess. When he takes the sugar, it feels like a kiss."

"Kisses are good. Even horses need love, right Aaron?" Carla smiled at the boys.

Around a huge bite of sugared bread, Aaron said, "I love Chess. And when I brush him, he knows."

"He smiles." Jaime piped up. "His lips do this." He pulled at the edges of his mouth with his forefingers to show a toothy grin. "And his teeth show."

Madge laughed. "Good thing those hands are washed."

"Baths next," Carla said.

"It's not even supper time," Aaron said.

Madge stood. "It's past five, and everyone will be in for dinner in another hour or so. They'll need to wash up, so bath time for both of you now."

The whine edged its way into Aaron's voice. "'Sides, I have to wait for my daddy."

"Not tonight. You're spending the night here," Madge reminded him.

His eyes lit up. "Can I sleep in Jaime's room?"

Carla stepped toward the table. "I don't know about—"

"Please." Jaime turned toward her.

Now how could she say no to that puppy dog look? "I guess it's all right. But," she held up her hand to stave off the joyful whooping. "We have rules. First a bath and pajamas, then supper in the kitchen. Then you can play upstairs. But you have to quiet right down when I say it's bedtime or Aaron will have to go into his own room."

The two exchanged knowing glances as they hopped down from their chairs.

"Am I in big trouble?" Carla asked Madge.

"Yup, but you'll love every minute of it." Madge smiled at Carla before marching toward the hall. "Come on boys. Tonight, you can have a bath in Grampa's big tub."

Chapter Fourteen

Carter stomped through the door, shucking his coat then his boots before proceeding down the hall toward the kitchen.

Madge looked up from the stove. "You're back early."

"Moved the herds around and fixed the fence in the north pasture. Enough for one day." He stretched his palms over the wood stove in the corner. "A bite in the air. Seems winter doesn't want to let loose yet."

"Good day for a stew then. It'll be ready in another hour."

Carter nodded.

"Something on your mind?"

Madge always sensed when he had a problem. Again, he nodded.

"Washup and grab some bread and butter—it's still warm, I imagine."

After he scrubbed away the dirt at the utility sink off the kitchen, he snagged a few pieces of bread Madge had sliced and slathered them in butter. When he leaned against the counter, Madge did the same, a few feet away.

"Well?"

"Carla and that kid—"

"Kid has a name."

He grunted. "Jaime. He's a good kid."

Madge tilted her head but said nothing. Her way of making him talk.

"You think if I offer to help, Carla will let me?"

"Why wouldn't she?"

"I haven't been welcoming up to this point."

"What is it you want, Carter?"

"I want my sister happy. And, I want her to know I support her career choices."

"Then tell her. And yes, offer to help with Jaime. Carla's an understanding and forgiving person."

Again, he nodded, before he stuffed the rest of the warm bread in his mouth.

Chapter Fifteen

With supper over, Carla herded two sleepy boys up to her room. Carter followed her up the stairs, lugging a folding cot. She'd been surprised when he volunteered to help.

She turned in the doorway of her bedroom and mouthed *Thanks*. He shrugged and scooted by her, as if he didn't want to be caught doing something nice for the *enemy*.

"Aaron, do you want to use my sleeping bag or have me put on sheets and a blanket?" Carla asked. She directed Carter toward the wall opposite Jaime's trundle bed. "Sleeping bag. Sleeping bag. Sleeping bag." Aaron pogo-jumped across her room toward the trunk at the end of her bed.

"I want a sleeping bag, too," Jaime said, tugging on Carla's hand.

"Honey, I only have one."

"I've got one he can use," Carter said.

Carla lifted a brow.

"It's okay." He raised both palms. "I'll be back in five."

Guess he figured it was time to tone it down a bit, especially with a kid. Jaime had been nothing but sweet. The father did not the son make. Carla sighed with relief that Carter was finally figuring out he couldn't take his beef with Ari out on an innocent child.

"Okay kids, jammie time. Then brush teeth." Giggles permeated the air, as the two raced to see who could win the jammie war.

"I'm finished." Jaime's voice rang out, at the same time Aaron shouted. "I win!"

"I'd say it's a tie."

By the time they brushed their teeth and Carla had wiped down dirty faces with a washcloth, they were both giggling again as Carter hauled the second sleeping bag into their room.

"Thank you, Mr. Carter." Jaime's voice was soft—tentative—as he squeezed Carla's hand.

Carter shrugged, as if embarrassed about getting caught in a gesture of friendship toward the boy. He glanced at Carla. "Need anything else?"

"Not that I know of. Thanks."

"Yeah."

With both boys zipped in, he issued a gruff uncle good night. Carla glanced at him, wondering at the softening of his attitude. "Carter?"

"Not now." As quick as a prairie dog ducking down a hole he strode from the room, leaving her to deal with the boys. And her questions.

With droopy eyes, neither boy asked for a story. "You guys sleep well. We have a full day ahead of us tomorrow."

"Night, Aunt Cal."

"Goodnight, Ms. Carla."

She turned on the butterfly night lamp. Pulling the door toward her, she left an inch or two open to give the boys a sense of security. The only light in her room shimmered softly from the lamp by her bed.

Carla settled in at her desk by the window and typed a list of questions and instructions she had for the school contractor. In the morning, she'd bring Jaime to their meeting. After the accident, she didn't dare let him out of her sight. Not that she didn't trust her family to care for him, but he was her responsibility, her job. If Ari ever found out she let her family watch Jaime, even for part of an hour while speaking to Giles, he'd throw a horse shoe, for sure.

Stretching, she kneaded the knot in her neck, the strain of the last few days creeping across her shoulders. Had bringing Jaime to the Peters Valley Ranch been the right thing to do? She and Giles conspiring against Ari. Endangering Jaime by trying to help him overcome his fear of horses…without Ari's knowledge. She had to trust Giles knew what he was doing. He had to know what caused the pain Ari tried to hide. And the same pain that affected Jaime.

Jaime was making progress, but at what expense? To Jaime? To her heart?

In the deep shadows of her childhood room, Carla's mind whirled, second guessing everything she'd done since she first confronted Ari about his son. She shook her head to get rid of what-ifs, to refocus. She had work to do.

As she finished her to-do list, her mind wandered back to the day spent with Jaime. They'd made more headway, thanks to Jack and Aaron. Tomorrow afternoon, she planned to continue familiarizing the boy with the horses in the barn. She prayed she did the right thing for Jaime. And for Ari.

She glanced out the window where the huge barn doors gaped wide and the stark overhead lights twinkled like stars against the dark interior. Carter strode, silhouetted, across the expanse between the house and the barn. His job was never done. Carla's gut clenched. She should be helping more while she was here.

Coming home made her realize how much she missed ranch life. The quiet of the barn after all the work was done, the only sounds from animals shuffling in their stalls and an occasional nicker or sigh as the horses settled in for the night. The gentle low of cattle coming from the nearby winter pasture. Maybe the quiet, soft sounds of the barn helped settle Carter each night before he retired.

She rose, the restlessness about whether she was doing the right thing eating at her. She'd check the boys, then head to the barn. She and Carter needed to clear the air.

As she neared the partially opened door to the boys' room, she heard whispers.

Aaron's hushed voice was clear. "Do you miss your mommy?"

Carla barely heard Jaime's faint yes.

"I miss my mommy tonight," Aaron said. "But Aunt Cal

will come in and hug me if I get scared." When Jaime said nothing, Aaron continued. "Aunt Cal would hug you too, 'cause my daddy says you're like family."

"Like your pretend brother?"

"We are like brothers. We like the same things—except horses."

Carla heard the rustle of the sleeping bags, as one of the boys moved. She pictured them facing each other in the near dark.

"Why don't you like horses?"

"Because...I don't." Jaime's voice hardened. Carla recognized his defensive tone.

"You can tell me. I promise, cross my heart and hope to die, I won't tell. We're friends...and brothers."

Silence hovered. Carla held her breath. Would she finally find out why horses frightened Jaime?

"Why?" Aaron's voice dropped to a low, coaxing tone.

"Because of my mother."

"Your mommy doesn't like horses?"

Carla heard the zipper on one of the bags, then the patter of bare feet. Jaime's voice was closer. "Can I sleep in your bed?"

Again, the rasp of a zipper cut through the silence. Carla caught a glimpse of Jaime's shadow as he climbed onto Aaron's cot.

"Now you gonna to tell me why your mommy doesn't like horses?" Aaron persisted in a raspy whisper.

"I hate horses. My mother loved horses, but the horse killed her."

What? Carla sucked in the urge to open the door and take Jaime into her arms.

A soft tap on the door and the squeak of hinges snapped Carla's attention from the boys' conversation. Carter stood on the threshold. He opened his mouth to speak, but Carla raised her palm, her finger slipping across her lips. Then she turned back to press her ear against the crack in the doorway. The almost silent footsteps, as Carter crossed the room, mingled with the soft murmuring as Aaron comforted Jaime.

"My daddy says horses don't hurt people on purpose. That's why I have to be careful. So there aren't accidents."

"There was lots of yelling and then the horse hurt my mother and she died."

"I bet the yelling scared the horse." Aaron said, with the authority of a seven-year old raised around horses.

When neither said another word, Carla backed away from the door and bumped into Carter. She swiped the unshed tears from her eyes. The last thing she needed was for Carter to notice her strong sentiments toward Jaime.

She turned and motioned him toward the wing-backed chair next to her desk by the window.

"You're letting that kid get to you, Cal. Be careful."

She shrugged, then sat in her desk chair. She swiveled it around to meet his big-brother look as he towered over her, as if she were ten. He did love her. Being bossy was his way of showing it.

"It's what I do. What I'm trained for. You can't help a kid unless you understand what he's going through."

"But you feel too much. You always have."

"For gawd's sake, will you stop hovering and sit."

The corner of Carter's mouth tipped. The closest he came to a smile these days. He plunked himself down. The chair that always appeared large, shrank in comparison to the cowboy.

"This why you came up here? To give me holy hello about my career...again?"

"Nope. I was pondering the kid and his fear. Suppose he'd get up on Chess if Aaron rode with him?"

"I don't know. I'm not sure it's a good idea to get him on a horse just yet." She wasn't about to tell him what she'd overheard. The death of Ari's wife was too personal to share with Carter, especially since he loathed the man. Before she told anyone, she should first confront Ari. Find out the truth from him. But how? How could she ask him how his wife died without stirring up a fury in the man?

She focused on the questions she could ask. "Why are your suddenly so fired up to help Jaime?"

"You're the one all bent out of shape that I'm taking my dislike of the prince out on his kid. Now he's hanging out with

Aaron, like they're best friends. If he's going to come around, least we can do is make sure the boys have common interests."

"Yeah, the least we can do." She stifled a smile, least Carter change his tune. "Go on."

"What if one of us held onto Jaime, rode with him?"

Carla laughed. "Poor Chess. You'd crush the little guy if you climbed on his back."

"Not funny." Carter chuckled just the same. "What about Snowflake? She's gentle and not too big. Maybe he would climb up there if it was you or Jack holding him."

"Jaime doesn't know Snowflake. We've barely got him to trust Chess."

"We could get Aaron on Snowflake tomorrow. Show Jaime how gentle she is. Have Jaime do the same you've done with Chess—give her some sugar cubes, learn to curry her. It might take a few days, but you can see his interest. Like he wants to not be afraid."

"Again, why do you care, Carter?"

"I hate to see any kid shy away from horses. Why the hell hasn't his father done something about this long before—"

"You have no clue what's going on with Jaime and Ari."

"And you do?"

She dropped her gaze to her lap. "Not yet. But I'm working on it."

"So, I'll ask you the same thing. Why do you care? What's this guy to you?"

This time, his question wasn't in anger. She was surprised by the gentleness in his voice. She wanted to rail at Carter. Tell him to mind his own business. But raising her voice wouldn't put him off. She sucked in a deep breath and decided to face this head on. "I know you believe Orula has done this family wrong. Why Carter? You insinuated the other night that Ari is stealing water. How can that be?"

"He's damned up the creek somehow."

"You have proof?"

Carter stood and circled back behind the big chair. "Why don't you take a ride out to the pastures? They're already dry as a bone. Yet he has water in his pond. What the hell do you think we're going to do come summer without water. All the snowmelt, it's going somewhere and it sure as hell isn't to our creeks. The spring has barely a trickle running toward the stream."

"What are you getting at?"

"Rumors around town, Ari made a deal with Duggans. That night we saw him at the Grill."

"Rumors? Then why did Duggans stomp out of there, mad as hell? You know how rumors go. They're just that—made up by some busy-body."

"Shawn? He's not a busy-body. Being down-stream from us, he's affected to. He's talked to others. The theory is—"

"Theory? You believe Ari's stolen our water? And that's all you have to go on...theory?"

"I've ridden up to the north pasture. I can see that pond of his—it's now a lake, Cal. Where the hell do you think he got that water?"

Carla stood to face her brother. "But why? Why would Ari do that to us?"

"You can be so trusting. He wants our land. Wants it cheap. Why else?"

"We run cattle, not horses. Why would he want to steal our land? He's got plenty of his own to take care of his horses. Have you even talked to him?"

Carter walked toward the door, as if he'd leave without answering, then paced back again. "Once was enough. He offered a lot of money for our ranch when he first moved in. We refused. Now he's trying to drive us out. And you're working for the bastard—" His voice rose. "— siding with him against your own family."

"Carter. The boys. Keep your voice down."

"Tell me why—"

Carla placed her hand on his forearm to stop the momentum of his tirade. "What I'm doing isn't about Ari. It's about his son. A boy who is so afraid of horses, he's almost afraid of his own shadow."

"And you're going to ride to his rescue. Cal, Jaime isn't your fight. Not when helping him hurts your own family."

"Carter, listen to what you're saying. You're equating helping a six-year old kid get over a life-numbing fear to helping his father steal our land. One has nothing to do with the other." She sighed and stepped back. "I'll do my job with the boy and then leave. It's temporary. His father doesn't factor into this at all, except he's paying me a bundle—all of it going into my dream school. Can't you understand what that means to me?"

"Your own family can help you. You don't need a prince's money."

"How? You just told me the ranch is hurting. I'm not taking money from my family. I'll earn it the way I see fit."

"And...meanwhile you're falling for the kid. And the goddamn prince."

She shook her head. And shook away the image of Ari kissing her. He was a fantasy. And he was coming between her and her family. Time she brightened up to the fact that falling for a rich prince would do her no good. And the prince reciprocating any imaginary feelings she thought she had for him wasn't going to happen. The aborted kiss told her all she needed to know. A shudder ripped through her at the memory of Ari wiping that kiss from his lips.

She looked at her brother. "Carter, stop worrying. You know family comes first for me. I'd never do anything to hurt our family or the ranch."

He nodded. "I know." He stuffed his hands in his pockets, like that might stop any more hateful words. "I'm sorry I get bent out of shape. But that guy has rubbed me the wrong way more times than you know." He paused. "You know I have to look after my only sister."

She smiled up at her oldest brother, the one who was always so serious. "You always have. I might kick and scream, but I wouldn't have it any other way. But Carter, you need to learn to trust that I can handle myself. My goal is making money and helping a child. Nothing more."

"I know. I know. I'll help the kid too. Do what you can to get him off this ranch and back home sooner than later, though."

After he left Carla sat on the edge of her bed, booted her slippers off, and sank back against the pile of pillows, another at her elbow to balance her iPad, which she didn't open.

She thought back on the last few days. Jaime had been nothing but sweet.

She couldn't fault Carter for his prejudices. They stemmed from his passion about their land and livelihood. But he was so narrow-minded about Ari. And Ari was narrow-minded about the people of Mineral Springs. They each had a lot to lose if they trusted the wrong people. For the life of her, Carla couldn't conjure up the obsessive mistrust that Carter managed to have about their neighbor.

She'd watched Ari when he met with Duggans at the Grill. He looked as disgusted with Ken as everyone else in town felt. Not once did he smile or shake a hand or show anything but disdain. Even when Carter was rude toward Ari, he neither flinched nor retaliated.

If Ari was such a badass, wouldn't he have reacted in some way to the bad behavior of both men? Instead, he'd retained his infamous princely cool. And when she observed him in his home with his son and Giles and the people who worked for him, they all loved and respected him. He had even slipped from his royal demeanor to show his humanity.

Sure, he was standoffish and pompous, but there was nothing about Ari that inferred he couldn't be trusted. That he wouldn't fight for his family and friends and land. Just like Carter.

Maybe that was the problem. They were too much alike. Both had been groomed for their family roles. Carter as the next patriarch of the Peters. Ari wasn't first or even second in line to run his country, but it was blatantly obvious that he did everything with a passion toward a goal that related to his role in his family.

Just one more thing compelling her to dig deeper into what made Ari tick.

She put her laptop on the table beside her, threw the pillow aside and got off the bed. Pacing, she periodically glanced at the iPad, shook her head, and continued back and forth across the room.

No, she couldn't Google Ari. She wouldn't Google Ari. She promised Carter to put family first, stick to her goal of helping Jaime, and nothing else. *Only temporary, remember?*

One more glance at the iPad and she wasn't so sure she could keep her promise to Carter. She wanted to discover everything she could about the man. But in person, not through the internet. And, she desperately wanted to help Jaime.

Carter wanted her to walk away—from Jaime and his father. Carla wasn't so sure she could.

Chapter Sixteen

Ari stared out the floor to ceiling window of the nineteenth-floor penthouse on 5th Avenue, over the tree tops of Central Park in full spring dress, to the vista of skyscrapers on the other side of the city. His stomach flip-flopped, a throwback to his childhood of straddling life between Manhattan and Portega, as he listened to his mother's high-pitched and incessant complaints.

Pushing his fingers through his hair, he tried to tamp down his agitation. He should have been in California two days ago to bid on a prize mare. Or in Colorado with his son and his horses and the work he loved. All the things he loved more than life itself. Now, three days into the continuing argument with his mother, he distracted himself with the skyline view and battled against reliving every childhood hurt meted out by his mother's insane lack of empathy and his father's rigid upbringing.

"Your father, he's never treated you like an equal to his other sons."

Her ridiculous tirade permeated his thoughts. He'd heard this over and over since he was able to understand the meaning of her words—drawing a line between him and his father. So much that he came to believe her declarations. And if he were honest, to this day believed them.

Time to rethink those perceptions. His father had sent him a prized mare. As Giles pointed out, that in itself was a show of faith and confidence in Ari's skills. And now he'd begged Ari to intervene between his difficult ex-wife and the NYC financial advisor he'd hired to keep mother-dear on track with her budgeting and curtail her out-of-control expenses. It wasn't the first time his father had begged Ari to step into the fray. But it was the first time his father had thanked him. And let him know Ari was the only one who could handle dear Grace, and help Valerio choose reductions in *dear Mãe's* budget that she would unlikely notice.

Lulled out of his thoughts as the shrillness of his mother's voice escalated, he homed in on her words.

"As if I was not of the same caliber as his first two wives. Maybe *I'm the one* who should have died."

Obviously, she wanted him to sympathize.

He had no more patience for her rubbish. He wanted to curse. In its place, he muttered under his breath, *I should have sent Giles.* Let him deal with her *all about me* attitude. He turned from the window to see his mom posed on her gaudy, gold brocade chaise. "What in the world does that have to do with anything, Mãe?"

He hoped to catch her off guard, calling her Mãe instead of Mother, and curtail the tirade.

Her chin lifted. "He would have revered me like he does his dead wives."

"And you would have been dead. Do you not see the folly of your reasoning, Mother?"

"Oh darling, he would have treated *my* son with the respect he deserves."

"*He* deserves? I am standing right here. Did you forget my name?"

She laughed and waved his comment away with the swish of a wrist. "And I appreciate you being here."

She said the words but had no idea of the meaning. She had never known the meaning of appreciation or any form of gratitude. It had always been about her. Even when she acted the demur wife of the crown prince, knitting and entertaining, she'd displayed her *all about me* persona, albeit toned down. No more, today she was in full form.

Again, Ari returned his gaze to the expansive view and wished he were anywhere but here.

"You must help me."

He turned. "Mother. Stop."

"How could your father do this to me? Cut my allowance when I have obligations." Her bejeweled and painted fingers waved and fluttered in time to her words.

He couldn't feel sorry for her dilemma of suddenly being forced into living on the paltry allowance of a little less than a million a year, in a Manhattan penthouse already paid for. "Father has been more than generous. Valerio says you can be perfectly comfortable. You only need to curb some of your expenses."

There was a time when his mother had been content to be his father's hostess in Portega. When she would knit and fuss about Ari's schooling and wait for his father's return from a business trip, a glass of whisky prepared for the moment he walked in the door. Things he was sure normal wives did. Now, she flaunted her position as ex-wife of a crown prince. Flaunted her wealth. Flaunted her ability to hold court in her own right.

"Valerio. What does he know?"

He turned from the view of the vibrant city below him, its people scurrying by and yellow taxies weaving in and out of heavy traffic. Real life compared to his mother's cocooned view on the world.

She rose from her chaise lounge, slow and graceful and fluid like the stretching yawn of a bored cat. Slipping on her heeled gold slippers that matched the gold and black swirl of her silk robe, she strolled across the expansive living room toward him.

He wanted to laugh, wishing like hell Giles was here to see the performance.

With her chin lifted, her voice cunning and smoky, she said, "I have no more use for Valerio. Dismiss him. Then you talk some sense into your father."

His mother was nothing, if not a woman always looking for the next prize to further her mission—living a lifestyle of the richest of the most famous. And she thought nothing of using her son.

"Valerio is in father's employ. You dismiss him and you will have nothing from father. You do realize that, do you not?"

"It is my money."

"Only because father bestows it upon you." Ari was beginning to understand his father's aloofness. Maybe living with this woman had caused his father to raise a shield of self-protection. As a boy, he learned to emulate the aloof behavior. Like father, like son. Yes indeed, he had learned from the master how to relate to people, keep them at a distance. He had tried like the devil was on his heels to never show that side to his son or his Colorado *family*.

"I will spend it however I wish."

"What?" Ari pulled his thoughts back to earth and this ungodly conversation with his mother.

"My money. I will spend it however I wish."

"And have nothing to show for it—the reason father hired Valerio as your accountant."

"Oh, posh. You will talk to him."

"Do you really believe I have pull with Father? Learn to live within your means, Mother. You might be happier, you know."

"Happier?"

He'd spent a lifetime hoping his mother would find internal happiness, not be dependent on indulgence and the misguided worship of those who surrounded her for her contentment. Did she not realize she had friends only because she spent heaps of money on them? The money his father—and Giles father, and her first husband's estate, a mere but wealthy business man—gave her.

He wasn't going to argue with her or explain.

But standing there, listening to her tirade, only reminded him he was much like her. Always striving to accomplish something so his father and brothers would notice him.

Over the last month, he had spent much less time on those pursuits. Now he wanted to prove to himself, and to Carla, that work wasn't nearly as important as being a good father to a son who needed him. It was time to end his mother's theatrics so he could go home where he belonged.

"Mother, listen to me. You have no choice but to live within your means." He tried not to stumble over the absurdity of that concept, as he thought about the abject poverty of many who lived in the squalor of this city or the rural lands near his Colorado ranch. Those who scratched out livings to meet the most basic of needs. His mother's idea of basic needs...well, he wouldn't go there.

Her neck stretched, as if a bird trying to defend its nest against a predator.

He lifted his palm to stop the bird-like shrill of the next rant sure to follow. "Valerio and I will meet today to come up with a monthly budget. You will never notice the difference. Believe me."

After spending four long days with his mother in Manhattan, and with his executive jet at the mercy of Giles in California, Ari climbed aboard a commercial flight headed to Denver. Once he tucked his bag overhead and sank into the front aisle seat in first class, his shoulders dropped.

Home.

He missed his son. He missed the ranch and the life he'd built. He missed Giles. He refused to admit the envy that churned in his gut when Giles had called to say he'd outbid everyone for the new mare. Or the resentment that settled deep.

A dream of a lifetime and Ari had missed it because of his mother's frivolous temper tantrum. At least he could be guaranteed he would not hear from her for many months to follow. She was nothing, if not predictable, as she moved on to absorb herself in wooing her *friends* until the next perceived crisis arose.

As the plane lifted to the clouds, Ari's heart and spirit lifted.

He awoke, hours later, to the bump and thrust as the plane landed and slowed in front of the cloud-like encased terminal standing majestically against the plateaued vista of the Denver skyline. The craggy, snow-capped mountains of his home rose in the distance, mimicking the roofline of the airport terminal.

Home.

He disembarked and looked around for directions. So close to home. With renewed energy, he quickened his stride as he headed from one end of the concourse to the other and to the flight that would take him on the last leg of his journey to the Aspen-Pitkin County Airport and his ranch nearby.

Carla straightened her spine. Her lungs expanded as she gulped in air to calm the flutter tap-dancing in her belly. She must be strong so Jaime would not sense her worry.

Carter sat astride Cupcake, a sweet chestnut, his arms dangling at his sides, his fingers outstretched in a nervous wiggle. Aaron sat on the saddle in front of him, holding the reins.

Carla laughed, as she held onto Jaime's hand.

"What?"

The edge to Carter's voice came through loud and clear. He wasn't used to giving up control to another.

Carla refrained from calling Carter on his attitude. She winked. "This will work. What fun. Right, Aaron?"

She glanced at Jack. The opposite of his older brother, relaxed, not seeming to carry the weight of the world on his shoulders. He sauntered toward Carla.

"Ready, sweetie?"

Jaime squeezed Carla's hand and she squeezed back. "You'll do fine. And it you don't want to ride anymore, Jack will bring you back."

"That's a promise." Jack reached for Jaime's hand and led the boy toward Snowflake, as if he didn't have a care in the world. Shorty, their grizzled cowhand who'd worked on the ranch as long as Carla could remember, held Snowflake's reins. He handed them up to Jack once he mounted. Then Shorty hoisted Jaime into Jack's arms.

The kid pivoted in mid-air to fling his arms around Jack's neck, Jack now face to face with Jaime.

Jaime's hands slid down to rest against Jack's chest. Carla

wished she could have heard what her brother whispered. Then Jack hollered *one, two, three.* He lifted Jaime in the air, turned him, and settled him on the saddle in one swift movement. With his arms around Jaime's waist, Jack leaned toward his ear. Carla imagined a horse whisperer calming the boy's fears.

Jaime glanced her way. She waved and beamed the biggest smile she could conjure, rewarded by Jaime's wide grin. *So far, so good.* No jinxing this. She knocked her fisted hand against the wooden slats of the fencing.

Aaron and Carter nudged Cupcake toward the edge of the corral and out the gate. Jack eased Snowflake into their wake. The horses swayed and lumbered along the fenced-in lane running straight down the middle between the paddocks on either side. Between the gentle, soothing gait of the big horse and Jack's words, Jaime's shoulders settled.

Her heartbeat tripped with a mixture of pride and nerves. She envied Jack taking Jaime for his first ride, but trusted he was the better fit in case Jaime panicked. He and Aaron had worked with Jaime the last several days easing him into his comfort zone, first with the pony then with the small, gentle mare.

Carla stepped on the first rung of the fence, leaning against the top to watch the parade of men and boys. Jack, Jaime, and Snowflake followed Cupcake, hugging the rail as they walked down the lane. The plan was to end their journey in the far paddock. If Jaime did all right, they would walk the rim and head back.

When they reached the gate, Carla sighed in relief. Obviously, Jaime was all right or they would have turned around by now.

Her cell buzzed in her pocket. She jumped from the fence, answering as she strode away from the barn to the sweet spot in the yard where she'd get the best coverage.

"Carla, I just landed in Aspen," Giles said.

"Do you want me to keep Jaime until Ari is back?"

"No need, Ari just texted. He's—" The line crackled before silence descended. *Ari what?*

She raced toward the house and the landline so she could call Giles back. Halfway there, the rumbling sound of a truck, weaving its way up the pass dividing the ranch from the highway, grew louder. As she topped the steps, a familiar black SUV rolled around the last corner and slid to a stop in front of her.

Well, well. The answer to her *Ari what?* question.

She glanced toward the paddocks. Would Ari be mad Jaime was here at the ranch? Before she could fathom the answer to her own question, he climbed down from the truck. All tall and lean and dressed in a crisp white shirt, black jeans, and those hand-tooled boots that set him apart from every other cowboy in town.

It was so cliché, but Carla felt the flutter and falter of her heart as he strode around the front end of the truck. She'd missed him.

Then it all came back. Their final minutes together, the kiss and the obliteration of the kiss. It was all written in his ebony stare, intent and angry.

Before she could say hello, he started in. "I arrive home to find my son gone. *Without* my permission." His clipped tone had her stepping back toward the door.

"Didn't Giles tell you?"

Ari moved up the stairs, each step matching her retreat.

When she backed into the screen door, Carla came out fighting. "Giles asked me to keep Jaime."

"Not to bring him to your home."

"Yes, to bring him here. It was all arranged so Giles could do *your errands*." She moved toward him. She was being condescending, but who better deserved that treatment than Prince High and Mighty. When his face reddened, she thought better of her words. But they were out. She couldn't take them back.

"Giles is my partner. *Not* my errand boy. You had no right to—"

"Papa, look at me."

Ari whirled around at the sound of his son's voice. His jaw

dropped. Like an attacking mountain lion, he turned to Carla and growled. "You have allowed my son to ride a horse? Without. My. Permission?" He didn't wait for an answer but spun on his heel, jumped off the porch, and strode toward the gate to the lane.

He had never once said what his son could or could not do. And never once had he mentioned a ban against horses. Carla started down the steps, then thought better of running after Ari. He would settle down once he realized how irrational he was being.

The parade of Cupcake and Snowflake lumbered toward the front gate. Carla watched as Jack helped Jaime down. She was surprised when Ari came to an abrupt stop fifteen feet away. What was going on? He had his own horses. Maybe he didn't trust someone else's. Or, he had no desire to get near her brothers. She studied his face, trying to read him.

Of course. Ari had told her he no longer rode for pleasure. Curious.

No wonder the boy had not been able to get over his mother's death. His father may have perpetuated the fear. His own fear or reluctance.

The gate to the paddock lane opened and Jaime ran toward Ari. "Papa. Papa, did you see? I rode a horse." He was panting by the time he ran into Ari's arms, a big smile on his face. Ari scooped him up in a hug, and Jaime flung his arms around Ari's neck. "I missed you, Papa."

"I missed you, too. Are you ready to come home?"

The boy shook his head. "Madge has cookies. I helped make them."

"I am sure she will pack one up for you. Come, we will get your suitcase."

"But Papa," Jaime said, as he wiggled out of Ari's grasp. "We have milk, too. Please, we must wait until we have our cookies."

Jaime skipped across the packed dirt and up the walkway by the lawn, followed by Aaron. When he climbed the stairs, he flung his arms around Carla's legs and looked up. "Did you see me?"

She tousled his ebony hair, just like his father's. Glancing up, she caught Ari's stare, his eyes leveled at the hand on his son's head. With her gaze on Ari, the right side of his jaw twitching, Carla answered the boy. "Yes, I saw you. I'm so proud of you, Jaime. You were very brave, and you rode so well."

"I did, didn't I?" He backed away and turned toward his father for further affirmation. "Didn't I, Papa?"

Carla prayed Ari would let go of his anger long enough to validate his son's accomplishment.

"Yes, Jaime. I am proud of you, too. But we must go now. I have work to do. Gather your things."

"But the cookies—"

"We always have cookies," Aaron said as he scooted through the door, letting it slam behind him.

A few seconds later, the screen door banged again behind Carla.

"Prince Orula, I wondered who was out here." Madge reached back to remove her apron, bowing her head slightly. "Welcome to Peters Valley Ranch."

"Ms. Madge, do we get cookies? My father needs to go home to work."

Madge glanced from Jaime to Ari. "I'm sure your father can take a few minutes while you have cookies and milk. After all, as we say, all work makes a man dull."

Carla tamped down a grin as she watched Madge morph into her *five-foot three ranch wife and grandmother* mode, the one that made even Carter and her dad toe the line.

Madge leveled a look straight at Ari, her brows raised, daring him to deny his son cookies. "Come." Her gesture pulled Jaime toward the door.

Carla waited for Ari to explode at Madge's command. But he stood rooted to the spot. Seemed he'd met his match.

As Madge opened the screen door and herded Jaime in, she looked over her shoulder and smiled her *hostess with the mostest* grin. "Hot coffee, Prince Orula?"

He merely nodded, as he climbed the steps and followed her inside.

"Boys, hands. Don't forget to scrub all the way up to your elbows." As the boys raced to the bathroom down the hall, Madge headed toward the kitchen. "Cal, plate those cookies and take them and the coffee into the living room. You and the prince have some things to discuss."

Carla stopped dead in her tracks, but not fast enough. She plowed straight into Ari's back as he stopped, too. When he turned, she swore a look of amusement flittered across his now tight-again features.

"Now I see where you get your spirit and...bossiness."

She seriously wanted to knuckle-punch him in the arm, like she would have if he was one of her brothers.

Madge reappeared in the doorway, her hands on her ample hips and a twinkle in her eye. "As her step-mom, I can't take any credit for her bossiness. But we love her just the same."

Ari's deep laugh ricocheted off the walls. He didn't appear a bit embarrassed at being overheard.

Madge had spun her magic. Carla shot her a huge smile of appreciation. Madge winked and went back into the kitchen to ready cookies and milk for the hungry horse-back riders.

With his anger on the back burner, now was the time to plead her case. "Are you willing to listen to my side?"

His smile disappeared, but he nodded.

"Good." She pointed toward the living room. "I'll be right back with coffee and cookies. If you need to freshen up, follow the boys' laughter. And you might as well give them a push to hurry up with the hand-washing."

Chapter Seventeen

Moments after Ari turned his back and strode down the hall to check on the boys, Carla drew in a deep breath through her nose and expelled it slowly through her mouth.

By the time she entered the kitchen, she had regained her composure. Madge had a tray ready with coffee cups, napkins, cream and sugar, and a plate. Carla removed the cream and sugar. When Madge raised a brow, Carla said, "Ari takes his coffee black."

"Aha," Madge said.

"What are you up to?"

"Me. Just trying to get you two kids on the straight and narrow. You're so intent on bickering rather than listening to each other, it's time someone sat you down and made you talk to each other like adults."

"We talk." Carla placed six cookies on the plate.

With a slight nod of her head that made her salt and pepper bangs bob, Madge arrowed *the look* toward Carla. The kind a mother hen might use to shoo her chicks in the right direction. The look that made every kid, even after you'd grown to adulthood, sit up and take notice. The mother-look of all looks—*listen-and-do-as-I-say* look. "I know a stubborn man when I see one. After all, I'm married to Mitch." She smiled, as if that would ease the imminent lecture. "You both want to be right. Go on in the other room and really listen to your man. Maybe you'll realize he has reasons for his reaction."

My man? Carla sucked in the response poised on her lips. Madge wouldn't appreciate the interruption.

"And, once you listen to him, you may want to insist he give you the same courtesy. It's called *communication*. All couples need to communicate."

"We are not a—" Carla swallowed the word as the boys burst through the doorway and climbed on to the kitchen chairs. She helped scoot in Jaime's chair, then Aaron's. She looked up to see Ari standing in the doorway, the narrowing of his eyes telling her he'd heard part of the conversation.

Great. She pressed fingers to her belly to quiet both the race of her heart that skipped a beat or two and the jagged edge to her breathing. Madge could handle communication between couples. Carla had heard her stand up to Mitch and watched her father actually listen with respect. If only she had mastered that confidence. With Ari, the communication game always turned into a sparring match.

Madge lifted the plate of cookies and handed them to Ari, smiling that Cheshire grin when she thought she'd won a minor skirmish. "Go on. You two need some privacy. I'll take care of the boys." She shooed Ari out of the kitchen.

"Madge?"

"What sweetie?"

"Thanks."

"Don't thank me yet." She poured coffee, then handed the tray to Carla. "You let me know how the listening goes and then we'll talk. Now git."

Carla paused outside the double doors to their great room. This is it. Remaining calm and collected meant she might get through that thick head of Ari's. And listening—well maybe if she kept her mouth shut for a change, Ari would open up.

She set the tray on the coffee table. Once Ari settled on the overstuffed couch, she perched on the edge of the matching chair next to him. Relaxing meant letting down her guard. She handed Ari a mug full of black, steaming coffee, then passed the cookie plate.

He hesitated.

"You have to try one. Chocolate chips and dried tart cherries. Jaime helped Madge."

"My son has learned to cook?"

His black eyes bored a hole through her. She couldn't tell if he was mad, his mood always difficult to read. His standard pattern of responses rarely showed emotion. Madge said to let him talk and she should listen, so she nodded, studying his face.

But he only bit into the cookie and remained his usual standoffish self.

She asked, "Does it bother you that he helped Madge with the cookies?"

"Of course not. Why would I be bothered?"

"I don't know. You appear to be bothered. That's why I asked."

Ari shrugged. "He helps Giles make sandwiches. And Cook." Then he sank back against the deep cushions and stretched his arm across the back of the couch, as if recognizing he'd been too stiff. "There is no harm done. It is a good skill to know." He finished off the cookie. "These are very good. Madge will give this recipe to Giles?"

Was he laughing at her? His smile showed no condescension. Could it be a lesson learned from the overheard kitchen conversation with Madge, that he should also learn to listen?

"I will suggest she email the recipe to Giles."

He winked. *Winked*! Never did she imagine her staid prince winking about anything.

Madge emphasized communication between *couples*.

The thought sent a cozy flutter straight to her belly. She'd promised Carter she wouldn't act on her feelings for this man. But it was hard not to. Not after she watched him hug his son and tell him how much he missed him. How proud he was. Not when he teased her about sharing cookie recipes. And not when he let her take the lead in the conversation, rather than bite her head off about the horseback riding, as she had anticipated.

She hated breaking the light moment by asking, but she had to. "Why are you upset with me for allowing Jaime to ride a horse? If I'd known how you felt, I never would have—" she waved her hand toward the barn and corral.

"He is frightened of horses." The rapid blink of his eyes told a different story.

She said nothing.

"When one is frightened, it is harder to concentrate and easier to become injured."

Was the death of his wife why Ari was so fearful of allowing Jaime near a horse? "He's not frightened anymore. You saw him. He did fine."

Ari leaned forward. His eyes squeezed shut for a moment. "He should not have been on that horse."

Carla mimicked him, leaning forward against the arm of the chair, trying to go for casual. But her gut twisted at his unspoken accusation. "I didn't just plunk him on a horse. We spent many days helping him get used to horses. He fed them sugar cubes. H-he said it felt like a kiss on his hand. We brushed them. We didn't let him ride by himself. We eased him out of his fear first." Drawing in a slow calming breath, she said, "I asked him, Ari. I didn't force him to do anything."

"It was not up to you to help him through his fear."

Carla reached across the divide between them and placed her hand on his arm. "Who then? You hired me to help your son. Ari, you are as fearful of letting Jaime ride as he is. I thought I was the right person to help him."

"You are not the right person to help him."

"Then tell me why." She'd overheard Jaime tell Aaron about his mother, but she wanted to hear in Ari's words what happened and why they were both so frightened. She silently pleaded with him to trust her.

Silver specks swirled among the black coal of his eyes. His lips parted, reminding her of the night they kissed. The night she moved toward him, into his arms, into a kiss she would never forget. And in kissing him, she'd done the one thing that would make Ari believe she wasn't right for his child. The one thing to make him distrust her. She'd abandoned common sense and followed her passion. Now, she'd done it again by letting his son ride a horse.

But he'd also followed his passion that night. Had their kiss been so wrong, when they both wanted it? And was she so wrong now, to use passion along with common sense to help his son overcome his fear?

Biting her lip, she waited.

His mouth closed in a straight line across his face. Ari stood. "You do not understand any of this, Carla."

She sucked in a breath but remained seated, even as he towered over her. He met her gaze. Deep, dark anguish radiated from his eyes, but a blank expression reminded her of a primitive clay mask, void of emotion. She held her breath.

As soon as he turned away from her, her entire body shuddered.

He paced to the center of the room and back and stopped in front of her once again. He hauled in a breath with such might, she feared he thought it was his last.

She should never have pressed him on this.

In a methodical voice, he explained, "It is *not* that you are not the right person. It is *not* the right time."

At least he had thrown her a bone. She wanted so much to ask him why the timing was not right. Against her nature, she didn't say a word. Madge suggested she learn to listen and if it killed her, she would.

His chest heaved before he slowly expelled the breath. "The boy has suffered great trauma."

She wanted to touch him. Give him comfort. Ease his pain. She stood, her knees pressed back against the chair.

"His mother, my wife...." He turned toward the window as he spoke. "She was killed by a horse."

Carla wished she could see his face.

"All my fault. Jaime witnessed the accident." He turned. His voice continued the methodical beat, his blank expression holding everything in check. "You see why I cannot allow him to ride without me or Giles. It is not time. Not yet."

Carla walked toward him, her voice soft. "Not time for you. Is that it, Ari?"

She came to a sudden stop when he looked away. He stretched his hands in front of him and stared down. Carla stared too. His always steady hands shook. Shook so hard, she wanted to grab hold of them to stop the motion. His hands were the only part of his body to show he suffered in telling her what happened.

"If I had not shouted at Arianna, the horse would not have reacted."

A look of utter despair and guilt clouded Ari's entire face, from shadowed eyes to the straight set of his mouth.

Carla stepped to him and gathered his hands in hers. "Can you tell me what happened?"

"There is nothing to tell."

Ari pulled his hands from Carla's, unwilling to accept the comfort.

"Surely—"

"Nothing." He had to stand tall and confront this latest situation head on. The guilt ate at him. But his anger won out. Only Giles understood the truth about his wife's death.

Carla was trying to worm her way into his life. He'd vowed to keep his distance from this woman. For some reason, since the day they met, he hadn't been able to completely raise the barrier to keep her out.

This is why he told Giles no. And when he'd lost that battle and hired her, and then kissed her, he told Giles to relieve her of her duties. And now what he feared most had happened. He'd let the woman in. He had to shut the door. Shut the door for good.

He curled his hand into a fist before he reached into his pocket. The small, smooth stone was warm against fingers numb with cold despite the spring day. He rubbed his thumb against the grooved edge of the stone that always reminded him of a half-formed heart—a heart that matched his own. Broken and closed to love.

His childhood, vying for his father's love. Watching his mother close herself off. And now finding herself in the unhealthiest of ways. His mother, who had gone through three marriages, each to a wealthier and more powerful man. Trying to mold herself into the woman she thought they needed. Each time giving up a little of herself for that man. Each time left with a bigger allowance and *friends* who surrounded her for her money and influence. Both his parents had taught him to close his heart. A heart he never fully opened to his wife. And then....

Giles once told him this secret ate a hole in his heart, the hole growing wider every year. In his sage advice, he told Ari the truth would set him free.

Maybe now *was* the right time. Maybe he should confide in Carla rather than push her away. She was like no other woman he'd ever met. She was fond of and respectful of his son. And that in itself sent his heart to pound and more fear raced through his blood stream.

This notion of opening up went against every grain of self-protection he'd built into a solid wall. Everything he moments ago argued against in his head. Shut the door for good. But it was too late. He would finally speak the truth.

Ari could only hope Giles' advice rang true.

This was his duty, to set free the broken heart of his son, so Jaime could move on. Even if this confession ended up irreparably breaking his own heart and driving Carla away.

Head on, he reminded himself.

For Jaime.

He released the stone in his pocket. Pulling his hand out, he spread his fingers wide, as if that would free him from his past. Now was the time to give Carla the truth of what held him back. Held Jaime back. "Arianna's death was my fault."

Carla stepped back. The tilt of her head and the question in her warm hazel eyes indicated not disgust, but perhaps caution.

With her weight on one foot, she tucked her hands discretely into her back pockets. "So you said. I don't believe you."

"You were not there." He raised his voice in defensive anger. "I should have protected my wife, even after she deceived me. That is my code, the code of my father, the code of my brothers."

"She deceived you?"

Of course, Carla would focus on the deceit and not the avoidable death.

He stepped toward her, his hands flexing at his side, trying to contain the percolating anger always threatening to overtake his better judgment. He had not meant to mention Arianna's deception. Carla picked up on everything. "Why must you delve into my life, my secrets?"

Her mouth opened, then snapped closed. If he hadn't been so filled with anger and guilt, he would have laughed. Her passionate and caring side warred with her need to know. He'd seen this same reaction several times, as if she bit down on her tongue to keep from asking.

Maybe she was taking Madge's sage advice.

"*Now* you are quiet?"

She shrugged. "You obviously don't want to tell me."

"No, I do not. But I have learned that you do not give up. You will ask another time, will you not?"

"Probably." The tentative smile lifted the corner of her mouth. Then she grew serious again. "What can I do to make you trust me? Make you understand that I care deeply about Jaime and his well-being. I believe—" She glanced at the floor, before looking back up at him. "The secret you hold so close is destroying you...and Jaime."

She moved close enough for him to catch a hint of her fragrance—fresh and alive and so familiar now, like springtime. As if he'd known her forever rather than several weeks. She lowered her voice. "But you need to talk. To someone. If not me, Giles."

"Giles knows all."

She nodded, as if she already understood the trusts they shared.

Ari swallowed his anger. His son's wellbeing depended on how he handled this situation. "I am grateful for what you have done for Jaime."

"He has had the chance to be a child these last few days, laughing and playing and not so fearful. Do you understand what that means?"

"I do understand. However...I am his parent." Why did he insist on being so stubborn? He too had never had a childhood.

Even as the eighth born prince, he'd been trained for royal duties. Why would he wish to imprison his son in the same box? The reason he'd moved far away from Portega and the prison it represented. "The good results of your actions do not negate the fact that I gave no permission."

"You hired me," her voice grew stronger. "You asked me to help your son. You entrusted not only me but Giles. *We* decided, in *your* absence, how to care for Jaime."

His anger returned. Not at Carla or at Giles. The two of them were not faultless in their decisions, but reality directed his anger at his own indecision and inaction. That he could not trust anyone with the secret that gnawed at his gut, affected every decision he made. And in turn made him so vulnerable he'd closed off his heart to all he cared about.

So he repeated, "I am his parent."

"And you avoid the original question. *How* is the death of your wife your fault?"

Her voice, steady and strong, gripped his heart. She cared about his son. Did he dare entertain the idea she might care for him, too? "Arianna was unfaithful."

"So I gathered."

"I followed her to the barn where she was to meet her lover. I vowed to make her choose and to stand by the consequences of her decision."

"Did you love her?"

He nodded. "That was my greatest weakness."

Carla flinched. For a minute, she said nothing. Just stared. Then in a calm, whispered voice she countered. "Love is not a weakness, unless you make it so."

He shuddered. His visceral reaction to—what?—her detached assessment and bull's eye accusation? He hated himself for how he'd reacted to Arianna. All he wanted that evening was justice. Justice for him and his son against a woman who had no qualms about betraying both. It was the only way he knew. Face a situation head on, solve the problem, and then move on. His father had taught him that from an early age. *You are royalty. You must take action. And you must be resolute in your decision and accept the consequences.*

Did Carla not understand this? Resolution made a person strong and self-reliant. He tolerated nothing short of being steadfast in his own convictions. And trust. Trust was paramount.

To love whole heartedly stripped a person of that fine-tuned edge of reason. Reason where you could distinguish between trust and deceit. "I cannot agree. Unbridled love exposes a person. Causes a person to second guess his principles."

"Did it ever occur to you that you may have loved the wrong person? That love wasn't what exposed you. But your wife's betrayal."

He stared at her. Carla's fierce proclamation caught him by surprise. He'd always been dazzled by Arianna's beauty. Been intrigued by her passion and her gypsy-like spirit. Blinded by her adamant claim of love for him. But had he actually loved her? Or had he been so enamored by the idea of love that he had been broadsided by the deception?

All his life he'd reached for that perfect love. Despite what his parents had had, he wanted to believe true love was there for the taking. Wanted to believe that when he found that sort of love, it would be fair and just and truthful.

Arianna's deception had broken him and stolen all trust. All that he thought love was. Because as much as he had a hard time accepting love and loving, he had loved Arianna…once.

Opening his heart fully had been his downfall.

Ari's chest tightened. He couldn't breathe. He had to get away from this woman who opened up his heart to believing in love again. To protect himself, he turned away from her. "You have managed to change the direction of this conversation. Jaime's welfare is what is important now. I must take my son home." He moved toward the door and the freedom of the hallway.

"Ari." Carla's voice shouted in command, causing him to stop and turn. "Answer one more question before you take Jaime. What have I done to erode your trust? Was it the—" He watched the mask of self-protection and doubt cross her features, her eyes lowering to the floor to study her dust-caked boots. "The night of the kiss? I know it was unprofessional." Her gaze snapped back to his. "But it won't happen again, I can assure you of that. You are my boss. And you're right—Jaime's wellbeing must come first."

He'd instigated that kiss, against all his own rules. *He had wronged her*

If he talked about the kiss, he would betray his own insecurities. He believed strongly that falling in love again was a weakness he could not afford to indulge. All he worked for and all he prized could crumble if he let passion and impulsiveness rule his decisions. She was correct. A kiss between them would *not* happen again. That was why he must take Jaime home. And leave Carla behind.

Without a word, he turned once again and strode out the door.

Chapter Eighteen

Dang. As hard as Carla tried to be the woman Madge had coached her to be, she wasn't capable of shutting up and listening. She forced Ari into talking about his wife. Which of course didn't help her cause. To top it off, she had no clue about the whole story of the woman's deception. And now, she had no chance of finding out.

At times like this, Carla longed for her mother. But what would her mother have done differently than Madge? A woman whose strength was hidden beneath her easy-going and motherly disposition. As much as Carla had wanted to have as little to do with Madge when her father married her a year ago, having known her for only a week, this last week had cemented their relationship. Madge had proven her loyalty to the Peters family and reached out in friendship to not only Carla but little Jaime.

Of course, liking Jaime wasn't difficult. The kid was loveable.

Now, she'd let Madge down. And everyone else. Jaime. Giles. Even Ari.

Rooted to the spot in the middle of the living room, she teared up. She swiped at her cheek, feeling foolish for the vulnerability that shrouded her. The click of Ari's boot heels sounded right above.

He was upstairs.

In her room.

The last time he'd been in her room had been at his ranch. The night she threw herself into his arms.

Like a fist, anxiety pushed against her chest. She convinced herself she could make a difference in their lives. She wanted so badly to help Jaime and show Ari she was the one to help.

Holy hello. Today, she'd blown it.

Now he was in her childhood bedroom, probably looking at her trophies and her stuffed animals. Noticing...*oh crappola.* She'd left her room a mess this morning. Her night clothes slung across the unmade bed, the plans for her school laid out on her desk, and by the bureau...*Oh gawd,* the laundry basket filled with under-things, including her new day-glow colored thongs.

She hoofed it across the living room, down the hall, and up the stairs. No way was she leaving him alone in her room to snoop. It was like letting a long-tailed weasel into your life. He'd find things, use them against her, and suck the life out of her.

Okay, maybe an exaggeration.

Because Ari had never done that before. The night he *rescued* her from Shawn she told him things she'd told no other, but he never turned her vulnerabilities against her. No. He used his royal attitude to close himself off. Used his parenthood as a weapon when he didn't like the decisions she made. But he never used anything she said against her.

Carla marched down the hall toward her room, determined to hold Ari's feet to the fire for Jaime's sake. She'd confront him on the real issue of why he insisted Giles replace her. The kiss and his regret instigated that decision, she was sure of it. Although now, she'd added another excuse to his arsenal.

She stopped in the door and propped her shoulder against the doorjamb.

When Ari glanced up from one of her books held open in his hand, he acted surprised to see her.

"I asked the wrong question downstairs. It wasn't about me, was it? Not about what I did to erode trust? It was all about you."

His brow lifted before he lowered his eyes and flipped a page, as if more interested in some random book than in what she had to say.

"What are you afraid of? Why did you tell Giles to get rid of me?"

He snapped the book shut and tossed it on her bed. "He told you?"

She nodded, biting her lip as a sharp reminder to listen.

"When?"

She blew out a sigh. "The morning you left." But she wouldn't explain or ask more questions.

The silence spread like low lying fog eating up the space between them.

She was tempted to cross her arms over her chest. Trying to play it cool, she willed her hands to lie at her side, leaning against the threshold as if she had not a care in the world.

The question had been as much risk as she could take. If he was ever going to throw something back in her face, now was the time.

Or, he could come clean. Confess it wasn't anything she'd done, but what was happening between them.

She waited.

And watched.

He rolled his neck before settling his gaze on her. His chin rose slightly in counterbalance to the lift at the corner of his mouth. Would he play the parent card or the royal card?

"Why do you do this, Car...la?"

As if drawing her name out might intimidate her. *No luck, buddy.* She channeled Madge and kept her mouth shut. She had his number. He was bluffing.

"Why do you say nothing?"

She shrugged and smiled, trying to convey she didn't want to argue. She needed the truth to move forward. And she waited. Waited for him to talk. Waited to prove she could listen and not be the loose cannon, ready to explode with each opportunity to make a decision about his son.

"What do you wish *me* to say?"

"Answer my question. Why did you tell Giles to get rid of me? What do you fear?"

He straightened—puffed up was more like it—into a princely posture. "I fear nothing. Certainly not you. It is simple. You are no good for my son."

"Really?"

"Well, I admit you have done some good."

"Like what?"

"Another question?"

She nodded. And waited.

Ari paced across the room to stand in the doorway of Jaime's room. "Are you ready to go?"

"*Sim*, Papa. Almost."

The zip echoed as Jaime closed his duffle bag. A shiver spiraled through her. They were leaving. The reality hit her stomach in a painful thud.

"We have much to do. I must work. You must bathe and eat your supper."

"*Sim*, Papa." Jaime's voice was thin and sad and a bit wavy, suggesting he may be close to tears.

"Good then." Ari turned back to her, his expression veiled again.

She hadn't moved. She'd waited and listened. And what she heard was panic in Ari's voice as he tried to pretend all was normal in his conversation with his son.

She started in again, daring him to finally answer. "What was wrong? Answer me, Ari. If you don't, I'll know you're afraid."

He strolled across the room to stand within a breath of her. She started when he reached for her short braid. Fingering it, he lifted his gaze to hers and paused. "You have taught my son to laugh again."

Not what she expected.

Carla forced herself *not* to leap into his arms. The same zap of wanting jolted down her spine as it had the night he'd kissed her. But she vowed not to make the same mistake again. Sucking in a breath to steady her nerves, she whispered, "So, what was wrong?"

"Wrong?" His raspy voice echoed her words. "I am the one who is wrong."

Amazed at his admission, she didn't move away from his heat, but waited and listened. The seconds ticked by.

"He is all I have. I must protect my son at all costs."

As he dropped the end of her braid, she wrapped her fingers around his wrist, fearful he would leave without finishing.

"I am afraid I have been overprotective."

She nodded. "When you love someone, it's natural."

"I have hurt him." Ari glanced over his shoulder. Jaime stood in the doorway with his duffle at his feet. "Go. Tell Madge thank you. I will follow with your bag."

"And Ms. Carla?"

"She will come say goodbye."

Jaime looked back and forth between the two of them. Blinking back tears, he picked up his stuffed stallion and crossed the room. As he walked by, Ari curled his hand over his son's shoulder. "I promise. You will see Ms. Carla."

The little boy, tears in his eyes, nodded and left the room.

As Jaime's footsteps faded down the hall, Ari turned back to Carla. Her heart thudded. Always so stoic. Ari hid much, but he loved deeply.

Without preamble, he answered the question that had eaten at her. "Jaime saw his mother die."

His eyes scanned hers, focused and serious. She kept her gaze fixed on him, trying desperately to keep her mouth shut.

"I arrived home early from a trip. I found out Arianna was in the barn. She cared little for our business, never bothering to go to the barn which was much too dirty for her. Did not know or care about our horses. So...I wondered. No, I knew. When I reached the barn, I found her in the arms of my brother's best friend."

She'd vowed to listen only, but she had to react. Placing her hand against his chest, she whispered, "I'm sorry."

"Yes, well *I* was angry. Too angry. I should know better than to approach a problem when my blood runs hot."

He sounded so calculating, as if finding his wife in the arms of another was like finding out a business competitor had outbid you on a project. As if he could simply stand back, out

169

plan and outmaneuver the competitor, and all would be back to normal.

"They stood in the corral, just outside the barn. None of us realized that one of the stable hands had opened the opposite gate to let in my stallion. When I yelled in rage at Arianna and Stefan, the horse startled. He ran toward my voice. I shouted a warning, but he reared up. Arianna screamed and the horse reared again. It was over in moments."

Carla didn't have Ari's ability to remain unwavering and unemotional. She wrapped her arms around his waist, surprised when he enveloped her and pulled her close. His heartbeat raced against her cheek, a contradiction to his cold, steady words. He acted the prince, but his heart beat out the rhythm of his grief and lost love.

She lifted her head. "And Jaime?"

"I had been gone several days. He saw me go to the barn and was too excited to wait. He begged his nanny to walk him to the stables. He arrived just as Arianna was knocked to the ground."

Carla gasped. Jaime had said a horse killed his mother, but she had assumed it was a riding accident. This was different. No surprise Ari didn't want Jaime on a horse. She pulled her arms from around Ari's waist to place her hands on his chest. His hand shook as he lifted it toward her cheek. But he didn't touch her.

"I killed my wife. My son saw her die."

Scalded by the cold and self-deprecating heat of his words, she stepped back. "You...you didn't kill her, Ari. It was an accident."

"An accident that should not have happened. I am at fault. I will never forgive myself."

"Even now, you love Arianna." She could see it in his eyes. Now she understood all that had happened between her and Ari. Or hadn't happened. The kiss. And his hasty retreat.

"Until now, I thought it true."

"And?"

"Now, I am unsure I ever loved her." He paused, looking

beyond her shoulder as if gathering courage. "I wanted to love. Convinced myself I knew how to love. But…neither of us loved the other. The accident—the situation—never would have happened had we loved one another."

"But you feel guilty." She wanted to touch him so badly. Wrap her arms around him again. Feel the heat. Soothe his shaking by pressing her body to his. But she didn't dare. He was the type of man who needed to work things out on his own.

Sadness etched his eyes, tiny lines stretching from the corners. Carla suspected this was the first time he'd admitted he hadn't loved his wife. She was sure he thought confessing or asking for help portrayed weakness. Ari hated to show weakness. Yet with all he'd endured, he was the farthest thing from weak.

"Why?" She let the word sink in. "Your wife was the one who betrayed you. Her death was not something you meant to happen. You must know that." She slid her palm up his arm and back down in a gentle caress, silently willing his clenched muscles to relax.

"I never wanted Arianna to die. But the fact remains, I did not hold my temper."

"Ari." The soft whisper of his name floated between them.

He closed the inches. Her hand moved from his upper arm, her fingertips brushed across his chest. "Do you really believe you are any different from others? No one would be able to hold back their anger. Really."

"Not true. I know many men who control their passions."

"And you don't?" She laughed, despite the serious situation. "You of all the people I know, except my brother Carter, guard your emotions so close to your…" Her fingertips tap-danced on his chest before she pressed her palm against the soft linen covering his heart.

He didn't retreat. His eyes softened to smoky charcoal, one hand covering her hand over his heart. "*Sim*, I do try. Sometimes too hard." The start of a smile fanned out from the corners of his eyes. "Giles says it will be the death of me."

"He's probably right. You could learn from some of our

rowdier American cowboys." She let the tease linger and sucked in her lower lip in an attempt to stop chattering. What he had told her was serious business. She shouldn't have teased. But the air had been so thick between them, she wasn't sure what else to do.

The corner of his mouth twitched in response. "Really? How so?"

"There's a place for serious. And then there's a place for playfulness." She swallowed, fighting the huskiness in her voice. "Giles is right. I'm not sure you know how to play."

"And you will be the one to show me?"

"I, ah…" She tried to pull her hand from under his, but he held it tight against his chest. "Maybe I shouldn't throw stones. I'm not so good at, ah…playing."

"Ah, but you are *Ms.* Carla. Look what you have done for Jaime. You have a natural way of making a man—a boy—want to play and laugh and forget his troubles."

For a moment, she obsessed on his words *a man*. Was it only a slip of the tongue, or had he really been talking about himself before he attempted to back away from the dangerous thread of conversation?

As she tried to figure out how to respond, Madge's voice played in her head. *Wait. Listen.*

The thump of his heart quickened beneath their entwined hands.

For the briefest of moments, he stared directly into her eyes before he released her hand and raised his to her mouth. The pad of his thumb warm against her lips. "I do not regret our kiss, you know."

She shook her head. He had deeply regretted the kiss. But now his thumb moved across her lips, along her jaw, and down the column of her neck. She shivered beneath the heat and forgot all about regret.

"Car—la." His breath, soft and warm, caressed her lips before his mouth melded with hers.

Her entire body melted. She sank against him and into a kiss she'd vowed to avoid.

His arm looped around her waist to pull her tight, as his lips and tongue played a heady game with her mouth. Carla shoved the little voice telling her this was a mistake to the far reaches of her brain.

With his other hand wrapped around her braid, he tugged to tilt her head as he deepened the kiss. Lost in his scent and warmth and sensations of coming home, all rational thought disappeared. The kiss lasted forever, as each fought against spoiling the magic moment by taking a breath.

"Papa?"

Ari jerked back to look over her shoulder.

She felt the loss of warmth before Jaime's soft voice penetrated the cloud of passion.

"Are you ready to go home, Papa?"

Ari's gaze snapped away from Jaime. "We must go." His whisper, practiced royal speak. But this time, he didn't wipe his hand across his lips. Nor did he step toward Jaime and the door. A moment of indecision hung between them, contradicting his words.

Lifting her hand, she gently pushed against his chest. "Yes, go."

She turned away from Ari to face the boy. Immediately, she piled bricks of protection around her heart. They were leaving. She couldn't bear the thought.

Kneeling, she pulled Jaime into her arms. His warm, little hands surrounded her neck. "I loved having you visit. I'll miss you." She glanced over her shoulder at Ari as she continued talking to Jaime. "Maybe we can talk on the phone every once in a while."

Ari nodded, and Carla turned back to Jaime.

The boy's arms tightened around her neck. "I love you, Ms. Carla."

When he pulled away, tears edged his lids. She was lost. Rocking back on her heels, she swiped at her own eyes. "I love you too. I'll call you. I promise."

Jaime smiled.

Ari picked up Jaime's duffle bag, grasped his son's hand,

and walked out of her room without a backward glance.

Deep in her heart, Carla understood this was the end of her nanny job. Once Ari thought about their conversation and kiss, he would shore up his heart the way he always did. With royal aloofness and the protection he wore like a ceremonial glove.

Chapter Nineteen

Ari strode through the front hallway, his and Jaime's bags tossed by the front entry. Sénhora Adélia had taken Jaime by the hand to see Cook, while Ari headed straight to Giles' office.

Without knocking, he barged through the opened doorway. But before he could open his mouth, Giles stood, fists planted on the desk. "What have you done?"

"I might ask the same of you. You betrayed me. Conspired with Ms. Peters."

"Conspired and betrayed are strong accusations. For your own good, I might add." Giles straightened, a smile working at the corner of his mouth. He walked from behind the desk, opened a cabinet to grab two glasses and a bottle and poured both a shot of Portega brandy. "Sit." He thrust the glass at Ari.

"And let you have the upper hand."

Giles plopped into one of the chairs in front of his desk and stretched out his legs. "Now you can sit, I have nothing to lord over you. Only concern for my best friend. Although at times, I marvel at why I bother."

That stole the ire from Ari's anger. Resigned, he sat, slugged his brandy, and leaned back in the chair. "Well?"

"What do you want from me? The same tired argument? She is good for you. She is good for Jaime. Until you admit that, what else can I say?"

"You manipulated the situation."

"That I did, mate, and I would do it again. You see the good it's done Jaime. He's made a friend his own age, he's conquered his fears about horses and people and, without having set eyes on him yet, I would bet he's put on a few pounds."

Ari raised a brow.

"I heard about the chocolate chip pancakes, fresh baked bread, and the cookie recipe. All of which Jaime was proud to have helped with."

Snifter in one hand, chin resting in the cup of his palm, Ari tossed his brother a half-lidded look. "You are proud of yourself, are you not? I turn my back—"

"You're a stubborn man. Someone must play games to get you to listen. To see. You do see now, right?"

"I am beginning to."

"Ah, so your stubborn nature precludes you from fully admitting your big brother is right. From admitting your fears hold you back from any happiness."

Ari sipped from the snifter to brace himself and leaned against the high-backed leather chair. "Yes, you were right. She has helped Jaime. No, you are not right that she belongs here. I stand by my assessment that we must find another nanny until Sénhora Miranda returns." He refused to address the fear comment. He'd gone through enough *fear confessions* with Carla to last a lifetime.

Giles straightened. "Really? You continue to stand by your ridiculous assessment of Ms. Peters. What aren't you telling me?" Giles raised his palm and stood to walk around his desk. "Never mind. Unless I resort to torture, you will never admit you have developed feelings for the lovely, compassionate, and smart woman. Now if you'll excuse me, I have work to do."

"You are dismissing me?"

Without raising his head from the desk, Giles muttered a *yes* that sounded like the buzz of a flustered and frustrated bee.

Back in his own office, the half-finished brandy on his desk, Ari scrubbed a hand through his hair. He could not concentrate on his work. Soon, he would have dinner with Jaime in his suite and then put him to bed. He missed tucking his son in, having Jaime rest his head against Ari's belly as he read to him. The sweet scent of newly bathed child working its way under his best defenses to open his heart and dispel the constant fear that something, at any moment, could go wrong.

Carla was right. As was Giles. He used his fear as a shield against the world. Carla knew his secret now. She had not run away. She leaned into his embrace, his kiss, and kissed him back. Despite his constant blustering, she did not fear him, or blame him for Arianna's death.

She had soothed him without pity. And…he had walked away. For her own good, he told himself. To protect Jaime, he told himself. All the while negating the ache of loneliness and what Carla's presence in their lives had done to assuage a throbbing need for someone who cared.

He had learned much visiting his high-strung and manipulative mother. It finally made sense why he craved his father's attention. And why he had subconsciously chosen to wed a woman who turned out to be so much like his mother. Arianna was someone he didn't have to wholly open his heart to. Vulnerable had not been in his vocabulary since boyhood. Not allowing anyone to get close had carried that self-imposed protection to adulthood.

Carla was right. He did push her away. He wasn't ready to allow anyone to breach his protective wall. Although, if he dared speak the truth, she already had.

And…being vulnerable hadn't destroyed him.

This time.

He pulled the black stone from his pocket. He studied it, remembering the day he found it half sticking up from the sand. The day he fought with his father and listened to his mother as she ranted on and on about how little the crown prince cared for his eighth son. How his father never believed he would amount to anything. His mother's words. He'd believed them. Continued to at times. The tiny rock had served as his protection all these years. A way to ward off his own beliefs that his mother's words were true. A way to quell the fear and give him courage that, yes, he would someday prove all the adults in his life wrong.

Maybe Giles was right. His father had reached out. Did

honor him by trusting him with a prized mare. Could it be Ari was the one keeping his father at arm's length?

He glanced around his room at the photos he'd taken of his homeland, remembering Giles grabbing the photo album to show proof his father did value him. Now, a grown man, cognizant of his mother's exaggerated sense of reality, he had to acknowledge she may not have been right about his father. In fact, she may have deliberately turned the young Ari against his father. The thought turned his stomach.

"Not time for you. Is that it, Ari?"

Carla's voice, her spot-on assessment, echoed in his brain. She was right. He hadn't let go of that fear. The fear that his father saw him as worthless. The fear that he'd be hurt emotionally, and perhaps physically, if he put himself or Jaime in harm's way. The fear that he now instilled in his own son. Yet, he had a tough time surrendering to anyone who made him feel again. That fear hit hardest, because it dug deep into his psyche.

He ran his thumb over the surface of the stone. Turned it to and fro. Studied it. His fist tightened around it. He tried to crush the constant reminder of his failures. His insecurity. His inability to fully love. He wanted to throw the small stone across the room. But not now. He wasn't ready to discard his talisman. The one he'd carried since he was seven. The one that motivated him to do the best he could. To reach his one goal. To prove himself to his father.

He stared at his clenched fist and then opened it. Slowly. Deliberately. He gazed at the stone. He had proved himself. His father did trust him, evidenced by entrusting his prized mare to Ari's care.

He plunged the stone back into his pocket.

And what did he prove? That his son should not trust either. That his son should not believe in challenging himself. That his son should stay stuck in the past, just as his own mother had taught him.

Ari pulled the stone from his pocket again, opened the bottom drawer of his desk and tossed it in. The stone bounced against the wood.

Straightening his back and squaring his shoulders, Ari prayed he could summon enough strength to quash the fears of his childhood and show his son life was meant for living. And loving. Again.

For a moment, he stared at the bottom drawer. Ached to pull the stone back out and put it in his pocket. The stone that had acted as a guardian angel against every self-inflicted doubt or insecure emotion he'd had since childhood. The stone that had rescued him when he wanted to shout out in terror or anger or love.

He stood, ignoring the temptation to pull out the stone and carry it with him, emptied the brandy snifter in one gulp. With glass in hand, he strode back to Giles' office.

"We need to talk," he said.

Giles merely raised one brow. Without raising his head from his keyboard, he said, "Again."

"Our mother."

Giles shut the lid of his laptop and stood. "Does this call for more brandy?"

"Probably. Definitely."

Giles retrieved the decanter, sitting right where he'd left it on the corner of his desk. Ari thrust his glass forward, and Giles poured another shot for each of them. "Do we need to toast? Or drink heavily after this conversation?"

Ari failed at suppressing a grin before he morphed in serious prince tone. "Our mother."

"You've already stated that."

"Yes, of course. She has poisoned us against our fathers. Do you realize this?"

"I'm sure you can guess why I always *allow* you to be the one to *soothe* her tirades."

Ari glared at his older brother. "And here I thought it was my great negotiating skills."

"That too." Giles leaned forward to slip his glass onto the desk. "Yes, I realized that, but it never stopped me from blaming my father. Or you either."

"Do you believe it is past time we both remedied that?"

"Probably." Giles stood to pace.

Ari drained his glass and followed suit. They soon came face-to-face in the middle of the large office. Ari reached into his pocket and regretted leaving his crutch behind in the desk drawer. They each shrugged.

"In due time," said Giles.

"In due time," mimicked Ari, before he strode across the office and out the door.

Carla sat cross-legged on her bed, leaning against the plump bolsters that transformed it into a couch.

It felt right to be back in her apartment. She turned to stare at her wall of photos, those of her family and those representing her personal history.

The same photos Ari had studied so carefully. He'd felt free to ask about her life. And here she sat, feeling guilty about digging and pushing until he had no choice but to tell her his secrets. Stupid really, that she felt so guilty. But her meddling had shoved Ari and Jaime right out of her universe.

There had been no word from Ari in three days. Giles had called once, apologizing for the outcome of their efforts and to tell Carla about the new nanny. And to tell her she had a check coming in the mail.

Dig. Dig. Dig. Her own fault. She'd signed up for one week, a boatload of money, and then planned to get back to her own life. That one week had turned into more. And that more had turned into setting herself up to getting her heart broken.

Dang. Carla swiped at tears. She missed her family, and she missed Ari and Jaime. Emptiness seeped through her veins, leaving her bare and exposed. She should get off the couch and move around. Stop wallowing in this brew of self-pity. It would get her nowhere.

Half her life had been spent pinning hopes and dreams on what she thought was love and eventual marriage. But it never would have worked with Shawn. She heard he asked out the new-in-town waitress at Comfort Food. She hoped it worked for him. He was a good guy.

And during the last several weeks...well, she'd been filled with an unreasonable hope for a new and exciting future. But Ari couldn't give her what she needed.

Obviously, she couldn't give either man what they needed.

Wow, batting a thousand. Two men, both gone.

She had her school.

Uncrossing her legs and scooting to the side of the bed, she vowed to be productive today. That meant leaving the apartment. Minutes ago, this space had been a comfort. Now, claustrophobia clawed at her.

Her cell jingled. She searched for the phone, finding it buried under three days' worth of unread newspapers on the kitchen counter.

"Hey, girl. We need to talk," Betsy said. "Dear hubby has some news for us."

"The school?"

"You bet. Meet us at Comfort Food at noon. We'll do lunch and fill you in."

An hour later, Carla strode into her favorite eatery. Granted, she worked there occasionally, and it was owned by Meloney, Tina's sister, but it served the best, guaranteed-to-make-you-feel-better food. Exactly what she needed right now.

The white walls were covered with brightly colored prints painted by local artists. The chairs, a motley selection of second-hand finds, were also brightly painted and placed around equally mismatched tables. An arrangement of well-worn leather couches and a coffee table, covered with magazines and copies of the local and state newspapers, formed a meeting place in the front bay window. Old, wood-framed windows, paint splattered as if an artist had painted them that way on purpose, hung as dividers separating the large room into several smaller seating areas and providing a semblance of privacy.

Kyle waved from a corner table. "Want coffee?"

She nodded as Tina scribbled on her order pad. "How's the

new job going with the prince?" When Carla didn't answer, Tina said, "Uh oh. What happened?"

Carla flipped her wrist in the air. "Don't wan'na talk about it."

"We'll do beers at the Rustler's Grill. Tuesday work?"

Carla rolled her eyes before nodding. Once she had a beer, she'd spill her guts. With a satisfied smile, Tina sashayed away. Carla glanced over her shoulder toward the front of the café to determine the reason for Tina's feline walk. Ore swung around on the lunch counter stool to watch Tina's approach, a hungry look in his eyes. She wanted to yell *get a room*, but there were too many locals around for her to risk embarrassing her friend and her brother. Besides, the burgeoning relationship was only in the flirting stage. Of all her brothers, Ore was the worst of the commitment-phobes.

A tiny spark of jealousy ignited as she watched the mating dance between the two. She wanted a man who inflamed her interest and her libido. A man that might promise a future. Unfortunately, the man who currently turned her insides upside down was off-limits.

Shrugging those thoughts to the side, she turned to her friends. "So, what's the news?"

Betsy elbowed Kyle. "You tell her."

"We have a silent partner. I know we have enough through county grants and tuition, but the extra funding means we can rev things up. Everything we planned as long-term improvements, we can do right away."

"You're kidding. Who?"

"What don't you get about silent—as in confidential?"

"Yeah, I get that, but I'm a partner."

Kyle mimicked turning a key to lock away his secret.

"So exciting," said Betsy. "Now we need to put some major elbow grease into renovations and move forward quickly."

Carla sighed, then plastered on a smile. "I've all the time in the world. Let's get to it."

Betsy glanced at Kyle, then at Tina who now stood by Carla's elbow with the coffee pot. Out of the corner of her eye,

Carla saw Tina shake her head before she refilled cups and set the pot on the edge of the table. Obviously, they all wondered why she suddenly had so much time.

She didn't want to get into specifics. "Assignment over. It stretched over the one week, but now...." She leaned in and cradled her cup, "So, ready to roll on the school."

Betsy again glanced toward Tina.

Tina tapped the menu in Betsy's hand with her pencil and waited for their orders. Her friends were treading lightly, thank goodness. She didn't have the energy to explain her Ari situation, not that they had a clue there was a *situation*. But...they'd known her forever. They suspected there was a story.

"I'll have Meloney's blue plate special."

"Me too," said Kyle, as he snapped closed his menu.

"Ooh, I love her gourmet version of mac and cheese. Count me in." Betsy handed her menu to Tina.

Despite being down when she walked into Comfort Food, Carla was happy to be surrounded by friends and excited to dig into Meloney's Italian mac and cheese laced with diced tomatoes, grated carrot, steamed broccoli, and fresh oregano with the side of browned spicy-Italian sausage. The almost-good-for-you version of comfort food to beat back the blues. She'd fill in her friends soon. Just not today.

"So. Aren't you going to tell me who our knight in shining armor is?" Carla couldn't help bugging Kyle, even though he sported a veiled expression of being sworn to secrecy.

"Can't."

"Kyle, we can't accept money from a stranger. What if this person doesn't agree with something we do? They could pull funding at the last minute, and we'd be stuck with a hefty bill. Besides, we don't need another partner."

"More a silent donor, not partner. You and Betsy have carte blanche. It's in writing. We've gone through an attorney. And it's already in the bank. This money is a donation to your non-profit, no strings attached."

"None? Really?"

"In writing. Now, are you two ready to move forward?" Kyle leaned back in his chair, his arms crossed and a self-satisfied grin on his face.

What Kyle forgot was that Carla did the books. She'd figure out who the donor was soon enough.

They spent the next hour laying out a rigorous work schedule.

As they finished up, Meloney came out of the kitchen to say hello. Sliding into the school-bus yellow chair between Carla's purple one and Kyle's red one, she said, "You guys have to come back a week from Saturday. I've got a great acoustical guitar player from England. I've ordered some English brews, and we're going to feature steak and kidney pie."

Betsy screwed up her face. "Kidney?"

"Don't even go there, Betsy. You haven't tasted anything like the way Meloney makes hers." Carla playfully nudged Meloney with her elbow. "Tell them the *secret* ingredients."

"Rosemary and garlic—tons. And stout." Meloney smiled.

"Some secret, if you tell us. But it sounds like a tasty gourmet version of the famous pub food," Kyle said.

"So, you'll come? It'll be fun. Spread the word."

They all nodded agreement as Meloney responded to an order-up call from the kitchen.

Chapter Twenty

Ari leaned back in the chair, his boots firmly planted on top of his desk. Twirling a pen between his forefinger and thumb, he tried for relaxed even though he was anything but. "Tell me, how is Sénhora Ferra doing?"

"First, I've come to invite you to Comfort Food on Saturday night. I'm playing and singing." Giles said, leaning against the doorframe to the office.

Ari straightened. "You? Singing? In public?"

Giles grinned. "Meloney twisted my arm. So, you'll come?"

"And mingle among the common folk?" Ari tried to maintain his royal-assed straight face to no avail.

"It'll be good for you."

"So you say. Now, tell me, Sénhora Ferra?"

"It's taking time."

"Why?"

"Why do you think? She's only been here a week. Plus…" Giles wasn't often testy, but his temper seemed to run short this morning.

Ari shook his head. "Are you going to answer me in questions as Carla does, or tell me what the problem is?"

A slow smile spread across Giles face, reaching all the way to his eyes. "So, Ms. Peters refuses to buckle under with your guff?" He held up his hand. "Not necessarily another question. Merely an observation."

Ari's boots thumped to the floor as he sat up. "No more games. Tell me about the new nanny."

"Jaime misses Carla. He'll get used to Sénhora Ferra

eventually. Give him time. He's had many adjustments the last few months."

"Is he misbehaving? Cook has indicated nothing wrong. And Jaime says nothing."

Giles nodded. "He defies her on every front—bed time, what to eat, activities. I'm afraid the Sénhora may walk out if we don't do something."

This time, Ari shot to his feet. "And what is it you suggest? I can tell you have ideas."

Giles strolled into the room and sat in the large chair in front of the desk. He crossed an ankle over his knee and leaned back.

"*Now* you give me attitude." But Ari couldn't help the slow smile, no matter how hard he fought. He walked around the desk and propped himself against the hard wood surface, arms crossed at his chest. He and his brother had been playing games for years. Ari hated to consider what a pompous fool he would be without his brother calling him on it whenever he pulled his high and mighty prince act. "You are lucky, you know. Even though I know you do not agree."

Giles sat forward, "What are you going off about?"

"Being sent off to England, to school and your father."

"I'm not sure I'd call that lucky."

"Away from mother and *my* father. Ah, but if you had stayed behind, you would know what I speak of. It is hard to undo an upbringing." Ari pushed away from the desk, taking a seat in the matching chair next to Giles. Why he'd brought up their childhood, he wasn't sure. Maybe it was his way of telling Giles they shared equally in childhood traumas. Giles with his abandonment issues. Ari with what always felt like the oppressive thumb print of the crown prince on everything he did or was. Not to mention his mother's manipulation that caused deep scars of resentment toward his father and feelings of inadequacy. And…Ari's way of telling Giles he was sorry for being that pompous ass he tried so hard not to be.

Giles pressed back against the leather. The lines emanating from the corners of his eyes smoothed out. "Shall we get back to the subject at hand, then?"

Ari nodded.

"The boy needs Ms. Peters back in his life."

When Ari shifted forward in his seat, Giles held up his palm. "All Jaime talks about is Chess and Aaron. And," Giles quirked a brow, "cookies. Of the home-made, Madge variety."

Ari couldn't help but laugh. "Ah, I must call Madge for her recipe."

Giles chuckled. "You? Calling for recipes? These Peters' women *have* created miracles."

Ari bit back a retort. He needed nothing from either Peters' woman except, of course, a cookie recipe.

To let Carla back into Jaime's life meant one thing. Letting her back into his life. *Impossible.* He'd revealed too much the afternoon they spoke. Then he kissed her. And she had kissed him back. A kiss so intense he thought he would never be able to leave her arms. Until Jaime interrupted them, and Ari regained his good sense. Carla Peters was a dangerous woman. To allow her back into their lives would be like knowingly sticking one's finger into an electrical socket. The zap would surely kill him. Or at the very least render him helpless.

"What? No comeback? She really has gotten to you, hasn't she?" Giles' grin stretched so wide Ari was sure his face might split in two.

"Must you be such a Cheshire cat? You know nothing."

"Ah, but I do, my little brother. I usually know what's best for you, long before you ever choose to admit I'm right."

Ari rose to his feet and walked back around the desk again. Restless. He shuffled notes from one pile to another. "No more talk about Carla Peters. What else do you suggest I do with Jaime?"

"What? Now I am an expert on childrearing?"

"You certainly act as if you know better than I."

"Pay attention to him. Take him to the corral to see your horses. Spend some time with him so you can both forget *your* fears." Giles stood and moved toward the office door. He tossed a look over his shoulder. "If you know what's good for you, you will heed my advice. You must get control of your fears before you can ever hope to open yourself up to your son. And if you refuse to acknowledge Ms. Peters' role in that healing, then…well, I'm at a loss as to what to do with either of you. Don't turn into your father, Ari." Giles pulled the door shut behind him with a resounding thud.

I have already turned into my father.

Ari dropped to his chair, plunked his elbows atop the desk, and lowered his head into his hands.

Tomorrow. Yes, tomorrow he would learn to be a better father to Jaime.

The ring tone for the Crown Prince pulled him from his stupor. He pressed the speaker-phone button. Perhaps he should vow to be a better son, as well.

"Hello, Father."

"What, no *Your Highness*?"

"What can I do for you, *Father*?"

The intake of breath echoed loudly over the long-distance line, as if his father stood in the very same room. "What is wrong?"

Ari straightened and stared at the phone. His father's voice didn't hold his usual gruff tenor. His question sounded very much like a father who cared.

"It is Jaime."

"Should I worry? I can be in America soon."

"No need. He misses Sénhora Miranda. Is her mother on the mend?"

"I am afraid her mother has a long rehabilitation before her. I have given Sénhora a job here until she can go back to Colorado, if she is able to."

"I will send her a note. And the reason for your call?"

"Only to say hello. How is my horse?"

Of course, the horse. "All is well here. I will have Giles send some photos. She has acclimated well to the altitude and temperature."

"Perhaps I will journey to the U.S. sometime. I miss…seeing Jaime grow. And I owe you a thank you for handling your mother. She can be, well, trying."

"That she is, Father." Ari tried to form the words to apologize to his father. But what would he say? *I have been a prick of a son. I did not understand how my mother may have sabotaged our relationship.* "I will send photos of Jaime, as well."

He would take Jaime to the stables and introduce him to Sapphire, his older and gentler mare. Maybe together they could learn to ride again.

"I, ah, miss everyone in Portega."

"Really? We also miss you, my son. But I, we, know you are doing a good job at your ranch."

Ari leaned back in his chair. "I am getting close, Father."

"I have faith."

"Trial and error take time. But yes, I too have faith."

"You will prove yourself with my mare."

"I plan to. I also purchased the Arabian you recommended at the California auction."

"Ah, you are building quite a stable. I must come and see the changes."

"As you wish, Father."

Ari said his goodbyes and reached to disconnect the call with a hand that shook.

Chapter Twenty-one

Shrugging off his sheepskin coat onto the back of his chair, Ari seated himself at the round table in the back corner of Comfort Food. The night had turned chilly. The air smelled like snow, a late spring storm predicted to start overnight. The long drive into town on such a night was his way of compensating for the hell he'd put Giles through lately and to support his debut musical appearance in Mineral Springs. Very few realized Giles played acoustic guitar for college bands and then for years after, on his own as a hobby.

Giles set down two mugs of ale. "Straight out of the barrel as it's meant to be drunk—room temperature. The owner knows her stuff."

Ari frowned. "I guess on a cold night lukewarm ale should hit the spot."

"Do I detect sarcasm? Would you prefer a hearty scotch?"

"Yes." He smiled at his brother. "But in honor of your performance, I'll will suffer the brew. You have time to eat before your set?"

"Of course. I've already ordered up the house special, steak and kidney pie."

Ari groaned. "How did I get stuck with an older brother who is all Brit. Although I admit, this beer is superb. Did not any of Mother's Manhattan side rub off on you?"

"When you're sent away for most of your childhood to boarding schools in dear old England, I'm afraid not."

Sorry he'd brought up his brother's painful past, he tried for a joke. "Ah, but I forget the theatrical side you inherited from

Mother."

Giles head fell back as he laughed. "I believe you're referring to Mum's theatrics not her theatrical talents."

Ari raised his mug and laughed. "Here is to your newly perfected British vernacular and to *Mum's* genes—theatrics and musical ability. None of which I inherited."

"Right'o," Giles said, turning on the accent. "You couldn't bust your way out of a paper bag with a tune."

"But I can appreciate a good one. How did you *score this gig*, as they say?"

"I stopped in for Meloney's home-baked cheese Danish and the richest coffee made in town, and she started telling me her dreams. One thing led to another."

"Meloney? Talk of dreams?" Ari raised a brow.

"You know old boy, you really need to get out and about more often. You come to town for business only. Do you ever bother to stop and look around you, talk to people? Do you good, you know."

Ari scanned the room. Tables were filling up. Everyone around him talked to their neighbors. He didn't know a soul. "You might be right." When it came to strangers, his social skills were next to nil.

Giles starred at him for a moment before he set his mug down. "You once were good at impromptu speech. Ever since Arianna—"

"That I will not speak of."

"Fine. Now's not the time. But you're missing out on much, understanding the culture of the state and town you've chosen to reside in. Making friends, so they know who the real Ari is. Someday, you'll need your neighbors. Consider that."

Ari simply nodded. Giles was right.

"And not to beat the subject dry, but Carla is the link you need to change your misdiagnosed reputation in this town."

"Most certainly not. I, ah…" True, now was not the time or place to get in this discussion with his brother. He lifted his mug, again. "Truce?"

As Giles lifted his to clink with Ari's, Meloney delivered

their steak and kidney pies. A smile as wide as the Mineral Springs' valley spread across Giles' face. "What are you doing out front on such a busy night?"

"It doesn't hurt to provide a little personal service to our star, now does it?"

As Ari suspected. Giles had a thing for the restaurant owner. And judging from her smile, it was mutual.

"I'll be back with my famous cabbage slaw. You want rolls?"

"No thanks, luv. You'll fill me up so, my vocal cords won't work properly."

As Meloney turned to leave, she waved at new arrivals. Ari looked toward the front and sucked down a groan. Carla had stepped through the door with her two friends. Meloney signaled the three over to the table next to theirs. Before he could say a word, Giles was on his feet.

"Carla, you came."

"I wouldn't miss it for the world." She accepted his outstretched hand.

Giles squeezed her hand in return. "Wonderful."

She rose up on tiptoe, leaned toward Giles. and planted a kiss on his cheek. "Good luck tonight."

"You have others joining you?"

Carla glanced at the couple she'd come in with. "Just the three of us."

"Then join us. We've plenty of room. I'll be up front most of the time, anyway."

Ari did not miss the quick glance Carla threw his way as her friends pulled out chairs at the table next to them. "No, no thanks, we're settling in." Nor did he miss the comradery between her and Giles.

"I insist. The evening for you and your guests is on me." Giles leaned toward Carla. "You'll not let the prince sit alone all night, will you?"

Ari wanted to growl at his brother. There was no mistaking what Giles was up to.

This time Carla looked straight at him. What could he do? He nodded and gestured toward the chair next to him. With her eyes pinned on him, she answered Giles. "You're sure we're not imposing?"

Damn Giles. Ari rose from his seat and pulled out the chair for Carla. "It would be our pleasure, Ms. Carla."

Her brow lifted as she moved toward him. "*Ms.* Carla?"

"Please. Sit." He hadn't intended it to be a command but, as usual, it came out that way. He lightened his tone. "Please Carla, I would enjoy the company."

Giles had already herded Betsy and Kyle to the table. "There, that's more like it. Much more fun to have a crowd."

Meloney returned with five orders of slaw and a basket of bread. She turned to the newcomers. "I've already placed an order for three specials." She looked at Betsy and smiled. "Try it. If you don't care for steak and kidney, I'll make you something else." Then she distributed five bread plates. "And Giles, there's plenty of bread. Just in case. No point in trying to watch your waistline tonight."

Everyone laughed at the joke, as the tall, slender man blushed. "You've got my number, Meloney. You know I can't resist your home baked goods."

"I'm counting on it."

Carla smiled at the flirtation. She watched as Meloney strolled away from the group, stopping at several tables to greet folks, and glanced over to see Giles watching her friend, too. Then she clasped her hands and stuffed them in her lap. The last thing she needed was to be stuck sitting next to Ari. For a week, she'd tried to put him out of her mind. Now, sitting close in the warm, crowded room, his spicy scent surrounded her in an unmerciful tease. Cloves and pepper. All Ari.

She closed her eyes for a second. Maybe she could plead a headache because right now, she could barely keep herself from leaning into his hard body and another one of his kisses.

"Please eat your dinners. Don't wait for us. We can start on our salad."

Carla's eyes snapped open when she heard Betsy's voice. She had to get a grip. For a second, she'd forgotten she was in public.

"This slaw is great," Kyle said around a mouthful.

Giles and Betsy had their heads together, talking about the new school. Carla realized she hadn't introduced anyone, yet they all appeared to know one another. Except Ari, who sat with his back to the corner taking in the scene.

"I should've—it wasn't polite of me not to introduce you." Carla leaned toward the middle of the round table. "Kyle, this is Ari Orula. Kyle and Betsy Sams. Kyle and Betsy are partners in our new school."

Ari simply nodded.

Kyle gestured with his fork. "Good to see you again."

The awkward silence filled the space between them before Giles and Betsy picked up the conversation where they'd left off. Betsy had on her motor mouth, telling them everything about their curriculum vision for the school, first year enrollment numbers, growth projections, even decoration plans and toy selection.

Ari leaned forward to rest his elbows to either side of his half-eaten dinner, effectively shutting Carla out. His head swung back and forth between the other three, as if the whole conversation was beyond fascinating.

She leaned toward him. "Are you planning to register Jaime?"

Ari looked at her. "Isn't he too old?"

"We're accepting applications for ages three through seven to start. That's the age group local parents feel is too young to bus to Aspen or Basalt. From our research, parents want something closer to home. Eventually, we'll expand up to fourth grade."

Their dinners arrived. Giles excused himself to start his set. Ari finished his meal while the others dug into their meat pies. Silence ensued, as they listened to Giles sing.

When Giles took his first break, Meloney joined them, crowding them all together around the small table meant for four.

Carla looked at Giles. "I had no idea. You have a beautiful voice. Why have you kept it hidden?"

"Merely a hobby. Not often I bring the guitar out in public."

Meloney leaned over and placed her hand on Giles' forearm. "I had to strong-arm him into playing."

"This should be a regular gig," Kyle said. "Once word gets around, you'll bring them in from up and down the valley."

Meloney's husky laugh rang out. "Are you kidding? Once word gets out, I'll be out-priced. Only places that will be able to afford him are the lounges up in Aspen."

Giles leaned in. "For you luv, I'll keep the price down and give you an exclusive. All I need is my steak and kidney pie and a few brews for payment."

Carla had never seen Giles' flirty side, nor heard the hint of cockney in his accent, a contradiction to what she understood about his background. Apparently, he was adept at acting, as well. His job with Ari dictated fierce seriousness most of the time. Giles usually acted the part of a prince's aid or a protective older brother with a British nobility accent to boot.

Carla glanced at Ari. The fine lines that emanated from the corners of his eyes and the upturn of his lips spoke volumes. She tried to imagine what he was thinking, this serious man who rarely played. At least not around her.

Then his eyes darkened as he looked toward the front of the restaurant. Carla glanced at the door.

Uh oh.

Carla groaned.

Carter strode through the throng of diners straight toward them. His lips set in a grim line and his eyes arrowing a path directly at Carla, then narrowing as his glance switched over to home in on Ari, squashed shoulder to shoulder with her.

Meloney stood and ran interference as Carter neared the table. "Hey there, handsome. Can I get you the house ale tonight?"

"Not now," Carter said, as he sidestepped her and stopped next to Carla. His hand wrapped around her upper arm. "We need to talk."

Now wasn't a good time to assert her independence with her big brother. Not that Carter would ever be violent but if he were a dragon, he'd be spitting fire. Carla shook his hand off her arm and pushed her chair back. She stood, her eyes level with his chin, then looked up. "You want to talk, it will be outside."

Ari stood. "Is there a problem?"

"Nothing I can't handle," Carla said at the same time Carter growled out, "None of your damn business."

Carla's gaze moved from Ari's startled expression to Carter's furious one. With her hands on her hips, she looked at her brother. "Enough. You don't air the family laundry in the middle of Comfort Food. Outside." She grabbed Carter's wrist and pulled him toward the hallway that led to the back alley.

She slammed her hand against the back screen-door and stomped into the alley. Only after she heard it bang shut behind her did she turn on her brother. "What the *hell* got under your saddle?" Wasn't often she allowed herself to cuss, not when she worked with kids, but Carter deserved her fury.

"*What* are you doing with him?"

"What does it look like? Eating dinner and listening to music." Probably a stupid thing to say, but she didn't owe Carter an explanation. It wasn't like she and Ari were on a date. She'd gotten thrown into a situation that wasn't her making. But Carter didn't need to know how she ended up seated next to Ari. None of his business.

"I thought we talked about this. That man is bad news. You owe it to your family to stay away from him." As he stepped back, the fight oozed out of him. His voice softened when he added, "You promised."

"Dang it, Carter." But the fight had left her, too. "I'm not out to hurt the family. I came in with Kyle and Betsy. Turns out Kyle knows Ari. The next thing I know, we were crowding in around his table." She watched his eyes cloud over. "You need to talk to Ari. You can't let this rivalry eat at you. I don't even know what the fighting is all about."

Carter stretched out his hands in front of him, his fingers spread, before he fisted them. "We're going to lose everything,

Cal. We can't fight it any longer."

Carla sucked in a deep breath. What could she say to ease Carter's mind? Nothing. He was shaking and hogtied like she'd never seen him before. As she stepped toward him, into the small circle of light cast by the bare bulb above the back door of Comfort Food, a shadow darkened the doorway.

Before she could warn Carter, Ari pushed open the screen door and stepped into the ally. By the time he'd taken two more steps. Carter had swung around to face the man he despised.

"Not now," Carla said, not sure who she directed the comment to. Neither paid attention.

"We must talk. In private." Ari stared down Carter, just out of reach, as if he waited for him to take a swing.

Carter turned to her. "Go on."

She flexed her fingers, willing her hands to relax. All she really wanted to do was curl them into fists and throw a punch at each of them. Carter was back in protective big brother mode and Ari in arrogant prince mode. And she...she was back to what-does-she-know,   she's-only-a-woman-and-a-little-sister status.

"Fine. Duke it out for all I care." She yanked the back door open and stomped down the hall muttering, "Dang men. Screw them all."

Ari swallowed, unsure if he was doing the right thing. One look at Carter as he peered through the screen door told him he must help Carla's brother. Her entire family thought Ari to be the very devil. They needed to know the truth. But could he trust Carter to keep the secret?

Surprised that Carter didn't take a swing, Ari stepped closer.

Carter squared his shoulders. "If you've come to gloat—"

"There is no reason to gloat. We are all in the same predicament." Before Carter could belt out another accusation, Ari stepped under the light and flipped open a slim, square leather case he'd tucked against his palm. "You want explanations..." Ari waited and watched.

Carter moved under the light and his eyes widened as he glanced at the case. "You're telling me you work for the feds?"

"Not for. With." Ari nodded.

Carter's eyes narrowed. "The difference?"

"I am a…as you would say, a snitch. They recruited me to make a deal."

"How? Why you? And why do you have identification?"

"For situations like this."

Ari glanced over Carter's shoulder into the darkness of the ally and beyond the dumpster that partially blocked one end. Out there the night seemed stagnant. The only sound, the low hum of voices and music drifting down the hallway from the restaurant. He turned his head toward the other end of the ally and the filled parking lot beyond before moving a step closer to Carter. He kept his voice low. "Duggans is my neighbor."

"Yeah, so? He's neighbor to all of us. And bad news."

Ari nodded in agreement. "My closest neighbor. And the source for all the water running down valley."

"You have water."

"I made a deal."

Carter stepped back. His hand scrubbed across his chin. "Duggans—he's the one siphoning off our water?"

"Not siphoning. Redirecting it south of here. Southwestern Colorado, where they pay big money for much needed water."

"Then why is your pond full?"

"I have told Duggans I will pay blackmail money. My ID was given to me for just such a case as you who will get in my face. Without it, I would have had to stand in the fire-line of your punch." Ari grinned. "They know Duggans will never search my pockets. He believes he has the upper hand. But he is nothing but an opportunistic drunk who has no brains for this kind of treachery."

"The feds—they know about the blackmail?"

"They encouraged the exchange of money. It keeps me—how you say it—dangling from the end of the fishing pole."

Carter stared at Ari, then punched his balled-up fist against his leg. "That bastard. I'll break his—"

"You will do nothing. Not until we can prove how he directs the water. And who pays this money to him."

Carter straightened. "We don't have time, damn it. My cows will die if I can't feed or water them."

Ari stretched out his hands to try and calm Carter's anger and offer an olive branch. "I have water in the southern valley pasture. My spring has held steady this year. Bring your cattle to graze there until this situation is settled."

Carter opened his mouth.

"There are strings attached, of course." Ari anticipated pride would goad the man into arguing against his gesture of friendship. He smiled, hoping Carter would understand. "He has been blackmailing me. I promised payment. He gives me water. Next, he will try the rest of you. If he should, let me know. The feds will hand over marked bills so we may make payments. You must go along with him. With your help we can nail Duggans."

"Won't Duggans question why my cattle are grazing on your land?"

"He is not a man smart enough to look at small inconsistencies and recognize them for what they are. Your land is next to mine. He will not know the difference. Nor do I believe he will see beyond his greed, thinking he has me on that hook."

Carter nodded.

"You must swear to tell no one. Not even Carla or your father. *Nothing* can cause jeopardy to—how do you say it—this operation."

Carter nodded again.

"Tomorrow, I expect to see your cattle in my pasture. In case this goes on longer than we hope—" Ari flashed his palms. "—you need the water. I have enough in my pond. Save your cattle."

Carter offered a hand.

Ari handed Carter his card. "Call me if you hear from Duggans."

Carter pocketed the card and slipped out of sight, down the alley toward the parking lot.

Ari returned to the table in the corner. As he pulled out his chair, Kyle motioned toward the front. "Hey Betsy, there's Tom and Abby." The two rose, leaving Ari alone with Carla.

"Did you leave Carter's dead body in the alley or at least clean up the mess when you finished with him?"

Ari stared down his nose at her, trying to contain his smile.

Her fingers beat a rhythm against the table, as if counting out the seconds before she would make a dash to the back alley to check on her brother.

"Naturally, I cleaned up the mess." He did his best to assure her in his perfected dry tone, hoping she would see the humor.

Her chin lifted. He watched the slow smile spread across her face before she laughed low and easy. "I'm surprised. I'd placed my bet on Carter. Like an enraged bull, he was primed to throw you and then round back to gore you."

He pressed his lips together to keep from laughing. "You believe I cannot handle a riled bull?"

"You never cease to amaze me, *Prince* Orula."

"We spoke only. No fists. No goring. Your brother and I have come to an agreement."

"Why wasn't I included in your little chat? What did you two decide to do with me?" Her voice, low and conspiring, murmured the questions. Even as her eyes blazed.

Ari reached out to cup her cheek. His shoulder pressed against hers as he breathed in her scent of sweet wild roses and pungent thyme. He ached to kiss her, try to wipe that smirk off her face, but he'd never get away with it. "Ah, if we had bargained about you, I would have won. You and I would be riding toward the sunset, as we speak."

Her eyes widened.

"We spoke only of ranch business. I assure you, you are *allowed* to make your own decisions." He slid his fingers down her cheek to trace a path along her chin. Avoiding her warm lips, he followed the path up the opposite cheek to sweep a lock of hair behind her ear and then caress her earlobe.

She shivered against his fingertips, her eyes smoky. Then, ever so slightly, she leaned into his touch. The soft lock of hair fell back against her cheek to tickle the back of his hand.

He dropped his hand.

Carla jerked, as though a branding iron had scorched her, and then retreated, leaving the cool air to heal her. She locked eyes with his, sure he wanted the same thing. A kiss. Another kiss. Maybe...more.

"Now is not the time," he murmured.

"I, ah, no, of course not." Carla leaned away from Ari, remembering the promise she had made to Carter to not get involved. She turned away to avoid the smoky heat of his gaze. Studying the group of people who'd come to hear Giles play was much safer. Anything to get her mind off the kiss that didn't happen. And...the ones that had.

Most of the crowd were ranchers from the area. There were a few she didn't recognize. A table with three young couples, all dressed in designer jeans, stood out among the cowboys decked in dress jeans—the newest of their Wranglers or Levi's. She glanced at Ari, comparing the young couples' dress to his, surprised to find he looked more like a local rancher than a moneyed tourist from Aspen or Denver. If it hadn't been for his sharp Mediterranean features, his dark eyes, and the new sheepskin coat slung over the back of his chair, he'd fit right in.

When Ari turned to catch her stare, his flinty eyes lit a match searing her with an all-consuming need.

The ache that had started in her stomach with his soft touch and now inched its fiery way to her heart, terrified her. Even as Ari maintained his steely stance, she couldn't pretend he didn't affect her.

The night was young. She must leave before she did something foolish. Looking around, she caught sight of Kyle and Betsy weaving their way back to the table. Good. She could say her good-byes and thanks for a—what—lovely? entertaining? disconcerting? evening. She reached down to find her purse, ready for her escape.

The music had stopped, and Giles was pulling out the chair next to her. "Carla, I was so bad you feel you must run away?"

She felt the blush rise on her cheeks. "You were incredible. I don't know why you've kept such talent hidden."

"Ah, there was a day when I thought myself a rock star. But life throws other opportunities your way and suddenly, you're off in a new direction."

Giles nodded toward Ari. She turned in time to see Ari return the nod. She interpreted his closed-mouthed smile as a subtle sign of respect for his older brother.

Dropping her purse to the floor beside her chair, she resigned herself to sticking out the evening a bit longer.

Chapter Twenty-two

Carter paced the length of his suite living room to dispel the pent-up energy, thankful no one had waylaid him upon his arrival home. Reality hit him straight on. He'd been all wrong about the Portega prince. The entire town had. But he could tell no one about his findings.

He strode to his private office, thankful for the lock on his suite door. The office he used when Mitch and Ore got on his nerves. He loved his family. Most of the time. But trying to run a ranch with his father looking over his shoulder at every opportunity and his brother taking very little seriously, made his life more difficult than it had to be.

He pulled up his spread sheet on herd rotation. Soon, he could take them up to the mountain summer pastures. Until then, he had to move one herd to Ari's land. A second herd to the vacated land. And somehow, he must figure out how to funnel water from Ari's pond to the herd without direct access. All without letting on Ari was one of the good guys.

In the wee hours of the next morning, he put his plan to bed and setup an after-breakfast meeting with Mitch and Ore on the ranch schedule app. Exhausted, he climbed into bed for some shut eye. At times like this, he wished for a wife. One who understood the rigors of ranching. One he could talk to about his problems and ideas. One who would reach for him, even in the early hours of the morning, to let him know someone cared. Someone was on his side. Finding such a woman who could put up with this family and the never-ending work of a rancher seemed a pipe dream. Until then, he was in this without an ally.

When the alarm went off three hours later, Carter groaned and rolled over. As he drifted back toward deep sleep, the ten-minute snooze bleated out its incessant blare.

After a quick shower and a hasty breakfast, he walked through the double doors of the main office, all business. Ore was lounged in front of the large oak desk, Mitch sat ramrod straight behind the desk. Carter swallowed his trepidation. It lodged like a boulder in his belly.

"We're moving the herds today."

"No. Too early." Mitch's fists landed on the desk as he half-rose out of his seat. "You'll jeopardize their survival, moving them this early."

Carter wanted to pound his own fists on the desk. When would his father let him run this ranch without interference? Mitch would not let go, even though he'd handed over the reins two years ago. "Let me finish before you go blustering like an enraged bull."

Mitch remained half-standing for a beat of a few seconds, before he huffed out a breath and plunked back down in the massive leather desk chair.

"We've been lugging what little water we have trickling into the creek for almost a month now and buying more to be trucked in. We can't survive any longer."

"So, the alternative is to send them to the mountains to freeze?"

He couldn't help tossing Mitch a glare. "You could give me a bit more credit than that."

Ore, in his usual manner, grinned as he watched the two set up for a major brawl.

"I've reached an agreement with our neighbor to use his lower pasture."

This time Mitch did stand fully and barreled around the desk, his fists planted on his hips. "You made a deal with that ass of a prince?"

Carter faced down his father with an identical stance. "We have no choice. Do you want to lose the entire herd?"

"How much did you have to pay him? We don't have that

kind of money lying around. If we did, we could buy and schlep all our own water. Not make a deal with the devil."

Carter bit down on his retort. He couldn't fault his father for his anger. Mitch didn't know the truth. He backed away, then plopped himself down in the chair next to Ore. As he did so, all the steam spouting from his father settled like ground fog. "We'll pay him once our beef go to market."

"How much?" Mitch asked.

"Less than it would have cost us to transport water in." The lie rolled out. He wanted to feel guilty, but he couldn't. He had to do what he had to do. "It's a fair settlement. We've already contracted to sell the beef to area restaurants, so we know the money's coming in. We'll make a profit."

"Just not as much," his father grumbled.

"We lose the herd, we make nothing," Carter spat out the words, rising again to his father's provocation.

"So, when do we move the herd," Ore asked, as he sat up straight.

Now he finally butts in to end the quarrel.

"Today. I need you to get hold of Jack. See if Carla is available. Never mind, first call Shawn and see if he can spare help. Carla's dealing with her— Other things. The three of you will each take a team. Move one third at a time. I don't want to lose any, you hear?"

"I got'cha. We should be able to get them all moved over by tonight." Ore stood. "Anything else?"

"Yeah. Tomorrow, we move the herd in the eastern pasture into the southern pasture. Then we figure out how the hell we water them."

"We've got spring storms in the forecast," Ore said. "That should set the creek to roaring for a few days. Once we get both herds shuffled around, how 'bout we rig up a make-shift dam to capture the water so it doesn't overflow the creek and seep into the ground? Buy us some time."

Carter nodded. He glanced at Mitch, knowing if he didn't, the infernal man would rail at Ore. "Dad?"

Mitch also nodded, then strolled back behind the desk to sit.

"Could work."

Carter wanted to criticize his dad, the perpetual pessimist. Instead, he turned to Ore.

"Good plan. When you talk to Shawn, ask him for his help. I think he did similar a few years back. Line up a few men to start on that tomorrow morning, as we move the second herd."

Once Ore left, Carter turned to his dad. His father looked ashen. "Dad, you taught me everything I know. Trust me." He wanted to beg, but that would give his dad the upper hand. Instead, he added in a confident voice, "I did what we had to do. We'll make it now."

"How long? What the hell happens if the rains don't come in strong this spring? We going to hand over all our earnings to our neighbor? Hell, he stole that land right out from under us. And what about next year?"

Carter shook his head. His dad was blaming him for bad decisions. Rather than engage him in yet another argument and churn up old family fights, Carter bit his tongue. "Have to believe it will all work out. We've been through this before." He strode to the door, not wanting to draw out the conversation. If he and his dad got into it, he'd blurt out the truth for sure. Better to live with his dad's scorn. He'd know the truth soon enough.

Gawd, he wished he had someone to talk to.

Chapter Twenty-three

Carla crouched next to the line of cubbies, brush in hand, carefully edging the shelves near the floor with peacock blue paint. They'd managed a lot of work in the last week.

"I love the colors," Betsy said. "It really livens up the room." She sank to the floor, folding her legs into a pretzel twist beside Carla.

"How's the pre-school room coming?"

"Finished. Kyle added the last coat of sunshine yellow to the cubbies. Looks great with the green apple trim."

"Do you suppose this peacock blue is too much with the orange sherbet?" Carla asked, as she rose.

"Absolutely not. Kids love bright colors." Betsy leaned over to point out a spot Carla had missed. "Here, give me the brush. I can reach it."

Carla handed her the brush and then, with both hands at the small of her back, leaned back in a much-needed stretch. "And I thought rounding up calves was tough work."

Betsy placed the brush on top of the paint can and stood. "Yeah, I…"

Carla straightened from her stretch as she waited for Betsy to continue. When Betsy remained silent, Carla glanced up. Betsy stared at the door. Carla didn't need to turn to know who stood in the doorway. Her sixth sense sent a tingle of anticipation, putting her entire body on alert. But she asked anyway. "What?"

"Well, back to work," Betsy said, darting around Carla as if the school had caught on fire. "Kyle and I are tackling the second-grade room next. Here we come, lilac and cherry."

Carla turned slowly, her eyes following Betsy's footsteps before she dared raise her head to look at Ari.

The large, first grade room shrank in size with each of Ari's steps. By the time he reached her, the room's bright colors had swirled together in a kaleidoscope mist, closing them in against the world.

What was he doing there? "Come to register Jaime? If so, you'll win the prize for being first." The nerves in her tummy fluttered in direct contrast to her cheery and, she hoped, nonchalant voice.

His lips barely moved at the corners. Just once she wished for a wide-open smile, but those were rare.

"Maybe I should. But I have other business today. I need you—your services."

She shook her head, knowing what was coming. She couldn't go back to being his employee. Not that she was anything else to him right now. That was the problem. He'd kissed her…twice. Then regretted it. But the other night at the restaurant she sensed he wanted to kiss her again.

They had sat wedged together at the corner table the entire night, as they listened to Giles play romantic folk ballads. At times, knees touching. Barely speaking. But glancing at each other. The whole evening felt like a chemistry experiment bubbling in a tiny test tube and finally pouring over the top. And then the explosion when Carter barged into Comfort Food. When Ari returned to the table, she sensed a change, as if he didn't want to hold back any longer. He—teased about absconding with her across the fields and over the mountain pass on what she pictured as a white Arabian.

Then there were the glances, barely noticeable, but for her alone.

If for no other reason, she had to stay far away from him.

I promised Carter, she repeated over and over, as if the mantra would help her keep her distance. But it didn't. When he stepped closer, she didn't move. He reached up to finger a wisp of hair that had escaped her ponytail. Heat shot through her. Today, his scent was not only pepper and clove, but leather and the faint aroma of hardworking man.

Before she could mind her mouth, she said, "You've been working with your horses."

He nodded.

"And Jaime?"

He nodded again. "Giles has him working with Bennie."

"Bennie?"

"Our resident pony."

"Good. A pony like Bennie should help ease his fears for a solo ride." She stepped back and then stepped back again. As long as she couldn't feel his heat or smell the scent that was all Ari, she might be safe. But with each step, he followed, until her back edged against the wall next to the newly painted cubbies.

"Yet, he acts out."

Her mind scrambled into a blur. What had they been talking about? "Jaime?"

"He misses you and the routine you've set for him."

She raised her palms to ward off his words. His last step crowded her, forcing her hands to rest squarely against the soft flannel on his chest. His heart beat under her palms. When he sucked in a breath, the thumping in his chest grew stronger, a steady drum beat. His coal black eyes turned to smoke, the silver specks swirling together with the onyx.

"This isn't a good idea—"

As he planted one hand against the wall beside her head, his mouth collided with hers, fierce and hungry. All thoughts of bad ideas vanished, as his other hand touched her waist and tunneled a path under her shirt and up her belly. Her fingers fumbled with the buttons on his shirt, aching to touch his skin. When she loosened the first two, she tangled her fingers through the hair on his chest, knowing it was coal black against his olive skin. Wanting. Wanting desperately to see all of him. Feel all of him.

His warm hand cupped her breast, his fingernail scraped across her nipple encased in sheer lace.

Her whole body jolted back against the wall, reality fighting through the haze of lust.

She shoved her hands against his chest. Each sucked in breath as their mouths parted.

Ari dropped his hands and stepped back, then he turned to pace away from her.

The shock of cool air hit Carla. She remained standing against the wall, an anchor for her shaking body and racing heart. And watched Ari's back as he retreated.

He stopped and turned to face her, buttoning his shirt. "I cannot help wanting you. But I vow I will keep my distance if only you will help my son."

She wasn't sure she wanted him to keep his distance. But he was right. They had to curb this lust that stretched between them, despite the need emanating from his eyes. Despite the heat that threatened to combust within her.

She understood the desperation that made him seek help for his son, that overrode everything else. Ari was right to withdraw. Her heart pounded. She sucked down the need to touch him one last time, before they both stuck to their vows to retreat. Still, she wanted him.

No. I promised Carter.

Carla's shoulders slumped, the small of her back pressing against the hard wall. There was no way she could keep that promise to Carter. She was in love with a prince. And his son. No matter how hard she fought to distance herself from the Orula's, her heart paid no attention.

Ari scrubbed his hand across the back of his neck, looking so needy and vulnerable. She couldn't abandon him or Jaime. But she could not help as the nanny. That job remained off limits—especially after today.

She straightened from the wall and moved into the room. Reaching for Ari's hand, she drew him toward the small, straight-backed, wooden chairs circling the center of the room. Holding his hand, they sat to face each other, knee to knee.

"Tell me what's happening with Jaime."

"He does not care for the new nanny."

"Is she strict?"

At that he smiled, fully this time. Carla's heart melted a little more. "Maybe that is all it is." Then his mouth straightened and his tone grew serious again. "He misses you."

"He said that?"

Ari shook his head. "Not in words, but I know he does. You know he rarely acts out. Giles is convinced that with several nannies lately, he needs stability. He opened up and responded to you."

"But this new nanny, she's only been with you a short while. You have to give her a chance. Have you talked to Jaime about his behavior?"

"Of course. He is only sullen in his answer. He offers no excuses. But when he judges me out of earshot, he talks of you...and Madge and Aaron."

Carla leaned forward, taking his other hand in hers. She looked into his eyes. "You know I cannot return to your ranch. Not now."

His mouth opened in protest, but she cut him off before he uttered a word. "I'm sure Madge would welcome Jaime for the day. I can arrange it with Jack and Aaron and then pick up Jaime. We can go riding in the paddock, and Jaime can see how the puppies have grown. Their eyes are open now."

"I cannot persuade you to come back?"

She shook her head. Dropping his hands, she stood. "I have only two months until we open and a lot of work to do here."

"Can you not hire people to do some of the work?"

Carla tilted her head, looking down at Ari sitting scrunched in the child's chair. "I have already used all my savings. Plus, I love doing this. This is my school, and Betsy's. It's important that *we* do the work to make this school the best it can be. Can't you speak to the nanny and ask her to be less strict? Tell her Jaime is smart and self-motivated...and creative. He needs a bit of freedom to explore. Not rigidity."

Ari unfolded long legs and rose. "Yes, I will do so, and I do understand. I am being selfish in my wish to have you back in my home."

"It's for the best." She wouldn't mention for her sanity and his. "I'll come to visit once a week. And I can take a day off here and there to take him to visit Aaron."

Stuffing his hands in his back pockets and looking every bit the cowboy, he didn't say a word. Then he raised his chin and morphed into his royal persona. His protection. Not one word about how he might want her to come visit him. Her gut twisted at the thought that what she felt for Ari was completely one-sided. Not the lust—that they both felt. But the love.

"You'll ask Jaime if he wants to spend the day with Aaron?"

"I will. I will call and make arrangements." He turned.

"Ari, one more thing. Thank you." When he glanced over his shoulder, brow raised, she moved toward him, but stayed out of reach. "For helping our cattle."

"Any neighbor would have done the same." With that, he strode out of her bright, new classroom, leaving only the memory of their passion-laden kiss.

An hour later, Carla reached high to paint the top of the doorway trim in the second-grade room with its last coat of lilac. She couldn't get rid of the tingle that rushed up and down her spine every time she thought of Ari's kiss. And his touch. And the look in his eyes when she'd pushed him away. From lusty smoke back to coal, it had only taken him moments to shut down. He'd perfected the art of hiding his emotions.

Was that all it was? Or did he really not have it in him to love? No, she'd witnessed the love lift the corner of his mouth when he spoke of Jaime and when he sparred with Giles, the flare of emotion enveloping his face. The emotions, she guessed, that whirled through his body like an eddy taking down his stoic wall when he looked at her with smoky eyes.

Carla shoved back her own emotions ebbing and flowing through her, *thunked* the paint can lid in place with her palm, and walked to the classroom sink to wash off her brush. Tomorrow, she could take up where she left off before Ari strode into her space.

But today, she would mourn what could never be.

Love. *Dang it all to holy hello.* This was so not what she bargained for.

Ari stared out the window of his second-floor office. Black clouds gathered at the tips of mountain peaks on the other side of the highway and Roaring Fork River. They swirled, ready to spill down the mountains and engulf the valley before churning their way back up the outcropping of hills where his house sat. The path was a well-traveled route for storms.

Carla had called twenty minutes earlier to say she was leaving and would arrive soon to pick up Jaime so he could spend the night at Peters Valley Ranch. It had been a week since he'd begged her to come back to work for him.

More days then he wished to count since he'd given in to his urges and kissed her again. And…who knows what would have happened in the brightly colored classroom if she hadn't put a stop to his madness. She was right to turn down his offer of employment. Getting closer to her, and inevitably making love, would mean commitment to Carla. And he had yet to believe himself capable of commitment.

His cell buzzed in his pocket. Without looking at the number, he turned from the impending storm and answered. "Carla?"

"Ar-ri." The familiar deep, accented, and royal voice boomed over the phone.

"Father?" His chest constricted like a vice clamping tight. How had he not noticed the ringtone for the Crown Prince? He'd been so lost in thought about Carla, that's why. Such debilitating temptation was wrong. Yes, a good thing Carla refused his offer of employment. "What can I do for you?"

"I have only now landed."

His mouth went dry. "What? You are in Aspen?"

As though his father hadn't heard a word, he continued, "But the storm has begun. Maximilian and I will go to the Ritz. We will arrive at Silver Mine tomorrow by noon." He hung up before Ari could take the next breath.

Forgetting the storm, he buzzed Giles and set to making a

laundry list of notes on things to be done before his father's inspection.

When the flash of lightening filled the room, followed quickly by a clap of thunder, Ari's head jerked up and toward the window. The sheet of rain obliterated any view of the mountain range that minutes ago had been visible. He glanced at his watch. A half hour since Carla had called. She only had fifteen miles to drive, all highway, until his long, winding road.

Giles strode through the door. "This will be a bad one. The groomsmen and stable boys have secured the horses and will stay in the barn until this is over."

Ari stood. "Carla has not arrived?"

"No. Should we try to reach her? Turn her back? With this rain, the creeks will rise quickly."

"She should be here by now." Ari pulled out his cell and hit number five. It rang and rang. "She does not answer."

"Maybe she's already crossed the Roaring Fork. There is a dead zone there. I'll go down to greet her."

Ari stepped around the desk. "I will go. Have Sénhora Adélia prepare a room. Carla is going nowhere in this deluge."

Giles nodded and left. Another flash of lightening streaked across the sky. A thunderous clap boomed before the flash dimmed. Right on top of them.

Carla's cell bleated beside her on the passenger seat. The rain had started only minutes earlier and the roads were already muddy. As she fought the pick-up's steering wheel, she cursed the distraction. Just around another bend and she would be in sight of the house.

She heard the roar before registering where it came from. Above her. Peering out the window, she saw nothing coming at her from the sheer mountainside. She pushed against the accelerator. One more turn and she would be out of this pass and away from the rock and mud slide churning somewhere above her.

And then it hit. Slamming into the tail end of her truck. She gripped the steering wheel as the front of the pick-up swerved, the hood careening toward the sheer wall of rock. She slammed her foot on the brake. But it wasn't her braking that stopped the truck. The mud and rocks jammed against the back end of the driver's side had stopped the pick-up on a dime.

She peered into the rearview, squinting through the sheets of rain. The truck bed was piled high with debris. Her hands shook, her heart already lodged in her throat on impact. Hitting the accelerator had put her seconds ahead of the slide. She sat staring out the windshield as the wipers slapped back and forth on high speed, fighting the torrent of rain.

More rock could tumble down at any moment. She couldn't sit in the truck. She had to get to higher ground. She'd call for help as soon as she escaped immediate danger. Grabbing the key from the ignition and finding her cell on the floor, she pocketed both before scooting toward the passenger door and shoving it open. As her foot hit the gravel road, now deluged with water and mud, she slipped and grabbed the door handle to keep from sliding straight under the truck.

Sucking in a deep breath to steady her pounding heart, Carla eased her way around the door, hanging on tightly until she could plant both hands against the hood. How was she going to make it out of this pass?

Very carefully.

She steadied herself by leaning against the front end of the truck. On a deep breath to calm her beating heart, she turned and eased away to sidestep up the steep incline of the slick road.

Despite the hood of her rain slicker pulled close to her face, pounding rain streamed into her eyes and down her face. The icy water began a slow and steady trickle around the inside of her collar and slipped down the back of her shirt, causing a shudder to ripple down her spine. She offered up a silent prayer, or was it an oath, that she'd make it out before more mud and rock let loose.

Up ahead, a hazy silhouette marked the edge of the rocky pass, and Carla breathed in deeply. Almost there. Only a walk across wide open space the size of three football fields without being struck by lightning. Easy.

As she rounded the bend and spied the outline of the ranch house on the hill ahead, she heard the steady roar of a truck engine getting louder. Closer. Stepping off the edge of the road onto a pile of small boulders, she grabbed hold of a scrub tree and shielded her eyes. The deep maroon of the truck with its gold Silver Mine Ranch logo stood out against the stark gray of the storm. She waved with one hand while clinging to the sapling with the other.

The Jeep crept to a halt in front of her. Thank goodness she'd worn her bright yellow slicker.

Clinging to the weak branches, Carla stepped carefully off the rocks to the gravel road.

"Do. Not. Move. I come to get you."

Her heart thrummed at the sound of Ari in royal rescue mode, his voice clear and strong. Her teeth chattered and her hand shook as she tried to maintain a grip and stand upright in the wind gusts.

The branch snapped. Arms flailed as her feet scrabbled to stay under her. Ari's strong hands gripped her waist, pulling her tight against his body at the same moment she lost her battle to the wind and mud.

"Careful. I have you."

Her body, rigid with fear and adrenaline, kept her from melting into the safety of his arms.

"Sidestep. We are only feet from the door."

Together, they worked their way to the Jeep. Ari helped her inside and slammed the door. The blast from the heater hammered into her, making her shiver all the more. A tug on the knotted ties, and she slipped off the hood of her wet slicker and absorbed the warmth.

Through the wash of rain on the windshield, she followed Ari's movement around the Jeep until he finally climbed into the truck.

With a slump of her shoulders and the shudder of pent-up breath, she allowed herself to believe she was out of danger.

Ari didn't say a word. It was as if he didn't even breathe. As if he had bottled up his emotions, as usual. The only sound of life was in the shifting of gears as he gingerly backed the Jeep around to head toward safety.

Carla stared at him, trying to imagine how he stayed so stoic no matter what happened. But then, in a flash of lightening, she caught a glimpse of his face. His lips were drawn taut, his complexion gray. In the waning light of another powerful flash he glanced her way. Then, just as quickly, his black eyes focused back on the road, intent on getting them safely to the house.

And she understood.

He cared.

Chapter Twenty-four

Giles opened the front door wide as Ari eased the Jeep to a stop.

Before Carla could untangle herself from the seat belt, Ari skated around the front end and opened the passenger door. The tinkle of ice hitting the roof and the pellets bouncing off the rim of his black Stetson signaled the turn from thunder and lightning to a late spring hail storm.

Carla swung around in the seat, ready to step down. As she flipped up her hood and steadied her palm against the doorframe, Ari wrapped his hands around her waist and pulled her toward him. She yelped in surprise. Before she could say Jack Rabbit, he slipped one arm under her legs, the other to her back and scooped her up.

Shaking so hard from the cold, she couldn't summon the strength to resist his chivalrous act.

The icy rain struck her cheeks and forehead, adding to the bone-deep chill, as Ari hunched over her in protective-mode, taking most of the icy assault.

He carried her to the open door. Only when they were well under cover in the room-sized front hall did he release her, letting her slip slowly down the length of his body until her feet hit the floor. She brushed by every hard muscle. And the shiver that shot through her wasn't from the cold.

For the briefest of moments, she leaned against the warm, protective wall of his body.

Ari had come looking for her. As if she'd swallowed a shot of warm brandy, heat pulsed through her. But she couldn't stay like this forever. She'd promised him, and herself, she would act the professional. Pulling forth every ounce of strength, Carla pushed away from the comfort of his body.

Her legs folded under her.

Strong hands grasped her waist. "You are dizzy?"

She shook her head, the motion driving her more off balance.

Giles immediately slipped the wet slicker off her shoulders and down her arms. He threaded his arm through hers, as Ari turned to do the same. Between the two, they walked her to the roaring fire in the great sitting room. A flutter worked its way through her.

Their relationship—it had all begun in this room, the morning she railed against Ari about wanting to help his son. And he'd stomped off. Less than six weeks ago. And now…she loved this man.

Love. Another shiver slipped down her spine.

"You are injured. No?"

"I'm fine," Her teeth chattered as she stretched her hands toward the flames.

"You are far from fine. Your truck is half buried in a mud slide. You are drenched and dizzy."

A full-blown shudder ripped through her. Only feet had saved her from being buried under a wall of mud and rock.

Ari's arms snaked around her waist and pulled her back against the hard planes of his chest. His scent wafted over her. "You should have turned back when you saw the storm clouds." His voice lacked the usual pompous accusation. She picked up on the concern in the words he whispered into her ear, his warm breath raising goose bumps across her neck. "You could have been hurt."

To hell with being professional.

Carla turned and wrapped her arms around his waist, leaning against the beat of his heart. Exhaustion and tension wound around her in a tight coil.

"Come. We must remove these wet clothes." He glanced at Giles. "Have some hot soup sent up to my room, and a decanter of brandy." He tugged on her hand.

Reluctantly, she moved out of his embrace and away from

the fire. At the bottom of the stairs, he scooped her once more into his arms.

"Ari, no way. This time I can walk." In truth, she wanted nothing more than to be in his arms.

"I am rescuing a cowgirl too obstinate to know she needs care."

She glanced up and, despite her exhaustion, laughed. His lips were drawn tight, his black eyes focused on his mission. He bore his princely duties a bit too seriously. "Rescuing?"

"I worried."

She heard the panic laced through the deep timbre of his voice. Her heart tripped.

She tightened her arms around his neck "What made you come in search of me?"

"Giles expected you any moment. We were about to seek you out. When I heard the roar of the rock slide, my heart dropped. I knew..." He looked away for a moment, as though showing vulnerability was not an option. "I knew trouble had found you."

Real fear twisted across his face in a heart-breaking grimace.

A sob clogged her throat. She couldn't even muster a thank you. She'd managed to rescue herself, but that wasn't the point. Ari had rushed to her when danger threatened. And now he insisted on taking care of her.

She brushed her fingertips down his cheek before she buried her head against his neck.

He carried her up the stairs and through the wide doors to his suite, then set her in a plush armchair next to the fire. "While Giles assembles some supper, I will run a bath."

She positioned her hands on the arms of the chair, ready to stand. "I am perfectly capable of—"

"For once, can you keep quiet and allow someone to take care of you?" His mouth lifted in a teasing smile, making his expression doubly appealing.

But she could only stand so much coddling. "I don't need a bath." Why she chose to argue, she wasn't sure. Except that sinking into a deep tub drawn by Ari hit her as way too intimate. How could she keep her promise to stay clear of this man when he insisted on being caring and...romantic?

Glancing toward the fire, she tried to gather her bravado and not reflect on romantic gestures. She, in reality, *was* frozen. And shaken. "I can shower and change down the hall, in my— my old room."

"And what do you expect to wear after you shower? Cold and sodden clothes?" When she stared at him, he reached out both hands, pulled her from her seat, and turned her toward the bathroom. "Get in the shower then. A bathrobe hangs on the back of the door. I will find you something to wear."

He pulled the door shut behind her. Too tired and cold to protest further, she shed her clothes and walked into the huge, tiled, room-sized shower. Turning on the faucet automatically started shower heads on either end and along the side wall. Definitely a shower built for two. Sitting on the bench, she luxuriated under the powerful pummeling that warmed her in minutes.

The door cracked open. "Are you all right?" His voice sounded much too close. Looking around for a towel, she realized everything was in the other part of the bathroom.

"Fine. Wonderful. I'll be out...soon."

"Hot soup is ready." The door *snicked* shut.

Breathing in a sigh of relief mixed with a bit of disappointment, she turned off the water.

Wrapped in the fluffy royal-blue bathrobe, and her hair done up like a turban, she stepped into the spacious living area of Ari's suite. She'd been there for meals, but always with Jaime and always fully dressed.

She spied Ari setting a small table between the two overstuffed chairs flanking the fireplace. As she walked fully into the room, he stood and motioned toward the other chair. "I put in a call to your family to let them know you are all right."

Her heart twisted, shifting away from vows she couldn't keep. Reaching toward him, she touched his forearm. "Thank you. I hadn't thought to—"

"As soon as the storm lifts, I will send ranch hands to assist your brother with assessing his herd. I told him you will be staying here."

She shook her head and regretted the movement immediately. She reached to steady herself on the high back of the chair. "I'm sure they can get the debris cleared off the road soon."

"Not with the Roaring Fork flooding its banks and the bridge washed out."

"Your bridge?" Her stomach plummeted to new depths. She could have been crossing when—

"Many inches of rain fell over one hour. The ice has caused more damage."

Sinking into the deep, cushioned chair, she let her head fall back. The heat from the fire spread through her.

"This will warm the inside." Ari lifted the lid from a bowl of steaming soup placed on a plate and handed it to her. "A specialty from my country. Much like bouillabaisse." His eyes shone bright as he mentioned his homeland.

"You must miss home."

"At times."

She ladled a spoonful of soup. The scent was incredible, like the ocean and spring vegetables and exotic spices from a land so different from her own. "Aren't you eating?"

"I will wait and eat with Jaime." He walked to the fireplace, grabbed a poker, and nudged the logs. Sparks flew and a lick of flame spread among the layered firewood. He turned back, his arms crossed over his chest. "But you need to eat. You have had a fright."

After several more spoonful's, she tilted her head and stared at him. "I'm not eating because of the mud slide. I never got around to having lunch." When concern etched his features, she anticipated what would come next—his need to protect and lecture—so she changed the subject. "Do you eat Portega cuisine often?"

"Some. Mostly we eat your western food and a lot of, what you call, Tex-Mex. Jaime's favorite. Now eat. Brandy?"

She pinched her fingers together, and he poured her a short shot, then handed her the snifter.

"Aren't you having any?"

"Later. First, I will find clothes. Yours are being washed." He strode to the attached bedroom.

Carla sipped another spoonful of broth, letting the hot liquid work its magic. But her appetite was diminished from frayed nerves. After she picked through the bowl for some seafood, she relegated what was left of the sumptuous soup to the table.

She tossed a glance over her shoulder. Ari had disappeared. For a moment she relished the quiet, if only because he was no longer near, tempting her. Which was ludicrous. The only way to resist temptation was to get out of this robe and into some clothes. Then go in search of Jaime—the reason she was there in the first place.

Standing, she scanned the room. She'd never seen the rest of Ari's suite. Did she dare? Curiosity got the best of her.

"Ari?" When he didn't answer, Carla padded barefoot across the plush carpet to the bedroom door.

His gruff voice made her pause.

"Do not call me again until you have a reasonable solution. I will not bend to your games." He tossed his phone on his bureau. A scowl marred his features as he turned before she could step back.

"Come. It is only regrettable business that must be dealt with, but not now."

"I didn't mean to intrude—"

"Nonsense." His mouth relaxed with that one word. He unfurled a T-shirt." Come. Look what I have discovered. This will fit. No?"

She laughed as he held up a long-sleeved, white T emblazoned with red *I ♥ the Big Apple*. "Not exactly your style."

"Mother's idea of a joke. Much too large to give to Jaime."

Walking into the room, she reached for the shirt and held it against her. The hem skimmed her thighs. "Perfect. Thanks."

"And these." He grabbed a pair of gray sweats with a drawstring. "You will not fit any of my jeans."

"And that's a good thing."

One brow arched in a playful tease, turning her insides to

mush.

"I do pride myself on being smaller than the average cowboy."

He took the shirt from her hands and tossed both it and the sweats on the chair beside them. "Average?" The rasp in his voice underscored the passion they both tried to keep in check.

"I—ah—didn't mean—"

The playful gleam in his coal black eyes turned smoky. He stepped close. His thumb stroked her jaw. "You frightened me today."

She nodded into his palm, now cupping her cheek.

A shiver, like a warm mountain breeze, caressed her skin. From her jaw line, down her neck, and across her collar-bone to settle with an aching need in her breasts. Forgetting all her vows to her family, and all her promises to herself to never step into a kiss again, she moved closer. Wanting him. Wanting the kiss…and more.

Both palms now hot against her cheeks, she ached to have all of him hot against her.

He leaned close and murmured, "You should change." He edged his fingers under the towel wrapped around her head and freed her hair.

The move startled her. "It'll be a frizzy mess."

"What is this—frizzy?" His fingers combed through her hair, untangling snarls strand by strand.

"Curly—uncontrollable—ugly."

"No. Beautiful." The whispered endearment feathered her ear, triggered shivers, assaulted senses, ignited sparks, heated her veins.

The press of his body, all solid planes and strength.

The familiar scent of pepper and cloves seeped into every pore. As if they were one. As if, maybe, they could forget all the forces trying to drive them apart. If only for a night.

His lips parted, but he hesitated. *Please don't back away this time.* Her heart couldn't take one more ping-pong volley of want and rejection. Not rejection of her. She understood that now. But of what he wanted to feel but couldn't allow himself.

She looked at him. *Really* looked at him.

Smoky eyes softened him from the rigid man she'd first met on the slopes. Powerful jaw and prominent cheekbones reminded her of his loyal strength. The firm set of his mouth that rarely smiled, disguised his pain—a vulnerability he stuffed deep inside. Despite knowing he kept his secrets close, she was confident he was a man she could count on.

He had proved it again and again.

His hands slid through her hair to cup her neck. His solid strength pressed against her, pausing again. His gaze arrowed into her, as if he wanted to confirm her agreement.

Is he trying to kill me?

She brushed her fingers over the stubble of afternoon growth. Resting her palms against his chest, her gaze lingered on his mouth. "Yes."

Carla had dared not say *yes* out loud. But there it was, loud and clear.

Tired of trying to keep her promise to Carter, she wanted to give this relationship a go. What would happen moving forward, she couldn't say. But for today, she could pledge full commitment to the man she'd wanted from the moment she set eyes on him.

His eyes shone bright and sure, his lips upturned in a half-smile. Yes, they were headed beyond a kiss.

With a slight nod to egg him on, she raised up on her toes.

The rough pads of his thumbs stroked her throat, burning away any doubt, before circling back to lay warm against her neck. With a force she ached for, his mouth met hers. His big hands cupped her bottom, pulling her toward him. She welcomed the thrust of his tongue. Liquid heat surged through her belly straight to her sweet spot.

Tangled in a dance of tongues, their mouths melded so close there was little room for air.

As if fate had finely said enough—get on with it—she pushed her hands against his chest, lifted her mouth from his, and stepped back.

Sparks of protest and puzzlement shot across his features,

until she unknotted the sash at her waist. She let the ties drop and the robe slip open.

The tell-tale tick throbbing along the edge of his jaw signaled *same page*.

He closed the inches between them and dipped his long fingers beneath the edges of her robe. Each cell inflamed with the slow slide of soft material as it slipped from her shoulders.

"Ari." She pushed his hands away to grab the lapels of her robe. They'd come this far. She couldn't wait any longer. She yanked the robe open, the motion allowing it to slide down her back to catch at her elbows.

His hands covered hers. "Not so fast." The rasp in his voice rippled through her, as he pinned her hands at her side. "My turn. I have waited, wanted to undress you since…"

Carla's hands tensed within his grasp.

He tightened his grip.

Ari wanted to relish every moment. Every taste. Every touch. Look his fill.

Make Carla mine.

"You are perfect." Waiting so long to touch, inflamed every inch of him. Lust easing into long-forbidden love, his deepest fear.

His deepest fear reflected from hazel-eyes that shone with wariness and passion.

He leaned into her, savoring the sweet and salty flavors of brandy and soup as he smoothed his tongue along the seam of her mouth. A purr of contentment whispered across her lips. He deepened the kiss against her soft sigh of urgent want.

Time stopped, as if they'd moved beyond the prerequisite to breathe.

In between hurried nips and licks and tangled tongues, the need to breathe resurfaced. He lifted his head to glance over her shoulder. The bedroom door stood wide. Pressing her palms deeper into the thick pile of her robe, he let go and stepped back. "Do. Not. Move."

With a wink, he strode across the room to shut the door, *snicking* the lock he'd never used.

Chapter Twenty-five

Carla turned toward him, eyes wide, lips parted ever so slightly in a smile. With her palms planted at her sides, the robe gaped open showing him everything he'd dreamed about. Now. All his.

Ari's gaze skimmed the body of this woman who had torturously invaded his thoughts. Hell if he could move despite the ache that seared every inch of him.

Slender neck, creamy shoulders, a dappled pattern of light freckles sprinkled across her chest like the sun's kisses. Breasts made to fit a man's big hands. The flat belly of a hardworking cowgirl gave way to the feminine curve of hips and strong thighs that he had so many times imagined settling his body between. A tangle of copper hair nestled in the V between long, muscled legs. The thought of those legs wrapping around his waist sent a shot of fire to his already hard erection.

Sucking in a deep breath of control, he moved toward her in slow, deliberate steps. Not as a tease, but to ensure he would take this first time in slow motion. "No interruptions this time."

She bit down on her lower lip, and he nearly lost control. Striding the last few steps, he reached for her hands, inched his fingers up her forearms to dislodge the robe, and watched it slide to the floor. His arms wound round her waist and he dragged her tight against him.

For the first time since leaving Portega, Ari had come home.

"Definitely no interruptions." She pulled at his shirt tails and slipped her fingers beneath the edge of the waistband of his jeans.

His skin flamed with her touch. When her other palm molded solid against his erection, he groaned. "Wait."

"No more waiting, cowboy."

"Carla, great gods, I want slow."

Her teeth grazed a path up his neck and nipped at points along his jaw. Determined to slow things down, he reached for her breast, cupping the weight, stroking the valley between with his thumb. Her mouth found his and he pressed into her, coaxing her lips to part for him.

He loved the taste of her, strong and sweet, like tart cherries covered in dark chocolate. But this time, this kiss had a new layer—heady, full-bodied brandy. Just like Carla, strong and sweet and rich. A kiss that was different from the ones they'd shared before. Tonight, everything would be different. No longer would he escape into guilt and fear. Carla had set him free with her spunk and patience and forthright questions.

As he caressed her curves, heard her soft moan, his heart filled his chest to exploding. Carla was one of a kind. In that moment, he realized he meant to make her his...forever. The word flowed through his heart and pumped through his veins. *Forever.* Forever. Forever powered though him like tiny licks of flame igniting into a full-blown blaze. He wanted to make slow, torturous love to her. Wanted to claim her. Wanted her forever.

That thought surprised him, scared him. But much had happened in the past few weeks. He had told her everything. He trusted her. Wanted her.

Ari pulled back from the deep kiss to graze upon her lips. To slow the momentum. Carla had other ideas. Her fingers worked the snap on his jeans and slid his zipper open.

Again, he captured her hand to stop the motion.

He caught the murmured *"Ari"* by sinking into her lips. Pressing his palm against the back of her hand, he wrapped his fingers around hers and tugged her hand higher. Together they cupped her breast. His kiss deepened. He let go of her captured hand, and his thumb and forefinger squeezed and rolled her nipple, eliciting a soft moan.

A moan that spread through him, following the same path *forever* had taken, pulsing a beat of lust and love and evermore. He understood Carla's rush. This moment had been a long time coming.

He wrapped his arms around her waist to lift her into the next kiss. Without hesitation, she answered his call to dance. She wrapped her legs around his hips. Her tongue sparred with his as he carried her to the rumpled bed.

Together, they fell across the mattress, her feet settling against the firm bed. With his weight supported on his elbows above her, he couldn't imagine crossing into heaven a worthier cause than settling his body in the V between her legs.

Fire raced through veins with Carla hot beneath him. The swirl of anticipation dancing among the colors in her eyes. He couldn't believe he'd opened to her, trusted her with his life and that of his son's. But he did trust her and love her and wanted her more than he'd ever wanted anyone. His heart swelled.

"You are sure?" Tracing his finger across the rise of her cheek and back down to outline her jaw, he vowed to savor this moment.

Carla nodded as she thrust her hips up, yanking him out of his nanosecond of reflection. She tugged on his shirt before slipping each button undone, lingering, meting out a dose of his own medicine—methodical and agonizingly slow.

"You think you are funny, do you?"

She teased her tongue across her bottom lip. "You wanted slow, cowboy."

Her husky voice sent shock waves through his system. "What I want is—"

"To get you naked." A gleam in her eye accompanied her interruption.

Rising to his knees he yanked his shirt open, sending the last few buttons skittering. Then he stood, toed off his boots, and discarded his jeans and boxer briefs in one fell swoop. He reached into the drawer beside his bed, grabbed a condom, and sheathed himself. No more slow.

"Happy now?" His voice a growl, he crawled back over her. Her grin lit the room.

His knees prodded her legs to open wider.

His weight pressed her deep into the mattress.

Her gaze lowered. "Oh, yeah."

He followed her glance down the length of them to where they were all but joined. "You…" Reaching between them, he eased two fingers into her already wet heat. "…Are a wanton tease."

She raised her hips, mimicking his thrusting fingers, and sighed his name. When he found her sensitive nub with his thumb, she gasped. The sound filling him to painful proportions.

Her eyes glazed over and closed as she opened herself up to him.

"Love, open your eyes." They fluttered and closed again. "I want to see you," he murmured, as he stroked her. When her eyes remained shut, he stopped the caress. Her eyes popped open and her gaze snapped to meet his.

"Much better."

"You…don't play fair."

"All is fair in war…and love." He thrust his fingers deep. She lifted off the mattress before tensing and breaking into a shudder.

"There you go, love." He rode out her explosion, basking in the feel of her tightening around his fingers. Knowing she would do it again once he entered her.

"I—oh—" She relaxed against the mattress, straining to catch her breath.

He pressed his lips against her neck, nuzzling her, as his erection probed her opening and she spread her legs wider to invite him home. He slipped into her, easing inch by inch into the soul-saving warmth of her. And struggled for breath as she closed around him.

Never had he wanted to mark a woman as his alone.

Never had he wanted to keep a woman under him forever.

Never had he wanted a woman like he wanted Carla.

It wasn't just the warmth, but the sense of peace and contentment…at last…followed by a sudden rush of devotion. As if he was being saved and protected and taken to a higher, deeper plane of existence.

Carla moaned his name, thrusting her hips to match his rhythm. "Please. Now."

Yanked out of the clouds, he needed no more invitation.

As he pressed his whole body against her luscious curves and into her warmth, he admitted he could never let her go. That he loved her. All his grumbling about love sucking the life out of a person had been wrong. *This woman* was what love was all about.

"Oh gawd, Ari. Keep… Almost." She convulsed around him, sending him over the edge with her into magnificent freefall. Wrapping his arms around her, he clung on for life, as if without her as his parachute, he'd plummet off the edge of the earth. The sudden fast drop eased into a lazy drift, and together they floated back to solid ground.

Entwined they lay against each other, content and sated.

He hated to leave the warmth of her body. With reluctance, to keep from crushing her, he rolled off to lie on his side. She turned to face him, pressing her curves into him. The remaining embers of the fire they tried so hard to extinguish reignited with her touch.

Ari kissed her, his lips grazing across hers slow and steady, willing his body to settle into the comfort of afterglow. "I want you…again," he mumbled against her mouth.

She pulled back a breath of an inch and grinned. "I noticed."

"You are pleased with yourself."

Her fingers smoothed over his lips. "Yes."

"I am glad you are so agreeable." He teased, watching the glimmer of playfulness turn her eyes a shade darker.

"Oh, I plan to keep right on being agreeable."

He fingered a wisp of hair—shots of fire dancing with sunshine. "If only we had time to test that premise—you being agreeable, two times in a row. But…"

"But?"

He hated to put a damper on their ardor. "Jaime finishes his studies soon, and he will expect to see you."

She pecked him on the cheek and sat up, grabbing the sheet to cover her breasts.

He slipped his finger under the edge and pulled it back to her waist. "Do not hide."

She laughed. "I'm not hiding. It's self-preservation. If we can't…you're tempting me, Ari." She pulled out of his reach and swung her legs over the edge of the bed. "We should get dressed."

Leaning back, his hands clasped behind his neck, he studied the arch of her spine as it sloped down to her backside before flaring into womanly curves. He shoved down the disappointment when she reached for the big T-shirt, the soft cotton now drifting down over her hips and delectable buttocks to settle above her knees as she stood.

She turned. "You plan to spend the rest of the day lolling about in bed?"

"I would wish to do that, yes."

When she blushed, his penis rose.

Her gaze darted from him to the wall, lighting on the panoramic photo that spread as wide as the king-sized bed. She strolled closer, her forefinger tracing the line of steps as they cut down through a bluff of volcanic rock to meet the beach.

"Is this your Portega?"

"I live at the top of the bluff."

"How many steps?"

"Over three hundred."

"Your sand is black."

"From basalt, the volcanic rock."

"Basalt? Very much like here."

"Yes, your near-by town of Basalt nestles against the mountainside, much like in my country."

"What are these flowers?" She pointed to the color cascading down the sides of the rocky cliff.

"Trailing roses and bougainvillea."

"This photo is fabulous." She turned to survey the rest of the room. "Many beautiful photos." She grinned. "I guess I only noticed you…and the bed when I first walked in here."

He pushed to sitting and slid off the bed. "Thank you." He started to reach out his hand, wanting to touch her. Again. But if he did, they'd never make it downstairs to see Jaime.

"For the compliment about the photos? Or for only noticing you and the bed?"

Resisting the tease and the need to touch her, Ari muttered *both* and moved away from her to retrieve the clothes he had left scattered on the floor. As he reached for his jeans, she leaned in to look at the bottom corner of the photo, the big T-shirt rising up her thighs as she read the signature on the corner of the picture. He summoned every ounce of willpower to resist the spunky and passionate woman half naked in his bedroom.

She turned to stare at him. "This is you. Your photos?"

"Yes." *Please do not pursue this subject.* He stepped into his pants and shrugged on his shirt, until he remembered the missing buttons. Discarding it on the chair, he moved toward the closet to find something to wear and escape her scrutiny of his photos and his love of photography. His interest had been a bone of contention between him and his father.

"Do you have any you've taken in Colorado? You could have an incredible exhibit."

"No." He disappeared into the depths of the walk-in, hoping to end the conversation. When he grabbed a clean shirt and turned, Carla stood in front of him, just inside the closet door.

"Why not? You have a gift. In fact…photos like these would look amazing in the entrance to our new school."

When he shook his head, she moved closer. "But why not? I know you don't need the money, but that's not the point. It's the beauty you've captured. You know the long hall with the bank of windows leading into the school. Can you imagine what I mean—huge photos of the mountains and our valley along that wall for all to see from the sidewalk?" She laid her hand on his arm. "You have a special talent."

He stepped back, then skirted around her. "I have no time for pursuing a trivial hobby that has no meaning."

Even though he didn't believe the words he said, he wished to end the discussion. He closed himself off for the same reason he gave in to his father—easier than going to battle over his *trivial hobby*. He no longer had it in him to expose the raw emotion that photography invoked—once his escape from the rigid life of royalty. Why had he bothered to sign his work before hanging them in what he deemed his private sanctuary in America?

Carla followed on his heels. "How can you call your work trivial? My gawd, don't you have a clue how breathtaking these are? And here in Colorado, the views are as spectacular. The lighting, the—"

Ari raised his hand to cut her off. "Jaime waits." And strode from the room.

He berated himself for reverting to his haughty royal stance. He wanted to turn. To apologize to Carla. He moved down the hall. Away from his wish to allow himself to love another woman. His wish to fit in with the people in his new country, now his home. His wish to be friends with his father, if it was not in the stars to be loved by him.

He stopped midpoint down the hall. Who did he kid? He had fallen in love with Carla. He ached to fit in with his Mineral Springs neighbors. And his father had come to visit with no bidding from him. They were finally starting to forge a relationship.

All the emotion evoked by discussing, or rather not discussing, his passion for photography ground a ragged hole deep into the pit of his stomach, as he sought escape. His wishes, his wants, and what he had started with Carla—now all in a forward momentum. Now unstoppable.

Chapter Twenty-six

Ari hid out in his office. He was a first-class chicken, as Giles reminded him several times throughout the day.

He couldn't tell Giles he'd made love with Carla. That he loved her. And that the thought scared the hell out of him.

Love.

He promised himself never to fall in love again. But it had snuck up on him. No, that was a falsehood. He should have recognized love was burrowing its way under his thin skin since the moment the spirited Ms. Peters had confronted him up on Silver Mountain on a perfectly glorious, spring day. And that despite his temper at being called out by her and then her insult to his fatherhood, he'd fallen immediately for her spunky independence.

He had no one else to blame but himself for what happened last night. He should have had Sénhora Adélia deliver Carla's soup and run her bath and make sure she was tucked in down the hall in one of their many guest rooms. Instead, he insisted on making sure she was recovered from her ordeal. He had been so afraid for her. Never mind his need to stay in rescue mode when she had looked at him wide-eyed and grateful for his help.

Stoking the fire and making sure she had clean dry clothes, it never occurred to him an hour later they would be falling into his bed.

And now what was he to do? Run beneath the scrub like a frightened Jack Rabbit and hide.

He glanced around his sanctuary. Yes, a chicken and a startled Jack Rabbit described him perfectly.

His interoffice buzzer sounded. Pulled from uncomfortable thoughts, he barked into the intercom. "Can this not wait?"

"My baby brother, your mood has deteriorated since this morning. That is quite a feat."

"I am tired. And busy."

"Your father has been trying to reach you. I told him you had an appointment. I did not tell him it was with Jaime. Fair warning, he will call again this afternoon. You might want to answer and get it over with."

"Must I?"

"You do reign in your own *palace*, so no. But it might be prudent. You know your father. It will only be worse if he must call and call. He is anxious to get to the Silver Mine Ranch."

Ari scrubbed his hand through his hair. "He must think me a god who can control the weather and hurry along road repairs."

Giles laughed. "He is nothing if not predictable and single-minded. Thought I would give you fair warning."

"You are right. I have been ignoring his calls all day. I will answer the next time."

"Then call me so we can review the agenda for his visit. The roads and bridge should be repaired by tomorrow."

"So soon? I had hoped—"

"To keep your Carla prisoner a bit longer?"

"Must you always—"

Giles laughter faded with the click of the intercom.

Carla grabbed Jaime's hand. "Let's go to the barn. Show me your papa's stable."

"*Sim.*" Jaime tugged her hand. "See Bennie."

The warm, spring sun blazed the day following the ice storm. As Jaime stroked Bennie's forelock, joy swept through Carla like a fast-moving stream bubbling over bare toes. He stretched, offering up a sugar cube. The little pony lipped the sweet offering from Jaime's palm before nuzzling the boy's neck.

"See. He eats just like Cupcake."

Her heart almost missed a beat when she thought about how far Jaime, and Ari, had come after the traumatic death of Arianna.

Yeah, she had a part in their healing, but she had to give Ari credit. Despite his usual arrogant stance about anything, underneath all the bluster beat a caring and loving heart.

Loving. Did he realize he had the capability to love again?

She hadn't seen Ari since dinner the night before. He'd begged off any interaction, claiming too much work. Carla read Jaime his story and put him to bed. Giles had said she was to sleep in Ari's room. She'd fought the blush, but Giles features gave no indication he had a clue what had transpired earlier.

The lonely night she spent tossing and turning in Ari's big bed alone had crushed her spirit. Had he regretted making love as he once regretted kissing her?

No. He had been as fully involved as she. And not in the physical sense. This had been different. She'd seen it in his eyes. Felt it in his slow and deliberate attention. Careful. As if he treasured her.

He hadn't run until she dared question him on his photos. And pushed. When would she learn she couldn't push Ari about revealing the troubles that lay deep within him?

But she wanted to know everything about him. The photos had been a side of him she hadn't imagined. Passion displayed in every picture on his wall. A passion for his homeland. A passion for life, if he'd let the veil of self-protection drop. She'd caught glimpses of his desire to show his true self. But then he clammed up and turned into his haughty, closed-off persona.

Despite the valiant battle to remain uninvolved, making love committed both to try. They weren't there yet. Ari's shield remained solid and bullet-proof, hiding one more secret about his relationship with his father. His photography triggered some fear.

She hoped space would help him process all that had happened between them. And, with patience, Ari would come around. Right now, though, she had no choice but to wait him out—battered bridge, washed out roads, and a crushed truck had seen to that.

To quell her questions and insecurities and quiet her mind, she focused on her visit with Jaime, fully engaged in *his* new passion around the stables and Bennie. She listened to his excited chatter as they made their way to the gardens and the wooden table nestled under the overhang of the shed.

"Look how they've grown."

"And they survived the storm. It's a good thing we put them against the wall for protection."

With a gentleness not common for a six-year old, he fingered the slim stalk of the newly rooted sunflower they'd planted. "How tall will they get when they finish growing?"

Carla raised her hand as high over her head as she could reach.

Jaime jumped up and down. "That tall?"

"Probably taller. Then the big, beautiful flowers will bloom—like sunny faces."

"I can't wait. How long?"

She ruffled his soft hair. "You'll have to wait until the end of summer. It takes a long time to grow that tall." His dejected face made her laugh. "Honey, maybe next time I visit we can plant something else that won't take as long to grow."

"What?"

"I'm not sure. Tell you what. I'll surprise you with seeds."

"Can we plant pretty pink flowers?'

"We can, but those won't grow fast either."

He lowered his gaze.

"What's wrong?"

"My mommy liked pink flowers."

She knelt beside him and cradled his hand in hers. "We can find some seeds for pink flowers. Until then, would you like me to buy some pink flowers so you can have them by your bed?"

He nodded and shuffled his toe against the dirt. "I miss my mommy."

She tugged him to her and pulled him into her arms until his head lay against her shoulder. "Of course you do. But remembering she loves pink flowers is like having her with you in here." She tapped his heart. "You'll always have your love and memories, Jaime."

A minute later he pulled back. "Soon, we'll have pink flowers in the garden, too." And with that, he skipped down the path toward the gate. "I'm hungry."

After lunch, Jaime dragged Carla down the hall toward his father's study.

Carla pulled back, stopping halfway. "Your father is working. Maybe we should go to your room and clean up before dinner."

"No, Ms. Carla. Papa expects me every afternoon. It is past time for our chess game."

Her heart tripped at the thought of Ari teaching Jaime to play chess.

"Come, Ms. Carla." Jaime tugged her toward the closed door.

Nerves skittered up her spine. How would he feel when she invaded his space today? She'd give anything to watch the chess match, but she would duck out and give them time together.

The tug on her hand became more insistent. Jaime delivered them just as the door swung open.

Ari nodded toward Carla, then directed his gaze toward his son. "You have had fun today?"

"*Sim*, Papa.

"Ah." Laugh lines formed at the corners of his eyes. "I could tell. You are late for our game." His mouth straightened, but Carla noted the glint of a tease emanating from his eyes.

Obviously, Jaime saw through Ari's game, as he laughed and raced toward the chess board set up in front of the leather couch. A small wooden chair with a matching cushion was positioned on the other side of the low table. The boy sat. "Come, Papa. Today I'll win."

Ari backed away from the door, his dark gaze never lifting from Carla's mouth.

"Papa?"

"One moment."

Ari's gaze moved slowly up to meet hers.

Carla's heartbeat thrummed a path from her chest to lodge in her throat. She backed up. "I should go...let you have time together."

"You do not want to miss a game where Jaime beats his father, do you?" His mouth quirked in a lopsided grin. He reached for her wrist and drew her through the door.

Maybe he didn't regret yesterday. Maybe he was running scared. She got it. The fear of what lay ahead versus the tingle of immediate need that arched between them.

An hour later, the game ended with Jaime losing, but barely. Jaime's head bent in disappointment.

Ari motioned for the boy to come to the couch. As Jaime leaned against his knee, Ari ran his hand through the boy's hair. "Look at me. You have learned much about this game. Yes?" Jaime nodded. "Sooner than you know, you will win."

A tentative smile formed. "*Sim*, Papa. I'm much better than I was, even last week."

"Yes, you are. Have you been going behind my back and playing with Uncle Giles?" Ari's brow lifted, as he smiled.

Jaime laughed. "How do you know *everything*, Papa?"

"Ah, when you become a father, you will know the answer to that question. Now go, get cleaned up for dinner."

Carla rose as Jaime raced for the door.

"He does not need your assistance. Right, Jaime? You can wash up on your own and look at the clock to know when dinner is served."

"*Sim,* Papa." His chest puffed, as he stood tall. "I can do this all by myself." And he disappeared, his feet pounding down the hall in proud retreat.

Carla wasn't sure what to do. She started babbling. "Jaime knows so much about your horses. He's much more comfortable in the stables. He told me each of their names and what each like best for treats. Sugar cubes and carrots and apples—"

She stopped the litany mid-sentence, as Ari rose from the couch. He stepped around the coffee table and stood, feet planted wide. His gaze traveled over her. Her body reacted.

When he moved toward her like a mountain lion stalking his prey, she willed her legs to hold her upright.

He stopped a breath away and pressed his warm finger against her mouth. "I've wanted to do this all day." Replacing his finger with his lips, he nipped and licked, feasting on every inch of her mouth.

Sagging against him, she moaned her impatience. Why did he always want slow when her body channeled an exploding furnace? He continued to test her willpower. She clasped her fingers at the base of his neck and seized the moment to deepen the kiss. His pleasure throbbed against her belly.

"Maybe you should lock the door, cowboy." She purred in her most sultry voice.

He mumbled agreement against her lips. She gloated at her success to hurry things along. But rather than moving toward the door, he found the hem of her shirt and trailed hot fingers across her belly. As his hands moved up, the phone on his desk trilled.

He stepped back, regret crossing his face in the purse of his lips. "Business." He dropped a quick kiss on her mouth before turning toward his desk. "Remember where we left off."

Answering the phone in crisp efficiency he listened for a moment, then his tone deepened, and his voice dropped. "I see."

Carla moved toward the door, but Ari held up his hand and mouthed *stay*.

"It is impossible. Tomorrow we hope for access." Again, he listened. "I understand." When he hung up, the receiver sounded a loud thud against its cradle.

She could tell he was no longer in a good mood. "I should go. You have work."

Ari scrubbed his hand through his hair and moved from behind his desk. "Not work. Family. Dealing with father and his impatience at the weather."

She stopped in the middle of the room, not sure how to

respond. Anything about his life in Portega appeared to be off-limits.

She tried for lighthearted. "And what can you do about the weather?"

"Exactly. He arrived in Aspen right before the storm yesterday. The Crown Prince is highly perturbed he cannot reach the ranch." This time, his voice sounded downright cheery. Perching on the front edge of his desk, he smiled and held out his hands.

She walked across the room and placed her hands in his.

"You will help me enjoy my last day of freedom?" His eyes lit, as he pulled her into the V of his legs.

Letting go of one hand, she stroked his mussed hair back from his forehead. "Freedom? The Crown Prince can't be that bad."

"He is not a bad man, merely a man with high expectations for his youngest son."

"And his reach stretches all the way to Mineral Springs?"

He rubbed his thumb in circles on the back of her hand. It wasn't sensual. The soothing gesture was contemplative, as he watched the motion of his own thumb. He looked up. "In a way. He has no say in my operation."

"Then why is there tension between the two of you? You mentioned—" She bit her lip, not sure whether her comments would ruin the conversation and Ari's good mood. "Your photos. He doesn't approve of your interest?"

"He wants me to succeed here at the ranch. Any distractions are trivial."

"You use that word again. Trivial. The photographs reflect your passion for life. Plus, all work and no play—have you heard that idiom?"

"Forget the photos, Carla."

Her stomach churned. Again, she pushed. When would she learn to keep her mouth shut?

"I hang them on my walls to remind me of my home and of my goals here. There is nothing else to them."

She didn't believe him. But she would drop the subject for

now. "What are your goals?"

"To perfect breeding methods. An important business in my homeland. I wish—" He looked away, as if seeing his own office for the first time, filled with bookshelves and dark leather and portraits of horses and the accouterments of running a business. Carla followed his gaze. Very little in the boldly masculine decorated room said much about who Ari really was as a person. She imagined his bedroom reflected more of his spirit than he cared to admit—romantic, family first, love for his country, and an eye for understanding the world and nature surrounding him. So different from the businessman persona who must succeed at all costs.

"Tell me about your father." She softened her tone to let him know she wasn't demanding an answer. But wanted one, if he cared to divulge. She wanted to know all about their relationship. It could explain a lot. Like why Ari continually shut down.

"Not now."

She persisted. If they were to go on as lovers, she needed to understand. "Why is he here?"

"To check on me. He does care." He shook his head. "Never mind."

"Sometimes..." she placed her fingertips under his chin, "Our parents forget we are adults."

He gave her a tentative smile. "My father sees it as his duty to have the last word on much of what I do."

She sighed and placed her arms around his neck. "I can relate to that."

He cocked his head.

Laughing, she said, "Not only my father, but all four brothers believe they must have the last say in what I do."

"But of course, you are a woman."

Annoyance punched into her.

He laughed, placing his large palms at her waist and pulling her flush against him. "I jest. Dear Carla, you are your own woman, of that I am positive."

"You're lucky I didn't break your nose with that comment."

His eyes turned smoky, as his palms cut a hot swath from her waist to rest on her hips. "I have no doubt I am lucky. You are a woman filled with much passion." His hands moved around to her backside. "Passion that draws me to you, no matter how hard I try to resist."

"You didn't resist yesterday."

"No—" His mouth edged closer. "I did not…and I am glad of it."

She pulled her arms from around his neck and cupped his face. Brushing her mouth across his warm lips, she whispered, "Me too."

After dinner, Ari and Carla walked upstairs hand-in-hand. Jaime skipped ahead of them.

"Come." Jaime gestured toward Carla as he ran into his room.

She stood against the doorframe and shook her head. "This is your time with your Papa. I will stand right here."

Moments later, Carla could guarantee Jaime forgot she stood close by.

He bounced from his closet to his dresser, disagreeing about which PJs he should wear to bed. "I wish the ones with the stars and moon."

Amazed when Ari finally calmed him down enough to hop into bed, she agreed to take turns reading the three books Jaime had chosen. Halfway through the third, he nodded off.

Once they turned out the light and crept into the hallway, Carla paused in front of Ari. She stood on her tiptoes and kissed him on the cheek. "Thank you for rescuing me yesterday."

His soft chuckle brushed her ear. "*Now* it is fine with you when I rescue?"

"All right, don't rub it in. I do like to take care of myself."

He skimmed the back of his hand down her cheek. "And you did. But the weather was a mighty foe. What else would I have done but come for you?"

Two days earlier, she would have busted him for being a chauvinist. But now?

"Yesterday, I didn't know what to think. Today, I know I can count on you." She looked down the hallway toward the suite of rooms she'd stayed in weeks earlier, now occupied by the new nanny. "I'm a bit tired. If you can let me know which room I can use tonight…"

He stared at her. "Mine, of course."

She shook her head. "Not a good idea—with Jaime, and…"

"Did Jaime find out you were in my bed last night?"

"Ari, I was alone. You slept in your office."

"To allow you to rest after your ordeal."

"After you *ravished* me, you mean."

"As I recall, you ravished me, as well. That is not the point. You needed your rest."

"Really? Tell the truth. You were mad because I asked about your photos."

"Not angry. I am prone to bad moods when my father is nearby. And worried about what he will say when he inspects the Silver Mine operations."

Resting her hands on his hips, she couldn't help but ask, "Why do you give him so much power?"

"Why do you give your family power?"

"Stop with the answering my question with a question."

"I recall you are an expert at the same tactic of evasion."

She laughed. "I believe we are talking about you now."

He pulled her against him. "The truth? I am a perfectionist. I need to prove myself." She looked up at him. Saying nothing, she lifted her hand to stroke his jaw line. "You are right. I do let him have the power. I should take lessons from you on how you handle those brothers of yours."

"Once I moved away from the ranch, I was able to gather my nerves to face them down."

"You did. And they admire you for your independence."

"I'm not so sure." She sighed.

"Ah, but they do. However, their respect does not stop them from wanting to protect you."

"Isn't that the same as not believing I can take care of myself?"

He brushed her hair back off her shoulders, sending a shiver slipping down her back. "Men will always want to protect a woman, no matter how capable she is. You must understand it is not that a woman is helpless, it is that a man must feel strong and competent enough to protect his woman."

She leaned back to look into his brooding eyes as he admitted what he perceived as his weakness, and his way of overcoming such faults. Like father, like son. "Have you considered your father must protect and instruct you for the same reason, so he continues to feel capable and powerful?"

Ari's eyes grew as large as an onyx gem.

"It may be his way of staying connected to you, now that you are so far away."

He cocked his head, glancing at the wall sconces. His eyes narrowed, as he obviously thought through her observation. "You may be right. Perhaps I should not take his criticisms so personally."

"Make him feel needed when he comes tomorrow. He may lighten up a bit."

"Perhaps." He tugged her closer. "Now, back to the subject of sleeping arrangements."

Much as she wanted to crawl into his bed and stay there forever, she said, "I'll sleep in the guestroom."

His hand swept down her neck to rest at her collarbone, hovering above her breast. "You believe I would sleep with you as, how do you say, in the moment and then let you go? No. That is not the way of it, Carla. I do not intend to let you go. You will be in my bed tonight."

Before she could argue with him, his lips grazed hers. She tried to fight the want and need and belief that this thing with Ari was really happening—could work between them. And, that he wasn't telling her *what* to do, but what he *wished* she would do. Rather than fight the inevitable, she let him take her hand and lead her toward the other wing.

As she stepped into his sitting room, the photo on the wall

that she had somehow missed yesterday stopped her dead in her tracks. "That's taken from…" She turned to Ari. "When?"

"Last week. I just hung it."

"It's…well, stunning. You were up on Silver Mountain."

He nodded.

"Where we first met."

"I wanted to capture the valley after the snow melted."

"The lighting is spectacular."

"I caught it as the storm clouds moved in. The sun was low enough to skate under the clouds."

"And reflect the light in that weird and wonderful way. Talk about right place at the right time."

"That saying can be used many times over." He stepped between her and the photo. His knuckles trailed a path down her cheek. "The mud slide—you enough feet ahead of where it hit." His thumb traced a path along her bottom lip. "I am thankful you were in the right place at the right time."

Caught in his stare, she wanted to nibble on his thumb and draw it into her mouth. Better…she wanted to stand on tiptoe and suck on his luscious lips. "I'm grateful you sought me out to help Jaime. I've learned to value you and your son. More than you know."

"You refer to the day we met and you raised my ire by accusing me of being the worst example of fatherhood?"

"As I fought my attraction to you."

"That is the day I also fought my attraction to you."

His dark gaze raked over her as it had that first day. The day she was both frightened of and in lust with him. The day she vowed to help his son no matter how much he intimidated her. "Now you exaggerate, *your highness*, as you well know."

"As do you. But knowing of my anger did not preclude you from showing your passionate response."

"Passionate? Your anger—" She raised her arms and twined them around his neck to draw him close. "You love to push my buttons."

His cocked brow raised a question about her idiom.

"Push my buttons, as in poke fun at me to get a reaction."

"Ah, yes, that I do. I love to watch your eyes darken and blaze—as they do now."

"And what will you do about it, cowboy?"

"You dare to *challenge* me?" He grabbed her around the waist, then lifted her to carry her to the bed, where he deposited her smack in the middle. With a grin as wide as the Mineral Springs canyon, he fell upon her. "Now I show you what I will do about your *insolence*."

A sigh slipped from her lips as she stretched out her arms to encourage him.

Chapter Twenty-seven

Carla gazed out the window at the activity on the ranch grounds, before she headed to the kitchen for coffee.

By eleven a.m., the crews had cleared the road enough that the Crown Prince and his entourage would make it across the river and up the pass to the ranch house. They were due at noon.

Giles had towed Carla's truck to the large garage behind the estate. The damage to the truck bed and the axle, among other things, would be too expensive to fix. It was totaled and that meant Carla needed to scrape together the dough to buy another.

"I wish you didn't have to go. Jaime loves having you here." Giles slid in across from her in the breakfast nook.

Carla glanced over the top of her coffee mug suspended half-way to her mouth. "Ari needs time with his father. I'll be back next week."

Giles leaned forward, "I'll be frank. You have managed to lighten things up around here. Ari is less—" He picked his mug up and slugged back the last of his coffee.

"What? Ari is less what?"

"He's the happiest I've seen him in years. Please stay."

"I can't. My school." *My brothers. My father. My heart.*

"I've no doubt Ari would set you up with your own office. The nanny will be here for Jaime."

Carla shook her head. "We're so close. I need to be on premise, working with Betsy. Plus, I promised Jaime an overnight with Aaron."

"Why not bring Aaron here. You could stay on—"

"*So not* a good idea. You know that." She glanced at her watch. "In fact, I'd better call Ore and have him come for me. If I wait any longer, he'll be too busy."

"It is not necessary to call your brother." The deep voice came from the kitchen entrance leading out to the patio. The familiar click of boots crossed the tile floor. "I will escort you to town. As soon as my father has paid his obligatory visit, we can leave." Ari poured himself a cup of coffee from the carafe by the stove. Leaning against the counter, he added, "After lunch."

"No." Carla placed her mug on the table and stood. "I should go now, before your father comes."

"You will be here to meet the Crown Prince. He expects it."

"What? He knows about me?"

"Of course. Jaime talks of you often."

Carla glanced at Giles, who shrugged, before she swung her gaze back to Ari. She bit her lower lip. She thought they had come to some sort of understanding about over-protectiveness and control. *Guess not.* His words, and stance, commanded she stay and meet his father.

"Also…" Ari's lips parted as if he fought a smile. As if he read her mind. "I may have mentioned you, as well."

"Really? And specifically, what might you have mentioned about me?" She imitated his formal tone, forgiving his royal command moments ago.

Giles stood. "My cue to leave."

She ignored Giles' exit and watched Ari take a sip of coffee and place his cup on the counter. "Come here."

"No." If she went anywhere near him, he'd distract her and never answer her question.

"Do not act the child, Carla. Come here so I can tell you what I told my father."

"I can hear you fine from here."

"Then I shall not tell you what my father and I discussed."

"Now who is acting childish?"

He grinned. "One must fight fire with fire." He pointed his forefinger straight at her, then crooked it to beckon her.

Dang. She was in so much trouble. Despite her argument that she needed to be in town to work on her school, she didn't want to leave the Silver Mine, or Ari, or his big bed.

She strolled toward him, stopping just out of reach and crossing her arms over her chest. "Tell me."

He reached across the divide between them to snake his arm around her waist and pulled her closer until she stood between his legs. "I told him…" He bent, nibbling a path along her collarbone.

She shivered and tried to push him away before he totally distracted her.

"I told him I have met a woman who gives me a run for my money." He nipped at her jaw with his teeth. "Tests me every step of the way." Soothed the tiny bite with a lick. "Makes my blood boil when she lies across my bed—"

This time, she shoved hard with both hands against his chest. His arms, now anchored at her lower back, made it impossible to escape, so she leaned back and looked into his eyes. Tiny lines radiated from the corners and the silver flecks danced. "You did not say that. Did you?"

"Most of it. I did not mention the last part, although it is true." He bent his head and feathered his lips across hers.

Carla walked her fingers up his chest, then wrapped her arms around his neck and melted into his kiss. She was doomed. Gawd, she loved—head over heels—the eighth son of the Crown Prince of Portega. For a woman who did not want a strong, possessive man in her life, she couldn't get any deeper in trouble than with this man whose tongue now tangled with hers.

The kiss seemed to go on and on and on, until both were breathless.

Ari reveled in the feel of Carla's fingers tangled in his hair, the taste of coffee on her lips, the warmth of her body pressed against him. He never wanted this kiss to end.

He hung on to Carla as if his life depended on it. Maybe it did in some convoluted way.

In two days, she had indeed gotten under his skin. He felt

more alive than he'd felt in years…maybe in forever. Carla Peters was a different breed of woman. She challenged him. Made him laugh. Made him think about life that included many pleasures—his photography and his horses and, of course, his son. And now Carla. Made him want to believe in love and forever.

And made him want to get to know his father. Really get to know him. And work to forgive his father for all the transgressions he'd imagined all these years.

"I do wish you would stay," he murmured against her lips. "Please stay and meet Father. It's important to me that he get to know you."

She pulled back, her beautiful eyes flashing. "Really?"

"Of course. Why would you not believe that?" He fingered the tip of her side braid, the color of a late summer wheat field, that rested against her chest. "Did not the last few days convince you of how I feel."

"I-I, yes, but—"

"No buts, Car-la. Either you believe in me—us—or you do not."

She fingered the lapel of his dress shirt, the one he rarely wore anymore. A shiver reached deep inside him at her tender touch. "I do."

"That is good. Because, I do too. Believe in us." He glanced at the stucco kitchen ceiling that reminded him of home. "And therefore, it is imperative that you meet Father."

"Imperative? I do love it when you use those royal-ordered words."

"Ha." He threw his head back and laughed, as if all the joy that had been bottled up in him for years burst out at her words. "Oh, yes, you do challenge me at every turn. Father will be enthralled."

She glanced down, then lifted her gaze to meet his. "Really? Enthralled is such a…powerful word. One that must be lived up to. You put a lot of pressure on me, Prince Orula."

"You doubt your appeal? Since the moment I met you, you have captivated me. And I would add, held your own. Made me work to deny myself your company, despite your tendency toward irritating me." He grinned. Grinned. Carla made him grin, not offer his usual stiff, and seldom dispersed, smile.

She reached up on tiptoe, her palms resting firmly against his chest, and kissed him. Lightly. The barest of touches. And smiled. "I supposed I can no longer deny you either."

He pulled her closer, rested his chin on the top of her head. "Thank you."

The Crown Prince strode toward the stables on Ari's heels. Carla hung back, watching the similar gait, as if in competition to see who would reach the goal first.

They needed time alone. But since his father had arrived, Ari had insisted Carla join them for everything. Lunch in the formal dining room with Jaime, a business chat with Giles in Ari's study, and now a tour of the horse breeding operation.

Maybe they wouldn't miss her if she turned back to the house.

The Crown Prince stopped and glanced back. He beckoned to Carla. Ari had already reached the double doors to the barn, unaware either of them lingered.

"You and Ari should have this time. I'll wait back—"

"Nonsense. I enjoy your company." The Crown Prince strode toward her, on a mission. "Ari is more relaxed with you here."

"Relaxed?"

The man bellowed out a laugh. "As relaxed as he can be. He takes life so seriously."

"He is conscientious about everything he does. He takes pride—"

"That I know. But sometimes it is too much. He is never satisfied with what he has accomplished." The Crown Prince smiled. "You must know of what I speak."

"Yes. But it's not a bad trait."

"No, it is commendable. Of all my sons—"

"Father?"

Carla looked over the shoulder of the Crown Prince. He wasn't as tall as his son, but just as imposing with the same onyx eyes and regal stance. Ari stood behind his father. His eyes shone with the intensity that signaled he was in his royal mode. His shoulders tight, his back stiff, and his lips drawn straight. His posturing was an attempt at self-protection. She feared he might crack.

"You were telling Carla?"

For a moment, the Crown Prince looked taken aback. But then he threw his head back and laughed. "Ah, my son. I was telling Carla nothing she did not already know. But if you must hear what I have to say, I will tell you." He glanced back at Carla, winked, and snagged her hand before turning to face Ari's stony glare. Carla felt the gentle squeeze of the older man's hand. "Of all my sons, you have made me the proudest. You ask nothing of me. You must do it all on your own."

Ari's mouth opened like a gaping river trout stunned by capture.

"I pushed each of you to find your own path. But you are the only one who did so with no help from me or advantage from your position."

"I always thought…"

"That I did not love you? That I did not respect you?" The Crown Prince shook his head. "This is my fault. Trying to give you independence. All I wanted was for you to find your heart, your passion. I have noticed your prints. I was wrong. Your excitement lies not only with your horses, but with your photography. You have found your passion here in Colorado." His other hand swept toward the stable and the Colorado vista beyond. And then he looked from Ari to rest his gaze on Carla. "And right here in Mineral Springs."

Chapter Twenty-eight

Ari cradled the phone tight against his ear and glanced back at the partially closed door of the bedroom. He was surprised the trill of the phone hadn't awakened Carla.

He worked to keep his words firm yet conciliatory to a certain degree. All the while his insides churned at the situation, and his wish to *kill* the inane man who bothered him at this hour. The man who had caused him to lie to Carla. Not betray her, because what he did was the opposite. Yet when she found out, she would view it as betrayed trust.

He wanted this ruse over and done with.

He'd been pulled from the depths of sleep, cradled against Carla's firm bottom, his face buried in her hair that smelled like rosewater and wild, sweet thyme. Wrung out from a long day working with his father's mare while wanting desperately to be in Carla's arms. They had finally calmed an excited Jaime who had read them a book, stumbling over only a few words in English. He had been proud and hard to coax to sleep. When Ari and Carla finally found his bed, they'd been frantic to make love.

He scrubbed his hand across his face. *Damn this blasted Duggans.*

Now, the infernal man insisted on a final meeting to squeeze what he thought was a bottomless pit of money that Ari would give up to ensure he had water on his ranch.

"Duggans, you better not be screwing with me this time. You do and the deal is off."

Tonight, they would nail him red-handed. The first

installment of coded money Ari had handed over had been traced by the Feds to the bank account Duggans had opened with an alias. From there, the Feds also had traced the route back to the outfit who paid Duggans to siphon and divert water down state.

The man had made a strategic mistake by blackmailing one customer while taking payment for delivery of the same commodity with another. Not only that, but they believed Ari that the man had a third scheme up his shady sleeve—cripple his neighbors so he could buy their properties to obtain mineral rights. Now, they would nail Ken Duggans once and for all. And Ari could get back to concentrating on his son, the job he loved, and the woman who had stolen his heart.

He thumbed off his phone and dialed the Feds. "Midnight. Rustler's Grill." A Pause. "I will wait until you are in position and then go in the front door." Another pause. "Yes, I will call him next."

In seconds, his thumb moved across the lit screen and dialed. He hated to wake others at this hour, but it was necessary to carry out the plan.

"Midnight. Rustler's Grill." He paused. "Meet in the garage in five." Again, a pause. "The SUV." That was Giles taken care of. He tapped the phone again.

In hushed tones he spoke. "Now. The others will meet you at the end of your drive. They'll issue further instructions. You can follow them in."

Ari set the phone aside, curious at the rustle he thought he heard from the bedroom. Had he awoken Carla? He extinguished the lamp in the sitting room and strode toward the half-open bedroom door. She was right where he had left her, curled in a ball under the covers. He wanted nothing more than to crawl in beside her, wake her slowly with his fingers and his lips, make love to her again. But he had a job to do. With stealth, he entered the bedroom. He pulled on black jeans and a black turtleneck. Lifting his boots, he carried them to the open door, grabbing his wallet off the bureau in passing.

When he got to the doorway, he turned.

Carla kept her eyes squeezed shut and her head buried under the edge of the blanket. She counted to one-hundred, before she heard the *snick* of the suite door. She counted to another hundred to be sure. Then she threw off the covers, intent on following Ari.

What the *holy hello* had he been doing talking to Ken Duggans? In the middle of the night? About a deal?

Duggans had always been bad news.

Fingers of nausea curled in her belly at the thought the man she loved was indeed working with the man who they suspected stole their water. But why had Ari then turned around and helped Carter? It made no sense at all. She tiptoed toward the windows in Ari's bedroom.

She couldn't see the front of the house or the garage from his room. But she would be able to catch the beam of his lights as they wove down the road toward the Roaring Fork River.

Her hands shook as she pulled on jeans and a flannel shirt to cover her tee. Her toes were stiff as barn boards when she tried to stuff them into cowboy boots. *Relax.* She sucked in a deep breath and willed her toes to curl enough to slip them into her boots.

The minutes ticked by in slow motion.

Her heart pumped a harsh beat inside her chest. She wanted to crawl back under the covers and hide. She had trusted Ari with her body and her heart. She loved him. Now, she was about to follow him into town and possibly witness his betrayal of her family.

She glanced around the room at the reminders of their lovemaking, and what she thought was commitment after the four weeks since the ice storm. Her book on the side table. Her robe casually thrown over the hassock at the end of the bed. The side-by-side indents of their heads on pillows lying close. The empty condom wrapper tossed aside, reminding her of their rush once they'd tucked Jaime in.

Carter's warnings flooded her brain. She couldn't stop his voice. His pleas to stay away from Ari. His rationalization that Ari had somehow set out to take down the Peters family and business. And now, Ari was on his way to make a deal with Duggans.

But why? How? Carter said he and Ari had settled things. The Peters Valley Ranch cattle now grazed on Ari's land. She'd watched them from the windows at Ari's, some meandering toward the pond, others with their heads bent to mow the grass. Because of the peace she thought the two families had finally reached, she'd let her heart take over and accept that maybe she and Ari could make this work. *With* the blessing of her family.

Carla freed her thoughts of the idyllic and neighborly scene of Peters' cattle grazing in Ari's pasture as the scrape and whine of the garage door, followed by the rev of an engine, brought her back to the now.

Anger replaced regret, as she moved back to the window, heard the crunch of tires on gravel, and watched the beam of lights illuminate the long drive. Ari. On his way in the middle of the night to meet with the enemy. She waited until the tail lights were pinpoints in the dark night and then turned to leave.

The battered truck she'd borrowed from her brother Cole sat at the end of the curved drive, facing downhill—on purpose, since the truck had trouble starting on occasion. She pressed the clutch, let go of the brake, then popped the clutch to set the truck in motion. She turned the key. The truck growled to life in the silent night. She rolled down the hill past the first turn using the light of the almost full moon, before turning on her headlights, even knowing by now Ari had reached the highway.

As the road dipped toward the low-lying river, she downshifted. the tires thumped across the new wooden bridge. She'd driven for years over dark and lonely roads, never before noticing how loud everything sounded in the dead of night. Adrenaline, a raw sense of betrayal, and heartache played havoc on her self-control, heightening her senses and eating away at her gut. She willed her stomach to calm, her heart to stop racing.

Once she drove into the parking lot of the Rustler's Grill, she'd figure out next-steps. Until then, she had to imagine she was psyching herself up for a horse show. Sucking in quick, shallow breaths, she panted the way her mother had taught her to do before every competition.

If her mother had been there, would she have discouraged Carla from chasing a relationship with Ari? Madge had encouraged her. But she couldn't fault Madge—she had a romantic heart and wanted everyone to have what she had with Mitch. A strangled giggle filled the cab. Her dad in a romantic marriage. Like his oldest son, Mitch was a solid and staid man who valued his family and ranch above all else. He would die for either. But a romantic? *I guess if a man can die for you, he is a romantic.* Go figure. Madge had it right.

But not when it came to her faith in Ari, and the relationship she encouraged Carla to explore.

Carla reached the highway. The Rustler's Grill sat on the far edge of town, just this side of her family's spread. *Dang.* She should have called Carter. But how could she explain this craziness?

It's nearing midnight, and I'm on my way to the Grill where I believe Ari is about to sell us out.

No. She'd wait until she found out for sure. Then she'd tell the sheriff and Carter—in that order. No sense having Carter land in jail for roughing up Ari and Duggans, or worse. Carter prided himself on his cool demeanor, thoughtful decision-making, and above-the-board business dealings. But when it came to Ari and stealing water from the ranch, Carter's reaction would not be pretty. Quil could handle it. Ever since they were kids, the sheriff had known how to tame Carter's temper.

A niggle of a thought wormed its way into her brain. Why *had* Ari let them use his pasture? And why had Carter relaxed his stance of abject hatred against the prince?

Because of her. He had fooled them all. And it was her fault for agreeing to work for Ari in the first place.

Chapter Twenty-nine

Carter had stumbled out of bed after the late call from Ari, pulled on jeans and a quilted shirt, and tiptoed to the first floor.

This was it.

He stifled a yawn. Five a.m. had been a long time ago and the next five a.m. lurked a few hours away. He was getting too damn old to be playing cops and robbers in the middle of the night.

His heart pounded at the thought of his role in taking down Duggans. The plan had been in place since the day after Ari brought him into the fold. Not sure he was a good enough actor for this job he suppressed a yawn and pulled forth his inner thespian.

He shrugged into his coat, grabbed a cup of cold coffee from the fridge, and headed to his truck. As soon as this charade was over, he'd soon be in the quiet of his barn doing his morning chores. Back on familiar turf.

He straightened and climbed into his truck to meet the federal agents at the end of the drive, as instructed.

If he could pull off his role, their ranch would have back the stolen water. And soon…he would fill his family in on why he accepted the Prince's help. And…give his blessing to Carla and Ari's relationship, a fact that might throw Carla into apoplexy or a state of shock. Maybe this was the first step in getting not only his family, but the entire valley to accept Ari Orula as part of this community.

Carter's fury at Ken Duggans spurred him on. He wouldn't let the team or his family down.

Chapter Thirty

Carla pulled into the far end of the parking lot of the Rustler's Grill.

She stopped beyond the reach of the circle of lights that flooded the front entrance, scanned the row of parked cars and took inventory. Ari's black SUV parked near the back alley. Shawn's beat up pick-up and a few trucks belonging to other friends in the well-lit parking area out front.

At least she wouldn't be alone.

A big, black car with tinted windows sat with its parking lights on at the entrance to the back alley. Strange.

As she looked for Duggans' slick, black jeep, beams of light swung into the lot. Another black SUV edged toward the front door.

Carla rolled her truck closer to the building where she could watch the front. Backing into a spot just outside the ring of light, she instinctively locked her doors, turned off the engine, and waited.

Should she go in?

If she did, Ari might spot her. She'd never get close enough to hear what he and Duggans were discussing. Should she have stayed put at Ari's and confronted him when he returned home? *No.* She couldn't bear the thought of being at his ranch, much less in his bed.

She glanced toward the back. She could slip into the Grill through the alley door, but she'd have to walk by that idling car. One she didn't recognize.

She reached toward the door handle, then thought better of

her plan to enter the Rustler's Grill. If any of her friends saw her, they'd out her in seconds flat.

Pulling her flannel shirt tight around her, she shivered. Not from the night's chill, but from the betrayal unfolding inside the Grill.

She drummed her fingers against the steering wheel. Patience—not her best virtue. Unless she thought things through, she always got herself in trouble.

But she had to do something.

Carla jumped to the ground. When she reached the front bumper of her truck, a familiar midnight blue pick-up barreled into the parking lot. Ducking back, she squatted between two vehicles and waited.

Carter swung open his door. As his boots hit the ground, he was already in full stride toward the black SUV now parked cross-ways to the front door. The passenger door opened and a tall, shapely brunette in a slinky, red leather skirt, black tank, and red four-inchers that screamed do-me, emerged. In seconds, they were arm in arm and staggering toward the front door.

Staggering? Carter was drunk and meeting up with a loose woman? On a week night? Did she not know her brother at all?

Before she could holler his name, they'd worked their way to the front door, Carter whooping it up and the woman pressing her breasts against his arm and giggling.

Now what do I do?

Barge through the front door. If Ari saw her, so what? She could claim she heard about Carter and had made a beeline to the Grill to save him from himself. That excuse might not cut it with Ari, but it didn't matter any more.

She waited in the shadows for a few more minutes, until the damp and cold tunneled through her and sent a shiver down her spine. She moved from foot to foot. She had to do something or freeze to death ducked between two trucks in the Grill's parking lot. She glanced around. All was quiet except the purr from the engines of the two black cars.

Straightening her shoulders and lifting her chin, she

gathered her courage. Now or never. She moved out from between the trucks and strode toward the door.

Within steps of reaching the entrance, the doors of the idling car flew open and three men in black windbreakers emerged, guns drawn. "Duck," one of them yelled. Her heart beat in her throat. She turned toward the Grill, only steps away, and reached for the safety of the handle. The door banged open hard enough to smash against the side of the building.

Face-to-face with Duggans, his eyes blazing, his lips drawn in a feral rage, she stumbled back. He grabbed her arm and pulled her to his chest, locking his arm firmly around her ribs. He pressed a gun against her side and yelled "Move," as he pushed her into the parking lot.

The three men from the black car dropped to their knees and sighted their guns. One of them hollered, "FBI. Drop your gun, Duggans. Let the woman go."

The woman in red leather barged through the open entrance, gun drawn. "Drop it, Duggans."

He snarled in Carla's ear as he lifted the gun to plant it against her temple. "Make one move and you're dead. Ya hear me?"

She executed a curt nod. The cold metal scraped against the skin beside her eye. His arm tightened. She tried to suck in a breath, but his arm was a vice across her chest as he dragged her backwards. Four guns followed their movement.

Think. Think. Think.

He was headed to his truck. He'd have to lower his gun, or the arm holding her, in order to open the door. When he did, she'd go limp. He'd have to let go. She would duck and roll away from the truck. The FBI might get a shot off to disable Duggans.

She prayed they'd miss her.

The roar of an engine sounded behind her. Duggans turned toward the sound, the gun digging into her temple.

"What the hell is going on here?" Carter's calm voice, in control and cold as ice, came from behind them. He sounded perfectly sober. Where had he come from? "Duggans. Hurt my sister and you'll feel the pain."

Duggans stopped in his tracks as he yanked Carla tight against him. His putrid, whiskey-laced breath hot against her neck.

She panted tiny breaths and willed herself to remain calm. She'd get through this. Carter had her back.

"Drop the gun." Carter sounded closer.

Planting her feet, she prayed she could keep Duggans from turning and shooting her brother.

Duggans' heart beat drummed against her back. His gun hand, steady until now, began to shake as his grip tightened around her arms. His hot breath scorched her neck as he growled, "I *will* shoot you. I have nothing to lose." He stepped back, jerking her along the pathway between two pick-ups barely wide enough for both.

All her senses on alert, Carla heard the soft purr of a vehicle driving slowly through the parking lot. It edged closer as Duggans dragged her back away from the lights, away from the men with guns, and away from her brother.

They were close to Duggans' truck and almost out of clear sight of everyone. *Now.* She bent her knees, all her weight dragging Duggans' arm down. He stumbled and struggled to regain his balance.

A truck door slammed behind her. Duggans jerked back at the sound, his arm tight around her waist again. She twisted, wedging her shoulder into his chest.

But Duggans was back in control, shoving the gun against her side. "Ya damn bitch. What the fuuu—"

And just like that, Duggans let go.

Carla dropped to the ground and rolled toward the front tires of his truck. Scrambling to her knees, she scurried backwards until she could no longer see anyone.

"You bastard. Picking on a woman." The royal accent, deep and righteously pissed off, echoed in the dark. "You will hurt this valley no more, Duggans."

By the time she pulled herself to standing, men in black had converged from all sides to surround Ari and Duggans.

Ari had Duggans bent backwards in a neck hold, with one of Duggans' arms twisted behind his back. A man in black grabbed Duggans other arm and slapped on the handcuffs. Others moved in to seize each arm and haul him toward the Sheriff's car that had just arrived. They shoved Duggans into a cruiser and Quil slammed the door. He instructed a deputy to take *the shithead* to the holding cell and strode toward the gathered group of law enforcement.

A shudder moved through Carla. Her legs trembled so badly, she reached out to grab the massive side mirror of a truck to keep upright.

Quil stood with Ari, asking questions. Behind the two, at the edge of the crowd of law enforcement, Carter and Giles stared at her. As Carter moved toward Carla, the woman in red and black sauntered toward him, rested her hand on his forearm, and smiled.

They were all in on this.

Oh my gawd. Her entire body trembled, as she clutched her flannel shirt against her chest to control the panic.

Ari turned, his dark stare piercing the armor she'd built around her heart in the hour since she heard him talking to Duggans. The little hole in her self-protection spread wide open. He strode toward her, worry etched across his features.

Before Carla could step out in the open, he had her in his arms. Holding her up. Whispering in her ear. Feathering kisses along her temple. His mouth descended on hers, his kiss demanding and protective all rolled into one. She sank against him. Needing his protection. Needing his love. Needing his forgiveness for not believing in him.

He pulled back, one arm tight around her waist. With infinite care, he moved his fingers to skirt around the throbbing area where the gun had pressed. "*Minha querido.* He hurt you. I thought—"

She reached up and smoothed her fingertips over his high, strong cheekbones. His onyx eyes shone like polished stone. "I'm fine. Shaken, but fine."

He blinked and said nothing.

"Really. Ari, I'm fine."

His eyes narrowed, his lips pressed together, and his features changed from worry to anger. "What were you doing here? You could have gotten yourself killed."

She opened her mouth to explain. To apologize for doubting him. "I heard you on the phone—"

His eyes widened. And if possible, they darkened as he stepped backward. "You are impulsive. You never think before you act. Did you not trust me?"

Carla shook her head, not in answer to his question but to deny his accusation. To let him know she did trust him. She loved him. She owed him her life. But nothing came out of her mouth.

His arms stiffened by his side, before his fists clenched. "*You* do not trust me."

"Ari, no. Yes, I do—"

"Then why did you come? Follow me?"

"Please, Ari—listen to me."

But he'd already called to Carter. Already turned toward his truck, idling beyond the glare of blue strobes and milling men in black and tan.

Her legs shook. Before they buckled, she folded herself to sit cross-legged on the ground. By the time Carter reached her, sobs consumed her very soul.

Chapter Thirty-one

Three weeks after they apprehended Ken Duggans for taking bribe money to restore water flow to Ari and the other ranches, while selling off their water downstate, Carla sat in the office off the main corridor of her new school. She poured over applications, making notes on each one before placing them on the growing pile. The stack should have made her happy.

The culmination of her dream.

In a little over two months, laughing children would fill all the colorful classrooms. So far, two new teachers and an administrator had been interviewed and hired. With their help, they'd bless their new charges with a stellar educational start to carry them through a lifetime.

Carla leaned back in the chair and sighed long and slow. She dropped her pen and stretched her arms out to the side, wiggling her fingers. On edge and restless, the simple exercise didn't help.

Standing, she walked to the doorway and scanned the corridor. Blank walls in bright yellow, soon to hold the children's colorful and original art, faced a bank of windows. For a split second, she recalled her plan to display Ari's photos on those same walls on opening day. Her stomach knotted at the lost opportunity. If only Ari could have learned to let go of his fears and anger and restrictive expectations on trust and loyalty.

He and his father had finally reconnected, his father proud of what he'd done at the ranch, and amazed at Ari's perfected skill. She smiled. Despite what happened between them, Ari and Jaime could move forward. Together. She had a hand in that. And maybe, she could continue to help Jaime. If Ari decided to enroll him. She glanced at the list she'd memorized.

Jaime's name was missing.

Ari's mistrust was his issue. Nothing she could help him with now.

Already the townspeople were buzzing about the new business in town. But none of the excitement permeated Carla's dark mood. Nor did it override the constant nausea that overtook her every day right before lunch. Nerves and a love-sick heart. Yeah, nerves and a lovesick heart.

She leaned against the doorway, hand against her belly, ready to bolt for the bathroom. Reaching into the giant pocket of her cowl-necked shirt, she extracted a baggie filled with saltines and nibbled on one. After the third cracker, the queasiness waned.

She hadn't yet admitted out loud what her heart told her. She carried Ari's child. And he no longer wanted her. She thought back seven years ago. History *could* repeat itself. That time, she'd lost the baby in the second month. Shawn never knew.

Carla's chest tightened. Now reaching her second month, eventually she'd have to tell Ari. Because, no matter what, she was carrying this baby to full-term. She imagined a child like Jaime, dark hair and eyes. Or a child resembling her nephew Aaron, the epitome of Peters' coloring with copper hair and hazel eyes. She tried to envision ebony hair and hazel eyes, or copper hair and onyx eyes. No matter the combination, the child would be beautiful.

Around the corner from Carla's office, the double-wide, glass fronted door *snick*ed open. "Betsy?" The two were meeting to go over applications. When she heard no answer, Carla straightened from the doorframe and wandered down the hall. "Betsy—that you?"

As she rounded the corner, she came face to face with Ari. He held a fistful of papers.

"Carla." He nodded a restrained greeting. A reminder of how he'd been when they first met.

So, he hadn't forgiven her for not trusting him. Truthfully, had she been in his position, she might have been slow to forgive as well. But now they had a shared commitment. Although she dared not tell him about the possibility of a baby—not yet.

Shawn and her brothers were macho and controlling, and they'd do the right thing if they ever got a woman pregnant. Ari tended to be ten times worse. Whether or not he loved her or had forgiven her, in less time than it took to leap off a spooked horse, he'd drag her off to Portega for a royal wedding.

And that she didn't want. They would share in their child's care, but no way would she marry a man who didn't love or trust her.

"Ari." She nodded, too. Might as well get on with it. "Have you come to hear me out? Or are you so stubborn that giving me a second chance is not an option?"

For a fraction of a second, his wounded animal look disappeared with the nearly imperceptible rise at the corners of his mouth. "You come right to the point."

"And?" She tilted her head, as if the stance might relax them both.

"You broke my trust. I have no tolerance for such behavior."

Her gut tightened at the roundabout reference to his wife. She couldn't believe what she had done reached that level of betrayal. Not when worry for her family clouded her judgement for a mere hour out of all the time they had known each other.

"And what about my trust? Did you not have enough faith to tell me the truth about Ken Duggans? Especially when you understood how worried I was about my family's ranch."

"It was not for me to reveal the details of an investigation."

"You told Carter."

"We believed he could help us."

"How, Ari? Tell me how my brother could help."

"By selling Duggans the Peters Valley Ranch."

She gasped. Carter contemplated selling the ranch? "No way he'd ever agree to that."

"A ruse, Carla. See—the very reason I did not tell you. You are incapable of a poker face."

269

"Are you saying I'm too emotional?"

"Yes."

Now she was pissed. "Not too emotional to have an affair with you, but too emotional to trust—is that what you're trying to tell me?" She had fallen into his trap, reacting the way she did. She could blame it on hormones, if she wasn't positive she would have reacted emotionally no matter what. "You didn't mind my *emotional instability* the three days I was stuck at your ranch. Or the weeks after."

He stepped toward her. Reached out to cup her cheek, his eyes softening to pencil lead gray, as if he truly regretted what was happening, or not happening, between them.

She batted his hand away. "Why are you here, Ari?"

Stepping out of range, he didn't miss a beat, as if their affair had been an insignificant gnat buzzing around his stallion. "To enroll Jaime in your school." He thrust the papers into her hand. On the top lay a check for full tuition.

She glanced down at the address across the top of the check, before thrusting it toward him. "Keep your check. Jaime must be accepted first." She was being a bitch, but he had no more pull than any other applicant. He didn't need to know she would do anything to ensure Jaime a slot.

He grabbed for the check she offered. She pulled her hand out of range, clutching the check, the application papers in the other hand. She glanced down again. "Silver Equestrian Conglomerate?" Where had she seen that name before? When she looked at him, his eyes narrowed. "It's you?"

He nodded.

Crushing the check, she threw the ball of paper. It bounced off his chest before it hit the floor.

Without a glance at the discarded check, he turned on his heel and strode down the hall.

Her heart broke into a million pieces.

Their silent partner. It had been Ari all along, rescuing their school. Looking back, it was no surprise Kyle and Ari had been so chummy that night at Comfort Food. Now Ari wanted nothing to do with her. Why had he gone behind her back?

Obviously, he wanted the leverage to control his son's education. He did not trust her to do the right thing for Jaime.

Trust. That's what it all rounded back to. Neither of them trusting the other.

Nausea worked its way from her belly to her throat. She turned, making a beeline to the restroom. As she reached the bend in the hallway, pain ripped through her gut. She doubled over and cried out. Grasping the windowsill, she fell to her knees.

"Oh no. Oh no, not again." A moan replaced her cries.

Footsteps pounded toward her. Ari's boots slid to a stop in front of her. He crouched and cradled her head in his hands. "What is wrong?"

"Ambulance."

In one fluid motion he rose, scooped her into his arms, and strode toward the door and his SUV.

"Ambulance," she begged.

"This is faster." He laid her across the back seat and was on his way to the hospital before she cried out in pain again.

Ari's heart raced as he pulled away from the school, Carla huddled across the back seat. She had been pale when he first encountered her in the hallway. Why had he once again acted the ass? His pride. He couldn't be the first to confess he missed her. Had understood that her transgression of not trusting him had never neared the level of Arianna's.

He, who never could distinguish between gradients of trust. Or refused to distinguish that one could be major and one easily forgivable with discussion.

Yes, his pride continued to rule his emotions.

Carla groaned.

"Should I stop the car?"

"No," she murmured, her voice weak with a tinge of desperation.

"We are almost there."

He summoned Siri and barked the command for dialing the hospital ER. The phone rang and was answered immediately. He called in his ETA and explained the problem. The personnel assured him they would greet him at the ER entrance where the ambulances pulled in.

"One minute, Carla. We will take care of you. I promise."

In minutes, they whisked her into a treatment room. He was left to fill out admittance paperwork and call Carter.

Then he sat and waited. Maybe paced more than sat. Then in royal decree, demanded to be let in to sit by her side.

"Are you family?"

"I am her—" He scrubbed his face with nervous fingers. "—significant other. I must be beside her. Hold her hand."

"I'll check with the doctor."

A minute later he was ushered into the cubicle filled with machines, many hooked to his Carla. When he pulled his chair close and reached for her hand, she recoiled.

"Carla, please. I care about you. I want you well. And, until your family arrives, you need someone beside you."

Her head turned. Her copper hair spread across the pillow in a mash of tangles, the colors shimmering under the harsh light. Her beautiful hazel eyes, usually brilliant with green flecks, had dulled. Anger clouded her features. "You called my family?"

"Of course. What would you have me do?" He smoothed the damp shank of hair off her forehead and stroked his finger down her cheek. Machines beeped and hummed around him. His stomach heaved at the thought of Carla in distress.

She closed her eyes and turned her head away from his caress.

Moments later, the doctor appeared. "Ms. Peters." He sank to the stool next to her head, opposite Ari. "We're going to admit you. Keep an eye on you for a few days. At this point, your baby is fine. We want to keep it that way."

"*Baby?*" Carter's bellow, as he stood in the doorway of the ER treatment room, echoed Ari's own.

Chapter Thirty-two

Carla awoke to mumbled voices outside her hospital room where she'd been stuck for too many days.

"It is better this way. I have the staff to take care of her." The accent, deep and commanding, moved through her.

The harrumph sounded distinctly like her father, settling in to argue to the end. "Madge can handle taking care of Carla just as well."

"We can take care of her fine," Carter's bellow mimicked her father's.

"That I know, but it is my baby. I will see that both remain safe. You are welcome to come and go as you wish."

Holy Hello. Ari and her family deciding what was best for her. Ready to stick up for her right to make her own decisions, she pushed herself into a half sitting position before plopping back against the pillows. How right she'd been to not tell Ari or her family. They were doing as she predicted. Only now, she was much too weak to argue her case. She closed her eyes.

She was jostled awake, as they wheeled her down the hall, Ari by her side, and loaded her into a private ambulance.

Before Carla could rally to protest transport to Ari's, the ambulance was on the move. It wasn't long before she was off-loaded at the Silver Mine Ranch, where a bevy of medical personnel and staff now flitted in and out.

Her rebellion, since no one bothered to listen to her, was to shut down.

Now she had Giles planted in a chair by the side of her bed. The *armed* guard, back-up to Ari the warden.

273

Adélia summoned Giles with a wave of her hand. Giles stood. "Excuse me, Ms. Peters. I will send Sénhora right back to sit with you."

He insisted on calling her Ms. Peters ever since the night Ari had decided she betrayed his trust at the Rustler's Grill. "Not necessary. I prefer to be alone."

"But Ms.—"

She turned her back. The gesture was rude, but she couldn't deal with the constant babysitting. And the fact that Giles apparently no longer considered himself her friend.

All she wanted to do was go home and crawl under her own comforter, in her cozy little nest above the feed store. Back where the smells were familiar—pepperoni pizza and the sweet scent of baled hay mingling with the dust of the back alley. So, with her back to Giles, she closed her eyes—tight.

She heard the intake of breath, as if he wanted to argue with her. Then the *snick* of the door.

She let out the pent-up air in her lungs and breathed in the feeling of freedom, even if only for a few moments. The hovering made her crazy. The doctor said bed rest. He didn't say she was dying. He didn't say the baby was dying. Only ordered her to keep her feet up—all the time.

With the blessing of her entire family, Ari had whisked her straight from the hospital to his ranch. She was royally pissed. And if she dared get out of bed without jeopardizing the health of her baby, she'd be certain to pit her *royal* attitude against Ari's and drive herself home.

To make matters worse, the Crown Prince had landed his private jet in Aspen hours earlier. Now there would be no peace with both families hovering and pressuring her to do the right thing. Marry Ari.

He'd made it clear that's what he intended. Carter and Mitch had agreed that was for the best. Once again, everyone dismissed her feelings by not even asking. They only told her what to do.

No, they hadn't *told* her. Only discussed the matter in front of her, as if she wasn't there.

Carla rolled over on her back and wiggled up to rest against a pile of pillows. Before she could get comfortable and enjoy the quiet without anyone hovering over her, she heard the distinctive tap of Ari's boots.

She closed her eyes, feigning sleep. She had yet to speak to him since the ER. And he had not uttered a word, even as he sat by her side throughout.

The click of his boots closed in on her. The scrape of chair legs on the tiled floor warned her he was settling in. She turned her head toward the window, her eyes shut tight.

His big palm settled against the side of her head. His fingers combed through her hair to rest against her neck. She shuddered at his touch, wanting him so much she thought she might die. But he didn't love her. She overheard him admit so to Carter in the ER. She had betrayed his trust. And he had betrayed hers.

His deep sigh moved through her.

Carla couldn't ignore him any longer. She wanted to go home, away from him. Rolling over she opened her eyes, blinked, and stared into dark eyes filled with worry. He was hurting. Not something she expected. His pain made her heart ache all the more.

Reaching up, she clasped his wrist. The pulse beat fast beneath her fingers, the rhythm matching her own beating heart. "I'll, we'll both be all right. I promise. I'll do what the doctor says."

He nodded. But his expression told her he might not believe she could sit still. Was that why Giles and Adélia guarded her, in case she attempted to bolt? Yet, that had been her plan.

"I want to go home. Sleep in my own bed."

Again, he nodded, his thumb stroking the side of her neck, his gaze steady on his own hand. Carla wasn't sure he'd heard.

"I don't belong here."

His gaze snapped up to meet hers. "What is it you wish?"

She turned her face away, resting her cheek against the cool pillow, wanting desperately to bury her face in the soft pile and forget about Ari and the baby. But that wasn't really what she wished for. She wished to believe so deeply that Ari cared enough about her that he'd get up the gumption to argue with her. Command her to stay, in the way she'd learned to love. Promise to care for her, even though she'd railed against all the men in her life when they did just that.

Carla groaned.

He moved quickly to sit on the edge of her bed. With his thumb and forefinger at her chin, he turned her head so she had to look at him. And what she saw scared her. His face was ashen.

"What is wrong? Where do you hurt? Shall I call the doctor?"

Unable to hold in the three scariest words any longer, she blurted them out. "I love you."

"You groaned. What is wrong?"

"That is what is wrong."

He sat back a moment. His eyes widened. "That you love me?"

She nodded.

He leaned in and brushed his lips across hers. "And I love you. Tell me how to help you? You are hurting."

"I'm fine."

"You moaned. You are in pain."

She shook her head. "It is the two of us that pains me. And my heart aches because of what we could have had."

"No, Carla, do not say such things."

"I betrayed you by not trusting you. I can never gain that trust back. I'm so sorry, Ari." On a roll, she couldn't stop. "You never gave me a reason to distrust you. But my family—all these years, we've struggled to—"

Again, he brushed his lips over hers. "Hush you."

Wait. "What did you say?"

"Hush?" His fingertips brushed across her bottom lip.

"Before that. Way before hush."

He stared at her. "I—I love you?"

"Do you? Really?"

"Yes, Carla, I do love you."

"Then why—"

His mouth melded with hers, his scent surrounding her in a protective cocoon, until she forgot what she wanted to ask him. His kiss gentle, unhurried, loving. They stopped for slow breaths and then kissed again. Committed and trusting. So different from the kisses they'd shared in their frenzied lovemaking.

"I have been so worried." His warm hand engulfed hers. "I am the one who must apologize. I should have told you of my work with the authorities. I should have included you in my plans. And I should not have taken out my fury on you. It is I who has never learned to trust. And...I feared for your life. It was too much to bear. Those feelings so deep—"

She stroked his cheek, rubbing her thumb against the stubble, rougher than usual for late afternoon.

"You haven't shaved."

"This is what you worry about?"

"You always shave."

He laughed, released her hand, and sat back. "Not when I have you to worry about. There was no time to shave."

Oh gawd. She loved him more than she could ever imagine loving anyone.

"You will stay here now? Not run off on me? Let me take care of you?"

She laughed for the first time in weeks. Her strength rushing back. "You are asking me, Prince Orula? Not commanding me?"

He smiled. "I have learned my lessons with you. I love you and I trust that you know what is best for you." His grin disappeared as his eyes darkened. "That you will choose to stay here with me...and Jaime."

She barely heard a word past the *I Love You.*

"You love me."

"I do."

"I can't get enough of hearing those words. Why did you never tell me? Not once."

"I did not trust myself. By doing so, I did not trust you. I have been wrong."

"Wrong?" She sighed, too tired to laugh. "You have never been wrong."

His low laugh spoke of pain and worry. "Carla, I am many times wrong. Even my father thinks I am wrong in this. He adores you. One of my many faults is to neglect to admit when I am wrong."

"And now you do?" She couldn't help the tease. She reached out to caress his forearm, as he continued to stroke the damp hair from her brow.

"Love has changed me. And now our families have come together. My father shows his love. Your father, too."

Her lids drooped as she fought to stay awake.

"Carla—answer me this. Do you wish to stay? Or do you wish to go to your home? I will send Senhora Adélia to stay with you. Whatever you wish. I was so worried, but now I think you believe I hold you hostage."

"No. What I thought was that all the men in my life, including you and my father, were dictating what I should do. Not letting me care for myself. Know my own mind."

"We cannot help protecting those we love. All the Orula and Peters men, we are from the same mold."

"Unfortunately," she murmured.

"Yes, unfortunately. Does it not help that we have all learned our lesson?"

His eyes, the black overpowering the striations of silver that often appeared, told her what she needed to know. He loved her and he tried to hold back the possessiveness, his need to control and protect.

"Have you? You will not nag me anymore? You will allow me to make my own decisions?"

"Yes. What do you wish? Your apartment? Your ranch? Here? I will make sure you are well cared for wherever you choose."

"Here." She mumbled as she pressed her cheek against the cool pillow.

Chapter Thirty-three

After a long week in the hospital and a month at Ari's, the doctor finally permitted her get out of bed if she was careful. Both Ari and Giles stuck close, questioning everything she did. And then there were her brothers, especially Carter who stopped by every night after a long day on the ranch. Never mind the Crown Prince, her dad, and Madge, who hovered the most and spent many nights in the guestroom next to hers.

The saving grace was sweet Jaime, who would read to her, hold her hand, and report in on his chess games and the growth of their seedlings. She loved the little boy and decided not to regret the time spent immobile, since it gave her time with Jaime. Not as his nanny, but as his friend.

One afternoon, when she'd promised to rest by sitting with her legs elevated on a pillow, she watched Ari's head bent over a grid having something to do with horse insemination cycles.

Jaime knocked on the open door to the office. "Papa. Look."

Ari waved him in. "What is this you show me?"

"A sunflower, Papa."

"I do not see a flower."

Jamie giggled as he hugged the clay pot to his chest, dirt streaking his T-shirt. "Ah, Papa, you are silly. It must grow much bigger, then the flower will come. We must plant it in the ground first."

"Ah, I see." Ari winked at Carla. She giggled along with Jaime.

"Can we grow a garden, Papa?"

"And where do you propose we grow this garden?"

"Outside the kitchen door, at the edge of the flower garden.

Ms. Carla says—"

"Ah, so you got this idea from Ms. Carla."

The boy's grin widened. "*Sim*, Papa."

"And what will you grow?"

"Tomatoes and salad and melons and popcorn."

"Popcorn and salad?" Again, he glanced at Carla, a huge smile filling his face. "So, you have thought hard about this garden?"

The boy nodded, his head bobbing in excitement.

"And if you grow this garden, will you eat all your vegetables?"

Jaime's eyes shut, the moment stretching out before he slowly opened them and nodded. "*Sim*, Papa."

"Well, then, I believe a garden is an excellent idea."

Jaime hugged the pot to his chest and ran across the room toward the door.

"Will you not say goodbye?"

He turned, breathless, and said, "I must tell Cook. Bye."

Carla looked at Ari and laughed. "He has grown out of his shell."

Ari met her gaze and laughed, too.

It lightened his heart to see Jaime so full of joy.

And Carla. Resting on his sofa. Committed to Jaime and to him. Ari couldn't get enough of her smile and her laugh and her presence in his life. With the baby growing and her belly only now beginning to show the tiniest bump, he had decided to wait no longer.

He watched her, as she relaxed on the sofa and returned to scanning a magazine filled with teaching tips. Occasionally she scratched out a note on her laptop. His breath caught deep in his chest, squeezing the life out of his confidence.

Rising from his desk, he swallowed hard. Maybe he should have waited for the perfect moment. He'd always been a man who planned and followed up with action. But now he loved her, and he wanted to make it official. He could no longer wait. Today was the day. This was the reason he'd insisted she rest in his study.

His heart beat an erratic tap-dance in his chest. This wasn't a business decision. This decision came from deep in his heart. He'd thought about it long and hard, as he did with anything he set out to do. But this moment was different and bigger and more overwhelming than anything he'd ever done in his life.

Ari walked to the door and shut it, *snicking* the lock in place. Her gaze snapped up to meet his. Her smile, sure and strong, melted his heart.

"What's up?"

The last time he'd proposed it had been more like a business deal laced with a healthy dose of lust and infatuation.

Looking at Carla's fresh face, her cheeks rosy with the blush of the sun, he reaffirmed his trust in her. "You know I trust you. And I am deeply sorry for letting you imagine differently."

"Ari, we are beyond that. I know. We both mistrusted. And...we both forgave. Right?"

He walked to within feet of the couch, as she struggled to sit taller against the arm. "You see my best side, despite the bad side I insist on showing to the world." He knelt beside the couch.

"What is this about? I'm fine. I don't know why you hover so."

He laughed. "I am not hovering...this time. I have something important to ask you."

The hazel in her eyes danced with a swirl of colors. The emerald green specks stood out in merriment.

He bent to kiss her, a quiet touch of the lips. Then he drew both her hands into his. He'd never been more nervous in his life.

"What are you up to?"

"Please...do me the honor of being my bride."

Her hands tensed beneath his. Looking straight at him, she said nothing.

Carla had never seen Ari's eyes blacker. A small tick worked its way along his jaw as it tightened and relaxed. Ari, her strong and steady prince, was nervous.

She choked back tears. She'd wished for a fairy tale

romance ever since she was a little girl. Big dreams for a cowgirl brought up in a tiny town where everyone knew one another, and you were expected to marry your brother's best friend.

Ari's eyes grew wider. She hadn't yet given her answer.

She pushed herself to sit straight and swiped away a tear with the back of her hand. "I'd be honored."

As relief rushed across his face, she couldn't help laughing. Her serious, perfectionist, always-in-control prince looked flustered. "On one condition."

His brow lifted and his royal attitude charged back to settle in the straight lines of his mouth. "Condition? You put conditions on my proposal?"

The attitude that had once made her angry, now made her feel cared for and loved. She leaned toward him. One hand cupped his cheek. "I most certainly do."

"Elaborate."

"My condition is that we ask Jaime to give us his blessing before I say *I do*."

"Ah, my Car—la. You have such little faith in me." The tease lit his eyes. Relaxing, he placed his hand against the couch and pulled himself up to sit next to her. "Jaime has known for a week."

"A week? And he kept the secret?"

"Yes. In fact, we have a surprise for you."

"I love surprises. When?"

"Lunch first." He kissed her long and hard before standing and holding his hand out to her.

"What—you aren't going to sweep me off my feet and carry me?"

"You wish that I do that?"

"I'm teasing."

"Will I ever get used to your tease?"

"I hope not. It keeps you on your toes."

He escorted her to the sun room, insisting she link her arm through his. "I'm perfectly capable of walking on my own. I'm not sick, just pregnant."

"With my baby."

"Our baby."

"Must you always have the last word?"

She squeezed his arm. "You should know me well enough by now not to have to ask that question."

As he pulled her chair out, Jaime scampered into the sun room. "Papa?"

He nodded. "Carla will marry us."

Carla wasn't sure whether she'd ever seen such a huge grin on Jaime before he ran toward her and flung his arms around her waist. "You said yes? You'll marry us?"

She gathered the boy in her arms. "I sure will. How could I resist marrying my two favorite guys?"

"We have a surprise—"

"Jaime." Ari's voice startled Jaime. He pressed his hand to his mouth. "Oops, I almost told. But you must wait. Right, Papa?"

"Soon. I promise. After lunch."

Jaime bounced throughout the meal. When they'd all cleaned their plates, Jaime asked, "Now can we show the surprise?"

"Now is an excellent time."

In jumping jack mode, and holding both their hands, Jaime led them to the barn.

"My surprise is in the barn?"

"Two surprises," Jaime said, barely able to contain himself any longer. As they walked through the door to the stables, Jaime let go of Ari's hand and pulled on Carla's. "Over here."

"Careful," Ari instructed as Jaime hauled Carla toward the other end of the barn.

They neared the stall at the farthest end. A brand-new sign hung from the rafters just above the stall door. "Sundancer?"

Jaime's head bobbed up and down. "Wait until you see." Jaime pulled Carla closer. "Papa and Uncle Giles got her for me."

Carla sucked in a deep breath. "Your own horse? She's beautiful, Jaime."

"We named her Sundancer, 'cause look—she looks like sunshine."

"Indeed she does." Carla leaned over the door and stroked the beautiful, strawberry roan from forelock to nose. "Does she dance, too?" Carla teased the little boy.

"She does dance. Wait until you see. Papa, can we let Sundancer out?"

Ari strode toward them. Once he had the horse ready, he led her from the stall to the corral.

"Come on, come on, there's one more surprise." Jaime grabbed Carla's hand and tugged.

"Did you braid Sundancer?"

Jaime nodded. "I worked hard. Do you like the red ribbons?"

"They're beautiful. She looks like she's dressed up for a celebration."

"She is."

Once they reached the corral, Jaime let go of Carla and ran toward his dad. "Papa, it's my turn to lead Sundancer." Without question, Ari handed the lead rope to Jaime.

Jaime advanced several steps before he stood quietly holding the horse, motioning for Carla to step forward. "This surprise is for you."

"For me?"

"You have to find the surprise. It's in Sundancer's mane."

Carla glanced at Ari. He shrugged as if he had no clue what Jaime was up to.

It didn't take long. As Carla approached Sundancer, she noticed a small red velvet box intertwined in the braided ribbons. Pretending to look, as the horse danced from side to side, she dragged out the excitement for Jaime, finally holding up the end of one ribbon. "Is this for me?"

Jaime jumped up and down. "She found it."

Ari stepped forward and reached over her shoulder. He untangled the little box from the ribbons. As Carla reached for it, Ari pulled it from her grasp.

He turned to his son and offered his hand. Jaime skipped

over so Ari could enfold his small hand in his. They each dropped to one knee.

Carla lifted her hand to cover her mouth. She couldn't cry or she'd scare Jaime. The scene was one she would never forget.

"Ready," Ari asked, and Jaime nodded.

Ari flipped open the lid of the red box and together they said, "Will you marry us?"

Carla sank to her knees. She enveloped Jaime into her arms. "Oh, yes, I will. Thank you so much for asking me."

"We had to," Jaime said, looking up at her. "Papa said even if you said yes to him, we had to be formal when we gave you your surprise."

"Your papa is a very smart man."

When she turned toward Ari, he lifted the antique-set ring from the box. The emerald, surrounded by diamonds, was exquisite. "My grandmother's."

He picked up her hand and slipped the ring on her finger. She'd never take it off.

"The stone matches the tiny green flecks in your eyes."

She flung her arms around Ari, almost knocking him to the ground.

"I love you, Prince Ari Orula." She pulled Jaime back into the hug. "I love you, Prince Jaime Orula."

Then she planted her lips on Ari's and kissed the blazin' saddles out of him.

The Rancher Needs a Wife

The Cowboys of Mineral Springs, Book 2

Coming in 2020

Wanted: A Suitable Wife

*Workaholic cowboy needs hardy woman to
manage household and motley family.
"Girly" widows, with small children,
who sell naughty lingerie need not apply.*

Overprotective big brother and ranch owner, Carter Peters, draws the short straw at a contrived family meeting, to buy his stepmom's sixtieth birthday present. He never imagines while on the present-buying quest he'll get zapped with cupid's arrow by a feisty southern belle, single mom, and lingerie shop owner who is so wrong for him and has off-limits written all over her. He has no time for romance—he has a ranch to run and a father who, despite being "retired," can't help micro-manage. Dad insists Carter's new-fangled ways won't work.

Lynette Mercer wants nothing to do with the tall, sexy, and slightly bashful cowboy who walks through her door. Okay, maybe just a little. They *could* be friends. After all, she's vowed not to date until her four-year old reaches the ripe age of thirty-six. She's recovering from the death of her husband in a marriage that had turned bad. With new friends and Carter's family determined to marry him off, neither stand a chance against cupid or a town full of caring folks.

Reviews of Other Books by Delsora Lowe

Praise for *A Serenity Harbor Maine novella series.* All three, sweet with a bit of heat, novellas may be purchased individually, as a Serenity Harbor, Maine novella (books one through three in the Starlight Grille series), or purchased together in *Starlight Grille, a Serenity Harbor Maine Collection*, which includes all three novellas (*The Legacy of Parkers Point, Come Dance With Me*, and *Moonlighting*), with a bonus short story, *Welcome Home*, and Gray's recipe for the Starlight Grille's famous adaptation of the Reuben sandwich).

The Legacy of Parker's Point
Starlight Grille Book 1

...a feel good story, full of love and romance and hope....no game playing, no lies, manipulation or underhanded deceit to win affection....just two strong people finding love, learning to trust, and trying to make it work.

The author depicts life in a small town with memorable characters and descriptive scenery. Lauralee and Grayson are two beautiful people inside and out. Their chemistry heats up the pages.... The secondary characters are well written and the next book in the series is about the piano player, Luke, at the Starlight Grille.
Dianamcc - Romance Junkies – Five Hearts

Set on the picturesque sea coast of Maine....a heartfelt tale of helping and healing.... a delightful, emotional read.
N, Amazon Reader – Five Stars

This is a sweet story. The romance is a well-written small town story where two people learn to trust both each other and themselves. I highly recommend the story.
Mainer, Amazon Reader – Four Stars

Come Dance with Me
Starlight Grille Book 2

[Sam] is multi-layered, gorgeous and plays jazz like the superstar he is. Yet, something is eating at him. Then he meets Ashley Sullivan, the uptight high school teacher, riddled with fear and reluctance to join in. Sam doesn't give up on her and the push-pull of these two is charming. Give yourself a treat and read Come Dance With Me. It's a winner
Kat Henry Doran, Amazon Reader – Five Stars

Before I had even finished book one, I bought books two and three! Very entertaining and captivating!
Kate, Amazon Reader – Four Stars

Moonlighting
Starlight Grille Book 3

Delsora Lowe gives you an intimate look into a couple's meeting and falling in love with a background you want to live in.
CCMO, Amazon Reader – Five Stars

Really great, quick read! Well written with a great storyline. Bunnie is definitely older and wiser than her years and adds a nice dynamic!
Kate, Amazon Reader – Four Stars

Starlight Grille
A Serenity Harbor Maine Collection

Small town, big heart. All of the stories in Ms. Lowe's collection center around the fictional Serenity Harbor, a sleepy little community that is hiding secrets and more. She has woven so much into each story that I find myself wanting to know more after it is done.
Harbor Girl, Amazon Reader – Five Stars

About Delsora Lowe

From Cabins to Cottages…Keep the Home Fires Burning

A transplanted big city gal, world-wide traveler, and foreign-service brat, who now lives in a coastal Maine town, Delsora Lowe loves to write about small town heroes from the cowboys and ranchers of Colorado to the game wardens and lobstermen of Maine. Her work in the hospitality industry, rape crisis, admissions, alumni relations, and women's advocacy has allowed her to interact on a daily basis with real life heroines and heroes. Lowe's family visits to Colorado are the inspiration for her *Cowboys of Mineral Springs* series. And her daughter's wedding and her son's home on the coast of Maine provided plentiful ideas for the *Starlight Grille* series, as well as the *Galway Cove* series, currently being written.

DelsoraLowe.com

Keep up with Delsora's news by joining her Mailing List

Want to be first to hear about my upcoming books? Sign up for Dels's Reader Alert on my website. My promise to you is to only contact you when new books are released, books go on sale, or new covers are previewed. I will not share your name or email with anyone, nor will I overload your mail box.

When you join my mailing list, I'll send you the recipe card version of **Gray's Famous Maine Reuben** from the Starlight Grille.

You can also find her on social media:
Facebook: @DelsoraLoweAuthor
Amazon: Delsora Lowe
Bookbub: @DelsoraLoweAuthor
Goodreads: @Delsora_Lowe

Consider Writing a Review

Thank you for reading *The Prince's Son*. I hope you enjoyed my story as much as I enjoyed writing about Ari and Carla overcoming their fears and finding their home together in Mineral Springs.

It would mean so much to me if you would consider leaving a comment or review about *The Prince's Son* on Goodreads, Bookbub, and on the retailer site where you purchased this book. Reviews help other readers decide which books to read, and help authors spread the word. I thank you for taking the time.

Made in United States
North Haven, CT
07 April 2022

18022464R00163